# THE SIREN

ALSO BY KATHERINE ST. JOHN

*The Lion's Den*

# THE
# SIREN

## KATHERINE
## ST. JOHN

**GRAND CENTRAL**
**PUBLISHING**

New York Boston

Grand Central Publishing
Hachette Book Group
1290 Avenue of the Americas, New York, NY 10104
grandcentralpublishing.com
twitter.com/grandcentralpub

First edition: May 2021

Grand Central Publishing is a division of Hachette Book Group, Inc. The Grand Central Publishing name and logo is a trademark of Hachette Book Group, Inc.

The publisher is not responsible for websites (or their content) that are not owned by the publisher.

The Hachette Speakers Bureau provides a wide range of authors for speaking events. To find out more, go to www.hachettespeakersbureau.com or call (866) 376-6591.

Library of Congress Cataloging-in-Publication Data

Names: St. John, Katherine, 1979– author.
Title: The siren / Katherine St. John.
Description: First edition. | New York : Grand Central Publishing, 2021.
Identifiers: LCCN 2020053572 | ISBN 9781538733684 (hardcover) | ISBN 9781538733660 (ebook)
Subjects: GSAFD: Suspense fiction.
Classification: LCC PS3619.T2484 S57 2021 | DDC 813/.6—dc23
LC record available at https://lccn.loc.gov/2020053572

ISBNs: 978-1-5387-3368-4 (hardcover), 978-1-5387-3366-0 (ebook)

Printed in the United States of America

LSC-W

Printing 1, 2021

*For Alex*

In the future, everyone will want to be anonymous for fifteen minutes.

—Banksy

# THE SIREN

# The Biz Report

## COLE POWER TO PRODUCE AND STAR IN *THE SIREN*

## (EXCLUSIVE)

The first film slated for production by **Cole Power**'s fledgling Power Pictures will be a thriller starring Power, written and directed by Power's son, **Jackson Power**. The younger Power is a recent graduate of AFI whose thesis film has been racking up accolades on the festival circuit this year. Also joining the cast is **Stella Rivers**, who starred opposite Cole Power in 2006's box office hit *Faster*. The two were married from 2006–2007. Power Pictures is independently financing the venture, and **Taylor Wasserman** (formerly of Woodland Studios) has been brought on to produce.

*The Siren* follows a photographer (Power) married to a model (Rivers), living an idyllic life in the islands until they hire a beautiful young nanny to look after their baby. The nanny replaces the wife as the photographer's muse, sparking a war between the women that eventually brings them all down.

The film is slated for production over six weeks beginning in June, on the southern Caribbean island of Saint Genesius, west of Saint Vincent and the

Grenadines, where Cole Power owns the exclusive Genesius Resort, made famous as the on-screen resort owned by Power's character in the Gentleman Gangster series. Power purchased the resort and the neighboring film stage last year after wrapping the fifth installment of the wildly successful Gentleman Gangster series, shot partially on the island.

# PART I:

# The Calm before the Storm

girl lounged. All up and down the shore, our crew frolicked in the sultry Caribbean sun, tossing Frisbees and floating on their backs in the crystal-clear bay as if they were in a Corona beer commercial.

This was the sort of island paradise featured on office screen savers, where rich people came to decompress in seclusion and honeymooners could enjoy the ocean without ever leaving the privacy of their luxurious accommodations. Nature was king, the rhythm of the day was determined by the weather, and no one was in a hurry.

I would've been bored to tears if I weren't producing a movie.

What can I say? For better or worse, I'd never known what to do with myself in the absence of a mission. Everyone talked about the importance of meditation or yoga to relieve stress, but I found stress *useful*. Pressure kept my feet on the ground—without it I feared I might float away. My therapist had tried in vain to convince me otherwise in recent months, but what did she know? I could only assume the entertainment industry was far more cutthroat than the mental health industry.

At any rate, I simply wasn't made for a tropical environment like rock girl obviously was. My curly mop of dark hair didn't do that beachy wave thing; it frizzed. My lily-white skin didn't bronze; it burned. Also, was allergic to sundresses, especially those in bright colors.

"You're staring."

I spun to see Jackson Power's lopsided grin. A pair of black Wayfarers d down his nose, revealing mirthful muddy green eyes.

"Hard not to," I admitted.

"I'll say." He dropped his backpack and towel on a lounger under of the ten or so straw umbrellas that dotted the beach and pulled T-shirt over his head, revealing sun-kissed olive skin. Jackson was ny, to be sure, but not unattractive. He was our director though, I would never cross the line with someone I was working with. ever again.

hy didn't you come fishing with us yesterday?" Jackson asked.

et seasick," I lied.

*Not So Long Ago on an Island Not So Far Away…*

# Taylor

*Sunday, June 16*

S he was perched on a rock like a siren the first time I sa
upturned to the sun, copper skin wet with sea spray
dangled languidly into the mottled azure water while palm
tered overhead, casting pom-pom shadows on the powdered

I wondered who she was, how she'd gotten in. I'd pers
every member of our cast and crew, and she wasn't one o
from fifty yards away I could see she was a stunner, wit
the right places and an angelic face framed by jaw-skin
waves and a heavy fringe of bangs. No, this girl was
Perhaps she was an employee. A desk clerk or maid
lunch break. We'd reserved the entire resort and it was
uniformed guards with giant guns slung casually o
as they ate brown-bag lunches in the shade, so she

The beach was so shockingly vibrant it bo
postcard-perfect crescent of bleached pink sand
marine sea, rimmed by an assortment of palms
green leaves that concealed pathways to the po
Ripples tickled the shore of the tranquil bay,
island guide in my glorious over-water bunga
the surf by coral reefs just beyond the outcro

5

Jackson watched our mermaid stretch her long limbs out like a cat, her chestnut locks tousled by the steady midday breeze.

"Who is she?" I asked.

"Stella's new assistant." He tossed his sunglasses into his bag. "She always did like the pretty ones."

I opened my mouth to inquire what he meant, but he was already off, diving horizontally into the shallow water.

Annoyed Stella had somehow hired an assistant I knew nothing about, I collapsed on a chair in the shelter of an umbrella and gladly shed the black sun hat I'd thought ideal back home in Los Angeles last week. I'd since come to understand why everyone wore light shades in the tropics, but the appropriate hats in the gift store were so exorbitantly priced that I had yet to bring myself to buy one. I blew down my black T-shirt and tugged at the damp waistband of my jean cutoffs, which I'd taken scissors to only this morning. Denim: also inappropriate for the Caribbean. My suitcase of dark T-shirts, jeans, and cargo pants was going to have to be amended.

I'd slathered myself in SPF 70 and worn a sporty black one-piece beneath my clothes in hopes of perhaps going for a swim, but as I gazed upon the goddess on the rock, I thought better of it. Not because my sense of self-worth was tied up with my physical appearance—which it wasn't—but because I was only human, and while the curves on my vertically challenged frame were kept mostly in check by daily CrossFit torture, I knew when I was out of my league. Not that anyone was looking. Not that there was anyone on the island I'd have wanted to look. Still, vanity.

Was vanity permissible these days? I wasn't sure. I knew I was supposed to be self-assured and body-confident, everyone else be damned—and that sounded fantastic—but it was also a tall order for a girl who'd grown up in millennial Hollywood (oh, the midriffs!) with a misogynist father. So I buried my shameful insecurity beneath an industrial-strength steel facade and didn't let anyone in. According to my therapist.

I observed from behind my Ray-Bans as Jackson and the girl pretended not to notice each other out in the bay. Assistant, my ass. This chick was an actress preening for the director if ever I saw one. And I'd seen plenty.

A soccer ball landed next to my chair with a thwack, sending sand flying. Even in my foul mood, I could see it was a sign too obvious to ignore. It wasn't the crew's fault I hadn't been invited fishing yesterday; I shouldn't take my anger out on them. Anyway, I enjoyed soccer.

Gathering my wild curls into a ponytail, I dribbled the ball over toward a sound guy, two grips, a PA, and an electrical engineer. "Room for one more?" I asked, squinting into the sun.

"You're on our team," Sam, the scrawny sound guy, called. "That's our goal." He indicated two orange plastic cones about fifty feet away.

I threw a thumbs-up and kicked him the ball. I hadn't played seriously since high school, but I was a decent defender and could pull off a few tricks that made me look cooler than I was. In no time I was sandy and sweaty, my foul mood forgotten.

We'd stopped for a water break when I saw my boss emerge bare-chested from a pathway cut between the red-flowering trees. Cole Power, the Sexiest Man in Hollywood twice over: first after his breakout role at twenty-five—thick dark hair falling in front of stormy blue eyes, cigarette dangling from pillowy lips, T-shirt sleeves rolled to display bulging biceps—and again three years ago at forty-six, in a slim-fit black suit this time, close-cropped hair accentuating a square jaw, and one of the most recognizable faces on the planet, made only more desirable by age. A distinctly male advantage.

These days the hair was back, and thicker than ever. Navy board shorts rode low on his hips, threatening to slide off as he sauntered along the shoreline toward me, his bronzed chest cut by minimum two-hour workouts with his trainer every morning. He was a gorgeous man with charisma to spare, not to mention an icon: the original Out-sider, a rebel artist with a dimple and a penchant for fast cars, expensive wine, and beautiful women. But I'd been working for him only three

*Not So Long Ago on an Island Not So Far Away...*

# Taylor

*Sunday, June 16*

She was perched on a rock like a siren the first time I saw her, face upturned to the sun, copper skin wet with sea spray. Her toes dangled languidly into the mottled azure water while palm fronds fluttered overhead, casting pom-pom shadows on the powdered sugar sand.

I wondered who she was, how she'd gotten in. I'd personally vetted every member of our cast and crew, and she wasn't one of them. Even from fifty yards away I could see she was a stunner, with curves in all the right places and an angelic face framed by jaw-skimming brunette waves and a heavy fringe of bangs. No, this girl wasn't one of ours. Perhaps she was an employee. A desk clerk or maid, tanning on her lunch break. We'd reserved the entire resort and it was gated, secured by uniformed guards with giant guns slung casually over their shoulders as they ate brown-bag lunches in the shade, so she had to belong.

The beach was so shockingly vibrant it bordered on lurid. A postcard-perfect crescent of bleached pink sand swaddled the ultramarine sea, rimmed by an assortment of palms and trees with waxy green leaves that concealed pathways to the pool, spa, and restaurant. Ripples tickled the shore of the tranquil bay, which, according to the island guide in my glorious over-water bungalow, was protected from the surf by coral reefs just beyond the outcropping of rocks where the girl lounged. All up and down the shore, our crew frolicked in the sultry Caribbean sun, tossing Frisbees and floating on their backs in the crystal-clear bay as if they were in a Corona beer commercial.

This was the sort of island paradise featured on office screen savers, where rich people came to decompress in seclusion and honeymooners could enjoy the ocean without ever leaving the privacy of their luxurious accommodations. Nature was king, the rhythm of the day was determined by the weather, and no one was in a hurry.

I would've been bored to tears if I weren't producing a movie.

What can I say? For better or worse, I'd never known what to do with myself in the absence of a mission. Everyone talked about the importance of meditation or yoga to relieve stress, but I found stress *useful*. Pressure kept my feet on the ground—without it I feared I might float away. My therapist had tried in vain to convince me otherwise in recent months, but what did she know? I could only assume the entertainment industry was far more cutthroat than the mental health industry.

At any rate, I simply wasn't made for a tropical environment like rock girl obviously was. My curly mop of dark hair didn't do that beachy wave thing; it frizzed. My lily-white skin didn't bronze; it burned. Also, I was allergic to sundresses, especially those in bright colors.

"You're staring."

I spun to see Jackson Power's lopsided grin. A pair of black Wayfarers slid down his nose, revealing mirthful muddy green eyes.

"Hard not to," I admitted.

"I'll say." He dropped his backpack and towel on a lounger under one of the ten or so straw umbrellas that dotted the beach and pulled his T-shirt over his head, revealing sun-kissed olive skin. Jackson was skinny, to be sure, but not unattractive. He was our director though, and I would never cross the line with someone I was working with.

Never again.

"Why didn't you come fishing with us yesterday?" Jackson asked.

"I get seasick," I lied.

Jackson watched our mermaid stretch her long limbs out like a cat, her chestnut locks tousled by the steady midday breeze.

"Who is she?" I asked.

"Stella's new assistant." He tossed his sunglasses into his bag. "She always did like the pretty ones."

I opened my mouth to inquire what he meant, but he was already off, diving horizontally into the shallow water.

Annoyed Stella had somehow hired an assistant I knew nothing about, I collapsed on a chair in the shelter of an umbrella and gladly shed the black sun hat I'd thought ideal back home in Los Angeles last week. I'd since come to understand why everyone wore light shades in the tropics, but the appropriate hats in the gift store were so exorbitantly priced that I had yet to bring myself to buy one. I blew down my black T-shirt and tugged at the damp waistband of my jean cutoffs, which I'd taken scissors to only this morning. Denim: also inappropriate for the Caribbean. My suitcase of dark T-shirts, jeans, and cargo pants was going to have to be amended.

I'd slathered myself in SPF 70 and worn a sporty black one-piece beneath my clothes in hopes of perhaps going for a swim, but as I gazed upon the goddess on the rock, I thought better of it. Not because my sense of self-worth was tied up with my physical appearance—which it wasn't—but because I was only human, and while the curves on my vertically challenged frame were kept mostly in check by daily CrossFit torture, I knew when I was out of my league. Not that anyone was looking. Not that there was anyone on the island I'd have wanted to look. Still, vanity.

Was vanity permissible these days? I wasn't sure. I knew I was supposed to be self-assured and body-confident, everyone else be damned—and that sounded fantastic—but it was also a tall order for a girl who'd grown up in millennial Hollywood (oh, the midriffs!) with a misogynist father. So I buried my shameful insecurity beneath an industrial-strength steel facade and didn't let anyone in. According to my therapist.

I observed from behind my Ray-Bans as Jackson and the girl pretended not to notice each other out in the bay. Assistant, my ass. This chick was an actress preening for the director if ever I saw one. And I'd seen plenty.

A soccer ball landed next to my chair with a thwack, sending sand flying. Even in my foul mood, I could see it was a sign too obvious to ignore. It wasn't the crew's fault I hadn't been invited fishing yesterday; I shouldn't take my anger out on them. Anyway, I enjoyed soccer.

Gathering my wild curls into a ponytail, I dribbled the ball over toward a sound guy, two grips, a PA, and an electrical engineer. "Room for one more?" I asked, squinting into the sun.

"You're on our team," Sam, the scrawny sound guy, called. "That's our goal." He indicated two orange plastic cones about fifty feet away.

I threw a thumbs-up and kicked him the ball. I hadn't played seriously since high school, but I was a decent defender and could pull off a few tricks that made me look cooler than I was. In no time I was sandy and sweaty, my foul mood forgotten.

We'd stopped for a water break when I saw my boss emerge bare-chested from a pathway cut between the red-flowering trees. Cole Power, the Sexiest Man in Hollywood twice over: first after his breakout role at twenty-five—thick dark hair falling in front of stormy blue eyes, cigarette dangling from pillowy lips, T-shirt sleeves rolled to display bulging biceps—and again three years ago at forty-six, in a slim-fit black suit this time, close-cropped hair accentuating a square jaw, and one of the most recognizable faces on the planet, made only more desirable by age. A distinctly male advantage.

These days the hair was back, and thicker than ever. Navy board shorts rode low on his hips, threatening to slide off as he sauntered along the shoreline toward me, his bronzed chest cut by minimum two-hour workouts with his trainer every morning. He was a gorgeous man with charisma to spare, not to mention an icon: the original Outsider, a rebel artist with a dimple and a penchant for fast cars, expensive wine, and beautiful women. But I'd been working for him only three months, and his mercurial charm had already worn thin, revealing an ego larger than his home state of Texas lurking just beneath the surface. It wasn't his fault, per se. If I'd had the entire globe sucking my dick on command and blowing sunshine up my ass for more than half my life, I'd probably be a narcissist too.

The immediate problem though—the problem that made me want to run and hide in my beautifully appointed bungalow—was the question I needed to ask him and the embarrassment it would cause me. He wouldn't spare me any shame—I knew him well enough to know that. But time was running out.

I signaled my teammates to play on without me and joined Cole beneath the shade of a thatched umbrella, where he flopped down on a lounger and groaned. A lanky waiter in a pink polo shirt with a name tag that read "Jamal" appeared holding a menu and a large bottle of spring water, which Cole immediately grabbed and began chugging.

"Good afternoon, Mr. Power," Jamal said. Like most of the staff, he was African-Caribbean with a lilting accent so musical, I could listen to him read the phone book. "What else can I get you?"

Cole wiped his mouth with the back of his hand, his eyes fixed on a cruise ship on the horizon. "I need a shoulder massage. From a woman." He threw Jamal a pained smile. "My head is pounding. Had a little too much fun in Gen Town last night—you know how it goes."

Jamal nodded, clearly pleased Cole had acknowledged him. "Yes, Mr. Power, I know how it goes."

Jamal turned and mimed a shoulder rub to a similarly dressed female employee hovering in the shade of the thatched snack shack at the edge of the tree line. She grabbed a bottle of lotion and started across the sand on sturdy legs, her arm raised to shield her eyes from the blazing sun. There went my opportunity to speak to Cole in private.

"Can I get you anything from the menu?" Jamal asked.

"A green shake," Cole replied, enveloping Jamal in the warmth of his famous crooked grin. "And Tylenol. Thanks, man."

"No problem." Jamal returned his smile. "Anytime."

"Good afternoon, Mr. Power," the female employee said, stepping under the shade of the umbrella. I scanned her name tag. Tina. I liked to learn names. It came in especially useful working for Cole, who loved to think he knew everyone's name but always got them wrong, and no one ever corrected him. He had confidently called me Tyler for the first month I worked for him, which I guess would have been an understandable mistake if I were a guy.

"Mr. Power needs a shoulder massage," Jamal told her before departing in the direction of the snack shack.

"Certainly." Tina displayed a gap-toothed smile. "How do you like the pressure?"

"Gimme everything you got. I can take it." Cole dazzled her with his brilliant baby blues before flipping onto his stomach.

Flustered, Tina sank to her knees in the sand and began rubbing Cole's shoulders. "You guys have fun fishing yesterday?" I asked.

He grunted confirmation. "Bartender last night just about killed me though. Kept making specialties he thought I'd like. He was right."

From what I'd seen on our golf cart tour when we arrived the day before yesterday, "town" on this tiny island was nothing more than one cobblestone road lined with local shops painted in bright Caribbean colors, anchored by a concrete-block post office so miniature it looked like a children's playhouse. "There are bars in town?"

"One. If it's still standing after last night."

"I'd have loved to join you boys," I said pointedly. "On the fishing trip, too."

"I didn't think you'd want to come."

I bristled. "Why, because I'm a girl?"

"Because you're a vegetarian."

"I'm pescatarian. And anyway, Francisco's vegan and you invited him."

"He is? I didn't know that."

I sighed. What could I do? At the moment I desperately needed the admittedly liberal paycheck that no one else was willing to give me, so I was stuck with him, and he knew it. Anyway, this certainly wasn't the first time in my career that I'd been excluded due to my extra X chromosome. Not so many years ago, I'm sure he would've said it outright (and would have also likely hired strippers). But times had changed: these days I wasn't explicitly uninvited; I was just left in the dark—a miscommunication, if anyone raised eyebrows. This move would have been impossible if the handful of other women on the crew were around, but their departments—wardrobe, makeup, script supervisor, and a lone female electrician—didn't arrive until today.

"You'll need to call the bar and give them a card. I didn't have one on me," he continued.

I was his producer, not his personal assistant, though he rarely seemed to know or care where the line was. Everyone in Cole's orbit simply did whatever he asked, no matter whether or not it fell within the jurisdiction of their job description. But a night on the town wasn't in our film budget. "Ben has your personal cards," I returned.

"It's a film expense."

I took a controlled breath. "This is an independent film. You know we're on a tight budget. Anything you spend on things like fishing trips and bar tabs, it comes out of what goes on-screen."

His laugh had an edge to it. "You gotta stop worrying about money, half-pint."

I hated the way he called me half-pint, but he claimed the nickname was a term of endearment and found it hilarious. "It's my job to worry about money."

He propped up on his elbows, his lips curled into a smile. "It's my money," he said lightly. "Just pay the tab and raise the budget. The more I spend on this movie, the less I pay in taxes. You have any idea how much I pay in taxes?"

"Roughly half, I'd guess," I muttered.

He chuckled. "Not if you have the accountants I do."

"If we're raising the budget, I have a list about a mile long of things we *actually* need that got cut after Steve—"

He held up a hand. "Enough about fucking Steve."

I bit my tongue. Fucking Steve was the line producer hired before I was brought on. He'd been used to working on much higher-budget films and had so grossly overpaid for everything at the top of the list that he ran out of money long before he reached the bottom, leaving us scavenging for crumbs to make up the rest of the cost. I'd recognized the problem early on and had wanted to replace him, but he and Cole had been "mates" (Steve was British) for years, and Cole wouldn't hear of it. In fact, Cole was so adamant that I had to wonder whether Steve had some kind of dirt on him that demanded Cole's loyalty. Suffice it to say that Cole was extremely protective of his image. Unfortunately, the satisfaction of being proven right about Steve's incompetence was far outweighed by the stress of having to clean up his mess.

Cole flopped back onto his stomach. "Get your thumbs between my scaps," he instructed Tina. "Yeah, that's it." He groaned. "You're an angel. Right there. God, I love a woman with strong hands."

I imagined her strong hands around his neck, squeezing.

But it *was* his money—all of it, including the part that paid my salary.

I'd been recruited to produce *The Siren* mainly because Cole had gotten flack in the media for his entertainment company being a boy's club, which it was. For my part, I'd gladly accepted Cole's offer not only because it was generous, but because it was the sole offer I'd fielded in the half a year since I'd been unceremoniously dumped from my prior job, and I was running out of money, not to mention losing my sanity to a deadly cocktail of inertia and depression.

Power Pictures was smaller than customary for entertainment companies owned by stars of Cole's stature and was yet to deliver anything when I came on board. He handed me *The Siren*—a low-budget, complicated, truly independent passion project without studio involvement or even outside money—while the rest of the team stayed in LA to develop bigger things.

Why Cole had given his son, whose life he'd never much been involved in as far as I could tell, a three-million-dollar budget to direct a movie as his film school graduation present was beyond me. He and Jackson were far from chummy, and it was certainly a lot of trouble to go to for a tax benefit. But then, God only knew how much he had in the bank after the box-office-smashing success of the Gentleman Gangster series. (The fifth installment, for which he'd been paid thirty million plus an unheard-of percentage of the back end, had opened last month to even bigger numbers than any of the previous four.) The world was head over heels for the vicious yet charming anti-hero Gentleman Gangster. In a time of ever-declining ticket sales, Cole Power was one of the few movie stars whose name still drew a crowd.

Not only was father-of-the-year Cole Power financing *The Siren*, but in an even curiouser move, he'd agreed to star in it. It would be the lowest-budget film he'd done since before his first turn as Hollywood's Sexiest Man. Of course, his appearance in it all but guaranteed the film's success, which boded well for me and everyone else working on it, so I wasn't protesting. I was now one of the many, many people whose livelihood depended on audiences continuing to fork over their hard-earned cash to see Cole Power smolder *"A gentleman never shoots a man in the back."*

Tina continued to rub Cole's shoulders as he squinted across the water at the siren on the rock, now leaning out over the water to converse with Jackson, her breasts dangling before him like ripe grapefruits. "Who's that?"

"Stella's new assistant."

"Of course." He sniggered.

"Funny. Jackson had the same reaction." I raised my brows.

"Did he?" Cole eyed the two of them, the corners of his mouth downturned. "What else did he say?"

"Nothing."

I contemplated. I'd just pissed him off by reminding him the movie had a budget, and I certainly couldn't care less about Stella's preferences, but if a known pattern indicated there might be a problem, as producer I needed to know. I'd had a hell of a time getting Stella insured to play Cole's wife after her checkered past, and the insurance had caveats—like her staying sober. "Is there something I should know?" I ventured.

"No." He suddenly rose to his feet, leaving Tina kneeling in the sand with no shoulders to rub. She looked to me for direction. I knew he'd probably want her to hang around, but I saw a chance to handle my sticky business with him and decided to take it before we were interrupted again.

"Thank you." I dismissed her with an apologetic smile, pressing a fifty into her hand. Cole had an accurate theory that people rarely had anything bad to say about stars who were generous, so he insisted everyone around him always have cash on hand to grease the wheels.

"Hey, handsome!"

"Speak of the devil," Cole said under his breath.

Seriously? Was I ever going to get a moment alone with him?

Stella traipsed across the sand toward us, her slender frame clad in a turquoise caftan, wide-brimmed white sun hat covering her expertly highlighted honey-and-milk-chocolate waves. She was still beautiful at what she claimed was thirty-six but I knew from processing her paperwork was really forty, her heart-shaped face and delicate features offset by large, come-hither green eyes. I also knew after seeing her barefaced at the makeup test that even with the aid of fillers and Botox, the years of partying had taken a toll. She'd mastered the art of camouflaging the fine lines around her mouth and the hollows beneath her eyes with foundation and contouring, but our cinematographer would have to be incredibly careful how he lit and shot her.

Cole fired up his megawatt smile. "Stella! Gorgeous." He slid his arm around her and gave her lingering kisses on each cheek. "Good to see you. Mmm, you look good enough to eat."

"Oh, stop it!" Stella swatted at Cole. "You know you're more gorgeous than I am."

Stella and Cole had been an item way back when, and the scandal surrounding their breakup had been massive, but that was a long time ago and Cole was so insistent on hiring Stella that I'd figured they must have made peace since. Anyway, as skeptical as I was about casting her after her multiple, very public breakdowns, she'd been nothing but agreeable thus far. It had been nearly a decade since her last stint in rehab, and all her party-girl friends seemed to have gotten it together and moved on with their lives. Maybe her troubles really were in the past. She and Cole certainly appeared chummy enough now, play-fighting about whose abs were tighter.

I stood outside the circle of mutual admiration sweating in my inappropriate clothes, my curls sticking to the back of my neck. "Glad you finally made it," I said. "How was the flight over?"

"That little plane, my God! I don't think I've ever flown on anything that small...Landing on the water was crazy. I thought I might die."

Cole snickered. "Glad to hear your flair for the dramatic is intact."

"This place is amazing." Stella swept her arm toward the horizon. "The water is just...so blue. I can't even. I've always wanted to live on an island, drink from a coconut. So romantic. I love it."

Out in the bay, Jackson splashed the girl on the rock, eliciting a cascade of squeals. We watched as she stood, laughing, then dove into the sea.

# CELEB SPOTTER

## STOLE GETTING MARRIED?

t was a wet-n-wild weekend for Stella Rivers, 27, and Cole Power, 36. The two, who have been hot and heavy since playing opposite each other as star-crossed lovers in the film *Faster*, were spotted Saturday in Miami, lounging on Power's yacht. Rivers flaunted her toned figure in a barely there white bikini, while Power helped lube her up with sunscreen [picture]. Later that night, "Stole" were spotted in the VIP room of Thrive nightclub's annual white party, dancing the night away to the sound of DJ Hall with a group of friends that included actress Hannah Bridges and her boyfriend, Chad Young. But the biggest news came on Sunday, when Stole were spotted canoodling at brunch at hot spot South Shore, Stella wearing what appears to be a square-cut diamond solitaire on her ring finger [pic]. According to our source, the ring is startlingly similar to the engagement ring Cole's character gives Stella's character at the end of *Faster*. Could wedding bells be in their future?

# Stella

F elicity!" I called, waving my hand overhead.

She glided in with the surf like Aphrodite, only way hotter. I'd seen the paintings—I knew. One wealthy Austrian I dated in my early twenties *who shall remain nameless* even had a museum-quality *Diana* hanging in the entry hall of his country estate, by one of those famous Renaissance artists whose *objets d'affection* were always depicted as lumpy and pale—a reflection of the beauty standards of the time I'm sure, but Fee! My God. Greek goddesses had nothing on her. She was *TV pretty.* Though these days it did seem like every casting wanted "real people." As if having a symmetrical face and a trim waist somehow made you not a real person.

People might think I'd be jealous of my young assistant—and I'm sure some actresses would be—but you can't hold youth against the young. I am an Aquarius, after all; I've always valued aesthetics. And I understood what it was like to be splendor in the springtime of life. I was a girl like her not that long ago: hot without caveat. I knew I was still beautiful—it would be ungrateful and disingenuous to pretend otherwise—but I had to admit I was always a little thrown when I looked in the mirror these days. Like, *Who is this woman staring back at me?*

As much as I'd have loved to imagine myself aging gracefully like a sexy French dame, I lived in Hollywood, where women were put out to pasture at forty. Which is why I couldn't let anyone know I'd just turned forty. Forty! Lord, it sounded so *old*. The problem was, I'd been acting since I was a child, so it was hard to lie believably about my age. And it didn't help that I had to dye my hair every three weeks to keep the grays at bay. I did it myself so no one would know. You can't trust hair stylists. At least I still had my "captivating emerald" eyes (September 2005 *Vogue*'s description, not mine), though the crow's-feet drove me nuts, and I was afraid to get injections around my eyes for fear of looking frozen. C'est la vie.

I stepped beneath the shade of the thatched umbrella and fanned myself with my hat as Felicity sauntered across the pale pink sand, her thin beige bikini clinging to her curvy wet body like a tan line. I couldn't help but notice Jackson pretending not to watch from out in the bay. *Ooh…they would make a cute couple. Maybe I should play matchmaker.* I did want to help her any way I could. Contrary to popular belief, I was actually quite generous. "Come meet Cole," I continued. "And—" Oh hell, I'd forgotten the producer girl's name again. "And everybody!"

Felicity fluffed her bangs and ran her fingers through her short brunette waves, flashing a smile that warmed her cat-like dark eyes. "I just have to hug you," she purred, throwing her toned arms around Cole's neck. Accustomed to but never bored by the attention of beautiful girls, he inhaled her like a wolf would a rabbit, his hands on her back as she pressed her damp skin to his. "*Bad Boy* got me through high school."

"Glad to be of service." He fixed her with his mesmerizing gaze.

"I'm Taylor," the producer girl chimed in, extending her hand.

Wait a minute—*this* was Taylor? Surely she couldn't be the same Taylor the wardrobe girls were dishing about at my fitting. She certainly didn't look like a "devious little slut." She was diminutive and pale with messy black hair and brown eyes, wearing an unflattering mix of knee-length cutoff jean shorts and a bulky T-shirt that seemed specifically designed to repel any romantic interest.

The wardrobe girls were shocked I hadn't heard about the scandal— something about her being fired for embezzling from the studio run by her father while having an affair with a coworker—but after all the hurtful things printed about me over the years, I never read gossip. Which of course meant I shouldn't believe it either. So maybe this Taylor wasn't a homewrecking embezzler after all. But I kinda hoped she was. It had been my experience that devious little sluts were generally way more fun than upright citizens.

"I have to hug you too." Felicity beamed, wrapping Taylor in an embrace. "Thank you for having me down."

Over Felicity's shoulder, I could see a wave of discomfort pass over Taylor's face. I hadn't exactly told her I was bringing an assistant. But what could she expect? I was a star; of course I had an assistant. And the line producer had approved the cost last-minute without protest. She was lucky I didn't travel with a personal chef, a trainer, and a makeup artist, like some of my contemporaries.

Felicity fingered Taylor's curls. "Your hair smells amazing. What is that?"

"It's just the...uh, the hotel shampoo," Taylor stammered, her cheeks pink.

"It's delicious," Felicity breathed. "I'm gonna steal every bottle in my bathroom."

She released Taylor, leaving the impression of her wet swimsuit top on Taylor's black T-shirt, and swept her arm out at the brilliant beach. "Gorgeous day."

"So you're Stella's assistant?" Cole asked her, though I could've sworn I'd just clarified this. Maybe I hadn't. Sometimes the pills I took for my anxiety made it hard to differentiate between what I'd thought and what I'd actually said, but they made me feel so good I didn't mind. I'd snuck an extra on the plane ride over, and now I was wrapped up in its soft embrace like a baby in a blanket. I was supposed to be sober, of course, but the pills were prescription. No one but Felicity needed to know how many I'd taken or how delightful they made me feel.

Felicity nodded, batting her kohl-rimmed almond eyes at my ex-husband.

"She's the absolute best," I confirmed. "I don't know what I'd do without her."

I could see the edge of Cole's lip twitching like he was holding back a smirk. "And how long have you been working together?"

Felicity slipped her tanned arm around me and gave my shoulder a squeeze. "Feels like forever, doesn't it?"

"But how long has it actually been?" he needled.

What was he on about? "We met around the time the rains cleared," I offered. I'd thought that would be enough, but they were all still looking at me expectantly. "It must've been spring," I clarified, catching Felicity's eye for confirmation. "The jacarandas were blooming, remember?" She nodded. "I love the jacarandas, raining soft purple flowers all over the city..." Now they were eyeing me. Perhaps I'd said too much. It was so difficult to strike a balance between not enough and too much when you were floating on a cloud just above your body. "I'm so transported by beauty," I explained. "It makes me feel alive. It's beautiful here too though, isn't it?"

There, I'd brought it back around. I felt a trickle of sweat run down my back as we all took a minute to appreciate the gently lapping sunlit sea.

"Yes." Taylor nodded. "I love those flowering red trees."

"The flamboyant trees!" I exclaimed, proud I knew the name. "I love the flamboyant trees too."

"Flamboyant trees, what a great name." Taylor was smiling for real now. I could always tell when people were smiling for real. And I have to say, her wide smile made her much more attractive. "How did you know that?"

"I shot a movie down here—*Call of the Sea*? I played the daughter of a ship captain, learned to sail a boat and everything. But I just fell in love with those trees. Loved them so much I had one planted in my yard back in LA."

"I know *Call of the Sea*," Taylor piped up. "You were fantastic in it. Weren't you nominated for a supporting Oscar?"

"No." I sighed. It was a sore point. I shouldn't have brought it up. I got freshly angry anytime I thought of it. "I got the Golden Globe nom but was snubbed by the Oscars."

"That was one of the first R-rated movies I ever saw," Felicity chimed in.

"No need to remind us of your embryonic age, *babe*," I teased. "You exude youth like a virgin at prom."

Taylor laughed. "You're funny," she said in what I thought just might be an admiring sort of way. Maybe I was going to like this devious little slut after all. She was no beauty, bless her heart, but she was cute. She had spunk, and a little spunk goes a long way, especially combined with flattery.

"So, two months, then?" Cole was looking at me like he expected an answer; I had no idea what he was talking about. I would have raised an eyebrow, but I'd had my forehead Botoxed the previous week, so that was impossible.

Felicity pursed her full lips. "Something like that."

I was glad they'd settled it.

"Huh," Cole said. "And how did you meet?"

Lord he was nosy today. "Pure luck." I couldn't help but smile, re-membering Felicity silhouetted by the late-afternoon sun, the bracelet slipping from her wrist as she crossed the path ahead of me. "I was with Mary Elizabeth at Lake Hollywood—"

"She's still alive?" Cole spat incredulously.

"Who's Mary Elizabeth?" Taylor asked.

"Her Chihuahua," Cole clarified. "She must be a hundred years old—she's had her since we were together."

"Oh my God shut up. It wasn't that long ago."

He chuckled. "It was pre-Obama."

I rolled my eyes. "No need to date—"

"Oh, I'm sure it's all a fog for you, *darling*." Cole bared his teeth in what appeared to everyone else as a charming smile. And here I'd been thinking perhaps he'd changed.

But I wouldn't let him get me down. I opened my bag and gently lifted my sweet darling from her tuffet. She was shaking, unnerved by the sudden exposure to the terrible brightness of the beach and all the staring faces, her tawny fur raised in alarm. She reached her little paws for me, and I pressed her to my chest as she licked my chin. At least I wouldn't have to worry about her getting cold in this balmy climate.

Felicity reached over and stroked her head. "Hello, angel," she cooed.

"She's adorable," Taylor remarked. "She's so tiny."

"With such a big heart," Felicity agreed, taking her from me and nestling her between her boobs. Mary Elizabeth calmed down immediately.

"She loves Felicity." I smiled.

"I see," Cole said. His eyes were hidden by dark glasses, but I'd bet all the money I had left (which, granted, wasn't much) that he was staring at her cleavage. Honestly, it was hard not to.

I'd once had that effect on him. Not that I wanted to now—though I could likely still draw his eye if I tried. He was as handsome as ever and a dalliance *would* be good press. Felicity was insistent I shouldn't fear the press anymore; I was to court it, feed it, use it. I'd been out of the spotlight only a few short years—well, a decade, I guess—but *things have changed*, she said. I was to be proactive if I wanted to revitalize my career. I needed to get people's attention, show them who I was today. But I'd been hiding from the press since I was a teenager. Now suddenly I was supposed to embrace it? Wouldn't I appear desperate, fighting for attention like a reality star—or worse, social media influencer?

I was an actress, not a fame whore like whoever it was they'd hired to play opposite me. Madison somebody. Karanian? Karabian? Kasabian, that was it. *Madison Kasabian.* I'd never heard of her, but apparently she had over a million followers, whatever that meant. I'd looked her up and found hundreds, maybe thousands, of videos of an admittedly beautiful girl with perfect skin, long raven hair, enviable brows, and a full mouth, but no discernable talent that I could see, besides transforming her face with contouring and makeup. Which was certainly a great skill to have, but not the one you needed to be a real actress. What was this world coming to?

"So, you were telling us how you two met." Cole shifted his gaze from Felicity to me.

Why did I feel like he was challenging me? Had he only invited me here for his entertainment? It was hard enough trying to keep my chin up these days without my ex-husband taunting me. I'd only seen him a few brief times since I accepted the role, but he'd been so nice until now that I'd been hopeful he'd evolved. Alas, I probably shouldn't have taken the role—I knew better than anyone how changeable he could be—but I couldn't turn it down. I needed it. And he knew I needed it. The roof of my beautiful home was leaking, the pool was empty, my car was making a terrible noise. Luckily, I had a mechanic who always did the labor for free after I went to lunch with him, but still, Range Rover parts were expensive, especially on older models.

To be in a deferential position with Cole wasn't ideal, but I wouldn't bite the hand that fed me no matter how much it scratched. I fingered my crystal pendant: amethyst, for tranquility and sobriety. Regardless of his motivation for giving me this role, it was a godsend for which I was grateful. I would have an Attitude of Gratitude. He'd given me the opportunity; all I had to do was turn in a brilliant performance, and I would have my career back for real. No more low-budget indies with their cheap motels and pizzas for dinner. Pizza! I couldn't do the carbs. I really couldn't. The bloating, the lethargy...

Truth be told, I'd done only one of those awful low-budget affairs. A horror movie, of all things. But it took only one to realize that sort of thing was not for me. They didn't even have stand-ins—they expected me to stand there for hours drenched in disgusting sticky fake blood while they adjusted their shoddy lighting equipment. I shuddered at the memory. I'd gotten rave reviews though, by the handful of people who saw the thing. And it had helped me secure a part in a Lifetime movie. Not a large part, but a part, nonetheless. I recognized how depressing it was that I considered a small role in a Lifetime movie a career win these days, but I would stay positive. *What you think about you bring about!* I only ever thought of myself as a star and stayed far away from the forbidding stairwells that twisted downward into the dark recesses of my mind.

Which, of course, was why I hadn't made any progress on the tell-all memoir I was meant to be writing. In a moment of insanity during a promo I was contractually obligated to do for the horror film, I'd told the interviewer I was writing a memoir. To clear things up, in my own words. Put the truth out there, no reporters involved (and hopefully put a little money in my bank account). It was a good idea; Felicity agreed. Only, I hadn't yet been able to bring myself to actually write the damn thing.

My mouth was suddenly parched, and Cole was looking at me like he wanted an answer for something. Luckily, Felicity swooped to the rescue.

"I dropped my charm bracelet," she recounted. *Christ, are we still talking about this?* "It was from my mother and meant everything to me. Stella picked it up, and we started talking. I fell in love with Mary Elizabeth immediately and offered to help with her."

"And she was so much help, I realized she was the perfect fit to be my assistant," I finished, with what I hoped was an air of finality.

Neither of us mentioned that I'd yet to pay Felicity a dime of actual money. I had no idea how she was paying her bills; I'd been compensating her for her time with clothes and bags and jewelry. But now she was on the movie payroll, thank heavens.

"Welcome aboard." Cole flashed his dimple at Felicity.

"Thank you," she said. "I'm here to help, so if there's anything that any of you need, as long as I'm not busy with something for Stella, I'm happy to assist."

Taylor laughed. "Careful what you offer on a set. It's easy to get taken advantage of."

Felicity smiled. "I'm not worried about that."

---

# HORRORFANSONLINE:

## VIDEO INTERVIEW WITH STELLA RIVERS, STAR OF *BLOOD BOND*

**78 people like this**

[Time marker 4:57]

***HorrorFans:*** So you've never done horror before. What drew you to the role of Emily?

***Stella Rivers:*** No matter the genre, I always choose roles that speak to me on some level, and I really identified with Emily. It's not easy when your husband takes up with someone else. It makes you doubt yourself, leaves you feeling defeated, less-than... You start thinking self-destructive thoughts. It can drive you crazy, as it does Emily, and you become someone you don't even recognize.

***HF:*** It sounds like you have some personal experience with cheating.

**SR:**   You know I don't talk about my personal life, but I will say it's something I'm familiar with. Emily's not the kind of person who sits there and takes it, and that's something I can really appreciate. I'm like that too. Her anger transforms her. Of course she makes some mistakes along the way, that end up—not to spoil anything—adding to the horror element of the movie—

**HF:**   **Good catch. We don't want to give anything away. This one has a shocking ending you won't see coming. The raw anger you channeled as Emily was very believable.**

**SR:**   Thank you. I really felt like I could feel her pain, and it was cathartic for me. We've gone through some of the same things. You know how it is—you get angry and suddenly your anger takes over and maybe you do things you wish you hadn't. Then it's over and you look back and realize "Shit, I shouldn't have done that, and now I'm gonna have to live with it for the rest of my life," and it can really bring you down, make you crazy.

**HF:**   **(laughs) Wow, what are you trying to tell us?**

**SR:**   No, it's just sometimes—you know, sometimes good people do bad things. And bad people do bad things too, of course. And sometimes a bad person or a bad moment can influence a good person to do a bad thing.

**HF:**   **Sounds like you need to write a book.**

**SR:**   Oh, I am. You know, people look at me and they see all the outside things, the things the tabloids have printed. But they don't know the real story. And I'll tell you, it's not what it seems.

**HF:** So the famously private Stella Rivers is writing a tell-all memoir?

**SR:** I'm private because things get filtered and twisted by the press. But in my own words, I want to come clean, as they say, set the record straight.

**HF:** And when can we expect this explosive book?

**SR:** You know any good publishers, you send them my way.

**HF:** I certainly will. It's been great talking with you. Please come back when you release your book!

# Felicity

Iris stands in front of the mirror in her panties, painting her eyes black. I like them better plain like when it's just the two of us hanging out by the pool at the Super 8 next door or whatever, but she tells me I'm wrong. Men like mystery.

It must be true because every night she changes from my mom (which I am not allowed to call her except in my head) into this magical creature: glittering eyes, golden hair like a shampoo commercial, boobs spilling out of her dress, legs all tan and shimmery, balancing with ease on heels I can't walk two steps in. She's like a butterfly. Only, one time when I told her that, thinking it was a good thing, she wrinkled her nose and said, "Ew! So I'm, like, normally a caterpillar? Gross."

But she knows what she's doing because every night she gets a man. She doesn't usually bring them to our apartment unless they're special because I'm here and she doesn't want them seeing where she lives. But she tells me about them. What they do, what nice clothes they wear, what their fancy apartments look like. She doesn't tell me what they do with her, but I can guess. I've seen the internet. And also there was one time Miss Nina downstairs wasn't home, and she had to hide me in the bathroom when she brought one home.

Now that I'm ten I get to stay home by myself at night because I'm so responsible. And really I got to do that most of the time when I was nine too, and a little bit at eight. But before that I had to stay with neighbors and friends like Miss Nina or Mrs. Alvarez, who always had like a dozen kids there, so that was really fun.

Staying home alone isn't so bad though. I get to watch as much TV and whatever movies I want, even if they're R rated, with sex and cussing and people shooting each other. And I love movies. I think maybe one day I'll be a movie star. Mom says I won't be so pudgy when I grow up. It's just baby fat, she says. And I'll grow into my big nose, which must be my father's because it's sure not hers. At least I have her shiny blond hair and big blue eyes.

I grab one of her lip glosses and paint my mouth with it, making kissy faces in the glass. Suddenly my lips are on fire. "Shit!" I fan my mouth, tears springing to my eyes.

Iris laughs as I flip on the sink and try to get the gunk off. "Lip plumper," she says when I straighten up and wipe my face on a towel. "That'll teach ya to ask when you wanna borrow something."

"Why do you do that?" I blink away tears. "It burns."

She shrugs. "Beauty must suffer—haven't you heard?" She applies it to her own lips and smacks them without flinching.

"You look beautiful," I say. "Are you dancing tonight?"

She shakes her head, curls bouncing.

She's a dancer, but I've never gotten to see her dance because you have to be a grown-up to go to the place where she dances. But we like to dance together when we're watching *American Idol* or *America's Got Talent*, and I can tell how good she is.

"So, do you have a date?"

She spritzes herself with perfume that smells like jasmine. "You know it, girl."

The bathroom's so small that now I smell like jasmine too, which makes me feel like she's hugging me. "Who's the lucky gentleman?"

She likes it when I call her dates gentlemen. It makes her laugh.

"I don't even know if I should tell you." Her sky-blue eyes twinkle. "It's a secret."

"Why's it a secret? Is he a politician?" She's told me how much politicians love to keep secrets. Especially the ones who talk about Jesus a lot.

"Even better." She breezes into our bedroom and rifles through the overstuffed closet, pulling out a sparkly silver dress.

"Now you have to tell me," I beg. "I swear I won't tell anyone."

She shimmies into the minidress and offers me her back. "He's a movie star," she says as I zip her up.

My eyes go wide. "Which one?"

"Only your favorite." She grins.

"Cole Power?" I gasp. I don't even like boys yet, and I like him. I would have a poster of him above my bed if I didn't share a bed with my mom. "You have a date with *the* Cole Power?"

She nods. I spring onto the bed and start jumping and squealing. I can't control myself. "Oh my God, oh my God, oh my God! Holy shit, Mom!"

"Iris!" she corrects me.

"Sorry. I'm just so excited!" I bounce onto my butt next to her on the tired pink comforter.

"How'd you meet him?"

She removes a shoe box from a shopping bag and takes out a pair of sky-high silver heels to match the dress. "He came into the club last night and liked me so much he spent the entire evening with me."

"So that's how you got those new shoes." I laugh.

She slips them on and stands. "What do you think?"

"You look like a supermodel," I say. It's true, she's the most gorgeous mom anybody ever had. I'm sure of it. "Maybe he'll want to marry you." My eyes travel to the black-and-white poster of the Eiffel Tower hanging above our bed. "We could finally go to Paris!" But a cloud darkens my happiness as I remember the cover of one of the magazines sitting on our coffee table. "He's married already though. He got married to Stella Rivers, like, last month."

"That's why it's a secret," she says, stuffing things into her purse. "But don't worry. Celebrities have affairs all the time. It's no big deal. And anyway, marriage is overrated. Better to be the one he's cheating with than the one he's cheating on!"

She pulls me in for a jasmine hug and kisses me on the mouth, leaving my lips burning. But I don't mind. My mom is going on a date with Cole Power.

# The Biz Report

## TAYLOR WASSERMAN AND RORY WEXLER DUMPED FROM WOODLAND STUDIOS

## (DEVELOPING)

New details are emerging about Taylor Wasserman and Rory Wexler's abrupt firing from Woodland Studios yesterday. Former colleagues say each was escorted from the lot separately around 4:00 p.m., but no details were released until a company-wide memo went out this morning. According to the memo, Wasserman and Wexler were let go due to "misappropriation of funds" over a period of months. Sources say the creative accounting was to cover up an affair between the two that had been going on for over a year. Items under investigation include expensive dinners in London, New York, and Los Angeles, thousands of dollars' worth of clothes and jewelry, and personal use of the company jet. Wasserman is the daughter of Woodland Studios SVP, David Wasserman, who could not be reached for comment.

# Taylor

The thatched straw umbrella did little to cut the heat of the day, which had blossomed from warm to flat-out torrid as the breeze off the bay faltered. I'd been tracking the weather obsessively to ensure that production was prepared for whatever Mother Nature had in store, but clearly my weather app had misjudged the situation. High today of eighty with showers in the afternoon, my ass. It had to be at least ninety-five and not a cloud in the cobalt sky. I fanned myself with my hat as I tried in vain to concentrate on matching the list of script changes Cole requested with the script changes Stella requested before the shit hit the fan tomorrow with the first day of filming, but it was next to impossible with Stella perched on the edge of my lounger gossiping with Cole about famous people they knew and reminiscing about old times with strangely combative undertones.

It wasn't fair; I was here first. Sure, it would've been much easier to do my work in the privacy of my bungalow, but I'd hoped Stella would scoot so that I could ask Cole the dreaded question away from prying ears. That, however, was apparently not in the cards, and moving wasn't an option, as all the other sunshades were now occupied by cast and crew.

The camera and set design departments were recognizable by their tans, having been on the island with Jackson for preproduction nearly a month already, but everyone else had arrived today, and were making the most of the picturesque beach before being swept into six weeks of minimum twelve-hour days. Out in the bright bay, four guys attempted to race paddleboards, while the soccer game I'd been part of earlier had morphed into a boisterous game of football; the next umbrella over, someone was singing "No Woman, No Cry," strumming a guitar. Not an ideal working environment.

I closed the script and gathered my bag and towel. I'd have to corner Cole alone later.

"You taking off?" Stella asked, less than disappointed.

"Yeah. It's a little hot for me."

"Don't forget to pay that bar tab," Cole said.

"Already took care of it." I shouldered my bag as I stood. "See you guys later."

Intending to go for a dip in the pool, I strode toward the shaded path that led up the hill from the beach to the restaurant and infinity pool, but stopped when I spied Madison, our nanny actress, posing against a palm tree. She wore a red bikini that accentuated her curves, her long dark hair swept over one shoulder while making bedroom eyes at her phone, which was strapped to the branch of a nearby flowering bush with a GorillaPod. The GorillaPod slipped before the timer on the phone camera went off, and she cursed and reset it. I froze and quickly ducked behind a screen of dense leaves and white blossoms. I really didn't feel like getting conscripted into taking photos of Madison right now.

A YouTube star with only one season of a television show and a horror film under her belt, Madison had been a last-minute addition to the cast when the girl we'd originally chosen had unexpectedly dropped out a week ago. Madison was no one's first or even second choice, but she was the only actress on the short list available for the immediate start date and pitiful salary we were offering, so here she was, bringing her 1.1 million followers along for the ride. Fun fact about Madison: she'd been briefly involved with my father while she was on the television show—which was under the umbrella of the studio he ran—but as far as I knew, she was unaware of my knowledge of this, and I planned to keep it that way. Their affair had not ended well, and I knew my hiring her would irritate him, which in its own sick way made me happy.

Before I could slip away, Felicity sauntered up the path from the beach with a straw bag slung over her shoulder. She spotted me haphazardly hidden among the palms and gave me a quizzical look but thankfully didn't say anything. I pressed my finger to my lips, then pointed in the direction of Madison. She caught sight of Madison and took a step back, but it was too late: Madison had already seen her.

"Oh my God," Madison exclaimed, rushing over to Felicity. "What are you doing here?"

"I'm sorry," Felicity returned with a friendly smile. "I don't think we've met. Were you on the plane from LA?"

"No, no, I flew in from New York. I'm Madison. From the Actor's Toolbox?" Madison prompted. "We were in Lawrence's class together, like, two years ago. You're Nikki Nimes."

Felicity shook her head. "No. I'm Felicity Fox."

Madison peered at her suspiciously. "You're messing with me, right? You came over to my condo to rehearse. We did a scene together, from"—she snapped her fingers, trying to recall—"*Nine to Five*! With Belle—Isabelle Carter. Tall, southern brunette? But it was right around the time I booked *Dallas Divas*, so I had to drop out before we could perform it."

"I'm sorry," Felicity repeated. "I'm not an actress, and I only moved to LA a few months ago. I'm Stella Rivers's assistant."

"Huh." Madison tilted her head. "That's so weird. You look just like her. I mean, she had long blond hair, but like, I think I had blond hair then too, so... You have a sister or a cousin or something?"

"No. I've been told I have a familiar face," Felicity said. "People are always thinking I'm someone else. Sorry I'm not your friend."

"Oh, we weren't, like, *friends*. She was kinda weird, actually. She never hung out with any of us after class, like she thought she was better or something. And you know, I think she was meaner-looking than you. Maybe it's the nose. Yeah, you have a better nose for sure. Still. Pretty crazy. I'll have to find her on social to show you. Hey, speaking of, can you take a picture of me? I was trying to get one for my Insta, but the camera kept slipping."

Odd. Madison had seemed so sure she was someone else, it was unsettling. I hadn't processed Felicity's paperwork, but I felt like I would have at least been alerted if the name she was using didn't match her passport. I'd have to ask Francisco to check. I *had* pegged her for an actress immediately when I laid eyes on her. Perhaps she'd done an acting class under a different name and was now denying it? But why? Or maybe, more likely, it was simply a case of mistaken identity.

I took their distraction with the phone as an opportunity to slink off toward the beach, away from the crowd. I made my way across the downy sand to the shore, past the outcropping of rocks where I'd first spotted Felicity tanning, toward the end of the island, where a dock jutted into the sea. This was my first trip to the Caribbean, and I couldn't get over how bright the water was. I was used to the sapphire blue of the Pacific, but this was an aquamarine so brilliant it seemed lit from within, dappled with red patches of seaweed that looked purple beneath the waves and sprawling beds of coral that turned the sea above a light green.

And the sand! I'd never felt sand so soft, tinted the lightest pink with finely crumbled conch shells. Sure, I might not be a beach person, but I could admit the place had its perks.

Safely out of sight of my compatriots, I dropped my bag, stripped down to my swimsuit, and sprinted into the ocean with abandon. The water was what some might describe as too warm, but I've never been a fan of cold water, and it was enough cooler than the air to be refreshing. Little fish flitted between my legs; I could see my gunmetal-gray-shellacked toes as clearly as if I'd been in a pool. It was perfect.

I dove under. Light flickered across my closed eyelids as I glided through the water. Feeling reborn, I arose and floated on my back, shielding my eyes from the dazzling sun with a raised hand. Two white birds with black heads and red beaks circled overhead, periodically diving into the water to feed.

Admittedly, this moment of Zen was rare for me; I normally never relaxed at all during production. I'd come straight home from set and work until I fell asleep, sometimes upright, then wake up and do it all over again the next day. Days off were for stressing about the week ahead. I'd spent months shooting in places everyone told me were amazing and never left my room except to walk to the passenger van that couriered us to set. It was better this way; I stayed focused.

But perhaps this time would be different. I could imagine falling under the spell of this island, swimming here in this bay every chance I got, tasting the salt water on my lips. I'd make my therapist proud. Ha! She'd have a field day knowing that at this very moment, basking in the Caribbean sun on a tranquil sea, I could still hear my father's voice in my head loud and clear, reminding me that I would only ever be average, and if I wanted to get ahead, I'd have to work harder than everyone. A glimmer of guilt smoldered at the base of my skull for all the time I was squandering right now, floating around like a rich girl on holiday. I wasn't rich, and this wasn't a holiday. I had far too much riding on this film to fuck it up.

Who was I kidding? I'd already fucked up, and we hadn't even begun shooting yet.

Cole and I had arrived via chartered jet two days prior, our assistants and his personal trainer in tow. The assistant director and camera department were already on the island prepping with Jackson (as I should have been, if not for the budgetary crisis), but the rest of the cast and crew wouldn't show up until the following evening. Cole was early by design. He had a tradition of taking the camera crew to a rowdy dinner the night before everyone else arrived on set, ostensibly to thank them for all their preproduction work, but also to ensure he'd be liked well enough to be shot in the most flattering light. He'd do the same thing with the editors before postproduction commenced. No one ever said he wasn't smart.

I'd worked the entire flight and was so tired when we arrived that all I wanted was to lie on the cool glass floor of my bungalow and watch the fish in the ocean below, but Cole had other ideas.

First up was a tour of the verdant grounds conducted by smiling staff in a souped-up golf cart. Cole rode shotgun while I sat in back, wedged between our assistants. I adored my assistant. Francisco was the one good thing about my job. A twenty-five-year-old Mexican American with a small frame and a big smile, he'd become my confidant over the past three months; it always lightened my mood to gossip with him, trading stories about our terrible past boyfriends and nonexistent current dating lives. He was smart and hardworking, and even better, snarky, well dressed, and teaching me Spanish. He also had a mad crush on Cole's perennial cool-guy assistant Ben, though neither of us was entirely sure which team Ben was hitting for. Perhaps both, or neither. We'd come to the conclusion that it was likely even Ben wasn't sure.

We tooled around the small, roughly angelfish-shaped island, dazed by its surreal beauty; the Genesius Resort covered the head end, with the main road running the half mile down the center to the town and port at the tail end. The rocks where I first spied Felicity would be the mouth, and the pool and restaurant area the eye. On the back side where the dorsal fin might be was the golf course, and in place of the ventral fin on the belly side were the beach and over-water bungalows, with the dock on the crown side of the head. Lush greenery climbed up the hill from the beach to the shaded teakwood deck and infinity pool that looked out over the bay, presided over by a giant stone Buddha, behind which sat the spa. The restaurant, bar, and lobby were in an adjoining airy building with a view of the sea.

The setting was beyond gorgeous and all very serene, until Cole commandeered the golf cart and promptly wrecked it into a sand dune.

But he owned the resort—the reason we'd been able to reserve it for the duration of our shoot—so I guess he was allowed to wreck things.

After the golf cart tour was a sunset cruise on the resort's sportfishing yacht, Cole's jocularity greater with every cup of rum. I don't generally drink when I'm working, but I was stressed enough by the full day behind us, I acquiesced to his pleas and downed a fruity cocktail with him as we sped past dolphins into the tangerine sky. I could tell the captain, a fit Black guy about my age, was less than impressed by my boss's antics, his relaxed smile growing a little tighter every time Cole slapped him on the back and tried for the wheel, shouting, "Let's see how fast this thing can go!" But Cole himself was none the wiser, slinging an arm around the guy's shoulders and reminiscing about their past fishing trips like a commander recalling battles of long ago.

When we returned, Francisco and Ben were allowed to retreat to their rooms, but Cole insisted I join him for a chef's choice dinner on the porch of the charming restaurant, complete with some bottle of wine he insisted was too expensive for me not to at least sample.

This is where it got hazy.

I didn't remember leaving the restaurant but had the faint recollection of being carried somewhere—by him, I supposed—though I couldn't imagine how I could've let that happen. It must've been the alcohol, but all I could count were the rum drink on the boat and a glass of wine at dinner. Granted, the cocktail was stronger than I would have made myself, and my tolerance had likely plummeted in recent weeks. I'd had so much on my plate with preproduction that my social life was nonexistent, and at home I mostly abstained in favor of an early-morning workout.

At any rate, I remembered nothing from dinner until the following morning—when I awoke naked in my bed, covered in sand.

I was alone, thank God. Sun filtered through the slits in the wide wooden shutters, and I could hear the sea lapping at the pillars that held the bungalow above the water. The wood and glass floor was clean, the rattan chair empty; a dark-green T-shirt was crumpled on the bedside table. I felt a sinking feeling in the pit of my stomach as I recognized it as the shirt Cole had been wearing the previous evening. The clothes I'd worn last night were nowhere in sight.

I surveyed the platform bed. Pillowcase streaked with mascara, comforter pushed back, all the pillows rumpled. I wanted to think I'd slept alone, but evidence pointed to the contrary. I was alone now though, so that was something. Perhaps I'd just been so drunk, I'd slept wildly last night. The sheets were soiled and damp in spots; I put my nose to the bed and sniffed. Detergent, salt water, and sweat, I thought—though I couldn't rule out other bodily fluids.

I shuddered. I couldn't believe I'd let this happen. I hadn't blacked out since... I wasn't sure I'd ever blacked out. There were hazy moments in the back of cabs after long nights during college, but nothing like the dark hole that stretched from dinner until dawn. Try as I might, I could shed no light on how many times my wineglass might have been refilled or how the evening had ended. I could only assume stress had driven me to drink more than I remembered. I cringed to think what I might have said... or done.

A prickle in the back of my brain. If this had happened in a bar, I'd assume I'd been roofied. But here? The staff would never in a million years, and I couldn't imagine why Cole would roofie me. With a crook of his finger, he could bed anyone he wanted, at any time. I was hardly a prize catch.

I got up and showered, studying my alabaster body while lathering the suds as though I might be able to coax what happened from my thighs, but they were unusually silent, not even a murmur of admonishment about the plate of conch fritters I devoured on the speedboat.

*Why, oh why, is Cole's shirt on my bedside table?*

Did I have some deep subliminal attraction to Cole that I'd hidden from myself? I pictured his strong jaw, his toned body, imagined his lips on mine.

Nope, nothing.

Maybe I'd borrowed Cole's shirt for some reason. I was cold? Or wet? That could explain everything. I'd gotten drunk and gone swimming (in my clothes, hopefully), which would explain the sand and the slight wetness of the sheets, then borrowed Cole's dry shirt to wear home. Embarrassing, but not catastrophic.

Though I still had the nagging feeling I hadn't slept alone. Perhaps I'd brought home a waiter or a busboy? I scoured my mind for any detail, but it was useless. I just didn't remember.

I hadn't had sex since . . . wow, New Year's. Months ago. So I guess it made sense that I might be sexually frustrated. But Cole Power was the exact wrong person to fulfill that need. Some random resort employee would be better, though not by much. Was I sore? Maybe? Then again, maybe not. But I'd never really been one to get sore even when it had been a while, unless I'd had particularly rough sex, so my lack of soreness didn't mean much.

What a colossal fuckup, especially taking into account how my last job had ended. I needed to present myself as the consummate professional, not a professional who consummated her working relationships.

But I was getting ahead of myself. I would have to talk to Cole and find out what exactly had happened. Fun.

I prepared my speech to him while I towel dried my kinky curls, then wrapped myself in a plush white bathrobe and stepped into the living room. The decor of my bungalow was the same as throughout the resort: modern and minimalist, yet comfortable with a Southeast Asian flair in the form of Buddhas and orchids, carved teakwood, and colorful textile throw pillows to complement the neutral shades of the linens and furniture. There was no doubt the place was beautifully and expensively designed, but what made it so special were the unobstructed ocean views through windows that stretched from the floor to the soaring thatched roof. A ray of sunshine illuminated my open purse atop the dining table, and the black jumpsuit I'd been wearing last night was neatly folded over one of the chairs. Had I folded it, or had housekeeping visited while I slept?

I unpacked my suitcase and dressed, then ventured out into the bright, windy day. As I exited my bungalow, I spotted our bearded lumberjack of a cinematographer, Brian, and the wiry camera op, Adam, walking down the pier toward the sand with beach bags slung over their shoulders, but no one else was around.

I grabbed an iced latte from the espresso bar in the breezy lobby overlooking the sparkling pool and wandered the manicured grounds in search of Cole. I strolled through the empty restaurant and over to the gym—so air-conditioned the windows had fogged, but also empty. The woman behind the desk in the eucalyptus-scented spa hadn't seen him and didn't have any appointments scheduled that day—would I like one?

I considered; my knotted neck cried out for a massage and my nails were a wreck, but I had too much work to do to spare the time.

The day was beginning to heat up, the thick fleece of Caribbean humidity only sporadically interrupted by the flicker of a breeze as I trekked to the golf course on the far side of the property. No one had seen him there either.

Sweat trickling down my back, I descended the hill to the dock, where the fishing boat was just shoving off. I shaded my eyes against the morning sun and spotted Francisco waving wildly to me from the stern. I could make out Cole behind him, fiddling with a fishing line.

So the asshole was taking the guys fishing for the day and hadn't invited me.

I stalked back up the hill straight to the spa and had a ninety-minute Swedish massage followed by a mani-pedi, then spent the rest of the day working from my laptop on a cushioned lounger in the shade of an umbrella by the shimmering pool, uninterrupted. Regardless of my feelings about being left behind, I had to admit it was heaven. I nearly did a happy dance when the concierge who delivered my second strawberry smoothie and shrimp ceviche informed me that storms in Miami meant the rest of the cast and crew wouldn't arrive until the following morning.

I made sure to retire to my quarters for the evening before the boat returned. The light on my room phone was blinking with an earlier message from Francisco. "I'll work all day if you want. Anything not to go out and murder fish," he pleaded. I felt bad I hadn't heard the message sooner, but oh well. At least he'd been invited.

I lit one of the coconut-scented candles in my room and indulged in a long bath staring out at the placid sea, then ordered room service and set up camp in my cloudlike bed with a new romance novel from the secret stash I kept in my suitcase. I'd die if anyone ever found out about my guilty pleasure, but it was just that—pleasure. And escape, obviously, as my life was about as far from a romance novel as you could get. I didn't have the time or bandwidth for real-life romance these days, and besides, my taste in men had been proven to be terrible. I preferred to love vicariously through vivacious Vivian and her brooding boarder Benjamin. He had rippling muscles and a secret, and they would doubtless consummate their forbidden romance in an explicit encounter beneath a palm tree on a deserted beach, as I had specifically chosen this novel for its fitting Caribbean setting.

I knew I needed to get to the bottom of what the hell had happened last night but figured there were better times to approach Cole than when he'd doubtless been drinking all day. I'd do it tomorrow.

Only, now it was tomorrow, and I still hadn't quite worked up the courage. I realized, as I floated on my back staring up at wisps of clouds, that there was never going to be a good time to ask my boss what I'd done while I was blacked out. Problem was, I'd stopped taking birth control a few months ago because I wasn't having sex regularly enough to deal with how crazy the hormones made me. Worst-case scenario, if I had in fact slept with him and God forbid he didn't use a condom, I needed a Plan B pill and an STD test, stat. Could I even find a Plan B pill in this country?

I needed to talk to him now.

# *NOVA WEEKLY*

## COVER STORY: STELLA RIVERS ATTACKS PHOTOGRAPHER

Actress Stella Rivers was photographed accosting a photographer outside the Brentwood Women's Clinic in Los Angeles on Wednesday afternoon. Rivers emerged from the clinic at 2:40 p.m. to find a throng of paparazzi waiting for her. The Golden Globe–nominated actress was clearly upset and grew further agitated when the photojournalists began asking questions. She then allegedly shouted a string of expletives before shoving one of the photographers and hurling his camera to the sidewalk. The photographer, whose name has not yet been released, sought treatment at a nearby hospital and will reportedly press charges against Rivers.

The *Under the Blue Moon* actress married her *Faster* costar Cole Power in Las Vegas just over a year ago, but sources close to the couple say their marriage has been on the rocks for some time. It was earlier reported that the reason for their discord was that Rivers wanted to start a family while Power wasn't ready, but according to our source, the opposite is true: Power has been the one with the desire to start a family while Rivers is more interested in her career. A friend of Rivers speaking anonymously revealed to us exclusively that Rivers was at the women's clinic to undergo an abortion that Power was against, while Power sought consolation in Miami with their mutual friend Hannah Bridges, who reportedly tried to convince Rivers not to end her pregnancy.

# Stella

By the time I left the beach, I was beyond famished. It was mid-afternoon, and I hadn't eaten a thing since we left Miami at the crack of dawn. I knew I needed a workout more than a sandwich, but I was beginning to feel faint in the heat and my pills were wearing off, leaving me edgy. Clutching a sleeping Mary Elizabeth to my chest, I followed the signs for the restaurant along a shaded path and up wide wooden stairs around a wall of water spilling from the edge of an infinity pool.

I emerged from the leafy greenery into the full glare of the sun just as an oversize man cannonballed into the pool, splattering me with water. I took off my sunglasses and wiped them on my caftan as a production assistant who couldn't be more than eighteen rushed over, apologizing. I waved him away with a laugh. What, did he think I wasn't cool? I was cool. I'd partied harder than any of these amateurs in my time.

The pool was clearly where the fun was. Reggae music played and piña coladas flowed; a Ping-Pong game was in full swing under the awning of the restaurant. Most of the crew had to be here; there were at least thirty revelers, of which I counted one, two, three... four women, including Felicity and Madison, whom I had yet to meet.

Felicity floated like a mermaid on a swan-shaped lounger in the middle of the pool, and Madison posed in front of a pot of colorful flowers by the Ping-Pong table while some guy snapped photos of her with a phone.

My mouth watered as I watched Madison take a long draw of the pink frozen drink in her hand. Oh my God, I could almost taste it. Alas, I had to pretend to be sober the entire time I was here, like a teenager. So stupid. Thank heavens I had my pills and Felicity to secretly share her drinks with me. How was it possible I'd lived all my life without her up until a few months ago? Good help really was hard to find, especially on a tailored budget.

I placed Mary Elizabeth in my purse and shed my caftan, revealing the sexy white one-piece I'd splurged on last week. The neckline plunged near to my belly button, and the butt was a Brazilian cut that made all the Pilates I'd been suffering through totally worth it. I knew I looked hot in it, and sure enough from behind my sunglasses I clocked more than a few of the guys checking me out. It felt good. "Fee," I called.

Her head snapped up, and the swan nearly tipped over. She paddled slowly toward me, laughing. "This thing'll dump me into the water if I so much as breathe. You have a nice time at the beach?"

"It was beautiful," I confirmed. "It was lovely to catch up with Cole. We have so many friends in common, you know. And of course, our past..." My gaze drifted to Madison, now popping out from behind a plant over and over again. "What's she doing?"

Felicity followed my eyeline. "Boomerang. She's been at it since I came up here."

At that moment, Madison noticed us staring and waved brightly. She grabbed her phone from the guy and hurried over, thick dark waves bouncing. She really did have enviable hair, and her makeup was fantastic; I'd have to ask her for tips. Maybe we'd become friends after all.

"Hiiiii," she sang, perching next to me and holding her phone out. It was then that I noticed she was filming. "This is my costar, the talented Stella Rivers," she told the phone without looking at me. "It's so nice to finally meet her. Say hi, Stella!"

What a strange greeting. And I was not ready to have my picture taken. Heaven knows what I looked like after a sweltering day at the beach. I waved the camera away. "I'm good," I said. "Maybe later."

"But we're live streaming!" she protested.

No, we were not going to be friends.

" . . . with all my amazing fans," she continued. "How many of you are there? Wow, I see we have more than 143,000 watching right now. That is truly, truly amazing." She focused the camera on herself, batting her dark eyes flirtatiously. She was wearing eyelash extensions. Ugh, why hadn't I thought of that? "Thank you all so much for being here. I can't tell you how blessed I am to be in the beautiful Caribbean with such a talented cast. We have the camera-shy Stella Rivers"—she popped the phone over at me again, and I forced an uncomfortable smile—"and of course, Cole Power. Who doesn't love Cole Power? Well, I can name one person, but she isn't here now, is she?" She tittered.

As Madison rambled on about how amazing everything was, I fingered my amethyst pendant and threw Felicity a telepathic plea, silently begging her to get me out of there. I knew it was good for me to be in Madison's video in front of 143,000 fans—better than good. As much as I hated the fact that I was working with a YouTube star, she clearly knew how to court fans, and fans were what I needed. It really was so kind of her to include me, I chided myself. I should be grateful. I was grateful! Just not right now. I wasn't twenty-five with flawless skin. Sure, my mother's Venezuelan genes meant I was still getting carded at forty, but I needed to prepare to be on camera. I had an image to protect.

I was getting panicky, trapped half in the video with thousands of fans looking on. Felicity must've read my mind, because she pushed out of the pool and leaned into the shot between Madison and me, dripping all over her. "Oh!" Madison exclaimed. "Hi, Nikki!" She turned the camera on Felicity. "I'm so sorry, I can't remember your other name."

"No, I'm sorry," Felicity said, her cleavage filling the frame as she leaned in to grab my hand. "I totally forgot I was supposed to take Stella for a final wardrobe fitting. You'll have to forgive us." She pulled me up, and we both blew the camera kisses as we hastened down the teakwood stairs that led from the pool to the beach.

"Oh my God, that was intense," I breathed when we were safely out of earshot.

"Yeah, she's a little much," Felicity agreed.

"Why was she calling you Nikki?" I asked.

She shrugged. "Apparently she was in an acting class with a girl named Nikki that looked like me."

"Weird."

"Not really," she said, running her fingers through her bangs as we made our way down the shaded path that led to our row of over-water bungalows. "People are always telling me I look like someone else. It used to be annoying, but I've gotten used to it. I guess I just have one of those faces."

It was funny. I'd also noticed she resembled someone I knew in days gone by. But that someone was long dead, so I put it out of my mind.

Once we were safely ensconced in our gorgeous bungalow, I flung open the sliding glass doors that opened onto the wide deck and serene sea beyond and collapsed on the couch, releasing Mary Elizabeth onto the fuchsia silk pillow beside me. "That was terrible. They're all going to hate me. All 143,000 of them."

"No they're not," Felicity assured me.

I held my hand out. "Throw me my smokes."

She palmed the pack and shot me a look. "You sure?"

"Come on. It'll be my first of the day." I'd snuck one out the window when I took a shower this morning, but she didn't need to know that.

"But you're doing so great."

It was true I was smoking far less than I used to, but Rome wasn't built in a day. "For Godsake, just throw me one. My nerves are all jangled, and you're not letting me have a pill."

She extracted a cigarette from the pack and threw it at me. I caught it and strolled to the open doors, striking a light on a matchbox emblazoned with the name of the resort.

I inhaled, letting the nicotine do its work. The dive pool on our deck glittered invitingly, but I'd had enough sun for one day. The wrinkles just weren't worth it. "Madison has to be a Leo," I mused, blowing out a line of smoke that quickly dissipated in the breeze off the ocean.

"Why?" Felicity asked.

"She obviously thrives on attention. To court the public like that, inviting all those people into your private life to judge you?" I shivered. "I can't imagine."

"That's just Gen Z, everything is public. If a thousand people didn't see it, it didn't happen."

"But you're not like that," I protested. It was true, all her social medias were private, with only a handful of followers.

She shrugged. "I'm a private person."

"Which is why we work so well together," I said. "Why does Madison have so many fans, anyway? I mean, I know she's a YouTube star or whatever, but what's she famous for?"

"She had leukemia when she was a teenager and got a huge following blogging about her struggle with it."

My jaw dropped. "Okay, now I feel like an asshole."

"Her dying wish was to be on a TV show," Felicity went on, "so they gave her a walk-on role on *Dallas Divas*, which spiked the ratings so much that when she got well they made her a series regular."

"How do you know all this?"

She laughed. "The internet."

"I need a drink." I sighed, gazing out at the miles of turquoise water around us. "What do we have?"

She traipsed over to the refrigerator and opened the door. "Nothing."

"Order us something, will you? I'd love a chardonnay. Just get a bottle."

I stubbed the cigarette out in a shell ashtray as she dialed room service from the phone next to the Buddha-shaped lamp. I was grateful she had the sense to order a Chinese chicken salad for me as well (my favorite) and a club sandwich I knew was for her. The girl could eat bacon every day and never gain a pound, bless her heart.

When she hung up, she handed me a bottle of water and one of my A-pills, thank God. I'd lost my Screen Actors Guild health insurance when I didn't make the earning cutoff last year, and now my shoddy health insurance would only give me a thirty-day supply of my prescriptions, which wasn't enough to cover the six weeks I'd be on the island, so Felicity had procured the rest of the pills for me through a doctor she knew. Or was it a pharmacist? It didn't matter. She'd gotten them, which was what was important. Of course they were all generics with unpronounceable names, so we'd nicknamed each according to function. A-pills were for anxiety, D-pills for depression, P-pills for pain, and S-pills for sleeplessness. "Is it time?" I asked.

She nodded. "Past time."

Finally. I downed the pill with a gulp of water, relieved. That must have been why I was feeling so panicky. Managing the pills could be tricky because they all had different half-lives, so they had to be taken at different times, and the A-pills made time seem slippery and unimportant. I'd often lose track. But I'd been so much better since Felicity came along to keep up with everything.

The morning I met her in the park, my horoscope had said that a chance meeting could change my life. To expect help from unexpected places and that gold was a sign I was on the right path. I went out to walk Mary Elizabeth the same as I did every day, and all of a sudden there *by chance* was Felicity. When she literally dropped a gold bracelet on my path and Mary Elizabeth fell in love with her at first sight, I knew she had to be the "help from unexpected places." It was a miracle, really. A stroke of fate. And I believed in fate.

I'd gone to church sometimes growing up and always felt there was something out there bigger than myself, but I never had the time to explore it until I was in rehab the second time, after my DUI. The first time, rehab had masqueraded as an exorbitantly expensive "spa" for "exhaustion," but this time I had to satisfy the terms of the court and hadn't worked in two years, so it was stricter and less lavish. Though it ended up for the best and yet another example of fate stepping in because while I was there, I met a powerful psychic whose name was actually Faith, believe it or not. She shared her knowledge of metaphysics with me, and I've depended on her sage advice ever since. She's the one that gave me my amethyst pendant and the tigereye bracelet I wear for protection.

Faith had been telling me for years that everything was going to turn out fine if only I could be true to myself. Hiring Felicity was a step in the right direction, I thought. It was an example of being true to myself, because I was putting my needs first: I'd had the courage to hire her even though I didn't know how I was going to pay her. And now here I was, shooting a movie with my ex-husband, of all people, tucked away in an extravagant over-water bungalow with a jaw-dropping view. (I'd had Felicity check the prices. They normally went for $4,000/night minimum.) So everything really was turning out better than fine.

Felicity had been walking Mary Elizabeth for a solid week when I asked her to dog sit at my house while I was out for the day. By that time, my little darling was deeply in love with her, and Faith had read my cards and confirmed she was good for me, so I felt comfortable letting her into my sanctuary.

I came home to find her perusing the wall of framed black-and-white stills from films I'd done. She was so sweet and interested that I would have felt guilty not answering her questions, and before long I was thumbing through my old photo books, sharing stories I hadn't recounted in years while she hung on my every word. I'd had so many painful years that the memories of better times were often salt in my wounds and better to be avoided, but with Felicity lapping up the adventures of my former life like a kitten starved for milk, recollection suddenly became a salve.

The following week I asked her to dog sit again while I was out all day, and came home to both her and Mary Elizabeth on the kitchen floor licking Popsicles. It was an unseasonably sweltering day for May, and my air-conditioning wasn't working. I'd told Felicity I was waiting on the AC guy to come out, but the reality was, it had been broken for two years. I needed a new compressor, which was going to cost eight thousand dollars I never seemed to have lying around.

My home was a rambling Tudor affair in the Hollywood Hills, shaded by oak trees planted the year it was built, in 1928. I'd bought it outright for my twenty-third birthday, so all I had to pay were the property taxes, but I could barely manage those anymore. The house badly needed to be painted, and I'd stopped filling the pool a few years ago, but besides that and the air-conditioning, it was in pretty good shape.

I'd only just been cast in *The Siren* the week prior and came in buoyed by a conversation with Jackson to find Felicity there on the tiled floor fingering an invitation to a charity thing.

"Please don't kill me." She grimaced.

I hadn't been able to afford Botox at that particular moment, so I furrowed my brow. "Why?" I asked, alarmed.

She licked the Popsicle, taking her time before responding. "I kind of RSVP'd for us to this charity thing tonight."

My jaw dropped. How could she? It was *not* her place.

"I didn't mean to," she promised. "They called the house phone to confirm whether you were coming, and you'd told me to answer it."

"But…why did you say yes?"

"The lady was so nice, and she really seemed to want you to come. She said there'd be gift bags with that expensive face cream you were talking about the other day in them."

I sat in a chair in shock and scooped Mary Elizabeth into my lap. "I don't go to those things anymore."

"I know the press has been cruel to you, but you're different now, and they need to see that! If you start going out sometimes, people will realize how much you've grown. Public opinion changes. People's memories are short."

Maybe she was right. After all, I finally had something good to say when people asked what I was working on; I was once again relevant.

Before I knew it, we were playing dress-up in my closet like long-lost sisters. I may not have had cash, but I had clothes; my walk-in closet was just the start of it. The walls of my bedroom were lined with rolling racks, and I'd had a door put through to a guest room that was packed with more crowded rolling racks. Most of the clothes were at least a few years old, but they were all designer and half of them still had the tags on.

Felicity stripped off her sundress without an ounce of self-consciousness, strutting about in nothing but a yellow lace thong as she shimmied into dresses I hadn't worn since I was her age, which I figured to be somewhere around twenty-three.

I tried not to stare, but her body was a work of art—tan and toned and curvy in all the right places without an ounce of cellulite anywhere. Her full breasts defied gravity. A nipple grazed my bare arm as she reached past me to pull a dress off the rack, and I caught a whiff of jasmine. I suddenly grew light-headed.

"Are you okay?" she asked.

"Yeah, fine," I said, realizing I'd stopped breathing. "What's that perfume you're wearing?"

"Do you not like it?" she asked, worried. "I won't wear it anymore."

"It's nothing. Don't worry about it." I took the dress from her and rushed into the bathroom to change. When I returned, I noticed she'd spritzed herself with one of the perfumes from my shelf. I didn't say anything, but I was glad.

The light was fading by the time Felicity and I stepped out of our black limo into the balmy night. I was a little embarrassed to be arriving in a limo, but it was surprisingly cheaper than a town car and less than half the rate of a Suburban.

A single flame of jealousy flickered as I watched Felicity slink up the walk to the massive Mediterranean mansion in my low-cut emerald dress, the photographers eyeing her through the open door the way they used to eye me. But then she turned, engulfing me in the radiance of her smile. My envy evaporated, leaving in its place ghastly apprehension of the task at hand.

It had been ages since I'd set foot on a step-and-repeat. How I used to love it! Like standing before the sun if the sun shone only for you. All its white-hot energy directed at you, wanting your attention, calling your name, showering you with love and light. But in that moment that night, I would rather have had my fingernails pried off than stand before the flashbulbs. It was too much, too soon. I needed a cigarette, but I couldn't let any of these Hollywood health nuts see me smoking.

A woman with a clipboard greeted us at the top of the stairs and recorded our names, then conferred with the photographers while we waited.

"I don't know if I can do this," I whispered to Felicity.

The woman pointed at me and waved me forward impatiently.

"You're a star; go shine." Felicity gave me a little push.

My heart hammering, I stepped onto the red carpet in front of a backdrop emblazoned with the name of whatever the evening's charity was. I pressed my lips into a smile, feeling like a specimen under a microscope as the flashes popped. A man's voice yelled that I was looking good. Another wanted to see the back of my dress. The fear began to melt.

I stepped off the carpet dazzled, some part of my effervescence restored by the brilliance of the flashbulbs. Felicity linked her arm through mine and led me around a giant marble statue of a naked Venus and into an enormous living room, where a man in a tuxedo played Elton John on a white grand piano. Ornate chandeliers twinkled overhead, and endless pink roses gave off an intoxicating scent.

A beautiful girl in a black cocktail dress proffered a tray of champagne. Felicity accepted a glass; I sadly had to pass to maintain the illusion of New Stella.

"You can have some of mine when no one's looking," Felicity whispered.

Washed in the lavender of the fading sky, the rolling lawn was set with what must have been a hundred round tables covered with white tablecloths, each adorned with centerpieces of pink roses. At the far end of the lawn was a stage prepared for a band.

I was initially disappointed to find there was no one famous or powerful at our table, only a bunch of rich people who actually paid the $5,000 for their plates. But Felicity was undaunted. Before long we were drawn into a discussion about the continued relevance of my film *Under the Blue Moon* with the man next to me, who turned out to be a fan. His adoration warmed me like a sable coat.

At some point, Felicity returned from the bar with a sparkling water for me that turned out to be mostly gin. The band had started playing a song I heard on the radio ad nauseum, and most of our table had gotten up to dance.

"Wanna dance?" Felicity asked.

I pushed up to my feet. "I'd rather take a walk around."

The alcohol hit me as I stood; darkness vignetted my vision. I must've swayed, because Felicity caught my elbow, steadied me. Suddenly I couldn't breathe in my Spanx. The night was too close. I was suffocating.

As though reading my mind, she gently guided me between the tables toward the house. "I bet it's cooler inside," she murmured as we tripped across the manicured lawn.

Up two steps, and we were caught in the crowd gathered around the chocolate fondue fountain, inconveniently positioned blocking the French doors that led into the house.

Felicity's eyes lit up when she saw it. "We have to try, don't we?"

We'd just joined the jovial crowd around the fountain when I heard my name. I turned to see none other than that bitch Hannah Bridges, her thin lips curled into a cruel smile, her flat blue eyes directed at me. Her platinum hair was board straight, her skeletal frame draped in gray sequins.

Hannah, once my best friend and closest confidante. Hannah, never as famous as I until she sold the most hurtful story of all to the press and took up with Cole before we'd even divorced.

"So good to see you out and about," Hannah said as we air-kissed. "Rumor had it you'd died. Overdose, I think?"

I was meant to have overdosed on pills in a hotel in Rome. Why Rome, I wasn't sure (I'd only been there once), but I always did like the spirit of it. If I ever took a nosedive into the infinite abyss, Rome sounded like as good a place as any to do it. In my weaker moments I sometimes wished the rumors were true. Then at least I'd be immortalized, tragically preserved in time instead of barreling toward anonymity in middle age.

"The rumors of my death have been greatly exaggerated," I quipped gamely. It was my party line, designed to prove my sense of humor was intact, and generally got at least a polite laugh. Not this time. "I'm sober now," I added.

"Whatever you want to call it." She sniffed as though she smelled alcohol on my breath. "Good to see you're back from the dead. Maybe you'll book a Hallmark movie and finally refill your pool."

The air went out of me. How did she know about my empty pool? I was flabbergasted, acutely aware of the dinner guests watching our exchange like a tennis match but at a complete loss for words.

Felicity leaped to the rescue. "So thoughtful of her, right? With this drought, it's just terrible how some people continue to waste water. Stella was really impacted by all the work she's been doing building houses for refugees—"

Hannah stared at Felicity, confounded. "I'm sorry, who are you?"

I noticed more than one cell phone, angled vertically. At least one of them was likely live streaming.

"I'm her assistant." Felicity's hand flew to her mouth as she turned to me. "I'm so sorry. I know I wasn't supposed to say anything. But what you're doing is so amazing, I just—" She had the crowd eating out of her hand. "That's why Stella hasn't been acting," she explained to the sea of faces. "She won't tell anyone because she's so humble, but she's been using her time to do good in the world, building homes for those in need. That's all I'll say. Now we really do have to go."

She seized my hand and led me from the fountain into the house, through the foyer and out the front door. The valet signaled our driver, and we dove into the shadowy safety of the limo.

"I'm sorry," Felicity said breathlessly as we pulled away. "I couldn't stand to see her treat you like that."

"N-no," I stammered, still trying to wrap my head around what exactly had happened back there. "Thank you for standing up for me. But the refugee thing. I didn't—"

"I know." She laughed. "I don't know why I said it. It's just what came to mind. She was being such a bitch, and it makes you look like you're so much better than her, which of course you are."

"Yeah, but they're gonna ask questions now. They're gonna find out it's a lie," I protested, my thoughts spiraling into a dark hole.

"No, no, it's fine. It's better if you're mysterious about it. Makes it look like you weren't doing it for the press. We'll Photoshop a picture of you in a hard hat to look like it was taken in Central America and leak it. And if anyone pokes around, I have a friend with a construction company. He'll say you worked for him. No one will ever know."

"She used to be my best friend," I lamented. "Un-fucking-real, what she did. Sold horrible lies about me and started dating Cole before our divorce had even gone through."

"I know," she said. Then, off my look, "There wasn't much to do in the town I grew up in. I spent way too much time online and looked forward to my weekly tabloid delivery on Thursdays like it was Christmas. Embarrassing, I know, but I'm pretty much a walking encyclopedia of pop culture."

My mind reeled. "So what else do you know about me?"

"You were a super-talented kid who got famous young and wasn't prepared to deal with the stress of it. You suffered from depression, used drugs and alcohol to cope, and ended up losing your career in the process."

I gaped at her, stunned by the accuracy of her summary. There were parts she couldn't know, of course, that no one knew—my story behind the story. In the darkness I could feel her kind eyes on me. "You're not alone." She squeezed my hand. "It's actually super common among stars who made it really young. At least you're here now. You didn't lose your life or end up in some kind of conservatorship."

A tightness in my throat, and suddenly tears were pouring down my cheeks. She put her arms around me, and I bawled into her perfect breast.

"It's gonna be okay," she soothed me. "You'll see. You're gonna get it all back."

I was so inspired by her kindness that later that evening I put down the story of how Cole and I met for my memoir.

# *Love at First Sight:*

When I was cast in *Faster*, I'd just wrapped the last of the three Harriet films. As much as I'd enjoyed playing a bookish witch dealing with the pressures of college while hiding from an evil coven, I'd spent four years of my life on it and was ready for something different. Something meatier. So I was thrilled when the offer turned up to play an heiress seduced by Cole Power's con man in a gritty romance. The script was fantastic—something I could really sink my teeth into—and the costar... Let's be honest, who wouldn't want to spend a couple of months getting paid to make out with Cole Power? Like most of the girls in the world, I'd had a mad crush on him ever since I saw him in *Bad Boy* when I was thirteen.

I'd met Cole in passing a handful of times at events, but we'd always been on the arms of other people and had never had a chance to get to know each other. In fact, I knew his ex-wife, Bar Salmaan (the Israeli model with whom he shares a son, Jackson Power), better, which is to say we had mutual friends and had partied together on a couple of occasions. At any rate, when I came in to sign the contracts, my agent at the time asked for a word with me, off the record.

Andy had immaculately gelled hair and pristine suits, but he always reeked of cigarette smoke hastily covered up with cologne, so I generally tried to stay on the opposite side of his desk. However, this time he came around the heavy slab of glass and leaned in close, lowering his voice. "You know Cole was a client of mine for years," he began. Yes, I knew this. Not only had he mentioned it fifty times, but his walls were littered with posters of the movies Cole had done while they were working together. "I wouldn't normally share something like this, but I care about you, so I'm gonna tell you. But it needs to stay between us."

"Jesus, Andy, what is it?" I asked.

"Look, Cole's charming, right? But he's a method actor," he warned. I relaxed a little. I knew plenty of method actors. "And not just on set. He believes his characters live on inside him after wrap, so you can't ever be too sure what you're going to get. He can be incredibly sensitive, like Steve in *Bad Boy*, but he can also turn on a dime, like"—his eyes shot to the posters on his wall, landing on one featuring Cole with a smirk and a gun—"Wesley in *Snake Bit*."

"So you're saying he's an actor." I laughed. "Got it. We're all a little crazy, Andy."

"It's more than that." Andy pushed his glasses up on his nose. "Look, you're playing star-crossed lovers, right? I know how these things go. He's gonna want to sleep with you—"

I rolled my eyes. "Thank you for your concern,

Andy, but I'm a grown woman, and who knows? I may want to sleep with him too."

"I'm just saying be careful." He bit his lip like there was something else he wanted to say, but decided better of it. "Please."

I saluted him. "You got it, Captain."

Careful I was not.

When I arrived on the soundstage in Miami for our first read-through, Cole was already seated at the long table with his script before him. Someone called his name, and he turned, his gaze landing on me. He hastily got to his feet as I approached, never once taking his ice-blue eyes from mine. Everything went into slow motion, and suddenly the only people that existed in the entire world were the two of us. And then, like an idiot, I tripped over a wire that hadn't been properly taped down, landing squarely in his strong arms. My skin burned beneath his touch, as though the pull between us was so strong that our bodies set off chemical reactions in each other just by being in proximity.

During the read-through, everyone could see the electricity between us was palpable. So much so that afterward the director pulled me aside to request that Cole and I not spend any time together until after we'd shot our first love scene. I begrudgingly complied, allowing the chemistry to blossom between us on-screen while going home alone at night to the high-rise executive apartment overlooking the bay that production had rented for me. I fantasized about him so intensely in those first few weeks that I hardly slept.

When the day finally arrived for us to shoot our first love scene, I was a jangle of nerves. The scene called for Cole and me to tumble into bed together, tearing off each other's clothes, culminating with us wearing nothing but privacy covers as we writhed beneath the sheets. The nudity would all be tasteful, they assured me, and was necessary to the story—but that wasn't what I was worried about. I'd done love scenes before, situations ranging from awkward to gross to sexy, but had never had chemistry like this with a costar and was self-conscious about being that turned on by someone in front of the crew. I needn't have worried.

From the time our lips met in the first shot, everyone else melted away, and it was just Cole and me. All day long I ached for him as he kissed me and caressed my body in fits and starts between "action" and "cut." I'll leave the details to your imagination, but suffice it to say that by the time we wrapped that day, we were both so hot for each other that the idea of waiting any longer was unbearable. Without much regard for who might see or gossip, he slipped into my trailer and we ravaged each other for real.

From that day forward we were inseparable. We screwed on every surface of his yacht and his beautiful house on the bay, snuck into each other's trailers between setups, slinked off to the bathroom together in restaurants. When his character in the film proposed to mine, he asked if perhaps I might like a rock just like the prop stunner he slipped on my finger; within weeks, he'd given me a genuine five-carat square-cut diamond.

Andy, however, wasn't the only person who tried to warn me off Cole. Our director, while thrilled our chemistry jumped off screen, was visibly nervous about our relationship, doubtless concerned about what it would mean for the film if it burned out. An actress I'd worked with years ago called after seeing a picture of Cole and me hand in hand in the tabloids to say she'd dated him and it had not ended well. She'd signed an NDA so couldn't give me details, but she said she felt it was her duty to at least warn me to be careful. I kept my promise not to tell Cole she'd called but dismissed her claims, figuring she was just jealous. What Cole and I had was special.

The weekend after he gave me the ring, Cole and I went to the annual white party at Thrive, an open-air nightclub on the sand in Miami Beach with a VIP lounge situated on a high deck with daybeds and a view of the sea. Before the bouncer even lifted the white velvet rope at the top of the stairs, I spotted her: tall and gorgeous with bronzed skin and long straight chestnut hair swept over one eye, Bar Salmaan was the kind of girl who lived for the number of heads she turned, so it made sense that she was seated at the most visible table in the club, surrounded by her model-girl posse. I squeezed Cole's hand and nodded in her direction.

"Don't worry about Bar," he whispered, his breath hot on my ear. "I pay her a lot more alimony than the court mandated. If she wants me to keep it up, she'll have to respect you."

Regardless, I was glad our table was at the opposite end of the room, which allowed me to stay out of her way while she and her girlfriends flitted from table to table drinking champagne. By the time I visited the ladies' room toward the end of the night, I'd had enough tequila myself that I'd nearly forgotten about her, so I was dumbstruck when I opened the bathroom stall to find her waiting for me.

She grabbed my elbow and steered me back into the bathroom stall, locking the door behind us.

"You've been avoiding me all night." She pouted, lounging against the door.

"I didn't even know you were here," I lied.

"You're fucking my ex-husband," she said, her muddy green eyes full of mirth. "Of course you knew I was here."

I tucked a wisp of hair behind my ear with my left hand, displaying the rock on my ring finger. "I'd say it's a little more than fucking," I said. "But yeah, a lot of that too."

"God, I remember how hot it was in the beginning," she reminisced. "Like the sun shines only for you, right? You can't keep your hands off each other, and he's so naughty." She counted on her fingers. "We did it in bathrooms at restaurants, on the kitchen counter, on the deck of his boat just far enough out at sea that probably no one could see...It was a rush. And that four-poster bed of his comes in handy, doesn't it?"

She towered over me, a smile playing around her lips. I wouldn't be able to cook dinner in his kitchen again without seeing her spread-eagled on the center island, and she knew it. "Don't tell me you thought you were the only one he liked to cover in honey." She cocked her head, trying to read my blank expression. "Or has he not done that yet?" He had, as a matter of fact, just the other night. "It's a good one."

"What do you want?" I asked.

She took a little baggie of white powder from her bra and dumped a bump on her thumb joint, then snorted it. "I'm just being a friend," she said, repeating the process on the other side.

I crossed my arms. "How's that?"

Her pupils were the size of saucers. "I know I'm a bitch. But I like you, Stella. I really do. That's why I have to..." She lowered her voice. "It's wonderful now, I know, but when he loses interest—and trust me, he will, sooner than you think—it's like..." She snapped. "You know tarot?"

I nodded. "Of course."

"The tower card, the one where it's dark and the building is on fire and people are jumping out windows? It's like that." She closed her eyes and took a deep breath, letting it out through pursed lips. "I love our son. Jackson is the one good thing that came out of our relationship, but..." She clenched and released her jaw. "I just wish someone had warned me at the beginning what the end would look like." She swept aside her side-cut bangs from her forehead, displaying the faint trace of a white scar. "It's not worth it."

And with that she knocked back the latch and flung open the door, leaving me gaping after her.

I didn't listen. I wrote off her warning as envy. I wasn't sure where she'd gotten that scar, but I was sure it wasn't from my doting fiancé, and even more certain that he would never do something like that to me. He'd told me a million times he'd "never felt this way about someone."

In the months afterward, when Bar and I had to interact with each other while I was married to Cole, she was indeed a bitch, as, admittedly, was I. Still, I never mentioned our bathroom conversation to Cole. And years later, when he'd proved her right, I sent her a care package with a beautiful hand-painted set of tarot cards, to say thank you for her attempt to save me from the pain he ultimately caused me.

# Taylor

Rejuvenated by the sun and soft water, I felt as ready for my awkward conversation with Cole as I would ever be. All I had to do was pull him aside and ask what exactly happened the other night. Easier said than done, but I wanted to get it over with as soon as possible.

Only, when I flipped onto my belly to swim for shore, I found that the strip of white sand rimmed by green palms had receded. I was out far past the outcropping of rocks, drifting farther with every breath. My pulse quickened. Lost in thought, I must have floated into a current headed out to sea.

Alarmed, I tried to remember what to do. *Swim parallel to shore.* That was it. *Don't fight it.* But the shore was an island, its shoreline curved. Panic gripped my chest. I was a decent swimmer but not a strong one. I knew freestyle and breaststroke, but I'd never been on the swim team, never swam any distance. And certainly not any distance in the ocean.

I decided to make a go for the pier. I swam freestyle, kicking with terror-driven fervor, clawing the water with cupped hands. Was I even moving? I couldn't tell. I focused my eyes on the pier, where I thought I saw a man—but when I looked again, he was gone. I kept swimming.

My thighs and shoulders burned. I blinked seawater from my eyes and spat it from my mouth. My chest heaved.

I seemed to be getting closer to the pier but was still being swept out to sea. How wide was this current? I saw a WaveRunner in the distance and waved frantically, but between the waves and the salt water in my eyes, I couldn't tell whether whoever was on it saw me. My muscles were growing tired fast. I kicked harder, pushing with everything I had.

*Don't panic. Just swim.*

Were there sharks in the water? It was too deep to see clearly, which only added to my panic. I could die out here. I was completely beat, my energy consumed. But I had to keep going.

Suddenly came the heartening sound of a motor close by. The WaveRunner circled, throwing wake that crashed over me. Thank God. I sputtered as arms enveloped me.

"You're okay." A man's voice beside me in the water. "Just relax. I've got you."

Relief warmed my chest. I was saved. I did my best to relax as he turned me to my back, supporting my head and wrapping one of his strong arms around my chest while he swam us easily toward the WaveRunner.

He hoisted me up and set me astride the seat, then pulled himself up next to me. Wiping the seawater from my eyes, I recognized him as the captain of the boat from the sunset cruise. "You okay?" he asked, concerned.

I nodded, shaking. "I got caught in the current."

"I know." I faintly registered his eyes glinting caramel in the sun, muscles rippling under espresso-brown skin, like one of the heroes from my romance novels, as he wrapped a towel around me. "I'm glad I saw you."

I wiped at my face with the towel, trying to hide how upset I was. "Thank you, so much, for saving me." I choked back a sob like a damsel in distress. Was I dreaming?

"You were doing the right thing swimming with the shore, but it was a wide current." He shook the water from the short braids knotted on top of his head and ran a hand over the close-cropped sides. "I'm gonna drive us back in. Can you hold on, or you want to sit in front of me?"

"I can hold on," I murmured.

I folded my arms around his waist as he hit the gas and rested my face against his wide back, exhausted. In no time, we bumped up onto the sand and skidded to a stop just out of the water not far from where I'd left my clothes. Safe. He handed me down, but as my feet hit the ground, I found my legs had turned to noodles, completely useless for walking.

Without missing a beat, he spread a large towel emblazoned with tropical fish in a patch of shade and helped me onto it. I collapsed on my back, my body awash in the aftermath of adrenaline. His concerned face swam above me: high cheekbones, a strong jaw, full, kissable lips. I couldn't help but think if we were in a romance novel, what a perfect consummation scene this would make.

*Stop it, Taylor.*

He fished a bottle of ice-cold water from the back of the WaveRunner and handed it to me, then sat on the sand. "I'm gonna hang here with you for a while, if you don't mind."

I sat up to drink the water, but before I could even put the bottle to my lips, I found myself crying. My chest heaved as I sobbed uncontrollably. This was not a romance novel or a dream. This was real life, and it promptly hit me as I came back to my senses that I really could have drowned. I was that close.

He rubbed my back gently. "It's okay. You're okay."

"I could have...died," I managed.

"You didn't," he assured me. "You're here. You're okay."

But I wasn't okay. My life thus far was a waste, I suddenly realized. "All this time I've been thinking my life was out there somewhere...ahead of me...and just like that"—I snapped my fingers—"it could have..." I couldn't finish the sentence.

"I understand." He held my gaze, his eyes sincere, and I felt like I could tell him anything. But I also felt tremendously tired. So tired, I could hardly keep my own eyes open.

When I awoke, he was stretched out with a paperback in one hand and half a homemade sandwich in the other. "Hey." A warm smile lit his face. "You're up."

I nodded, groggy. "How long was I out?"

"Not long." He shrugged. "Maybe a half hour."

I flushed, recalling my outburst before I fell asleep. I must've been in some kind of fugue state; I wasn't sure exactly what I'd said, but I was sure it was embarrassing. "I'm sorry I freaked out earlier," I said. "Thank you for waiting. And saving me. That was terrifying."

"No problem. They need to put up more signs."

I followed his gaze to a sign that read "Warning: Strong current. No swimming," not twenty yards from where I'd left my things. It even had a picture of a swimmer crossed out.

"Oh my God. I didn't see that!" Feeling like an idiot, I made a mental note to warn the rest of the cast and crew at dinner that evening.

He took the other half of his sandwich from a brown bag and offered it to me. "You hungry?"

I was ravenous. "I don't want to take your sandwich."

"It's okay." His lips curved into an easy smile as he placed it in my hands.

"Peanut butter and jelly." I returned his smile. "I love peanut butter and jelly." I took a bite, then guzzled nearly the entire bottle of water. "I'm Taylor." I extended my hand to him.

He took it, laughing. "I remember. I met you on the boat the other day. Rick."

"I remember too," I said.

"You didn't want to fish yesterday?"

"I wasn't invited. It's kind of a sore subject."

"I'm sorry." He checked his watch. "I've gotta get the plane back to the port on Saint Ann by sundown—"

"You fly planes too?" I asked.

"Small ones," he replied. "I ferried Stella and her assistant over earlier on the water plane, but it can't stay here overnight. You gonna be okay?"

"I'm fine," I said. "Do what you need to."

He stood and pulled me to my feet. "If you ever want to go out on the boat—or the plane—tell the concierge and I'll take you."

"Thanks, but I'm gonna be crazy busy starting tomorrow." I furrowed my brow, frustrated with myself. This romance-novel-hot guy who just saved my life was offering to take me on a boat or a plane; no was *not* the right answer. "Sorry. What I mean is, thank you. Let's do it."

"Cool." He slung his towel around his neck with a grin, then jogged down the beach toward the dock.

Still dazed, I stumbled over to my clothes and sat down again. I could have drowned. It was surreal. I couldn't quite process it. Yet here I was on the beach in the glaring sun as though it had never happened.

I wouldn't tell anyone. I didn't want our cast and crew judging my powers of discernment, or worse, feeling bad for me. My grip on authority was already tenuous at best with all the disinformation about my firing from Woodland Studios swirling around out there. I knew the crew must have heard the stories and be wondering why the hell Cole would hire me. I'd wondered the same thing myself, and I knew firsthand how good I was at my job. I needed to start strong in the next few days if I wanted to win their respect.

I threw on my shorts, and not wanting to see anyone on my way back to my bungalow, took a detour down the shaded path that cut through the leafy green vegetation behind the beach. My skin and hair were sticky with salt water and crusted in sand. When I passed the wall of water that spilled from the infinity pool, it was all I could do not to press myself to it and allow the fresh water to wash over me.

As I meandered from the relative cool of the path to the sun-splashed over-water walkway toward my bungalow, I spotted Cole at his door at the far end of the pier, fumbling with the lock. As much as I wanted nothing more than to flatten myself in the nearest doorway and hide until he was safely inside, I screwed my courage to the sticking place and called out, "Cole!"

He turned, an eyebrow arched. I hurried up the pier, casting a glance around to make sure we were alone. He opened the door to his bungalow and I followed him inside, my heart in my throat. Through the walls of glass, the sun reflecting on miles of turquoise water was blindingly bright.

I launched into my practiced speech before I could chicken out. "The other night when—"

"You're fun when you drink, half-pint." He laughed and shook his head. "I mean, shit. I had no idea." He opened the refrigerator and took out a beer. "Want one?"

"I'm good, thanks." I tried my damnedest to stop my cheeks from reddening. "How fun was I? I mean, like..."

His eyes were full of mirth as he cracked open the beer. "You don't remember?"

I swallowed. "I remember the boat, and dinner, but...did we go in the ocean?"

"You did." He chuckled.

"In my clothes?"

"Oh no, you took those off first."

Shit. "All of them?"

"Oh yeah."

"Did anyone else see?"

"I was the only one around." He moved closer, looking me up and down with a half smile. "You have a rockin' bod you keep hidden under all those chunky sweaters and cargo pants." His breath was hot on my ear, his perfect superhero face inches from mine. I was suddenly overcome with the impulse to bite his nose like a deranged bird.

But he could shut the entire production down in a heartbeat. Not to mention fire me. Then where would I be? Working at McDonald's wouldn't exactly pay my mortgage, and I'd lose my shirt if I tried to sell my condo right now.

I swallowed my crazy and smiled. "What exactly happened?" I managed, hating myself.

"After you went for a swim, you refused to put your clothes back on, but I convinced you to at least wear my shirt to walk back to your room. You stripped it off the minute you walked in the door though," he insinuated. "You were a horny little tiger."

Oh God. So I'd gotten blackout drunk and thrown myself at my womanizing movie star boss, my worst nightmare incarnate. It wasn't like me, but *I* wasn't like me recently. The stress...I obviously couldn't trust myself. And the alcohol. I must've had more than the two drinks I could recall. *Keep it together, Taylor. What's done is done. Focus on the present.* I still didn't have the answer I'd plowed into this awkward encounter to obtain. "So the night we...um, we didn't..." I looked down at my hands, realizing they were making weird gestures.

"Fuck?" He laughed. "No. We didn't fuck. I was a gentleman. Tucked you in bed and walked my ass home, hard as it was."

There was a God in heaven.

"Okay, good. I just wanted to make sure."

"But I'm here for you, you know." He flashed that crooked grin, his eyes twinkling. "If you ever want to finish what you started, get rid of some of that tension you carry around."

"You know we can't be involved while we're working together—"

He held up his hands, laughing. "Whoa! Who said anything about getting involved? I was just trying to make you feel better about the whole thing."

Motherfucker. "Good, so we're on the same page." I forced a laugh, trying to regain my footing. "We'll keep it on the down-low, obviously."

"Yeah." He ran his fingers through his thick hair. "That Madison girl's already all up on me, and she doesn't seem like the type to make nice with the competition."

I furrowed my brow. The very thought of the drama that would come from a romantic liaison between Cole and Madison made me nearly break out in hives.

"What can I say?" He shrugged, sheepish. "I love women."

And women loved him. "Yeah, I've heard," I said. "But probably best not to hook up with anyone for the rest of the shoot, especially after what happened with Roxie. You don't need any more bad press."

"That was a bunch of bullshit." He groaned. "That bitch was nuts. I never meant to hit her. I was throwing the phone at the *window*, and she—"

"She got in the way," I cut him off. "I know." Like it was perfectly normal to be throwing your cell phone out a hotel room window. "But it's a good example of why you should probably just play it cool right now, at least until people forget."

People had already begun to forget, or at least forgive, after a "source close to the couple" revealed Roxie had been on hallucinogenic drugs and wielding a knife, a claim she vehemently denied. It wasn't the first time a romance of Cole's had been rumored to end badly. But the rumors were never substantiated, and the public never seemed to care. Somehow it was always the women he'd been involved with who ended up looking like the bad guy—the mark of either terrible luck or a talented fixer. Regardless, I didn't need celebrity antics throwing a wrench in our already tight schedule.

"We'll see," he retorted, tipping his beer to me. "I'm not the only one who doesn't need any more bad press."

I narrowed my eyes at him. "Touché." But he was right. Though the public didn't know me, I was without a doubt persona non grata in the industry currently, thanks to my father's lies in retaliation for my refusal to smear Madison after their dalliance ended badly. He had everyone believing I'd been skimming off the top while having an affair with my coworker, when the truth of the matter was, I'd had no idea the guy had reconciled with his wife, let alone that he was actively embezzling thousands of dollars from the company while we were together. My only true crime was playing the fool, a crime for which I was still serving my sentence.

"See you tomorrow, bright and early," I said as I turned to leave.

"Six a.m.," he confirmed.

I beelined for the door, breathing a sigh of relief when it slammed behind me. I couldn't imagine how I'd been drunk enough not only to skinny-dip, but to throw myself at my boss. And now I was stuck on an island with him for six weeks, not to mention the three-year contract I'd signed only a few months ago.

I should never have taken this job. *But my back was against the wall,* I rationalized for the millionth time. I was at the end of my savings with no prospects when the interview with Cole came in; I'd thought the opportunity a godsend. Up until now I'd willfully ignored the second thoughts I'd had from my first day in the office, but I'd almost died this afternoon. Perhaps it was time to start heeding red flags. Ha! Literally.

If the movie did well, I would break contract and leave. The success of the project would prove my worth and improve my optics; I'd no longer be radioactive. I'd cite creative differences and be done with Cole Fucking Power, get a job somewhere else. Maybe I'd even move to New York like I'd been talking about doing for years. Or New Orleans or New Haven...or anywhere new, really. Anywhere I could work. I did love my job. I'd just had the bad luck of being employed by toxic men. There were plenty of people in the film industry who weren't toxic though, and surely not all of them believed the lies about me—surely I could find some of them to work with. *If* the movie did well. That was a big if.

I pushed open the door to my tranquil bungalow and walked straight to the slate and teakwood bathroom, where I stripped off my wet swimsuit and stood beneath the cascade of the rainfall showerhead, staring out at the endless horizon. If only the warm water could wash away the deep disappointment I felt in myself.

# Felicity

*Thirteen Years Ago*

Ll the way home from school, I grip my report card in my fist as the bus bumps through the rain slower than a snail. I can't wait to show my mom I got all fours, the highest you can get. She promised if I did this good, she'd take me to see the new Cole Power movie even though it's rated R.

But when I let myself in, the apartment is dark, the curtains closed against the storm. I figure Iris has forgotten to pay the electric bill again, but when I try the switch, the overhead light works fine. On the coffee table I notice a copy of *Celeb* magazine, open to a page showing Cole Power on set, dressed as a cop. I drop my heavy backpack on the couch and pick it up.

> In *Bloodhound*, Cole Power plays a cop on a mission to find a serial killer who's been murdering prostitutes and covering his tracks by making it look like the women overdosed by their own hand. Power says the role has been challenging because the idea of violence toward women sickens him, but that's why he knew he had to take the role...

I toss the magazine back to the table and quietly knock on the closed bedroom door, my report card clenched in my hand. "Iris?"

Nothing but the sound of rain on the roof.

I open the door. The room is pitch black and freezing cold. All the covers are thrown off the bed, and my mom is sprawled across it, naked. I turn off the chugging window unit and sit next to her, allowing my eyes to adjust to the gloom. Her blond hair is dark with sweat, her cheeks flushed. I gently shake her shoulder. "I got fours on my report card," I say, setting it on the crowded bedside table.

Her eyes flutter, but she continues to doze. Worried she's sick, I shake her again. She moans and changes position, one of her arms flopping into my lap.

I trace the tattoo on her forearm with my fingers: a winged woman rising from flames. My mom loves the magical phoenix so much she named me for it. She sketched the one on her arm herself. She's an incredible artist. Or, she was. I haven't seen her draw in forever.

I fumble beneath the scarlet scarf draped over the bedside lamp, finally locating the switch. A rosy glow dimly lights the room. "Iris," I say softly.

She doesn't move.

I'm not sure what time she got home from Cole's last night, but I know it was late because she didn't budge when I got up and showered this morning. There was nothing in the house I could take for lunch and not a dime of cash in her purse, even though I know Cole's been giving her lots of money. I've seen her put it in the safe I'm not allowed to know the code for. Anyway, it's almost four now, and I'm starving.

"Mom." I squeeze her damp hand.

It's then that I notice the bruises. All up and down her forearm in shades ranging from green to purple. And the holes on the inside of her elbow.

Anger bubbles inside me. I may be young, but I'm not stupid. I know she hasn't been giving blood every day like Jewel's mom tried to convince her she was—before she never came home one night. Now Jewel has a foster family. She wrote me a postcard from Tallahassee.

She says it's nice and they have a real house and all, but she misses me and the rest of her friends in Miami.

How could I have missed this? I see her get dressed all the time; we sleep in the same bed. But actually, she's been sleeping at Cole's a lot. She's been sleeping a lot, period. And I haven't watched her get ready as much because she's always in a bad mood lately; she's no fun to hang out with. I would've thought she'd be happy she was dating a movie star, but she's been super bitchy and she won't even tell me anything about him.

Is this his fault? It *has* to be. She's been seeing him nearly two months, and in that time she's stopped dancing or going on dates with other guys, even the ones she used to see regularly—even the one that worked for a film studio and would always send home DVDs of movies that were still in theaters for me to watch.

All of a sudden I don't want to see Cole Power's dumb movie anymore. I want to punch him.

"Mom, it's late and I'm hungry. You have to wake up," I plead. She rolls away from me, taking her arm with her. "Mom! I'm serious!"

She turns her head slightly, wrinkling her brow. "I'm sleeping."

"It's four. I didn't have lunch. You have to feed me. I'm your child."

She pushes herself up to sitting, confused. "Four?"

"Yes."

"Shit." She jumps out of bed and crashes into a pile of dirty laundry. "I've gotta get ready. I have to be there."

"Where? Where are you going?" I chase her into the bathroom. She cringes like a vampire when I turn on the light. There's a giant bluish bruise on her thigh, a paler gray one on her hip. "Mom, I saw the bruises and the needle holes."

She squints at me. "Stop calling me that."

"No! You're my mother and you have to start acting like it." I stamp my foot, not caring if it makes me look like a baby.

She slaps my cheek hard, leaving it stinging. "How dare you talk to me like that, you little brat! I gave up everything for you!"

I stare at her in shock, tears in my eyes. "Oh, Phoenix, honey…" She crumples. "I'm sorry." She reaches for me, the anger gone from her like a popped balloon.

I notice I'm crying and run from the room. "I wish I'd never been born!" I yell as she chases after me into the living room. With nowhere to go but out into the storm raging outside, I turn to face her. "Then you'd have the life you wanted, and I wouldn't have to grow up with a druggie hooker for a mom."

She inhales sharply, her jaw slack. I can see in her eyes I've hurt her before she collapses in a puddle of tears on the stained carpet. Immediately I'm sorry. I love her. I do.

But also, I know I'm right. I'm torn between wanting to comfort her and wanting to make her stop this, whatever it is, at whatever cost.

I grab a blanket from the couch and drape it over her naked body, crouching next to her. "I'm sorry, Mom. But you can't do this to us. I don't want you to die like Jewel's mom. I don't want to have to go live with your terrible parents."

She snorts, wiping her tears with the back of her hand. "I'll never let that happen."

I've never met my grandparents. Never even saw a picture of them until I went to the library a few months ago and did a Google search with their names and hometown. *Fred and Ruthanne Pendley, Parthenon, PA.* There they were, smiling tightly in front of a dappled blue background in their Holy Cross Evangelist Church directory photo. He was seated, wearing a navy suit and squinting at the camera through rimless glasses, his brown hair thinning on top. She stood behind him in a matching blue flowery dress with her hand on his shoulder, her blond bob curled, the silver cross necklace around her neck lit by the flash. They looked to be in their fifties and were both a little overweight, but what struck me is how normal they seemed—like grandparents you'd see on TV. Not at all the monsters my mom had made them out to be.

Like me, my mom is an only child. She hasn't told me much about when she was a kid, except that it was really boring and she couldn't wait to get out of there. But she does like to tell the story about how I came to be. I'm not supposed to repeat it because she says most people wouldn't approve of her telling a story with sex in it to a kid, but she never wants to lie to me and also she wants me to know how it happened so I don't make the same mistakes. This is how it goes:

Iris was from a small town, and her high school had kids from a bunch of other small towns too. When she was a junior, she started going out with a guy named Danny, who was a senior and the coolest guy in school. He was a football player and drove a red F-150 pickup truck because his family had a lot of money from owning the big chicken farm a few towns over.

His parents didn't like my mom because her family was poor, but Danny didn't care. She was the prettiest girl for miles. They'd been together about six months when he knocked her up. She hadn't meant to get pregnant, of course, but no one had told her much about how to prevent it—except for not having sex, which she wasn't interested in. She didn't live under a rock; she knew about condoms, but Danny wasn't a fan, so they figured he'd just pull out.

My mom was raised super Christian and pro-life, so when she found out she was pregnant, she didn't even think about having an abortion. Besides, she'd always liked babies, and most girls she knew had babies by the time they were twenty anyway, which wasn't that far in the future. It was summer and Danny was going to Penn State in the fall, only a few hours' drive. They hadn't really talked about it, but she assumed they'd stay together, see each other on the weekends. Now she thought maybe she'd just move up there with him and get her GED after the baby came. She wanted to be an artist, anyway. Did you really need a high school diploma for that?

He was at the Jersey Shore with his family the week she found out about the baby, so she waited till he was back to tell him. They went to their special place on a lake where they liked to park and have sex in the bed of the truck. She meant to tell him as soon as they got there, but he was all over her. Afterward, he said he wanted to break up. He tried to blame it on going to college, but she pulled it out of him that he'd been screwing some other girl behind her back while he was on vacation.

That was when she told him about me. He was upset she hadn't been careful enough but said he'd drive her to get an abortion (because he was such a nice guy, he said). This gave her an idea. She told him abortions were expensive, and she couldn't afford it. He said not to worry, that he was sure his parents would give him the money, because he knew they didn't want her having his baby.

She agreed that would be fine, as long as her parents didn't find out. She knew they would eventually, since she wasn't really going to have an abortion. But she'd figure that out later.

As it turned out, she didn't have time to figure anything out. Danny told his father, who showed up at my mom's front door with an envelope of five thousand dollars' hush money for the abortion and a warning to her parents that this was all they'd get from them. Ruthanne and Fred were shocked, embarrassed, insulted, but most of all furious with my mother, not only for getting pregnant, but even worse, intending to have an abortion. They refused the cash and kicked her out.

So she had a friend drive her and her garbage bag of clothes over to Danny's to collect the five thousand dollars, then to the bus stop, where she bought a ticket to Miami and never looked back.

She hasn't been a perfect mom, but I know how much she loves me, and up until now she's managed to hold it in the road.

She gathers the blanket around her and kisses me on the head as she stands. "I'm gonna do better, Phee," she promises. "I just... He's giving us so much money, it's hard to say no."

"But can't you do—what you do—without drugs?"

She sighs. "It's complicated. If I can just stick it out with him another month or two, I'll have enough for a down payment on an apartment of our own. Something nice, that we can fix up just the way we like."

An apartment of our own! No scary landlord, no leaks that never get fixed or nasty carpet or roaches. But not if she has to do drugs to get it.

"Just please, Mom, please don't do drugs anymore."

She nods. "I have to get in the shower. You wanna walk down to the 7-Eleven and get food and stuff?"

She slides open the closet door and pushes aside the pile of old clothes that hides the safe. I've never tried to learn the code because she doesn't want me to have it, and I've always trusted her to take care of me. But I know when people are doing drugs you can't trust them anymore. I watch over her shoulder as she turns the dial. Seventeen. Thirty-five. Twenty-six. Four.

Seventeen, thirty-five, twenty-six, four. I repeat the numbers in my head as she opens the door. It's not a big safe, but it's completely full of stacks of cash, piled on top of one another. I have no idea how much money it is, but it's a lot. Seventeen, thirty-five, twenty-six, four. She hands me forty bucks and shuts the door.

"Thanks," I say, pocketing the cash. "Need anything?"

She shrugs. "You know better than I do, little bird."

The minute she steps into the bathroom, I run to where I dropped my backpack, get out a pen, and write the code on the back page of my math notebook. Heart pounding, I grab an umbrella and step out into the pouring rain.

By the time I return from the store, she's gone. I lock the bedroom door in case she comes back and kneel in front of the safe. Seventeen, thirty-five, twenty-six, four. I don't even need to look at the notebook.

# Part II:
# Atmospheric Pressure

# SPOTLIGHT ONLINE

## WHERE HAS STELLA RIVERS BEEN?

I t's no secret that famed actress and party-girl Stella Rivers had a break-down (or three) shortly after her split from Cole Power, but where has she been in the decade since? Spotlight learned new details about what she's been up to recently, and it's not what you might think!

But first...a timeline:

**1989:** A ten-year-old Stella Rivers appears in her first television show, *Meg & Co*, in which she plays the spunky title character.

**1997:** Eighteen-year-old Rivers plays the star-making role of Mary Elizabeth in *Under the Blue Moon*.

**2000:** Rivers does the first of three Harriet films.

**2006:** Twenty-seven-year-old Rivers marries Cole Power after meeting on the set of *Faster.*

**2007:** Rivers and Power divorce; she attacks a photographer outside a women's clinic in Los Angeles.

**2008:** Rivers pays the photographer $200K; releases the universally panned movie *Meg Grown Up* and goes to rehab amid rumors she was drunk on set.

**2009:** Rivers's midnight tantrum throwing pickle jars at a fan in a grocery store goes viral; she goes back to rehab.

**2010:** Rivers gets in a fistfight with the ex-wife of her trainer boyfriend that results in another lawsuit, which she settles for an undisclosed amount.

**2011:** Rivers gets a DUI and spends thirty days in jail, followed by another stint in rehab.

**2013:** Rivers stars in the reality television show *Stella's River of Wellness*, in which she opens a wellness center (that quickly goes belly-up, leaving her near bankrupt).

**2018:** Rivers resurfaces in a cult-favorite low-budget horror flick and a Lifetime movie.

**2019:** Rivers cast opposite her ex-husband, Cole Power, in *The Siren*, set to shoot over the summer on the island of Saint Genesius in the Caribbean.

So where in the world was Stella between 2013 and 2018?

Sources close to the star tell us she's been *busy working for charity*, building homes around the world for those in need. She apparently didn't want the press to know because she simply wanted to give back without fanfare. Now, that is truly heartwarming. We found this picture of her in Guatemala, and she looks right at home in a hard hat with a hammer in her hand [pic].

# Taylor

The sun had only just risen on the first day of filming, and we were already running behind. Stella's fault; she hadn't shown up until I'd sent a PA to drag her ass out of bed and escort her to set. Felicity apologized profusely for the both of them, saying they'd thought someone was going to pick them up—an offer Stella had turned down the previous evening in favor of walking the half mile to the soundstage for her morning exercise. (I say soundstage, but really it was nothing more than a converted warehouse on the far side of the golf course.) Covering my annoyance, I waved it off as a misunderstanding and assured them a production golf cart would be waiting at the end of the pier every morning from here on out, which seemed to placate Stella.

I didn't want to let the bumpy start ruin my day, but it pissed me off. We'd rescued the bitch from obscurity with a job I knew she needed, and one day in she was already acting like a diva, like she *deserved* to traipse in whenever she wanted while the entire production waited around for her. Though in the back of my mind I did wonder if Felicity was really the one to blame for their tardiness. In the brief interaction I'd had with the two of them together thus far, it struck me that Stella relied mighty heavily on this pretty young assistant she'd snuck onto the film budget last-minute. According to what Cole pulled out of them on the beach yesterday, they'd known each other only two months. How much could you really know about someone after two months?

I took a deep breath in through my nose and let it out through my mouth like my therapist taught me. Everything was fine. This was all part of production: anything that could go wrong would. Stella was in the makeup chair now, and the sun wouldn't set until six thirty, so we'd have enough daylight left to wrap the outdoor scene we had to shoot in the afternoon. We were so close to the equator that even in summer the days and nights were nearly even, which meant if we had anything to shoot outside, we had to run on time and pray the weather behaved. So far at least, the weather was behaving as predicted today.

"Nice cargo pants, half-pint."

I spun to see Cole, smirking as he eyed my camouflage cargo pants. "They're useful," I returned, patting the pockets. "Lots of places to put stuff."

"You should pick up a few things in the gift store." He gave me a friendly pat on the back. "Take whatever you want. Just tell them it's on me."

What the hell? Before I could think of a response, he was gone. I was insulted, but also begrudgingly grateful for the opportunity to buy a few things more suitable for the tropics without spending an arm and a leg. Though damned if I'd replace my beloved cargo pants.

I patted the sweat trickling down my brow with a napkin and smeared another bagel with cream cheese, not bothering to toast it first. I'd been up since 4:30 a.m., and I was starving. I knew that I was stress eating and I really should step away from the craft service table before my ass no longer fit in these cargo pants, but I gave myself a break. First day of shooting always tied my stomach in knots.

Normally the scenes in a film would be shot completely out of order, dependent on the availability of locations and actors, but the very few locations and actors we had on *The Siren* allowed us to shoot largely in chronological order, a gift for which all of us were grateful. So we were starting today with the scene in which Stella's character Marguerite and Cole's character Peyton first meet, on a photo shoot where he's the photographer and she's the model.

It was a set within a set, so the lighting was complicated and already taking more time than we'd allotted, which only added to my anxiety. Six weeks was such a short amount of time to shoot ninety pages; we'd need to shoot fifteen pages a week, or three pages a day. It might not sound like much, but when you added up the lighting setup for every camera angle of every scene—and judging by his storyboards, Jackson wasn't a director that skimped on angles—every minute was precious.

"There you are." Francisco appeared on the opposite side of the table in a pressed button-down, his swoop of black hair pomaded into 1950s Elvis perfection, an open MacBook Air perched on his forearm.

"Where's your walkie?" I asked.

"Oh, there aren't enough for me to have one. Bottom of the totem pole over here, you know."

"I'll fix that. What's up?"

"I just spoke to Tawny Crawford's people and she's confirmed for the role of Cherry. I'm booking her flights now. She's working in LA through Saturday, so I have her on the red-eye Sunday night to Miami, then the first flight out Monday to get here in time to shoot."

"Why the red-eye?" I asked. "That's gonna suck and could put us in a tight spot if her flight is delayed."

He rubbed his thumb and forefinger together. Money. Of course. "Okay." I sighed, frustrated. I liked treating my people well, and this budget austerity program brought on by Steve's mistakes was death by a thousand cuts. Of course, if Cole hadn't spent five grand at the bar on Saturday night, we could have afforded to ensure our actress arrived well-rested and in time to shoot her scenes. "Oh, I meant to ask you." I came around to his side of the table and lowered my voice. "You did the paperwork for Felicity Fox?"

He nodded, inclining his head toward mine. The great thing about us both being short was that we could easily whisper out of earshot of the taller people.

"That's her legal name, right? I mean, she's not using a stage name or anything?"

He shook his head. "No. I'd remember that. Why?"

"Nothing." I waved it off, not wanting to set off any alarm bells if she was in fact who she said she was. "She just looks like someone else. Can you forward me her paperwork?"

"Sure."

I noticed the sweat rings beginning beneath his arms. "Why don't you work out of the office in the hotel lobby today? Or wherever you want."

"Oh my God, that would be amazing. You sure you don't mind?"

"Not at all." I smiled. "It would be a travesty to ruin that shirt, and the Wi-Fi over here is spotty at best."

"Thank you, thank you! I'll keep you posted." He snapped his laptop shut and scurried away before I could change my mind.

My walkie crackled to life with the Irish brogue of our assistant director. "Two minutes for camera."

Price was a scrawny, ginger-haired Dubliner who was only in his late twenties but was probably the most mature person on the set. He had a wife and three kids back in Ireland and a head that remained cool as ice while the flames of hell raged all around him. I'd worked with him on a music video in the UK a few years ago and hired him every chance I got since. He made me feel calm. Calmer. No matter how I fronted, no part of me was actually calm.

Balancing my plate in one hand, I unhooked the walkie from my buckle. "How many minutes on Cole?"

"Five. Stella's double flying in."

We didn't have the budget for actual stand-ins, opting instead to use production assistants with vaguely similar build and coloring to the actors for lighting purposes, but after the snafu this morning, I graciously accepted Stella's offer of Felicity as her proxy while she was in makeup. Stella did not do her own stand-in work, she'd informed me in no uncertain terms. Irksome, but Felicity was game. I still wasn't exactly thrilled by her presence, but she was here now, and I could use all the help I could get. Also, I knew makeup would probably take a while, as Stella and Cole both needed to look fifteen years younger in the scene, so I welcomed the unpaid labor.

I stuffed a last bite of bagel in my mouth and dumped my plate in the trash, sneezing. The empty shipping warehouse we were filming in had briefly been used as a makeshift soundstage for the fourth Gentleman Gangster movie, and Cole had bought it when he purchased the Genesius Resort. But the stage was dustier than advertised, and the air-conditioning we'd paid premium for the benefit of using was so loud that we couldn't turn it on when we were rolling sound; nor could we run it at the same time as the lights because of the power pull, so we had to take AC breaks to cool the space down. At least the building was big enough to double as our de facto home base and storage for equipment, props, and wardrobe. Anyway, we'd be shooting out of here and on location most of the time, in the beach house meant to belong to Stella's and Cole's characters, Marguerite and Peyton.

I skated around a grip taping down electrical wires and threaded my way through a forest of light stands to join Jackson and Price at video village. Jackson sat in a director's chair staring at the set while Brian worked with the gaffers to light what was supposed to be a photo studio in New York for the flashback sequence. None of the three monitors were live.

"Where's the feed?" I asked.

"Communication problem," Jackson answered, tucking a wisp of dark hair behind his ear. His hair had grown out while he'd been down here the past month and was now nearly chin-length. "They're working on it."

A voice erupted from the walkie in Price's hand. "Makeup for Price."

"Go for Price." Price headed off in the direction of the makeup room.

I pulled up a director's chair next to Jackson. "How ya feeling?"

He'd become almost skeletal during the stress of preproduction. But now he looked healthier after a month on the island away from his father, who, I couldn't help but notice, treated him more like an employee he didn't particularly trust than his only son. One evening a few weeks ago, after they'd nearly come to blows over Cole's insistence on rushing to production despite it being hurricane season, I'd suggested to Cole that perhaps it would be better if he cut his losses and let the film go. Or at least delayed until the winter. He about ripped my head off, shouting at me that I had no idea what it meant to be a father.

He was right. Mine was hardly an example.

I'd made the same suggestion to Jackson the following day, even going so far as to volunteer to put the script in the hands of the few producers who would still take my phone calls, but was met with grim determination. "It'll come together," he'd insisted, rubbing his perpetually bloodshot eyes.

I felt bad for him. I guessed he wanted a relationship with his father and had thought the film would be a way for them to connect, but he was sorely mistaken. Today, though, Jackson's army-green eyes were clear. "Glad we're finally about to roll on this beast." He smiled.

"I was nervous about not being down here to oversee preproduction," I admitted, "but everything looks great."

"Yeah."

Nervous was an understatement. So far though, I was nothing but impressed with Jackson and his team and grateful for all they'd taken off my plate. The locations they'd found were perfect, the equipment had all made it through customs without a hitch, the permits were in order, and the craft services table was miraculously better stocked than on most higher-budget films I'd worked on.

Felicity emerged from the shadows onto the set wearing Stella's wardrobe for the scene: a gauzy silver dress that was nearly sheer beneath the lights. I noticed the crew guys trying not to heed her impossibly Barbie-like proportions as Price guided her toward the couch, where she curled into the corner and tucked her feet beneath her. One of the wardrobe girls covered her with a robe, but Felicity shrugged it off. "It's hot," she said. "I'm fine."

The monitors fuzzed, then popped to picture one after the other. "Monitors are up," I yelled to Brian. He gave me a thumbs-up.

The image on the monitors blurred, and when it refocused, Felicity's face filled the screen. It just wasn't fair. Somehow she was even more beautiful on camera than she was in person: her skin smooth and unblemished as a baby's, the light glancing off her cheekbones and the angle of her ever-so-slightly upturned nose, her dark eyes dancing when they found the lens. All of which only conspired to make me more suspicious of her.

"Jesus," Jackson muttered, transfixed.

She had undeniable star quality. Stella possessed that quality years ago, when she first began. But she'd been diminished by years of misfortune, made vulnerable and wary, and her light had dimmed. Her reduced state could work though, in this role. If she could pull it off without giving in to vanity.

"Find yourself a muse?" I teased.

He dismissed the idea with a wave of his hand. "Girls that pretty rarely have any talent."

I raised my eyebrows, taken aback. In the months I'd worked with him, I'd never heard him utter anything quite so spiteful. Regardless of how much I sometimes wished talent could be singular and evenly handed out at birth, I knew it not to be true. I'd seen far too many models become actresses who obtain degrees from Ivy League schools, then marry into royalty and raise more money for charity than any of their royal predecessors. Okay, maybe that was just the one— an unfortunately lovely woman who deserved it all—but there were plenty of other examples of successful multihyphenates, not all quite so lovely. I tried not to think about it too much; I found my own life tedious by comparison.

Truth be told, it was a little dispiriting working with the gods and goddesses of our time, no matter how nice they were—though of course it was always worse when they were awful. I'd read about the dangers of evaluating ourselves against the impossible ideals represented by magazines and social media feeds, but I liked to think that if I weren't shoulder to shoulder with celebrities all the time, I wouldn't be as vulnerable to comparison. Without Felicity lounging in all her glory out in the bay, I might've been excited to flaunt the fruits of my CrossFit classes. Without the signs of Cole's fortune all around me, I could've felt proud that my salary was above average for someone in her early thirties.

But Jackson had far less reason than I to bitch; he was in fact one of the gods, a prince of Hollywood. No other kid from his graduating film school class was directing a feature starring an A-list movie star. And on top of it, he was pretty good-looking too, with his father's square jaw and Roman nose and his mother's olive skin and deep-set eyes.

So while I myself was not thrilled that Felicity had hitched herself to our payroll without my noticing and I still wasn't sold on her motives, I felt compelled to say something.

"Killed by a model in a past life?" I asked.

He shrugged. "Raised by one. My mother had no soul until she developed wrinkles. Cole still doesn't, if you haven't noticed."

I stared at him, trying to think of a kosher response. "Sorry." He shook his head. "You're right. That was uncalled for. Don't listen to me. This is the closest I've been to my dad in a long time—or, ever—and it's... an adjustment."

I could relate. "If it makes you feel any better, I had a similar experience working with my dad," I confessed. "But let's not take it out on this poor girl." I gestured to Felicity. "Don't want to judge a book by its cover and all that. We don't know anything about her."

He nodded, and we turned back to the monitor, watching as Felicity's face broke into laughter over something a gaffer said. "There's something familiar about her," Jackson mused. "But I can't place it."

"Hmmm," I said. "Madison thought she was someone else too. An actress she'd been in class with."

"Well, she doesn't recognize me, so..." He shrugged.

Cole stepped onto the set swathed in the monochromatic black of his character and shaded his eyes from the lights, looking toward us. "Anybody have pages?"

Jackson groaned audibly. Of course Cole had put off memorizing his lines until five minutes before we rolled. Price called for pages over the walkie while Cole ambled over to Felicity and massaged her shoulders. On the monitors, I could see a flicker of distaste flash across her face before she quickly covered it with a friendly smile.

Shit. This wasn't the nineties. What the hell was wrong with him? Everyone knew his reputation as a "method" actor who didn't break character while on set, but come on. Felicity was just a stand-in, and the guy didn't even know his lines. He couldn't exactly claim to be living in the skin of his character. He had to step into the twenty-first century or we were going to get sued. Yet another fun conversation I was going to get to have with the boss I'd apparently attempted to bed.

Before I could come up with an appropriate solution that wouldn't get me fired, a production assistant mercifully handed Cole his sides, occupying his paws and rescuing Felicity from his clutches. He sank onto the couch next to her, his shoulder grazing hers.

Vigilance didn't come as naturally to me as it did most women in film, having been sheltered by my father's power my entire life. Until now I'd never been harassed by a colleague, sexually or otherwise, because no one wanted to incur the Wrath of David, who had quite a temper and an arsenal of dirt on seemingly everyone in Hollywood. Not that he would have noticed or cared. In fact, if someone assured him the molestation of his only child would ensure a profit for any of his films, he would likely give his famous half shrug, the left side of his mouth downturned, acquiescing with a dismissive flick of his wrist. *Whatever it takes.* In the long run, of course, he was the one I should have been afraid of.

How my mother was ever married to him, I had no idea. And from the time they finally broke up when I was four, she valiantly made excuses for every recital and birthday party he missed, never once attempting to correct my conviction that he was Superman. She enforced the rules and made my lunches, chauffeured me and helped with my homework, while he'd swoop in for a few hours every few weeks to take me to premieres where movie stars fawned over me, I realized later, to get into his good graces. Naturally, I wanted to work in Hollywood when I grew up, *just like him*, never be a teacher or a mom, like her. Even after years of manipulation and verbal abuse as his employee, I was not fully disabused of the illusion of his grandeur until he brutally murdered my career.

"Where's Stella?" Jackson demanded of no one in particular. "We need to get Stella in to do a blocking rehearsal. She doesn't have to be camera ready."

I activated my walkie. "Taylor for Price."

"Go for Price."

"We need Stella for blocking. Makeup and wardrobe can finish after."

"Copy."

Jackson strode onto the set and turned an apple box on its end to sit in front of Cole and Felicity. I looked on, curious, never actually having seen him direct outside of the audition room. I'd watched the experimental short film that had ostensibly convinced his dad to fund this, but I had no idea what his on-set style would be.

"Taylor."

I turned to see Price shaking his head. "What? Where's Stella?" I asked.

"She says she doesn't do blocking rehearsals until she's camera ready."

This wasn't normally the kind of thing that Price would come to me for. He would work it out, concoct a way to get her to set when the director wanted her. She must've really put her foot down. "That's crazy. Lemme talk to her."

We were spending about $100,000 per day, which meant every minute of each twelve-hour day was worth roughly $138. I'd done the math. We simply couldn't afford any diva antics.

I plotted how to convince the woman to do her damn job as I

trod toward the makeup room, tucked away into the darkest corner of the warehouse. Light spilled from underneath the closed door. The handle was locked. I took a deep breath and knocked more loudly than necessary. "Stella, Evelyn, Stephanie!" I called in a sing-song voice.

Nothing. I rapped again. "Ladies, open the door please."

"We're still thirty away," came Evelyn's voice.

I clenched my fists. "I know, I just need Stella for a quick blocking rehearsal."

"I told the AD already," Stella snipped, "I don't do blocking rehearsals until I'm ready. Use Felicity."

"Please open the door so we can talk about it."

The lock turned, and Evelyn's assistant opened the door. "Sorry," she mouthed. Stephanie was in the corner curling a wig, and Stella sat in the center makeup chair with her cocoa and honey hair in curlers, nursing a coffee while Evelyn contoured her face. She looked up at me, tired. The bright lights around the mirrors exposed the bags under her anxious red eyes, her uneven skin. Immediately I understood the big dark glasses and hat this morning, the locked door and camera-ready demands. I reached for the spiel I'd prepared about why she needed to stop acting like the Queen of Sheba and report to set immediately, but my tongue couldn't find the words. "I'll have Felicity do the blocking," I said feebly.

She nodded.

Jackson was waiting with his arms crossed when I returned to video village. "Well?"

"Not gonna happen," I said. "Rehearse with Felicity."

He threw his script on the ground. "You're fucking kidding me. Who's calling the shots around here?"

"Jackson," I warned with a small shake of my head. "You want the best performance out of your lead actress, don't you?"

He stared holes into me, rage bubbling from his eyes.

"It's gonna be okay." I patted his back like a baby. "You gotta let this stuff go. Inhale through your nose and out through your mouth." Surprisingly, he obeyed. "Now count to ten."

He closed his eyes, again inhaling through his nose and blowing it out slowly through his mouth. I bent to collect his script from the ground, hiding my smile. Perhaps he'd turn out to be one of the good ones after all.

I climbed into my director's chair to watch as Jackson walked Felicity and Cole through the scene. Jackson obviously knew exactly what he wanted, but he had a natural way of guiding the actors to make the discoveries themselves so they felt empowered. Cole was so fooled he clearly thought he didn't need any direction. After a minute, I noticed that Felicity wasn't holding her sides in her hand as she ran through the lines and hit her marks without missing a beat. She had the script memorized.

# Felicity

ris takes a swig of her Dr Pepper and lights another cigarette. "Fucking gorgeous day." She stretches out on the plastic lounger with her arms above her head. "Finally."

It is a gorgeous day, the first we've had after weeks of nonstop rain. I don't understand why we're the only ones enjoying it at the Super 8 pool, but we're glad because it means we can do whatever we want. Iris sings along to Nelly Furtado, "Maneater" blaring out of the boom box between our chairs.

I practice some of the moves I've been learning in the hip-hop class I finally got to sign up for last month, the concrete hot under my bare feet.

Iris claps. "Whoo-hoo! Get it, girl!"

I dance harder. "I'm gonna be a dancer just like you when I grow up," I shout over the music.

She laughs. "Don't even think about it. You're way smarter than me, girl. You're going to college. You're gonna have a real life with real money and never be anybody's bitch."

Hitch-kick! Shoulder isolation! I can feel my belly jiggle as I hop, but if I keep dancing like this I'll be skinny as my mom in no time. "We'll see." I parrot her favorite thing to say when I ask for something she doesn't want to give.

She sets her cigarette on the edge of the ashtray, and before I know it she's tackled me and we're both in the deep end sputtering water. "Gotcha!" She laughs.

I splash her, joining in her laughter.

She's been a different person since the day I found the holes in her arm. Or I guess the person she had been before the drugs, only better. And not exactly since that day but a few days after. I'm not sure what happened, but the holes were gone and she was glowing, whistling in the shower, giggling every time she picked up her phone. I knew what it had to be.

"You're in love," I declared one evening when she kept checking her phone even though we were watching our favorite show together.

She looked at me wide-eyed and started to protest, then laughed. "You're right. I think I am."

"With who?" I asked, though I could guess. Cole was the only man she'd seen in months.

She smiled secretively. "I'm in love with a movie star," she purred.

I grinned, my mind swirling with possibilities. "And is this *mystery* movie star in love with you?"

She nodded, her cheeks red. "I think so."

"Are you actually blushing?" I teased. "I don't think I've ever seen you blush before. Iris and Cole sitting in a tree, K-I-S-S-I-N-G. First comes—"

"Stop it." She whacked me with a pillow.

"So when do I get to meet him?" I prodded. "If he's gonna be my dad, I have some questions for him."

"All in good time," she assured me. "It's complicated right now."

Then I remembered. He was married to Stella Rivers. They'd just married when my mom met him, and I hadn't seen anything about them divorcing in the tabloids, so they must still be married. "He's gotta get divorced first, huh?" I asked.

"Something like that," she replied. "You don't—you haven't talked about this with any of your friends, have you?"

I shook my head. "No, of course not. You told me not to."

"Good." She nodded. "Don't. It's more important now than ever."

"I promise."

And I haven't said a word to anybody. The thing I find weird though is that the big pile of money in the safe hasn't been growing. In fact, it's been shrinking. But I can't ask her about it because I'm not supposed to know the code. I've decided it means that Cole is really in love with her. Maybe he's even set up a bank account in her name or something. It's the only explanation.

It's late afternoon by the time we get home from the pool, and I can tell I'm going to be sunburned. I'm usually so brown I don't get sunburned, but with all the rain, I haven't seen the sun in weeks. "Shit," Iris says, looking at her phone. "I didn't realize how late it was. I gotta hop in the shower. Can you handle dinner for yourself?"

I nod. "I gotta go to the store for aloe anyway. I'm sunburned."

I'm in line at the 7-Eleven with my frozen pizza, aloe, and Coke, when I see the front of *Celebrity* magazine. It's a picture of Cole and Stella that looks like it's been ripped in half, a jagged black line between them. The caption reads "OVER ALREADY? Cole and Stella reportedly headed for Splitsville."

I grab the magazine and start thumbing through it, unable to hold back my grin. At the register I don't have enough money for everything, so I choose the magazine over the aloe. Who cares about a sunburn. My mom's gonna marry a movie star!

I run all the way home and throw open the front door, panting. "Mom! Guess what?" I tear into the bathroom, where she's curling her hair, and slap the magazine in front of her, doing a victory dance.

But her response isn't what I thought it would be. She frowns at the cover, sets her curling iron down, and lifts the magazine, studying the picture intently. Without a word, she takes it over to the bed with her and reads the entire article without looking up. I try to peer over her shoulder, but she bats me away.

"Well?" I ask, holding my hand out for the magazine when she's done.

"I need it," she says.

"But I haven't even read it," I protest.

She throws the magazine at me. "Give it back when you're done." She picks up the curling iron and turns her attention to her reflection.

"Aren't you happy?" I ask, confused. "He's getting divorced."

She doesn't look happy. "I told you," she says. "It's complicated. That's all I can say right now."

I'm dumbfounded. "Seriously?"

"Sorry, honey," she says. "I promise I'd tell you more if I could. Soon."

I sigh and flop on the bed with the magazine, flipping to the article about Cole and Stella. The page features a picture of the two of them in front of a chapel, their clasped hands raised. She's in a white sequined minidress holding a bouquet of roses; he wears a cream linen suit and a shit-eating grin.

Is Hollywood's hottest couple divorcing after only ten months? Stella Rivers and Cole Power were already stars when they met on the set of their hit film, *Faster*, but their PDA-filled relationship has made them the most talked-about couple in Hollywood. After a quickie wedding in Vegas on Friday, July 13 (bad luck, we all said!), Stella reportedly moved into Cole's home in Miami [picture of mansion]. It's no secret "Stole" likes to party, and true to form, the two have been photographed together out and about in South Beach, Los Angeles, New York, and Paris. But after photos surfaced of Cole with a mystery woman in Miami [grainy photo of Cole leaning into a woman whose long blond ponytail spills out the back of a baseball hat] and reportedly getting cozy with his *Bloodhound* costar Noemi Calderon at a bar last week in Los Angeles, Stella was spotted out with a girlfriend, no Cole in sight [blurry photo of a woman that may or may not be Stella on a dance floor]. Now a source close to the couple confirms there is indeed trouble in paradise. Stella's reportedly jealous of his continued flirtation with various women while she's ready to settle down and have a baby. Cole already shares an eleven-year-old son, Jackson, with his Israeli model ex, Bar Salmaan. The source tells *Celebrity* that Stella's been wanting to start a family for some time and thought Cole was on the same page, but he seems more interested in continuing his bad-boy ways. With his philandering past and her reported jealous streak, we give this relationship a grade of FAIL!

"Mom, is that you in the photo with Cole?"

She grabs a powder-blue sundress from her messy closet and pulls it over her head. "No."

"But I don't understand. Is he seeing other women?"

"Don't believe everything you read. Especially that shit." She nods at the magazine. "Can you grab my perfume out of my purse for me?"

I paw through her giant white shoulder bag in search of the perfume, but my fingers brush something soft. Curious, I pull it out. It's a rainbow rabbit's foot attached to a key chain with a solitary key. I turn it over in my hands, noting the initials *CS* burned into the paw. Suddenly it's last Christmas, and Jewel's mom is once again alive, chasing us around her apartment with this same rabbit's foot while we squeal in terror.

"Why do you have Crystal's rabbit foot?" I ask.

Iris spins from the open closet abruptly, her eyes flicking to the rabbit's foot. "She gave it to me before she died."

I drop it on the bed, remembering how disgusted I'd been that Crystal carried some poor rabbit's amputated leg on her key chain. I also remember Jewel saying how attached her mom was to it and how much trouble she got in when she took it off the key chain once, because her mom never went anywhere without it. "But wasn't it, like, her good luck charm?"

"I guess she didn't need it anymore."

I snort. "Boy was she wrong about that."

"Phoenix. Not cool." She gives me a dark look before turning back to the closet.

I pick up the rabbit's foot again. "Why do you have her key?"

"She, uh...she gave it to me," she says, continuing to rummage in the closet, "in case she ever got locked out or whatever."

My mom doesn't lie to me much, but when she does, I always know. "You promised you would never lie to me."

"Phee." She takes a deep breath and turns to meet my gaze. "Some things are grown-up things that are hard to explain. So I have to leave it at that for now, okay? Please don't mention it to Jewel."

I drop my eyes, stroking the rainbow fur. "Phee, I need you to promise."

"I promise," I mumble.

"Good. Thank you. How about that perfume?"

I toss it to her, still mad about her lying to me. She spritzes herself, then holds up two different strappy flats. "Silver or gold?"

"Gold," I say.

I've hardly ever seen her wear flats or dresses that aren't short and tight until the past few weeks. Another sign Cole must really be in love with her for who she is and not only what she looks like. But what was that in the article I just read about him cozying up to some actress in LA last week? I know Iris saw him last week. At least she said that was where she was going. But who knows. She could be lying to me about that too. She better not screw this up by seeing some other guy behind his back while he's out of town.

Now I'm worried. I could ask her about it, but I don't trust her anymore. She obviously hasn't been straight with me about any of this, and I *need* to know what's going on. It's my life too.

I'm gonna find out for myself, and I know exactly how to do it. It's risky—she would kill me if she found out—but it's for her own good.

"I didn't have enough money for the aloe because I bought this stupid magazine," I say. "Can I have some money to go back to the store?"

"Sure. Grab a twenty out of my wallet."

"Thanks, Iris." I pocket the cash and give her a hug. "Have a nice night. I'll see you tomorrow."

She kisses my forehead. "Love you, little bird."

"Love you."

Leaving her in the bedroom, I quickly grab a bottle of water and a protein bar from the kitchen and roll a blanket from the couch under my arm before bolting out the door. I hurry down the stairs to her beat-up hatchback, which she always leaves unlocked. She'd rather they steal whatever old towels and T-shirts she has in the trunk than smash the window trying to break in again. I lie down in the way back, arrange the blanket on top of me, and wait for her to get in the driver's seat.

# Stella

'm pregnant." I tried to remember my next line without looking at the sides. "I know this isn't what we planned; it'll turn our lives upside down and probably ruin my career, but it's what I want."

Our script supervisor, Kara, held my gaze expectantly. She was of Japanese descent, with exquisitely delicate features and a face as symmetrical as a doll's. I'd always wished I had a face as symmetrical as that. "Aren't you going to say something?" she asked.

"What?"

"Your line... It's 'Aren't you going to say something?'" she said.

"Oh! Right. Sorry." I'd skipped my A-pill this morning because I wasn't actually feeling all that anxious for once and I wanted to be clear, but I still had a little residual fogginess from the S-pills I'd been taking before bed in order to ensure a good night's rest.

It was Wednesday, our third day of filming, and so far, so good. Cole and I had great chemistry (we always had) and were getting amazing feedback on our performances. It was wonderful to be working, and I felt such a connection with my character, Marguerite. It hadn't been all smooth sailing, though: Monday we'd done the scene where Marguerite and Peyton first meet as he's shooting photos of her, and suffice it to say Cole was not comfortable behind the lens. We'd ended up running an hour late because the set photographer had to give him a lesson in how to use a camera, which meant we had to rush the second scene of the day, where he proposes on the beach. Even so, it worked out in the end, because the sunset was fantastic. Then yesterday we shot a series of short montage scenes that took us through the rise of Peyton's career as a photographer and the decline of Marguerite's as a model, here on the soundstage. There were a lot of setups, but it went smoothly, besides Jackson and Cole arguing over every little stupid thing. They were always arguing. At any rate, the kinks were getting worked out, and I liked Jackson as a director, regardless of what Cole thought.

I cleared my throat and glanced at my sides to confirm my next lines. "Aren't you going to say something?" I read.

Kara slouched against my dressing room mirror and ran a hand through her short black hair. It was a boy's haircut, but it looked sexy on her. I could never wear my hair like that, but she was so dainty, it really suited her. "It's great news," she read Cole's line.

"But you don't seem happy," I returned.

She approached me and put her hand on my hip, looking deep into my eyes as she lowered her voice, imitating Cole's. "Perhaps we should celebrate."

We both laughed. "And then we kiss," I said.

A rapping at the door and she abruptly dropped her hand from my waist, returning to her post against the mirror. "Come in," I called.

Price opened the door. "Ten-minute warning," he said.

"Thanks." I gestured to Kara. "Kara was just helping me with my lines."

He nodded and left without closing the door. I grabbed my pack of smokes and a lighter. Kara raised an eyebrow. "I know, it's a disgusting habit," I admitted, "but better than some other habits I've had. Thanks for helping me."

She smiled. "Anytime."

I cut across the stuffy warehouse toward the exit, stopping for just a moment at the edge of the stage lit for the scene we were about to shoot, set to look like the bedroom of Peyton and Marguerite's New York apartment. Jackson looked on as Felicity stood in for me, running the scene with Cole as the gaffer adjusted the lights and the camera crew rehearsed their movement.

Felicity really was an angel, volunteering to work as my stand-in. She was always going above and beyond. And her idea to have makeup come to our bungalow every morning so I didn't have to worry about looking a mess in front of fifty people who all had cameras to snap unflattering pictures of me, at any moment, was pure genius. The Botox and fillers I'd had done in recent weeks were holding up nicely, and I swore my pores had never looked so good after the micro-needling and vampire facial, but still, I didn't like to be photographed without my total game face on. Taylor, of course, assured me that the crew had all been thoroughly vetted and none of them were leakers, but in my experience you could never be too careful.

I watched as Fee ran through the scene with Cole, hitting all her marks and nailing her lines like a pro. If she hadn't been way too young for the part, I would've been worried she'd steal my role—she was that good. She said the line about the pregnancy ruining her career with such unbridled glee, it made me stop to think about my own inter-pretation of the line. Perhaps instead of being afraid of the pregnancy destroying her career, my character was in fact thrilled by the excuse to end her career. She knew she was growing older, and stepping away from the spotlight would allow her to live her life in peace, without agonizing over every crease in her forehead. Achingly familiar, really. I knew as I opened the stage door that I was going to borrow it.

Temporarily blinded by the brutal glare of the morning sun after the dark of the warehouse, I stumbled over the lip of the door and plowed straight into Madison, who was standing on the small loading dock just outside. "Sorry!" I yelped. "Didn't see the step down."

Madison tittered and spun to face me, phone in hand. "Careful," she teased. "People might say you're drunk on set."

Noticing the live stream icon in the corner of her screen, I forced an awkward laugh. Did this girl ever stop filming? At least I was camera ready today. "Sober as Sunday morning," I quipped.

Of all the exits, why did she have to take up residence at this one? The side loading dock was tucked away from the hubbub of the craft services tents in the dusty parking lot on the other side of the building, shaded by big trees and overlooking a hill that rolled gently down to the rocky shore—a perfect place to take a break.

Madison's eyes flitted back to the screen. "I'm getting so many questions from you guys right now, I can't even keep up!" she exclaimed. "I'm gonna pick one at random. Here we go. Randy from Wisconsin asks 'Stella, these days, do you shave your pussy—' Randy! That is *very* randy of you."

I could feel the heat rise in my cheeks. A decade had passed; I shouldn't still be bothered, but when your most embarrassing moment is splashed all over the internet and proceeds to ruin your career, it's a little hard not to be. I didn't actually remember the night in question, but I'd never be allowed to forget it. It wasn't my fault, really. I'd been (what I didn't know at the time was clinically) depressed and really fucked up—uppers and downers paired with booze, an ill-advised combination in any circumstance. I was at Rock & Roll Ralphs on Sunset replenishing my supply of gin and snacks at two in the morning when I apparently caught a woman taking pictures of me. I was blackout drunk, so I have no recollection of it, but the video shows me yelling and throwing pickle jars at her, wearing a sundress with no underwear. The nail in the coffin: in my despair, I hadn't been taking care of my nether regions properly, hence Randy's comment and my perpetual shame.

"Stella?" Madison asked expectantly. "What do you think?"

I blinked at her, realizing she'd continued to talk after I'd stopped listening. I had no idea what she wanted my opinion on, but I was beginning to feel claustrophobic, trapped beneath the crush of her 143,000 adoring fans, and I needed to get out of there. "Sorry," I said as nicely as I could muster. "We're about to roll. I've got to prepare."

And with that I gratefully disappeared into the cavernous darkness of the studio. I hadn't gotten to smoke a cigarette, but it was probably for the best. It was a filthy habit.

"Oh, there you are!"

I turned to see Taylor, headphones around her neck and script in hand. "I got caught out there in Madison's live stream," I explained.

"She's live streaming here?" Taylor asked. She sounded as frustrated as I was by the whole thing.

I nodded and pointed to the door. "Out there."

Taylor put the heels of her hands into her eyes, sighing. "Okay, thanks. I'll deal with her. They're ready for you on set. The photographer is going to shoot some stills of you guys before we roll."

"Cool." I skirted around a collection of flags and scrims to land at video village, where I found Jackson and Felicity in deep conversation, the script between them. I watched his gaze soften, his eyes trained on her as she looked down at the pages, searching for something. I smiled to myself. Didn't look like they'd be needing my matchmaking services after all. The kids could evidently figure it out on their own.

Feeling my eyes on him, Jackson turned. "Felicity and I were just discussing a discovery she made about your character that I thought you might want to use."

"Oh?"

"You inspired it, really," Felicity rushed in, batting her long lashes. "I was thinking of what you've said about how stressful the limelight can be, and I realized that maybe Marguerite's actually not terrified but thrilled by the idea of leaving it behind."

"Of course she's thrilled," I snipped, annoyed. I saw Felicity's face fall, but it wasn't my job to coddle her. And clearly Jackson needed to be reminded that I was the lead actress here. "The spotlight eventually burns even the thickest skin. I of all people should know that." Avoiding Felicity's gaze, I shed my robe and draped it over the back of Jackson's director's chair, meeting his eyes with what I hoped was a convincing smile. "Ready when you are."

Cole sat on the bed beneath the lights, studying his lines. "I'm gonna cut that last line about wanting to celebrate and just kiss you after you ask me whether I'm happy," he said without looking up as I approached.

"You're gonna cut what?" Jackson asked, overhearing.

The prop master signaled to me as Jackson and Cole once again locked horns, and I gladly stepped away from their argument, joining him in the doorway of what was supposed to be our bathroom. "This is the positive pregnancy test you'll come out of the bathroom holding," he said.

I palmed the pregnancy test and inspected it. It did indeed have two lines. "Who's the lucky mother-to-be?" I joked.

He laughed as the sound guy approached with my mic. "You ready to get wired?" he asked.

"We're gonna shoot pictures first, so let's wait till after," I said.

"Stella." Jackson beckoned to me. I slipped the pregnancy test into the pocket of my pajama pants and joined Jackson, Cole, and the baby-faced set photographer at the foot of the bed. "We'll have you here. Cole, you're facing her with your hand on her belly."

Cole and I faced each other, and he lightly placed his hand on my stomach as Jackson moved over to the monitors. "Looking good. Pete's gonna take over from here."

The set photographer waved at the mention of his name. "Stella tilt your face up to the light, and, Cole, cheat out a bit," Pete instructed. "Nice."

We followed his directions as he clicked away. "Brings back memories, doesn't it?" Cole whispered.

"She would have been twelve now," I murmured.

"If it were a she," he returned.

Tears welled in my eyes. "She would have been," I said. I'd felt it from the beginning, that I was carrying a girl. But the day I went in for the blood test was the day we found out she'd left us, taking with her what was left of our shell of a marriage and leaving me crushed. I often wondered how differently things might have turned out if she'd stayed. Who she would have become, who I would have become. But dwelling on what might have been only drove me to drink, and evidently throw pickle jars at unsuspecting passersby.

"She would have been beautiful," he said, running his fingertips over my cheek. "Just like her mama."

Cole really could be sweet when he wanted to. These past few days I'd begun to remember what it was about him I had loved. And the chemistry. God, the chemistry. I couldn't believe I was still attracted to him after all that had happened between us, but my body seemed to have a mind of its own.

"Let's do a few kissing," Pete instructed.

Cole pulled me closer and covered my mouth with his. My head grew light with the smell of his aftershave, the roughness of his persistent stubble, the taste of his lips; the familiarity was dizzying, as though I'd stumbled into a time warp.

"Okay, we're good," Pete said, checking his camera.

Cole brushed my cheek again with his fingers and let his gaze travel once more to my lips before he turned his attention to his buzzing phone.

Flushed, I grabbed the bottle of water I'd stored behind a chair and gulped it.

"Everybody take twenty," Price called out. "AC break before we roll."

Film really was a lot of hurry up and wait. But I was glad to step away from the swell of emotion that threatened to breach the levees when I was in Cole's arms, and beelined for the door.

Outside, I found Felicity at a table under the giant pop-up tent in the parking lot, laughing with Kara. "What's so funny?" I asked, sliding into the seat beside them.

"Show her," Felicity said.

The image on Kara's phone was of a girl that strongly resembled . . . me. I squinted at it and looked at Kara quizzically.

"She's your doppelgänger!" Felicity exclaimed.

"Who is she?" I asked.

Kara flipped to the next picture, which showed her and the girl kissing. "My ex."

"Well, she's very pretty," I said. "If I do say so myself."

"Yeah." Kara gazed at the picture wistfully.

"What happened?" Felicity asked.

"She's an actress," Kara said, as if that explained it.

"And?" I asked.

"She fell in love with her next costar, naturally." Kara laughed.

"Then she wasn't worth your time," I said. "Anyway, not all actresses are assholes."

She brushed her hair out of her eyes and smiled enigmatically. "So I hear."

Felicity abruptly stood and beckoned to me. "I wanna shoot you while you're in this makeup. For your Insta. Grab your phone. I know just the spot."

She led me around the corner to the side of the warehouse that had a view of the sea. "I'm sorry about earlier," she said when we were out of earshot of the others. "It was out of line for me to discuss your character with Jackson. I wasn't thinking."

I nodded. "Okay."

Her big brown eyes were full of tears. "I've never been on a set before. This is all new to me," she explained, her voice shaking. "Please believe me, I never want to do anything that would hurt you."

I felt bad then; I'd obviously hurt her feelings more than necessary. "It's okay," I said. "Really. I understand. It's not your fault Jackson worships the ground you walk on."

"You think?" She wiped her eyes and looked at me sideways. "I don't see it."

"Riiiiight. I give it a week before you're knockin' boots." I wiggled my hips.

"That's not happening." She laughed, starting down the grassy hill. "Come here." She gestured to a large shade tree with a swing hanging from it. I dutifully handed her my phone and sat in the swing facing the sea. "No. Face the other way so I get the ocean behind you."

I adjusted my position and smiled. "No smile," she said. "And look wistful. You don't know I'm here."

I gazed over her shoulder toward where Madison sat on the edge of my loading dock with her computer in her lap, so wrapped up in whatever she was doing that she didn't even see us, thank heavens. I recited my gratitude prayer in my head, feeling the ocean breeze lift my hair from my shoulders as Felicity snapped pictures. This whole sharing culture was beyond counterintuitive to me. But I knew she was right: if I wanted the world to see a new me, I had to show them a new me. And she was actually a pretty good photographer, though I always made her shoot with my phone so that I could edit the photos. The whole unedited photos trend was another I simply could not understand. Why would anyone want to expose their flaws when it is so easy to simply delete them with the click of a button? Photoshop was like makeup, but for pictures. And I, for one, was grateful for it.

"What's this?" I heard the mockery in Cole's voice before I spun to see him striding up from the rocky beach. "Stella Rivers allowing herself to be photographed without a publicist present? I don't believe my eyes." He looked to Felicity. "You know she wouldn't even allow a photographer at our wedding for fear he would sell the pictures."

"And somehow our pictures ended up in the magazines anyway." I smiled tightly. "But I've changed with the times."

He gestured to Felicity and Madison, laughing. "Who are we kidding? We're dinosaurs compared to these kids." He threw his arm around my shoulder just as Felicity snapped a photo.

We glanced at her in surprise. "Great shot." She showed us the picture, which was indeed a great shot, and would be even better once I removed the crow's-feet from around my eyes. "You guys always were a good-looking couple."

Cole threw his head back and laughed. "I was never enough for Stella, though," he taunted. "Was I, baby?"

After the sweetness he'd shown me on set, his words were like a bucket of ice water. And just when I was beginning to imagine that perhaps we could put the past behind us. "I could say the same, I guess," I snapped.

His smile evaporated before he turned and sauntered away, leaving Felicity and me staring after him. "What the hell was that about?" Felicity asked.

I sighed. "He cheated on me."

"No surprise there," she said. "But why turn it around like that?"

"He's a dick, in case you haven't noticed."

She snorted. "Seems like he should be a little nicer to his leading lady if he's the method actor he claims to be."

"He doesn't need to go method on this," I said, rolling my eyes. "He *is* Peyton. A capricious artist who can't stay faithful and needs everyone to love him? Jackson wrote him a role he couldn't botch."

Felicity brushed away a piece of hair that had found its way into my eyes. "You okay?" she asked. I nodded. "For someone who's such a great actress, you're really a terrible liar," she breathed.

I watched Madison stand, smiling as Cole approached her perch. She showed him something on her computer and laughed flirtatiously when he made a comment.

I felt just like my character Marguerite, watching her husband hit on the nanny. Only he wasn't my husband anymore, and our child had never been born.

I forced the thought from my mind and looked over Felicity's shoulder as she thumbed through the pictures she'd snapped, stopping on one where I had a slight smile. "This is perfect. You look gorgeous."

It was a beautiful photo, but all I could see was how much I favored my mother. The resemblance was striking. I'd always taken after her, but now I was nearing the age she'd been the last time I saw her, and looking at the picture I realized I'd unwittingly styled my hair exactly like hers had been twenty-two years ago. I shook my head sharply and grabbed the phone. "Don't post it."

"Why? But it's—"

"I look like my mother," I cut her off. She wrinkled her brow. "What?" I asked.

"It's just—you've never mentioned your mother."

I sighed. If I couldn't even talk about these things, how was I supposed to write a memoir? Felicity had encouraged me, said it would be cathartic, not to mention instrumental in showing the world the new me. At least I'd written out the story of how Cole and I met. Though I'd probably have to completely rewrite it so I wouldn't get sued. Anyway, it wasn't like I had a deadline. I didn't even have a publisher. I did want to set the record straight though, and my mother was a subject ripe for the page. "She was my manager," I said finally. "Until I turned eighteen and discovered she'd spent every dime I'd ever made."

She nodded with sympathy. "Gotcha."

I kicked off and pumped my legs, the branch of the tree creaking as I swung. Felicity never pried, bless her. She sensed the subjects I was reluctant to talk about, and never pushed or prodded the way so many people did.

That was one of the strangest things about being famous: everyone felt they owned a piece of you. Your joy and pain were their gossip, to be examined and analyzed like you weren't a real human with feelings at all, but some kind of fictional character. Everyone had opinions about who you dated, where you went, what you ate and wore—and they had no problem informing you of these opinions while you were in line for an embarrassing medication at the drugstore or in the midst of an intense fight with your partner in the corner booth of an exorbitantly expensive restaurant on Valentine's Day. You were stalked like prey by paparazzi and vilified for having secrets, as though the public had a right to know everything about you. It was exhausting.

It all rolled off Cole's back like water off a duck, but I was too sensitive; it was my greatest strength as an actress and my greatest weakness as a star.

There was a time, before the press that had turned me into a star remade me as a pariah, before the film offers dried up and the glowing fan mail turned to vitriolic hate mail, when I'd relished interviews with friendly journalists, photo shoots for glossy magazines, getting all dolled up to walk the red carpet. But I learned the hard way that when you're on a pedestal, you have a lot farther to fall. And when you're down, those who once raised you up will be the first to spit on you. At my lowest point, my entire life was picked apart, my every mistake magnified and mocked, my pain warped into madness and reflected back at me from every newsstand, and it broke me.

Most people blamed the paparazzi for how invasive the press had become, but really, those who courted them were equally to blame. I detested influencers with their instantly targetable audience and guaranteed views. They weren't actors by trade, but they'd become our competition, their quantifiable numbers of fans trumping our years of training and hard work. I needed another anxiety pill just thinking about it. And now here I was working with one of them. All Madison wanted was to be famous. She wanted it so badly it was written all over her lineless, vapid face.

Wondering how much work she'd had done to perfect that face, I watched as she snapped a selfie with Cole, then checked the camera and snapped another one, repeating the process ad nauseum until Cole finally put a stop to it. I was simultaneously fascinated and repulsed by how she eagerly invited her fans into every nook and cranny of her life, shamelessly sharing every mundane detail of her day. She was so desperate for attention that she'd do anything for views, and it was obviously working for her. She was a walking, talking advertisement for herself. We were yet to shoot a scene together, and already I was sick of her. But more than that, I hated how much she got under my skin.

"What's wrong?" Felicity interrupted my reverie. "You're frowning. Or trying to." She laughed.

"Nothing," I said, watching Madison toss her wavy black hair in response to something Cole said. She'd be banging him by the end of the week for sure. And I wished to hell it didn't bother me so much.

Felicity followed my gaze. "Mmm-hmm. You don't still have feelings for him, do you?"

I grimaced. "And here I was, thinking how lovely you were for not prying."

She dropped her gaze. "I'm sorry. I didn't mean—"

Immediately I regretted jumping on her, especially after earlier. "It's okay. That was mean of me."

"All good." She forced a smile. "Do you want an A-pill?"

*Of course* I wanted one, but would I be able to remember my lines? I was feeling mighty clear now that the S-pill had worn off completely. And mighty sensitive, obviously. Some might even say irritable. Also, I was going to have to do a romantic scene with my ex-husband-turned-employer in five minutes. Screw it. Kara would be there to feed me lines if I needed them. "Yeah," I said, slowing the swing. She extracted the little blue leather bag she kept my medicine in from her purse and dumped the pill in my hand. I knocked it back dry. "And no, I don't still have feelings for Cole."

"Too bad." She smiled. "A rumored romance would certainly bring you back into the spotlight."

I gripped the ropes of the swing, suddenly dizzy. "You know how much I loathe the spotlight."

She laughed. "You know you love it."

I wished more than anything she was wrong, that I could simply walk away from fame without a backward glance. But the maddening truth is that once you've bathed in the warmth of the limelight, you find you're damn cold when it no longer shines on you, no matter how you despised its glare.

# Family Ties

Most people don't know that my mother's name is also Stella. That's right, she named me after herself, which tells you just about everything you need to know about her. No memoir is complete without a chapter on the mother though, so here goes:

Stella Rodriguez was born into a wealthy family in Venezuela that lost all their money when they fled to New Jersey when she was a teenager, for reasons I never learned. She was very beautiful though, and quickly married my dad, a successful American businessman fifteen years her senior, when she was twenty, and had me the following year. I remember how grand our gaudy mansion seemed when I was little—white columns, gold lion statues guarding the door, the Aphrodite fountain in the foyer. My mother never worked, but she spent money like it was water—which was fine until my dad got thrown in jail for embezzlement when I was nine.

They took the house. I remember my mom would

be sitting on the overstuffed paisley printed couch that was far too big for our rented apartment, drinking a screwdriver while watching a talk show when I got home from school at three in the afternoon. She was always dressed and made up like she'd gone to lunch somewhere fancy, but I knew she hadn't. All her old friends had dropped her, the same way mine would years later after my breakdown.

She said she didn't speak English well enough to hold a job and told me in no uncertain terms that I had to make money to support us. I had worked as an actress when I was younger, doing commercials and that kind of thing, but had stopped when she no longer wanted to drive me around to auditions all the time. Now we were back on. I can't say I wasn't glad. I'd always loved acting, and now I had the chance to do it full-time.

I booked *Meg & Co* when I was ten, and we moved to Los Angeles, where she bought a house for us with my money. She was my manager and guardian, so I trusted her to make all the business decisions while I worked hard on the show. Little did I know that right under my nose she was spending every last dime of it on clothes, bags, and cosmetic surgery, not to mention a staff that included a maid, a gardener, a tutor, and a cook.

When I turned eighteen and learned there was nothing left, I had to start over at ground zero. Well, not exactly ground zero, as I first had to climb out of the hole she'd dug by neglecting to pay my taxes for a couple of years running. My father, who'd been released from jail by this point, tried to talk me into forgiving her, but I suspected all he really cared about was that I continued to support them. So I gave them a choice: I would forgive them and remain in their lives but never give them another dime, or continue to pay for them but never speak to them again.

I kept my word. I paid for them until my bank account ran dry.

# Taylor

*Thursday, June 20*

The evening of the fourth day of filming, I'd just emerged from a steaming shower when I heard a knock at my bungalow door. I quickly threw on gym shorts and a worn T-shirt without bothering to put on a bra and flung open the door, expecting the fish tacos I'd ordered. Instead I found my personal hero, Rick, holding a conch shell in the soft night air.

"Oh, hi," I said.

My surprise must have shown in my face because he chuckled. "Expecting someone else?"

"Room service," I explained. "It's been a long day."

"How's the shoot going?"

"Surprisingly well," I said. It was true: the weather had behaved, we'd run largely on time, and after all her demands the first morning, Stella had actually turned in a fantastic performance thus far, while Cole and Jackson had managed to mostly be civil to each other—a win all around.

"Good," he said. Behind him I spotted the room service guy pushing his cart up the torchlit pier and waved. "I won't stay," he added. "Just wanted to check on you."

"It's fine," I said quickly. I knew better than to read into his impromptu visit, but I couldn't help it. I was flattered this tall, dark, and handsome stranger had stopped by, and I didn't want him to go yet. "Do you wanna come in and chill with me while I eat dinner? I have extra fries and a minibar. Sorry, is it rude of me to ask you to watch me eat?"

An unhurried smile spread across his face. "No. I already ate, anyway. But I'll have a beer."

I signed for the room service, and we settled into two cushioned loungers on the over-water porch, facing the horizon. The heat of the day had dissipated, leaving a balmy breeze in its wake. A half-moon shone overhead, reflecting on the calm sea, and lights beneath the cabin illuminated the water, making it appear an unearthly blue-green.

"What's that?" I asked, indicating the shell.

"This is for you." He handed me the perfectly formed conch. Delighted, I turned it over in my hands, noticing for the first time the almost erotic appearance of its rosy, smooth flared lip. "I found it this afternoon."

"Thank you," I said. "It's beautiful." I held it to my ear and listened to the distant sound of the ocean inside.

"Conch shells are symbols of spiritual awakening and strength," he said. "It goes deeper than that, but I don't know all of it."

"Wow, spiritual awakening and strength . . . I could use both of those."

He held my eye a moment too long before he took a sip of his beer, and my stomach did a somersault. I turned my attention to my fries, reminding myself not to misread it. He was just one of those guys who was so comfortable in his own skin, he didn't mind holding someone's eye longer than usual, or gifting them symbols of spiritual awakening.

"So, Taylor." That gaze again. My God. Like some kind of a big cat. I'd read about guys with a "glacier-melting gaze" in my romance novels, of course, had even occasionally come across them in real life, but that gaze had never been directed at me. I was the friend, just one of the guys—the cool chick they told about their exploits and shared bawdy jokes with, who they might hook up with but we'd both know it was only that and things would never get mushy. Even with Rory, it was never romantic. My therapist said because my father had never shown me love, I didn't think I deserved it, so I chose unavailable men and lived vicariously through my romance novels rather than risking putting my heart out there. I argued that I simply didn't have time for romance and I wasn't a sentimental person. But maybe she was right, because Rick looked at me like I was a woman and suddenly I was a freaking puddle. "Tell me something about you, besides that you don't read warning signs," he teased.

I giggled like a fool. "Actually, that says a lot about me. What do you want to know?"

"Where are you from?"

It had to be just the way he looked at people because there it was again. Hypnotic. *Focus, Taylor. He asked you a question.* "LA, born and raised. You?"

"Here. Well, there"—he pointed toward the horizon on our right, where lights of the main island twinkled in the dark. "Saint Ann."

It was my turn. I could do this. Carry on a conversation like a normal woman. "You have a big family?" I asked.

He nodded. "My parents and four sisters, three married with kids around here and one at medical school in Miami."

"Wow, four sisters. You must know a lot about women."

He laughed. "Not really. You have siblings?"

I shook my head. "Only child. My parents divorced when I was four."

"I'm sorry," he said.

"Oh, it was for the best. My dad's a total asshole."

He raised a single eyebrow. Why had I said that? Talking about my dad was a surefire way to douse any interest he might have in me.

"You don't wanna know," I said.

"Try me." His eyes danced in the reflection off the water. "Unless you don't want to talk about it. I don't mean to pry. I'm just interested."

*Why?* I wanted to ask, suddenly defensive. But I stopped myself. It wasn't his fault my dad was a scumbag. "It's okay." I sighed, crashing back down to earth. Despite my momentary fantasy of falling into his arms in the light of this beautiful moon and letting him ravage me while the ocean rolled beneath us, this wasn't a romance novel. I was me. There was no escaping it; I might as well be honest. "My dad's a studio exec. He's a total stereotype—the Hollywood shark, always wheeling and dealing, screwing people." I focused on the glimmering lights of a cruise ship way out at sea. "I took a job working for him right out of college—I'd only really spent brief amounts of time with him, so I had this convoluted idea of who he was and thought it would be amazing to work with him. I mean, I'd heard he was a dick, but surely he wouldn't be a dick to me."

"So what happened?" he asked.

I eyed him. The rest of the story required me to reveal way more of myself than I felt comfortable with, but what the hell; this guy had already witnessed me at my most vulnerable. "I was wrong. He showed me zero respect, continually promoted men with less experience over me...Bitch of it was, he made me doubt myself so much that I didn't think I could leave."

His gaze was soft. "He sounds like a real asshole."

"Oh, I haven't even gotten to the good stuff." I'd been reluctant to talk about it, but now that I'd started, I felt the weight I hadn't realized I was carrying begin to lift, and it felt tantalizingly good. "Last year I made a mistake," I admitted. "I had an affair with a coworker who'd told me he was getting divorced. Only he wasn't."

Rick tipped his beer. "Wow, another asshole."

"Oh, my life is full of them." Something about this honesty felt provocative, like some kind of perverse striptease where every secret I revealed was akin to peeling off a piece of clothing. "Anyway, shortly after I broke it off with Rory, my dad asked me to leak some compromising information on an actress he'd had a relationship with, which had ended badly. When I refused, he blackmailed me."

He knit his brow. "With what?"

I leaned my head back against the cushioned chair, looking up at the glittering sky. Way up high, a tiny plane cut silently through a field of twinkling stars. "Rory and I had traveled together a lot for work the previous year, and I'd stupidly trusted him to submit our expense reports. Turned out he was doctoring the books, using our work trips to embezzle money from the studio and implicating me in the process."

"How'd he get away with it?"

I shrugged. "He took advantage of how complicated the flow of money can be for financing the huge movies we were working on. There were multiple companies involved on each project, which allowed for a good deal of double-dipping—getting reimbursed from more than one company, that kind of thing."

He let out a low whistle. "Impressive. And this guy was your boyfriend?"

Had he been? At first the relationship was casual, but as time passed I'd believed we were only keeping it under the radar because we worked with each other. When I learned he'd reconciled with his wife, I was more hurt than I cared to admit; when I discovered that he'd implicated me in a crime, I was furious. Unfortunately, I was also too mortified to ever confront him.

But I didn't feel the need to share this information with Rick. I was exposed enough already. "I have terrible taste in men, obviously."

"That's too bad." His gaze was steady. "So how did your dad find out about the embezzlement?"

"I don't know, exactly. He always likes to have dirt on people and would go digging around sometimes. When he came to me, he'd already decided to fire Rory but offered to keep my name out of it if I'd do as he asked. I didn't."

"Good for you." He held up his fist, and I half-heartedly bumped it with mine.

"I guess," I said. "Hollywood is a hundred percent about optics, so after he fired me, I was screwed. As in, the only person that offered me a job before my savings ran out was Cole."

He had no idea I was completely naked in front of him now, and disconcertingly, more turned on than if I'd actually performed a strip-tease. The mind is a powerful tool. Maybe I needed to spill my secrets more often.

"Aha," he said. "I knew there must be a reason you were working for that particular asshole."

I laughed, enjoying the pleasure of being seen, the luxury of having someone on my side for once. "So many assholes." Emboldened, I met his eye. "Are you one?"

That slow smile. "I'm sure there are one or two people out there who would say so. I'm far from perfect." He shook his head. "But no. I don't think I am."

I assessed him in the moonlight, and I had to agree. Despite his rippling muscles and tiger gaze, he wasn't nearly brooding enough to be the romantic hero in one of my bodice rippers—which was a good thing, because despite my performance in the water the other day, I wasn't nearly helpless enough to be a damsel in distress. But perhaps a fling with a handsome stranger wouldn't be an entirely bad thing. It could never be serious since we lived in two different countries, but a distraction might do me some good. And he was definitely flirting with me, wasn't he?

My phone buzzed, and Price's number flashed on the screen. I knew he'd be wanting to go over the call sheet for tomorrow before sending it out. Rick noticed me glance at the phone with dismay and laughed. "You need to get that?"

I frowned. "It's work. I have to go over—"

"No worries." He stood. "I should be getting back to Saint Ann anyway. Thanks for the beer."

"Anytime," I said.

I walked him to the door, wondering whether he'd make any kind of move or say something about hanging out again, but he didn't. He simply gave a friendly wave as he strode onto the pier. I closed the door behind him, feeling as though a million tiny lights had flickered to life beneath my skin.

Once I got off the phone with Price, I grabbed my laptop and hopped in bed to indulge in some light Google stalking. I wanted to hunt down Rick's profile immediately, but decided to delay that pleasure in favor of exploring what there was to see about one Felicity Fox.

A search of her name on Facebook pulled up a list of Felicity Foxes all over the world, including three in California. One of the California profiles showed a picture of a smiling Black woman in her thirties, one a plump white woman in her fifties, and the last was a blank icon. Could that be our Felicity? But the page had no friends and didn't seem to have been used. Thwarted, I checked Instagram, finding again a long list of Felicity Foxes that were not my Felicity Fox. The only possibility was a locked California profile that showed a palm tree, but it had only fifty-three followers. Did anyone her age have only fifty-three followers?

I searched fruitlessly on LinkedIn, Twitter, and Snapchat. I wasn't a member of anything else, so my social media search stopped there. Google wasn't helpful either, turning up only advertisements for a Felicity Fox who was apparently a successful hair stylist in Bethesda, Maryland. I even went as far as to pull up the picture of her ID, which Francisco had sent me (issued two months ago, showing an address in Echo Park that turned out to be a charming blue fourplex), to search her driver's license number. Nothing.

The absence of her presence online was almost more alarming than if I'd found evidence she was... What? What did I think I was going to find, and why was I fixating on this? Sure, I was jarred by the fact that she'd slipped under the radar (after the business with Rory, I was a fiend for a tight budget), but the girl hadn't done anyone any harm.

I sighed, and feeling like a teenager, turned my attention to Rick. He wasn't hard to find. The website of the resort told me his last name was Hamilton and led me to all of its social media pages, on which he was featured heavily. He didn't seem to be on Twitter, and his Facebook page was locked, but his Instagram was open. The first picture was from a few hours before, of the conch he'd just given me resting on a white sand beach. Next were pictures of the fishing trip he'd taken the crew on, followed by him flying a small plane (God, he looked hot flying a plane), a group of guys in a bar, a girl he referred to as his niece graduating from elementary school, more fishing trips, dolphins at sunset...all totally kosher, confirming he was exactly who he said he was. My finger hovered over the "follow" button, but I held back. I didn't want him to think me too eager. Instead, I clicked on the page of tagged photos.

The top few were from fishing trips, but the next row down was a picture of him with his arm around a pretty light-skinned Black girl with long magenta-tinted hair, her head resting on his shoulder. I clicked on it. The caption was only a red heart, and it was dated six days ago. Shit. I stared at the picture, willing it to disappear, then clicked on her profile. @JeanieBabie24, tagline "keepin' it hot in the sun" had 1,476 followers, and her feed featured multiple pictures of her flaunting her figure in various skimpy outfits, interspersed with pictures of Rick. One of him shirtless on a dock with a fishing rod ("love that pole"), another a selfie of her kissing his cheek at what appeared to be a party, a third of the two of them smiling with a group of people at the beach ("beach daze r the best daze"), the same picture he had on his page of him flying a plane.

Two and two added up to he obviously had a girlfriend he'd failed to mention. My brain balked; he'd seemed so nice, so *not an asshole*. Had I misinterpreted his gaze? Had he only wanted to be my friend? But then why not mention the girlfriend? I thought back over our conversation. I'd run my mouth most of the time. So maybe he hadn't had a chance to mention her. It was true he'd done little more than ask questions—but that was also a classic player move. And it didn't bode well that he didn't have any pictures of the girlfriend in his feed. I could just imagine that conversation: *Sorry, honey*, he'd say. *I need to keep it professional for my job.* And having a hunch he might be acting shady with the hordes of horny girls on holiday he was likely to meet, she'd tag pictures of him to show up on his profile in case any girl he hit on happened to check his feed before diving in.

Like me.

I cringed. I felt so incredibly stupid for revealing myself to him, for feeling *seen* by him. Stupider than if I'd slept with him. I'd been so desperate for real human connection, I'd made myself vulnerable, and he'd played me like a fiddle.

No wonder I'd been attracted to him. He was an asshole.

# INDUSTRY STANDARD:

## STELLA'S RIVER OF WELLNESS RUNS DRY

S tella's River of Wellness has been canceled by WTV. The docu-follow series, which centered around actress-turned-spirituality-advocate Stella Rivers's attempt to open wellness center WelLife, selling crystals, life coaching, psychic readings, guided meditation, juices, and various dietary supplements, aired only seven episodes of a planned twelve-episode season.

The troubled Rivers found spirituality during her latest stint in rehab, after a string of incidents that included physically attacking a paparazzi, throwing pickle jars at a fan, assaulting the ex-wife of her boyfriend, and driving under the influence. From the beginning, production on Stella's River of Wellness was plagued by protesters supporting the neighborhood taco joint the spiritual center displaced in the hip Eastside Los Angeles community of Silverlake. But the bigger problem was Rivers's lack of business acumen and the public's distrust of her as a guru after her checkered past. One of the terms of Rivers's contract was that she would fund the spiritual center with her own money, and Rivers has filed a suit claiming the producers of the show intentionally sabotaged WelLife for ratings, causing it to go belly-up and leaving her nearly bankrupt.

# Felicity

*Thirteen Years Ago*

I've been sweating under the blanket in the trunk less than five minutes when Iris gets in the car and starts the engine. Thinking of how grounded I'll be if she finds me, I almost lose my courage and reveal myself, but decide not to. I have to know what's going on.

Trying to stay still as the car bumps over potholes and sloshes through rain puddles, I lose track of the turns she's making after a few blocks, but when the road smooths out and she hits the gas, I figure we must be on the highway.

After what feels like forever but is probably only ten minutes, she exits and makes a few turns on roads noticeably more even than the ones in our part of town. She stops and lowers the window, and I hear her keying a code into a security box, then a gate opening. She pulls through the gate, parks the car, and gets out.

I count to one hundred before daring a peek out the window.

It's twilight, and we're parked in the driveway of what I immediately recognize from the picture in *Celebrity* magazine as Cole's house. It's sleek and modern, all white and glass, surrounded by tall white walls and lush greenery. Relieved she wasn't lying, I carefully push back the blanket and lift the hatchback just enough to roll out onto the pebbled driveway.

The carport is empty; my mom's car is the only one in sight.

Terrified that Cole will drive up at any minute, I dart around the side of the house and flatten my back against the wall, panting. What if she decides to leave? Then I'd be stuck here. This was a bad idea. But I'm in now, so I might as well carry through with my plan. Only, I don't have a plan. I didn't think this through.

Okay. *Think, Phoenix.*

I want to see what's going on. That means I need a window. I move away from the wall to check out the side of the house. It's nearly all windows. The entire back of the place is like a greenhouse. I crouch behind a row of palms just taller than I am and inch toward the back-yard. A wide deck extends off the back of the house with steps down to a rectangular pool, and beyond that a narrow bay channel with what looks like a park on the other side.

The sliding glass door that leads to the kitchen is open; my mom is spotlighted under the bright lights over the island, chopping vegetables. I creep closer, fascinated. I've never in my life seen her do more in the kitchen than make spaghetti from a jar. But here she is with a glass of red wine (since when does she drink red wine?), humming along to something that sounds like jazz, and when she tucks a wisp of blond hair behind her ear, I can see she's smiling.

It's the weirdest feeling, watching her. It's like she's not my mother at all, but some happy rich lady in the movies.

She puts a pot of water on the stove and turns on the burner, then checks her phone and darts from the room as though she's forgotten something. I track her across the dark living room, but lose her once she goes into the part of the house where I'm guessing the bedrooms are. The curtains are all drawn on that side, but I figure she'll be back; she left the water boiling and her phone on the counter.

I hear the gate open and a car with a deep thrumming motor drive in. After a minute, Cole enters the kitchen. My heart flips, seeing him in real life. He's even more hunky than he is on-screen, just being himself in ripped jeans and a black T-shirt. He notices the pot of boiling water, the vegetables, takes a slug of wine. "Honey?" he calls out.

*Honey.* That's what people in love call each other.

He turns off the water and moves in the same direction Iris disappeared. "Hello?"

It's dark now, so I don't have to worry as much about hiding as I scurry around the pool in search of a window with a view of Cole and my mother. But the curtains at this end of the house remain drawn, and the glass must be thick because I can't hear anything. I crack my knuckles, frustrated. I'd wanted to see them together for peace of mind, and now I can't see either of them. But they're probably having sex, and I don't want to see that anyway. I got what I wanted: I know she's been telling the truth about coming here to Cole's house. I still haven't seen them together, but at least they looked happy.

I slink back to my hiding place with a view of the kitchen and sit behind an azalea bush to eat my protein bar.

"What are you doing in my yard?"

I spin to see a scrawny, dark-haired boy about my age towering above me. He pushes his glasses up on his nose and crosses his arms.

"Shhhhh!" I put my finger to my lips and pull him down beside me. "Are you Jackson?"

He jerks his arm away. "Yeah, so what? Why are you in my yard?"

"My mom's dating your dad," I whisper.

He looks confused. "Stella has a daughter?"

I shake my head. "No. My mom is Iris. The car that's parked in the driveway is hers. I'm a stowaway."

He tilts his head and squints at me, then laughs. "That's pretty crazy."

"So can you please get out of sight? She'll kill me if she catches me." He crouches next to me. "Your dad hasn't talked about my mom?"

He shrugs. "I live with my mom in South Beach. She just sent me over here because she's having a party tonight."

"Did your dad know you were coming?"

Again he shrugs. "Stella said it was okay."

My eyes go wide. "Stella's gonna be home tonight?"

"I think so. I mean, she told my mom she'd watch me."

"Oh shit." I panic. "My mom's up there having sex with your dad right now, and Stella's gonna come home and find them. This is bad. We have to stop them!"

He cocks his head. "I don't think—"

"I can't go. My mom can't know I'm here. But you have to. You have to go stop them before she gets here."

He looks at me like I'm crazy. "You want me to go bust up our parents having sex?"

I grab his hand and drag him to his feet. "Just—I don't know, knock on the door until they answer and warn them." I push him in the direction of the open door.

"What are you gonna do?" he asks.

"I'm gonna go get in her car so that when she takes off, I don't get left. Please," I beg, shoving him over the threshold. "Go."

"Okay, crazy." He laughs.

"Whatever you do, don't tell anyone you saw me!" I whisper.

He flashes the thumbs-up and jogs off in the direction Cole and my mom went. I dash through the dark yard to my mom's car, where I once again crawl under the blanket in the back, proud I've saved my mom from the wrath of the famously jealous Stella Rivers.

I haven't been in the back of the car for long when I hear the gate open and headlights sweep the driveway. I peer out the window to see Stella step out of a white Range Rover and rush into the house. Shit. This is bad. My mom is still in there. But what can I do? I wait on pins and needles, praying that Jackson at least had time to tell them she was coming so they didn't get caught in the act. Surely he had time.

Unless he chickened out.

Finally the front door opens back up and light spills down the wide steps. But it's not Iris. It's Cole, and he's—no. It's Cole and Stella, and they're carrying my mother.

My heart stops. He's holding her under the arms, and Stella has her feet. She's not moving. Oh God, what's happened? Is she sick? Is she hurt? Did Stella do something to her when she caught them?

Stella and Cole are arguing as they carry her down the walkway, but I can't make out what they're saying. She's hysterical, sobbing and yelling, dropping my mother's feet, and he's frowning, trying to get her to shut up. Suddenly the car door opens. I duck as they place Iris in the back seat, arguing about which hospital to take her to. She's a foot away from me, on the other side of the seat. "Mom?" I whisper. No answer. My breath is shallow. What do I do? Should I show myself? But what if they won't let me go with her to the hospital? I need to go with her to the hospital.

Cole slams the door, and for a brief moment I'm alone in the car with my mom. I listen for her breath, but the car is eerily quiet. "Mom?" No answer. "I'm here. I love you."

I peek over the seat and gasp. Her skin is ashen, her eyes open and unblinking. Rivulets of blood run from her bruised and swollen nose; the back of her hair is matted and red. My heart crashes. "Mom!" She doesn't move. I reach over the seat and touch her face. It's warm, thank God. But maybe it's not as warm as it should be.

What did Stella do to her? I grab her wrist, trying to feel for a pulse. Her hand is limp, and there's a new hole in her arm, but I can't find a pulse.

A spear of ice in my heart. I can't breathe; I'm numb, outside my body, watching as Cole opens the driver's door, and I duck under the blanket. He backs out of the driveway fast and hits the gas as soon as we're on the road.

I reach my hand around the side of the seat and find the top of my mom's cooling head, stifling a scream. I silently sob as I stroke her sticky hair, knowing she's gone by the gaping hole in my heart.

**Part III:**

# Turbulence

# Taylor

*Saturday, June 22*

T he last place I wanted to be on my day off was aboard a boat with my narcissistic boss, his delusional ex-wife, and the guy I had a crush on who had a girlfriend, but it was unavoidable. Things could have been worse, I supposed: the boat could have been smaller than the fifty-foot sportfishing yacht from which we were currently admiring the sunset. Well, they were admiring. I was hiding in the kitchen.

I'd tried to convince Francisco to come, but he'd begged off. He wasn't exactly Cole's biggest fan, and his darling Ben was spending the afternoon at the pool, so that was where he planned to be. "You do love a challenge," I'd teased him.

"Nearly as much as you love an unavailable man," he'd returned.

I snorted with laughter at that. Learning the truth about Rick had confirmed it: I only fell for unavailable men. "Oh, I don't love them; I just make love to them," I quipped, though it wasn't true. "Big difference."

"Touché."

I tilted up the remainder of my Kalik Gold, tossed it in the trash, and grabbed another from the refrigerator. Hiding in the kitchen had its advantages.

"You like Kalik?" I turned to see my personal-hero-turned-villain Rick, sporting a wide grin. I was dying to ask him about JeanieBabie24, but obviously I couldn't let him know I'd been stalking him online—which also meant I had to act normal around him. He clearly wasn't bothered by juggling women; he looked more relaxed than I'd felt in my entire life. I hated that I was so pleased he'd come down to say hello, if that was in fact what he was doing. I would not be the other woman ever again.

I nodded, struggling with the cap. "May I?" He held his hand out, and I placed the beer in it. In one swift motion, he knocked the bottle against the counter, sending the top spinning.

"Thank you."

"Imported from the Bahamas." He grabbed another one from the fridge and gave it the same treatment, tapping the label against mine. "How'd the rest of your week go?"

I shrugged. "Good." Truth be told, it had been tough in spots but nothing I wanted to discuss with him anymore.

"Not a very convincing performance," he noted.

"Yours?" I asked, ignoring his comment.

"Great. With you guys working all week, I didn't have any tours, so I took my nephews fishing and looked at a couple of boats for Cole."

I bit my lip, recalling my argument yesterday with Cole about his refusal to pay for the additional Steadicam operator our cinematographer had urgently requested. "What kind of boat?" I asked, hoping it was a fucking canoe.

"Pleasure yacht. You should see the ones I've been looking at." He let out a low whistle, then cut his eyes to me and abruptly dropped it. "But I can tell that may be a sensitive subject for you, so I'm gonna stop right there."

I swigged my beer, wondering if he'd taken JeanieBabie24 with him to see the yachts. "Thanks." I was beginning to feel a pleasant hum beneath my skin and was happy I'd tossed my no-drinking-on-the-job rule out to sea. "Sorry. He's been stressing me out, but I can't really get into it right now."

"Gotcha."

I indicated his beer. "Are you allowed to do that?"

"What?"

"Drink alcohol while driving a boat?"

He laughed. "We're not in the States, and I won't get drunk." He knelt next to the sink and opened the cabinet below, fiddling with one of the drainage pipes.

"What are you doing?"

"Sink's been draining slow," he said as he unscrewed the pipe.

It was really hard not to be turned on by a man who could fix things with his hands. Most of the men I knew were more helpless than I was. I hopped down from my perch on the counter and squatted next to him, watching as he deconstructed the pipe into three pieces. I was a homeowner now, and I should know how to do this kind of thing. "Show me."

His half smile said most girls wouldn't be interested, and he thought it was cool I was. "It's easy," he said. "First you've gotta make sure the sink is drained; otherwise you'll get wet. Then you unscrew the ends of the curved piece." He finished doing it and showed me as he gently pulled it down. "Make sure that's clear, then check the connecting pieces." He removed a mass of something nasty from the pipe, which he tossed into the trash. "Easy."

"Cool," I said. It did, in fact, look pretty easy.

"You're missing a beautiful sunset up there," he said as he fitted the sink back together.

"Yeah." I stood and stretched my legs. "But I'm close to the beer."

He raised his brows. "And not so close to your friends?"

"Coworkers," I corrected him.

"Mmm."

"What's that mean? Mmm?"

He shrugged.

"It's not like they've exactly made an effort with me either," I said.

"Okay." He closed the cabinet and washed his hands in the sink.

"I used to make an effort. At my last job. But when I got fired, all those people I'd thought were my friends dropped me like a hot potato."

"So, no more friends?"

I snorted. "What, are you my therapist?"

He raised his hands. "Just curious."

"Curiosity killed the cat, you know."

He held my gaze. "I'll take that chance."

Heat crept up my spine. "Anyway, shouldn't you be steering the boat?"

He shook his head, a twinkle in his eye. "We dropped anchor. Which you would know if you weren't down here belowdecks, sulking."

My jaw fell at his brashness, and I found, despite myself, I was smiling. "I like to think of it as pouting."

"Come with me." He turned and headed up the stairs.

"Do I have to?" I called after him.

"No," he returned, without looking over his shoulder.

But he was right. I was acting like a child. So I ascended the stairs after him, shielding my eyes as I emerged into the Technicolor rays of the setting sun.

"Up here."

I followed the sound of Rick's voice upward again to see him standing in the raised cockpit. I climbed the ladder with my beer in one hand, allowing him to pull me up over the last few rungs onto the deck beside him. The platform was just big enough for the two of us and a shallow bench, so high it felt like we were floating above the boat. The sky glowed coral and violet, reflecting in the calm sea. "You were right," I breathed. "This is spectacular. It's like we're inside the sunset."

He smiled that slow smile. "A little better than the view from the galley."

Below us, Felicity and Jackson leaned on the railing of the bow, looking out toward the horizon, their heads inclined toward each other. I'd noticed them spending more and more time together over the course of the week, which only made me more suspicious of Felicity's motives. But truth be told, Jackson *was* pretty lust-worthy, and Felicity had been nothing but helpful and gracious all week, so perhaps my paranoia was unfounded.

Cole and Madison reclined on a lounger at the stern with their backs to us, thankfully. The last thing I needed was shit from Cole for hanging out with Rick, and I knew he'd relish the opportunity to dish it out. I observed them for a moment, wondering what two narcissists could possibly be discussing so animatedly. Themselves, likely. For once Madison's phone was out of sight and she wasn't posing. On second glance, I realized she was posing, only not for the camera, but for Cole, doubtless hoping a dalliance would thrust her further into the spotlight. Great.

But where was Stella? I leaned over the railing and gazed down to see her laid out on the front of the boat, asleep. My stomach suddenly flipped at the height. Dizzy, I reached out to steady myself and found Rick's strong arms around me. "Easy there." I felt his deep voice reverberate in his chest. I eased myself onto the padded bench, flustered. He sat beside me. "You okay?"

I nodded, a part of me wishing I'd stayed sulking in the kitchen. "Not great with heights."

The sky reflected bronze in his concerned eyes, and I...couldn't look away. "Do you want to go back down?"

I shook my head, horrified to register that what I wanted, more than anything, was his arms around me again. But he had a girlfriend. I wouldn't make that mistake a second time. "I like it up here." I ripped my gaze from his and studied my hands. The manicure I'd gotten a week ago was ragged and chipped. "Sorry. I swear I'm not usually this incapable. First you have to save me from drowning, and now I can't handle a ten-foot height."

"No need to apologize."

God, he seemed so genuine. *But he's not.*

He pointed out to sea, blissfully unaware of the war going on inside me. "Dolphins."

Not fifty feet from our boat, a pod of dolphins played, their sleek bodies rising in crescents from the water. I heard a squeal of excitement from the deck as the others spotted them. We watched as four adults and two babies dove and jumped, kicking up glittering flecks of peach-tinted water.

"Beautiful," I murmured at their frolicking, feeling the tension drain from my shoulders. I was being silly about Rick. He was just friendly. And it might be nice to have a friend. A very attractive friend, yes, but as long as we were just friends, no harm done. I'd read too much into his interest in me, the result of too many romance novels and not enough actual romance. But this was neither the time nor the place. I took a breath and watched Felicity and Jackson laughing, their arms grazing each other, pointing at the dolphins. I lowered my voice. "What do you think of Felicity?"

"Which one is she?"

I indicated.

"Haven't talked to her." He shrugged. "She's hot, and Jackson's obviously into her. She's one of the actresses?"

I laughed. "Funny you ask. She claims not to be, but she's been working as Stella's stand-in all week, and..."

"You don't believe her. You think she's after something?"

"Too talented, too pretty, too nice," I confirmed. "I don't trust her."

Rick laughed so hard that Felicity and Jackson turned and looked up at us. I waved. "Nice view up there?" Jackson asked.

"Gorgeous," I confirmed.

"Too bad we don't have any scenes set on a boat," Felicity chimed in.

Jackson looked at her as though that were the most wonderful idea he'd ever heard. Oh Lord, scenes on a boat were the last thing I needed. I caught his eye and rubbed my fingers together to signify money.

Felicity said something to him that I couldn't hear, and he laughed, turning away from us. Despite my suspicions about her, I couldn't for the life of me figure out what it was she might want from Stella, who could hardly get herself a job these days, bless her heart.

"Not everybody has ulterior motives," Rick whispered, as though he'd been reading my thoughts.

Damn it, I liked his breath on my ear. It made me think of his breath on other parts of my body. I batted the thought away. If I couldn't control my attraction, then I wouldn't be able to hang out with him anymore, and that really would be unfortunate. I liked his company.

I leaned forward to see Stella still dozing on the cushioned nose of the boat below us. "She'll sleep it off by the time we get back," Rick said.

I sighed. "She's supposed to be sober. Her insurance requires it."

"Oh," he said.

I leaned my head against the railing and groaned. "I should have been babysitting instead of hiding."

"Give yourself a break. The insurance company can't exactly turn up without warning out here."

"I'm more worried that Madison will post something compromising. She films nonstop."

"Nothing illegal about taking a nap on a boat," he assured me. "I do it all the time."

"Did you notice if Felicity was the one giving her alcohol?"

He shrugged. "I wasn't paying that much attention. I did see her hand her a pill earlier though."

I felt a twinge of guilt for talking about Stella behind her back. She was fragile and not incredibly easy to work with, but she wasn't as demanding as I'd initially thought, and shockingly, was doing exceptional work when she could recall her lines. After reading about her antics in the past, I was pleasantly surprised by her professionalism, especially when playing opposite Cole, who seemed to run hot and cold toward her. She wasn't great at taking (or perhaps, remembering) direction, but she didn't need a lot—Jackson had clearly written the role with her in mind. She *was* Marguerite, an insecure star grappling with aging while watching her husband transfer his affection to a younger version of herself, and often the bits she improvised were better than the written dialogue. I could also tell that Stella liked Madison even less than I did, and I looked forward to watching her seek revenge on her younger nemesis in the later scenes.

"She may not be sober, but she's perfect in her role, and luckily the script supervisor's smitten with her, so she's always close by to feed her lines."

"You notice everything, don't you?" he asked.

"I'm sorry. I must be boring you to tears with my work drama."

"Not at all," he said. He pointed surreptitiously at Cole. "How's that one been?"

"Exactly how you'd think, I imagine," I returned. "Camera loves him and he was born to play his role as a temperamental playboy genius, but I'm still not convinced he's read the script, and he won't listen to a thing Jackson says."

To his credit, Jackson was apparently prepared for this reality—it was his idea to shoot in chronological order so his father would know what the hell was going on, and he instructed our cinematographer to roll early and cut late on every take, which would give the editors more to work with. Still, Cole's performance was haphazard, and the romantic scenes we'd shot all week setting up Peyton and Marguerite's love story, her pregnancy, and their move to the islands would require some heavy revision so he'd appear smitten rather than smug. We'd filmed only fifteen pages of a ninety-page script so far, and I could already tell postproduction was going to be a beast.

I drained the rest of my beer and rubbed my temples. "Be glad you're not in film. It'll eat your life."

"Then why do you do it?"

"I'm beginning to wonder that myself," I admitted. "I mean, I got into it because it's really exciting, creating a world from the ground up. Working with a team, everyone in on the same secret... It's fun, when you're working with the right people. And you know about my dad. I guess I always wanted to follow in his footsteps. But enough about me," I said, realizing I was running my mouth like I had on my deck the other night. "You have a dad?"

He laughed. "Yeah."

"Tell me about him."

"He's a fisherman. Taught me everything I know about boats. He's got white hair, a white beard, and a belly. The kids call him Santa."

I laughed. "Any of those kids yours?"

"No. I'm the last man standing."

"You don't want kids?"

"We'll see. I couldn't be birthing them myself."

*But JeanieBabie24 would be happy to oblige*, I thought.

"What about you?"

I shook my head. "I'm one of those career girls you hear about, shirking their reproductive duties to play ball with the boys."

That line usually elicited some sort of objection, but it didn't seem to bother him. "I see."

"It's hard enough trying to hold my own and take care of myself." I sighed, remembering my hazy evening with Cole. At least I hadn't slept with him, thank God. "I'm a mess."

His smile was enigmatic. "If you say so."

Out over the ocean, the sun melted into the horizon like a pat of butter on a hot pancake.

"Sorry for talking your ear off. Again." The beer had clearly loosened my tongue. Perhaps I should return to sobriety for the remainder of the shoot.

But once more, he didn't seem bothered. "Anytime." His gaze was steady. "No apologizing."

I nodded. "Right. Sorry."

June 22, 2019

---

@MadisonMadeit

[PICTURE]

♡ 100,364 likes   ☆

Poor @TheRealStellaRivers snoring right through the gorgeous #Caribbean #sunset and #dolphin spotting here off the coast of the beautiful #GenesiusResort. Obviously worn out from a long week shooting #TheSiren. Looking forward to joining her and @ColePower on set Monday. So excited to be starring opposite these super talented #actors!

#actress #model #me #survivor #warrior #blessed #yacht #movie #film #blogger #lifestyle #Madisonblogs #Madisonac-tress #MadisonKasabian

# Stella

I wasn't sure how long I'd been asleep on the bow when Felicity roused me, but it was dark, the boat had docked, and all the others had disembarked. I was disoriented and annoyed that she'd let me sleep in front of everyone like that. Had I snored? Was my mouth gaping open? God, how unflattering! It was humiliating.

The half-moon was low over the water, and the wind had picked up as we trudged through the powdery sand toward our bungalow. "No one thought anything of it," Felicity assured me. "You were tired. You've had a long week. We all have."

"But no one else fell asleep. What if I'm in one of Madison's stupid videos, snoring?"

I could sense her rolling her eyes in the dark. "People sleep, Stell. And you weren't snoring."

We walked along the shore past the rock outcropping that separated the tranquil bay from deeper waters, waves warm as bathwater lapping at our ankles. Clouds had gathered over the island, but the stars out over the ocean shone like diamonds flung across the sky. It was unfortunate that I could hardly appreciate the peaceful setting for the tension headache gnawing at my brain. "My head hurts," I complained. "Is it time for a pill yet?"

Felicity checked her watch. "You have an hour on the A-pill, two on the D-pill."

Ugh. The anxiety and depression pills were the best. "What about a P-pill?"

"Are you in pain?"

"I just told you my head hurts," I reminded her, annoyed.

"If you need it," she said. "But you know you can't mix it with any of the others."

I swore she wasn't this annoying back in LA. "Damn pill Nazi," I complained, kicking a shell into the sea. My tummy rumbled. "What time is it? I'm starving."

"It's past eight," she said as I followed her up the wooden stairs to the pier that led over the water to our bungalow. "Everyone ate on the boat."

I sighed, exasperated. "Great, so I missed dinner too."

"I'm sorry." She stopped to rummage in her bag in the soft glow of one of the tiki torches that lined the pier, finally extracting our room key. "I know you've been having trouble sleeping at night. I thought you could use the rest."

"No, you thought you could use some time off to flirt with Jackson." Her mouth opened, as if in surprise. But her stupefaction only irritated me further. "What, do you take me for a fool? You think I haven't noticed the two of you flirting all week? It's obvious."

She looked up and down the empty walkway and lowered her voice. "I wasn't trying to hide anything from you."

I raised my hands, unable to stop the words from tumbling out. "You don't want anyone to hear your secrets, but you let me fall asleep in front of everyone," I snapped.

"Can we talk about this inside?" she begged.

"No." I stood my ground. "I'm going to get something to eat because *someone* didn't wake me for dinner."

"It's going to rain," she said, indicating the clouds hovering over the resort.

I held out my hand. "My pills."

She sighed. "Which do you need?"

"All of them."

"You know it's not time," she protested.

"They're *my* pills," I hissed. "Hand them over."

She fished in her bag—an expensive YSL tote I gave her, coming up with the little blue leather pouch that held my pills. "Please don't do anything stupid."

"I'm not a child." I shoved the bag in my purse, then turned on my heel and marched down the pier. "Do you have a key?" she hollered after me.

"Don't need one," I called over my shoulder. "You'll be home to let me in. And make sure you feed and walk Mary Elizabeth."

I chuckled to myself as I tromped across the sand and threaded my way between the up-lit palm trees toward the restaurant. Any plans Felicity'd had to go out tonight were now ruined, and I wasn't sorry. Who did she think she was? She was here to take care of me, not the other way around.

A fat raindrop hit my face, and then another. I unscrewed the top of a medicine bottle without checking to see which it was and dumped a pill on my tongue as I plodded up the stairs to the pool, impervious. I wouldn't let a little rain ruin my night. I'd had a nap and I was going to enjoy myself.

Rain pocked the surface of the fluorescent blue pool, casting the courtyard in flickering luminescence. The two lone guys playing Ping-Pong under the wide eaves of the lobby waved as I passed, and I blew them a kiss. One of them pretended to catch it and slap it on his cheek. I laughed. I was feeling better already.

Energized by the prospect of a lively evening at a lovely restaurant, I threw open the door.

My heart sank. The scene was anything but lively. It was dark and quiet, illuminated only by the backlit bar that lined most of the wall to my right. The tables were empty, the windows that faced the beach closed to the coming storm outside. Caribbean jazz played softly over the sound system, barely audible above the sound of the rain on the roof. The lone man at the bar turned and raised his glass to me.

It was Cole.

My stomach did an unexpected flip. Sure, we'd been working together for a week—staring into each other's eyes, kissing, stroking each other's nearly naked bodies—and we obviously still had chemistry. But all that was pretend, for the cameras, in front of an audience. Up till now, we hadn't once been truly alone together.

In fact, I hadn't been alone with him since the night he left, thirteen years ago. I forced the memory from my mind.

"Come have a drink," he beckoned to me, slapping the leather barstool beside him. "No one's looking."

I sized him up as I crossed the room. Cole could just as easily play the villain or the hero, and it was crucial to know which you were engaging with. Though I'd often known the wolf in him to dress in sheep's clothing, so even when he was at his most charming, it was advisable to keep your wits about you. I slid onto the barstool next to his. "Where is everyone?"

"Most of the crew went to dinner in town. Everyone else from our cruise is a pussy." He laughed. "But not you!" He rattled the ice in his empty glass and called out to the invisible bartender. "Another! And one for this gorgeous lady."

So he was feeling agreeable, apparently. A bartender materialized from around the side of the bar and poured a heavy shot of Scotch into his glass. "What can I get you?" he asked me.

I glanced at Cole, unsure. I wasn't supposed to be drinking, and he was technically my boss. "Come on, I won't tell. Anyway, we all know you're not really sober." He poked me in the belly. "You were passed out on the boat like a frat boy after a kegger."

I shot him a dirty look. "I wasn't drunk. I was tired from the week." I shifted my gaze to the bartender. "Spiced rum with a splash of pineapple, please."

"You are a gorgeous lady, you know."

Seductive Cole, the most dangerous of all.

"Thank you." I smoothed my hair.

"Really." He locked eyes with me and placed his hand on my thigh. Could it be that this was the reason he'd wanted me on the film? I hadn't thought it possible, after everything that had transpired between us. But that was all years ago. We were different people then. I could tell from the softness of his gaze that he was somewhat drunk, but that wasn't exactly rare for him, and alcohol always brought out the truth. Maybe this was his truth. My horoscope this morning *had* said that cycles from the past that were left unfinished would be coming full circle.

"Cole," I warned, cutting my eyes to the bartender. But I didn't stop his hand.

"Oh, he won't breathe a word, or he'll be fired," Cole whispered into my hair.

The bartender slid my drink in front of me.

Cole threw him a smile. "Thank you, Darian. We'd like the room."

Darian disappeared through a door that led to the kitchen. I took a long draw of my drink and considered Cole. He was as irresistible as he'd ever been, and I'd be lying if I said that his kisses earlier in the week hadn't turned me on. He slid his hand farther up beneath my skirt, and I took a fortifying swig of my rum, remembering what Felicity had said, that a relationship with him would be good for my image. But it wasn't just about that. It felt good to be wanted, if I was honest. And not by any man, but by Cole Power.

"Where were we?" He fingered the lace of my panties.

My heart beat faster. After everything, how was it possible I was still attracted to him? He brushed the spaghetti straps of my dress from my shoulders. He was just so good-looking. "Cole," I protested. "Someone could come in. Some guys are right out there playing Ping-Pong."

"Even better." He pushed aside my panties and inserted a finger in me. I gasped. "There's my dirty girl."

He jerked down the front of my dress and covered one of my nipples with his mouth, his stubble rough against my skin. Feeling my body respond to his, I became suddenly panicked. This raw lust was how it had started before between us, and look how that had ended. I couldn't go there again. "Cole." I stopped him, lifting his face in my hands. "Not here."

He groaned. "You used to be fun."

"I am fun," I protested, stalling for time as my mind seesawed. "Just not in the middle of a restaurant in a resort you own, where we know literally everyone."

He pulled his finger out of me and drained his drink. "Got it. Never mind."

My resolution wavered. It had been so long since I'd been touched, and we were more mature now. This time would be different. "So let's go somewhere else," I suggested.

He leaned against the bar, considering me with those baby blues. I allowed myself to enjoy the attention, finally beginning to feel the effect of my extra pill mingling with the rum. "We can revisit old times," I insinuated.

"I heard"—he reached over the bar and grabbed a bottle of Scotch—"you're writing a book about old times." He raised a single eyebrow.

"Where'd you hear that?" I asked, taken aback. Though of course I'd said it in an interview, so it wasn't like it was a secret.

"But I knew it couldn't be true," he went on, tracing my jaw gently with his fingers. "I thought, Stella's not that stupid. She knows any secrets she might spill would implicate her as much as they would me."

"I wasn't—"

"And she knows how the press can be. She'd never in a million years give them an entire book's worth of confessions to prey upon." He held my chin for a moment before running his thumb down my throat, ending in the soft hole between my collarbones. "Would you, darling?"

Without a backward glance, he strode out of the restaurant and down the hallway that led to the lobby, leaving me alone at the bar. I took a gulp of my cocktail, considering his words. Was *that* why he'd asked me here? To ensure I wouldn't say anything in the book to damage his image? He had always been so protective of his image. I thought of what I'd written the other night about the beginning of our relationship. The bit about Bar's warning would definitely have to be edited out, but I knew that when I wrote it.

My intention with the memoir had only been to set the record straight (and hopefully make a buck); there was plenty to dish about without implicating anyone. My mother pushed me into acting and then stole all my money; my best friend sold my heart-wrenching miscarriage to the press as an abortion; my representation dropped me while I wrestled with depression; a reality television producer convinced me to put my life savings into a spiritual center that he had every intention of bankrupting for ratings, and then I lost my suit against him. I'd been victimized at every turn; my life story was a cautionary tale if ever I heard one—a tale I hoped would have a happy ending once the public understood what I'd wrestled with over the years and once again embraced me. At any rate, I never would have spilled the real secrets, the ones Cole was worried about. Those secrets didn't exactly cast me in the best light either.

Maybe it was the fault of the rum, but after a moment I decided to follow him and tell him all of this. The hallway was dark and empty, as was the lobby beyond. "Cole?" I called.

"Down here!"

I followed the sound of his voice down a stairwell that descended into the dark depths of the building, where I found him in a short cement-walled hall lined with movie posters of his films, standing before a giant steel door. "*Bad Boy*," I commented, studying twenty-four-year-old Cole on the poster. It was remarkable how much Jackson favored him. "What was your famous line? Wait, don't tell me. *I'm finished taking orders?*"

He shook his head. "*I'm through taking stock.*" He smoldered, exactly like he'd done in the movie half his lifetime ago. "Because my father had given me stock in his company as a bribe to keep quiet about a hit-and-run he was involved in."

"Right! I love a good double entendre," I enthused.

He slid a latch the size of a two-by-four and pulled open the heavy door. The room beyond was perhaps eight by twelve feet, with a flagstone floor and walls lined with bottles of wine lit by an eerie bluish light. I followed him inside, remembering what I'd come down here for. "Cole, about the book—I want you to know—"

"Shhhh..." He put his finger to my lips, turned me so my back was against the countertop beneath the rows of bottles, and pressed his hips to mine. My body tingled with anticipation as he kissed me deeply, cupping my ass in his hands. "Some things are best kept between us."

"I know."

He reached for a bottle above my head, pulled it down, and unscrewed the cap. "Fucking screw caps," he said. "Ruin the whole experience."

"But much more convenient," I pointed out, wrapping my arms around myself to control my shivering. "It's freezing in here!"

"Fifty-five degrees." He leaned against the granite-topped island in the middle of the room and poured us each a glass of red. "Temperature controlled. Flood proof. Safest wine room south of Miami. This entire building is made of concrete block designed to withstand two-hundred-mile-per-hour winds. Though there hasn't been a hurricane since I built it. And check this out." He pulled the door to the room shut and lifted an enormous latch identical to the one on the outside into place. "It works as a safe room as well, just in case."

"Gotta keep that wine safe," I teased.

"It's expensive wine," he said defensively. "And I keep other stuff down here too." He slid open a panel in the wall, revealing a row of antique handguns. "This collection is worth more than a hundred grand." He took a six-shooter out of the compartment and pointed it at the opposite wall. "This is the actual gun my character Bad Billy in *The Lone Shooter* carried in real life. He killed Wildman Sam with it in 1877."

I controlled my instinct to recoil like it was a snake. "Beautiful gun," I managed.

"Know how he killed him?"

I shook my head, but he'd gone to that place in his brain where he stored all his characters and was no longer paying any attention to me. I hadn't thought of it in so long, but I now remembered how he used to do that when we were married too. I'd think I was going to a nice dinner with my husband and end up dining with a vigilante cop or a rumrunner from the prohibition era. It was maddening.

"He didn't shoot him," Cole said, turning the gun over in his hands as though it were made of precious stones. "They'd been partners, Bad Billy and Wildman Sam." Cole's voice took on a gravelly Western drawl as he transformed into Bad Billy. "But I found out that Sam had double-crossed me and was working with the long arm of the law to bring me down, so I knew I had to kill him.

"A duel was too much of an honor for a man that snitched on his best friend. So I tricked Sam. Invited him to have a drink with me at the saloon we frequented. As Sam settled with his whiskey into his favorite chair before the fire, I confronted him—asked him point-blank what he had done, gave him a chance to come clean. Because that's what a gentleman does. But Sam didn't come clean. No, he looked me in the eye and he lied. So I took this gun." Cole gripped the gun in his palm and raised it. I flinched, but he was so lost in his story he didn't notice. "And I brought it down on Sam's temple."

I stepped aside as Cole brought the gun down hard on an invisible Sam, disconcertingly close to where I stood. "Beat him with it until the blood oozed from his ears. And then I tossed his carcass on the street so that everyone in Westboro would know Sam was a man who wasn't worthy of a duel."

"Wow," I breathed. "That's crazy."

"Anyway." He tossed the gun in with the others, his normal speaking voice restored. "Gotta keep the humidity under control down here so the metal doesn't oxidize. So." He laid a heavy hand on my hip. "You wanted to revisit old times."

It wasn't a question, but again I wavered. There was so much water under the bridge. Yet I knew he was giving me a chance to come in from the cold, and I was more than tempted. I called to mind the good times: how hot we'd been for each other at first, the warm glow of the spotlight, the insulation of a thick blanket of money. Perhaps it was synchronicity that the man who'd been my undoing could provide me with a second chance.

I widened my eyes and bit my lip, the signature sex kitten look that had hooked him all those years ago. He pulled my pelvis to his and breathed into my ear, his scruff coarse against my cheek. "You always were a little whore, weren't you?"

Oh. But it was just role play; he didn't mean it. He flipped me around and hiked my skirt up around my waist, yanked my panties to the side and thrust himself into me. I cried out in surprise and braced myself against the island, my mind racing to keep up with my body.

This was my passport to a better life. I wasn't a whore; he was my ex-husband, and he was gorgeous. I wanted this. I just wished it felt more pleasurable. I knew I should ask for a condom, but somehow the words didn't come. I was on the pill anyway. And who knew whether I was even capable of bearing children; I'd only ever been pregnant the once, and it had failed.

But God only knew where his dick had been.

"We should grab a condom," I managed breathlessly.

He didn't seem to hear, hammering away like a carpenter on a deadline. A stack of framed movie posters leaning against the wall clattered to the floor. "Cole..."

"Shhhh..." He placed a hand on the back of my head, pushing my cheek into the smooth, cold granite.

I suddenly remembered that after the first rush of heady infatuation had worn off, I'd never truly enjoyed sex with him, even when I was in love with him. It was always about his needs, never about mine. My life in and out of the bedroom had been ruled by his mercurial moods, which had nothing and yet everything to do with me. He was jealous and philandering, clingy and cold. I was always walking on eggshells trying to guess which version of me he might need next, continually trying unsuccessfully to relight the fire of our beginning.

The personal shit storm I'd been through since our breakup had cast a rosy light over everything that came before, including our romance. But I realized as he pounded away that it hadn't been great even before the things that came between us eventually drove us apart. There was a reason I'd had an affair—not just had an affair, but fallen in love—with someone else while we were married.

Even so, my life with him had been far better than what it had become after. I pictured my empty pool, the sagging garage roof. And if I were to be with him now, it would be different. I wouldn't care so much. I wouldn't be in love with him. I wouldn't let him hurt me. And it wouldn't be forever—just for a little while, until I got back on my feet. It wouldn't be the worst thing in the world to be back on the arm of Hollywood's Sexiest Man. Sometimes the right thing wasn't the easiest thing.

Maybe I was a whore.

He was pumping furiously toward ecstasy now. Pill or not, I didn't want his sperm inside me.

No time to think. "Pull out to come," I said. He didn't stop. "Come on my ass," I instructed, trying to sound sexy. Nothing. "Cole! Don't come inside me!"

He jerked his dick out and finished himself off, covering my ass and the hem of my dress in warm ooze. I used a stack of cocktail napkins to wipe myself off while he pulled up his pants. "You're on birth control, aren't you?" he asked. "Or are you too old now?"

"I'm only forty," I snapped. "And yeah, I'm on birth control, just being cautious."

I looked around for a garbage can to dispose of the soiled napkins. "You can leave them on the bar. The staff'll take care of it," he said.

Gross. I wrapped the napkins inside more clean napkins to dispose of upstairs.

"I'm gonna hit the sack." He yawned, opening the door.

"I'm pretty tired too." I followed him up the stairs and into the restaurant, where even the bar was now dark.

I grabbed my purse from the barstool where I'd left it. "That was fun," I fibbed. I leaned in to kiss him as he reached for his phone, landing the kiss on his cheek. "See you tomorrow."

I cast a flirtatious glance over my shoulder as I sauntered away, but he didn't look up from his phone. When I reached the door, he finally called out, "Stella."

"Yes?" I turned.

His eyes were in shadow, but a smile played around his lips. "If you ever did decide to spill things, it wouldn't turn out well for you."

My heart skipped a beat. Was he threatening me? I dropped my gaze to the floor for a moment as I tried to figure out how to respond. When I looked up, he was gone, the door to the kitchen swinging in his wake. My stomach felt suddenly unsettled.

Outside, the rain had stopped and the night creatures were singing. The luminous sea lapped at the shore, and the palm trees rustled in the wind as I scurried around the deserted pool, down the stairs, and across the torchlit pier toward my bungalow. I was already sore from the rough encounter. It had been so long since I'd bedded anyone that I'd lost track, and I'd always needed more foreplay for proper lubrication to begin with.

I entered the bungalow to find the ocean side completely open to the salty night air and some kind of chill trance music playing on the stereo. Through the rectangles of glass in the wood floor, submerged lights illuminated the water, sending liquid reflections dancing around the dimly lit room.

I dropped my purse next to the incense burning on the coffee table and grabbed my smokes, calling out, "Felicity?"

"Out here!"

I followed the sound of her voice to the glowing dive pool on the moonlit deck, where I found her floating naked in the tantalizing indigo water. She smiled, our earlier scuffle forgotten.

"Where were you?" she asked.

I sank into a cushioned lounger at the edge of the pool and lit a cigarette, inhaling deeply. "With Cole," I admitted as I exhaled.

She swam to the edge of the pool, resting her chin on her hands. "And?"

"We . . . rekindled."

She laughed. "I knew it! Tell me everything."

"I ran into him at the bar." I leaned back, staring up at the twinkling stars. It was truly amazing how many stars were visible out here in the middle of the ocean. So many, I couldn't even make out the constellations. "We had a drink and he confessed he never stopped loving me all these years—he'd always wanted to give it another go, but he knew he wasn't in a good place, you know. He's different now."

"What kind of person was he before?"

"Oh, I don't know . . ." I searched for the words. "He wasn't ready for a relationship."

"And he is now?"

"We'll see." The smoke from my cigarette hung heavy in the thick night air. "I told him he'd have to prove he's worth my time, of course."

"Of course," she said, smiling. "I posted the picture of the two of you that I took on set the other day. You've got a thousand new followers."

"Thank you." I smiled. She pushed off the side of the pool to float on her back again, her curvy body backlit purple. "You should come in. It's so warm from the sun, it's almost a hot tub. It feels amazing."

The breeze did feel delicious on my skin and the steamy water was tempting, but I was tired. "I'm sorry about earlier," I said. "I was hungry and irritable."

"No worries." She lifted a leg, pointing her toes at the moon. "There's wine in the fridge if you want a glass."

I felt a twinge of guilt, then, for lying to her, when she'd been so good to me. But it was better this way. If I started telling the truth, I might not be able to stop.

# Felicity

*Thirteen Years Ago*

I awake like rising from underwater to the sound of a siren. A dark-skinned man's unshaven face is inches from mine, haloed by a bright light. I start and try to move away, but find I'm tied down. Panicked, I fight against the ties.

"She's back," the man says.

Back from where? Where am I?

His face is replaced by that of a smiling Hispanic lady with bright pink lipstick, her long hair slicked back in a bun. "Hi, sweetie," she says, placing something on my index finger. She holds open my eyelids and shines a bright light in each of my eyes.

I feel whatever I'm lying on jostle beneath me and look past her to confirm I'm in an ambulance. Suddenly it all comes flooding back. Cole's house, my mom—

"Where's my mom?" I ask, alarmed.

"They'll have all that information for you when we get to the hospital. You've just had a head injury. Right now I need you to concentrate on staying calm so you can heal, okay?"

Fear rises like bile in my throat. I push down the half memory of her unseeing eyes, her cool skin, hoping against hope it was a dream. "But my mom, she wasn't doing well. She was hurt. We were taking her to the hospital."

"Mmm-hmm." She nods. "You're on your way to the hospital. Do you know your name?"

"Phoenix Pendley."

"What day is it?"

"Saturday."

I'm only getting more confused. "Where's Cole?" I ask.

"Is Cole your daddy?"

"No, my mom's boyfriend. He was driving us."

"You're saying there was another person in the vehicle?"

"Yes! He was driving. Cole—" I know Iris told me not to say anything, but surely now it doesn't matter. "Cole Power, the movie star."

The woman raises her eyebrows. "Cole Power the movie star was driving the car."

I nod vehemently. "Yes. He was taking my mom to the hospital. She was hurt."

I pray that was all. That she's at the hospital now, recovering.

The man leans in and whispers something to her. The lady nods, then turns her attention back to me. "We're almost there. I'm gonna need you to rest till we arrive, give that brain a break. Can you do that for me?"

Seeing no other option, I lay my head back against the thinly padded stretcher.

When we get to the hospital, they wheel me into a curtained nook and hook me up to a bunch of machines that beep. The nurses and doctors ask me the same questions about my name, address, and the date over and over again, but no one will give me any information about my mom or Cole.

At some point I'm so tired that my worry can't keep me awake anymore, and I finally fall asleep.

I awake to a nurse shaking my shoulder. "Some men are here that need to talk to you," she says.

Two cops linger in the doorway behind her, both of them bald and bulky in their uniforms. They move to the foot of my bed as the nurse raises me up to sitting.

"Do you know where my mom is?" I ask them.

"I'm sorry. We don't have that information," the taller, thinner one says. My chest tightens, and tears spring to my eyes. "We need to get a statement from you about what happened last night. Are you up for it?"

I choke back a sob, picturing her bruised face. Then I picture her healing in a curtained hospital room like mine. She's probably down the hall. "I want to know what happened to my mom."

"That's what we're trying to find out," he replies. "So why don't you tell us what you remember?"

I take a deep breath and tell them the whole story, up until hiding in the back of my mom's car while Cole drove her to the hospital. "That's the last thing I remember," I finish.

They're quiet for a minute, looking at each other like they know something I don't. "Did your mother have a problem with drugs?" the shorter one asks.

"She's been clean for weeks," I promise them.

"Okay," the taller one says. "That'll do it for today. Thank you."

"Can someone please tell me where she is?" I beg.

They nod. "We'll take care of it for you," the shorter one says, and then they're gone.

I never prayed much before, but this seems like the time to start. I hardly sleep at all that night, for praying so hard that she's okay. It's morning before anyone comes to talk to me. Not that there's any windows or clocks where I am. I only know it's morning because a nurse I haven't seen before comes in with a tray of food and says, "Good morning."

I'm eating my bland breakfast of oatmeal and melon off a mauve tray when another nurse comes in with a small blond lady. "This is Carol from social services," the nurse says, then leaves.

Carol from social services pulls a chair up to my bed and sets her briefcase at her feet. "Hi, Phoenix. I'm Carol," she says, even though the nurse literally just told me that. But she has kind eyes, so I don't protest. "I understand you've been through quite an ordeal."

"I want to know what happened to my mother. Where is she?" I say, fighting tears.

She takes my hand and bows her head. "I'm so sorry. Your mother...She didn't make it."

The air goes out of me. The world goes dark. Carol holds me while I sob into my pillow. My mother's gone. I knew it in my heart. I'd known since the car, but I'd held on to hope for a miracle until she said it. She pats my back as I cry so hard I can't catch my breath, handing me tissue after tissue. "What happened?" I ask when I can finally speak.

"She overdosed," Carol says. "Passed out while she was driving and wrecked the car into a tree in the Everglades, with you in the back."

I hold a tissue beneath my still flooded eyes. "But she wasn't driving. Cole was," I protest. "She'd already overdosed, I think, and there was something wrong with her face. He was driving her to the hospital."

She pats my hand. "Sweetie, your mom was behind the wheel when the car crashed. You were the only other passenger in the car."

I shake my head. "No! No, she would never drive like that with me in the car!"

"They found you under the blankets in the back. Maybe she didn't know you were there. Do you remember why you were hiding in the back?"

"Because Cole was driving and I didn't want him to see me. Something bad happened to her at his house, and he was taking her to the hospital. I wanted to go with her."

"I'm sorry," she says, her voice dripping with pity for me. "Cole Power never knew your mother. The police interviewed him this morning. He was with his wife and son at his home last night."

My head is spinning. "But that's not true," I cry. "They were dating for months. He was leaving Stella for her. She saw him all the time."

"Did you ever meet him?" she asks.

"No, but I saw him last night. I was at his house. His son was there. He saw me! Jackson. I talked to him."

But she's already shaking her head. "He was in his room watching a movie all night. He didn't see you or your mother."

"What about the text messages? Cole texted her all the time. It always made her laugh."

"They're looking for a phone, but they haven't found one. It may have been thrown in the accident, or she could have left it anywhere. Drug addicts sometimes—"

"She wasn't a drug addict!" I scream. "Stop talking about her like that. She was my mother!" And I'm sobbing again.

Carol tries to hold me while I cry, but I push her away. All these people think I'm making it up. They think I'm lying—or worse, crazy. But I know as clear as I know my name that my mother did not overdose and crash into a tree. Whatever happened to her happened before she ever got in that car. Cole and Stella are the ones who are lying, and I will do whatever it takes to find out what really happened.

# Taylor

*Monday, June 24*

The house stood atop a grassy hill that tumbled down to the turquoise lagoon below, where the waves crashed steadily against the shore. All the arched windows and French doors were flung open to the morning sun, white curtains fluttering in the breeze. The view was distractingly beautiful—a far cry from the dusty, dark warehouse we'd been cooped up in all last week.

I was sitting at a colorful chipped tile table in the shade of an oak tree, eating a breakfast of juicy pineapple, strawberries, and coconut flakes while watching the crew set up for the day when Stella breezed in. She was early—a first—and she was without Felicity. Also a first.

"What a gorgeous day!" She swanned through the house without removing her sunglasses, landing next to my table as she took in the view of the iridescent bay. "I could live here," she announced, to me, I guessed, as I was the only one there. "Perhaps it'll be my second home."

"It's great, isn't it?" I agreed. The house was a sprawling ivory Spanish Colonial affair with a red tiled roof and numerous patios and porches with archways open to the ocean breeze. "This is where we're shooting most everything from here on out."

"Wonderful." She looked back toward the crew, lighting the kitchen while "Three Little Birds" undulated from someone's phone. "Where's Cole?"

"Not here yet. Is Felicity with you?"

"I gave her the day off. Thought I'd do my own blocking to—oh, there he is!" She waved to Cole, skipping over extension cords spread across rolls of brown paper atop the terra-cotta floor to meet him as he strolled through the front door. Wary of her sudden change of heart, I craned my neck to watch her greet him. "Hello, darling!" She laid her hands on his biceps and leaned in to give him a lingering kiss on the cheek.

He didn't rebuff her, but he didn't return her enthusiasm either, giving her a quick dry peck without ripping his gaze from the game streaming from his phone. "Shit!" he said, still watching, striding past her to sit on the couch.

Stella hovered over his shoulder. "Who's winning?"

He grunted, noncommittal.

Price appeared in the doorway, brandishing two sets of pages. "One for you"—he handed a script to Stella—"and one for you." He held it out to Cole, who didn't look up. "Cole." Price snapped his fingers in front of Cole's phone. This was why I adored Price. No fucks to give. If only I could live my life that way.

Cole looked up at him, perplexed that someone was actually interrupting his game. "What the fuck, man?" Cole grumbled.

"Wardrobe is this way." Price pointed to the back of the house, where the bedrooms were. "Bring your sides. There are some changes I need to go over with you."

Cole pocketed the phone and swiped his pages off the couch, annoyed. Stella scurried to keep up with him as he strode down the hall, out of my line of sight. Clearly something had happened between them; her attitude had done a complete 180 overnight. Where she'd been guarded around him before, she was flirtatious today. More than that, she wanted us all to see the change.

He, on the other hand, seemed to feel differently.

I groaned. Just when I thought things were getting easier, the damn actors had to go and muck it up. Par for the course. Here I'd been worried that people might make something of my innocent flirtation with Rick on the boat yesterday, while our divorced leads were shagging under our noses.

It would be one thing if they were both into it. That would be good, even—making for steamy love scenes and chemistry that leaped off the screen—and it only had to last five weeks. Even actors could usually sustain a flame that long. But if it blew up, we were all screwed.

The fact that Stella had "given Felicity the day off" worried me too. I had the distinct feeling that Felicity, despite my uneasiness about her intentions, was all that held Stella together.

"Where's Felicity?" Jackson stood in the open doorway, shading his eyes from the sun.

"Not here. Apparently Stella gave her the day off," I returned.

The poor thing looked downright dejected at the news. It was all I could do not to laugh. "But girls that pretty rarely have any talent, anyway," I quipped.

He glared at me. "I didn't mean that. You know I didn't—and it was before I'd seen—you didn't say anything did you?"

"Say anything about what?" Stella appeared in the doorway behind him, fanning herself with the stapled sides in her hand.

"Nothing," Jackson snapped. She recoiled. "Sorry. I—I meant it's nothing to do with you," he backpedaled.

Hiding my smile, I gathered my bowl and followed them into the house, where the crew was setting up the kitchen for a scene where Marguerite finds Peyton and the new nanny, Olivia, playing with the baby and grows jealous. Today was Madison's first day as Olivia, and with the obvious real-life tension between Stella and Madison, I was anxious for it to go smoothly.

"I'm gonna need some time to study my lines," Stella said to Jackson as he squeezed past an eight-foot scrim into the large square kitchen, where the crew was nearly finished lighting. A heavy iron chandelier hung from the high-beam ceiling over the wood-block center island, and a royal-blue backsplash complemented the white cabinets. Through the picture window above the farmhouse sink, the azure sea sparkled beyond palms rustling in the breeze. "I didn't know we were doing this scene today," Stella complained, sidestepping a light stand. "It was supposed to be my scene with the other nanny, when she tells me Olivia is coming."

Brian looked up from the camera for just long enough to catch my gaze and smirk behind her back.

I cracked my knuckles, irritated. "It was in the email with the call sheet last night, and I left a message with Felicity just to make sure you were clear."

"She didn't tell me." Stella crossed her arms. "I'm not ready."

I wanted to smack her. "And what do you suggest we do then, Stella?" I smiled through my teeth.

Jackson was avoiding us, staring over Brian's shoulder at the controls on the side of the camera as though they held the secrets of the universe.

"I don't know." She scowled. "That's your job."

"Okay, great." I beamed like a crazy person. "Well, I've decided we're doing that scene. So go get ready."

"Jackson—" Stella protested.

It was at this point that Madison sailed into the kitchen, her phone outstretched before her. "Here's everyone, getting all set up to shoot my first scene today," she trilled into the screen. "Soooo exciting."

We looked on in horror as she extended her arm to sweep our unsmiling faces with her camera, live streaming to a gazillion fans, no doubt. I couldn't help myself; before I knew what I was doing, I'd grabbed the phone and hit stop on the record screen. "Taylor!" she cried. "That was—"

Still holding her phone, I threw up jazz hands. "Your adoring fans, I know." By this point, everyone was staring at me like I was holding a bomb. "But this is a movie, not a TikTok or a Snapchat story." I was vaguely aware that I was speaking to her like she was a not-bright child, but unable to stop myself. "If you want to shoot on set, you'll need to obtain written approval from production." I pointed at myself. "That would be me. Capisce?" She blinked at me, a deer in headlights. "That goes for photos too."

"Oh my God." She rolled her eyes. "This is so stupid."

I slammed her phone to the counter, blood rushing in my ears. "I know you're desperate to be famous, but have a little common sense."

"I am famous!" she cried. "I have more followers than anybody here except Cole."

"For fuck's sake, life isn't all about likes and followers," I snapped.

"Really?" She snorted. "Well, they'll all do what I say, so if you want me to tell them to watch this movie, you should show me a little more respect."

"If you want to keep your job, you should show *me* a little more respect," I retorted.

"Yeah," Stella piled on. "I really didn't appreciate that picture you posted of me sleeping on the boat."

"You should have," Madison taunted. "It got over a hundred thousand likes, which is more than the number of followers you even have."

Stella gasped.

"Enough!" I shouted. "No more posts of the set or anyone on it without their approval, Madison. *Or you will be fired.* Do you understand?"

She crossed her arms and jutted her chin out. "Fine. But it's only gonna hurt you. You'll see."

"Okay, okay." Jackson stepped between us. He placed a gentle hand on my shoulder, giving me a subtle look that said to stand down. "Madison, there are reasons we don't want anything shared without approval, so please, don't do it. And we will all"—he looked from her to me to Stella—"respect each other. Okay?"

It was all I could do not to strangle the bitch, but I swallowed the rage constricting my throat, clenching my fists.

I looked up to see Price standing in the entry to the kitchen, bewildered. "Now then, ladies." I forced enthusiasm, clapping my hands. "Price will take you to wardrobe. You can run lines while you get ready."

Wordlessly, Madison and Stella followed Price out of the kitchen, studiously avoiding looking at each other. Jackson peered at me from beneath a knitted brow. "You okay?"

"Sorry," I mumbled, knowing it was fairly obvious I was anything but okay.

"Maybe you should take a walk," he suggested.

I nodded. "I'll be back in—"

"Take your time," Jackson said.

"You're gonna shoot the scene on the schedule, though—"

"Yes. I can handle it. Go get some air." He pointed toward the door. "Breathe."

Brian was fiddling with the scrim as I squeezed past it, and his mirthful eyes caught mine. "That was kinda awesome though," he whispered. "You said exactly what I was thinking."

"Thank you," I mouthed.

Feeling out of body, I walked out the back of the house and down the grassy hill to the beach, where I shed my shoes and rolled up my jeans. The sun was too bright, the air too humid. I didn't know what had gotten into me. I'd never snapped like that on set before in my life, and I'd been in far worse situations, dealt with much bigger egos.

I picked my way across bits and pieces of broken shells to stand at the shoreline, staring across the blue dappled ocean. The warm water rushed over my ankles, excavating the sand from beneath my feet as it returned to the sea. Thunderheads gathered way out on the horizon, turning the morning's glassy surface choppy.

Why was I so on edge today? Maybe I was hormonal. I blocked the month in my head. I should be getting my period this week, and that often made me bitchy. But not psychotic. More likely it was the strain of the past few months finally taking its toll—at the very worst moment, of course.

My therapist said it was okay to be angry with my father; the danger was in allowing that anger to bubble over into other parts of my life.

Fifty yards out, a giant brindled gray bird dive-bombed the clear water, coming up with a silvery fish in its beak. It tossed its head back, swallowing the fish whole, and swooped away, wide wings beating. I wished I had wings to fly away.

The way I'd behaved with Stella and Madison was emotional and unprofessional—exactly how my father would have expected a woman to act, which made me doubly angry with myself, and them. Damn actresses.

There was a time when I'd wanted to be an actress when I grew up. I vividly remembered the moment I'd made the decision. I must have been about eight. I was standing in the dark drizzle outside Grauman's Chinese Theatre on Hollywood Boulevard at the premiere of some film my father had produced, my pink sequined dress heavy with the runoff from my flimsy umbrella, feet squelching in my kitten heels. Twenty feet away, the actresses posed on the red carpet under blazing spotlights in their beautiful gowns, protected from the rain by a maze of massive clear tents as reporters fawned over them and drenched fans snapped pictures from behind the barricade erected on the sidewalk. I was transfixed. They were like real live princesses, the mere mortals scurrying after them turned to mice by juxtaposition. Like any little girl, I didn't want to be a mouse. I wanted to be a princess.

My father was under the tent as well, of course, and at some point he remembered he'd left me out in the rain and had an assistant escort me inside. He didn't sit next to me, as there were far more important people to share his time with, but afterward, in the car on the way home, I told him my decision.

He laughed. "Sweetie, you're never gonna be pretty enough to be an actress."

The back of my throat closed, and tears stung my eyes. My mother had always told me I was beautiful, and I'd never thought to question her.

"Oh, come on," he said tersely. "Stop crying. You don't want me to lie to you, do you?"

I sobbed, embarrassed I hadn't realized my own homeliness.

"Get it together!" he snapped.

"But...not all actresses are pretty," I protested.

"You want to be one of the plain ones? Go ahead, if you think you can take it. But it's always going to be about what you look like. It's a visual medium. Plain actresses only ever play the plain girl until they get to the age where none of the other women are particularly good-looking anymore anyway. I'm just telling you the truth."

That was the end of my acting dream.

I didn't blame my father for what he said to me that night. For years after I was grateful he'd told me the truth; it was what I needed to hear. I wasn't plagued by imagining myself to be something I wasn't. I stopped messing with dresses and bows, because what was the point? If my own father didn't find me beautiful, I knew no other man would.

At school the girls ostracized me when I became a tomboy, so I hung out with the guys. I laughed at their fart jokes and, later, listened without judgment to stories of their escapades with the other girls. They picked on me, but I was tough and could give as good as I got. I won their respect.

I developed sizable boobs around the time I turned sixteen, but I kept them hidden under sweats and baggy T-shirts, never wore makeup or straightened my kinky curls, and never let on when I periodically crushed on any of the guys from our group. Predictably, I made it through high school with my virginity intact and not a single girlfriend to share secrets with. Not that I had any secrets.

I discovered sex in college, but after a quick and brutal heartbreak, swore off relationships. My tomboy persona worked so well throughout film school and beyond that even after I discovered the magic of high heels, flat irons, and eyebrow shaping—and to my surprise learned there were in fact plenty of men who found me quite attractive—I continued to fight for the respect of the guys I worked with by styling myself as the perennial cool girl. DTF but uninterested in anything further. Which was, of course, how I ended up having an affair with my married colleague and ruining my life.

I gazed out at the electric-blue sea and inhaled the salt air, turning my face up to the warm sun. Maybe my life wasn't totally ruined. Plenty of people who were told they'd never work in Hollywood again lived to tell the tale.

Out on the ocean I spied a fishing boat about the size of Rick's and couldn't help but wish I was aboard it. He'd laugh hearing about my outburst today. The thought of it made me smile. But no. He was taken, and admittedly, I didn't like him as just a friend. I had to stay away.

I looked up at the house on the hill, where a giant light was shining into the kitchen window. They must have started filming; I should get back. I'd eat crow, blame it on—sleep, or the lack thereof. Awesome.

I dusted off my feet, slipped on my shoes, and trudged back up the hill, dreading the task before me. I shouldn't have behaved the way I did, but really, Stella should have come prepared, and Madison should have known better than to live stream on set. Did she not remember the NDA she'd signed? I checked myself. No matter what they did wrong, it was on me to keep the thing running smoothly, which meant taking whatever they dished out with a smile. I was just so incredibly sick of taking people's shit. It was exhausting.

As I neared the house, I heard a baby squalling. So this day was only getting better. I found Price on the patio talking with Jackson while through the archway in the living room, three women tried to calm not one but two screaming babies. Madison, Stella, and Cole were nowhere in sight.

"Welcome back," Price said as I approached. "You're right in time for the latest crisis."

"The babies hate Madison," Jackson clarified.

I swallowed a chortle that didn't go unnoticed by the men. "Sorry. That's terrible." I peered through the open doorway at the twins playing Stella's child, both screaming bloody murder while a woman, presumably their mother, sat with them on the couch, desperately performing peekaboo while an older woman sang a lullaby. In the film, Marguerite had one child, but babies could only work for such a short time that it was necessary to cast twins.

"That's the mom and grandmother," Price pointed out. "And Tawny just arrived as well. Her flight got out after all." Tawny, currently waggling a ducky in the face of one of the babies, was the actress playing Cherry, the pregnant nanny replaced by Madison's character, whose scenes we'd planned to shoot today, before storms delayed her flight. She was a striking Black woman in her thirties with large round eyes, her long box braids swirled into a bun atop her head. "They like her a lot more than Madison, but not enough to stop screaming."

"How do you know they hate Madison?" I asked.

"They were the happiest babies on the block until they saw her. Each of them, in turn, lost their shit the minute they laid eyes on her."

I snickered, quickly covering my mouth with my hand. In the script, Madison was supposed to be the dream nanny that Stella's character had to hire regardless of her doubts because she was such a great influence on her child. "Perhaps we should have consulted the babies on casting." I laughed.

Both men stared at me like I'd lost my mind. "Sorry, sorry." I cleared my throat. "So can we hire different babies?"

"Casting is on it," Price confirmed. "But finding ten-month-old twins with working permits and passports is gonna set us back a week at least."

"How are they with Stella?" I asked.

"Fine, as long as Madison's not around."

I sighed, the producer in me rumbling to life. "Okay, are we lit for the scene in the kitchen?" They nodded. "Great. We'll shoot the baby only from behind or frame him out. After that, let's revert to shooting what we were originally going to do today with Tawny, since she's here and the babies like her, while casting looks for more twins. Until we find them, we film as much as we can without the babies. For shots where one is necessary, the baby will be sleeping or we can use a doll—"

"No doll," Jackson objected. "Fake babies ruin everything."

"Put that on his tombstone," I said, trying to lighten the tension. "Okay, no doll. We can shoot the baby's reaction shots without Madison present."

"But the whole premise is that the baby loves her." Jackson groaned. "It's the reason Marguerite keeps her around, even when she sees her husband become enamored with her. We have a ton of shots ahead where she's calming him, singing to him, rocking him…"

"Okay, for those we can use a baby that's not one of the hero babies as long as it's the same size and skin tone. Price will find one. Right, Price?"

He nodded. "On it."

"And for shots where the baby is featured, we'll use…" I peered through the doorway, and my gaze landed on Felicity, who had appeared out of thin air while we were talking. Odd. I could have sworn Stella said she gave her the day off, but there she was, crouched on the floor before the babies, a pinkie wrapped in each of their curled hands.

The crying had finally stopped, the babies hypnotized by Felicity singing softly, "Hush, little babies, don't say a word, Mama's gonna buy you a mockingbird…"

We entered the living room slowly and hovered inside the archway, not wanting to disrupt the equilibrium. The mother smiled at us, whispering, "They love her. We ran into her in the restaurant this morning, and she played with them the entire time they had their breakfast. They're enamored."

Of course. Once again Felicity saved the day. I knew I should be grateful to the Goddess Who Was Good at Everything, but what I felt was suspicious. Had she somehow turned the babies against Madison? I nipped my paranoia in the bud. That was impossible, of course. They were *babies*. I was losing my mind. I caught Jackson's eye and nodded toward Felicity. "Ask her to stand in for Madison," I whispered.

Felicity and Tawny now each held a smiling baby, bouncing ever so slightly and cooing at them with hyperfocus. Tawny looked up to see me watching her and flashed a warm smile. She bobbed over, waggling the ducky before the child on her hip.

"Glad you made it, Tawny." I returned her smile. "Did someone get you all set up in your bungalow?"

"They took my bags, but I came straight here. Wanted to say hello to everyone before I got settled."

"Do you mind working today?" I asked. "I know it's a quick start, but with the situation with the babies—"

"No problem. I'm totally prepared."

I sighed with relief. "Bless you."

"Only thing is I haven't had a fitting."

"Your wardrobe is scrubs, so I think we'll be okay."

The baby in her arms gazed up at me, and for a moment I was terrified the screaming would start again, but instead the child giggled and reached for me. "She likes you."

"Go on. You can hold her," the mother encouraged as Tawny held her out to me. "She loves people."

*Everyone but Madison, apparently.*

"Hi there," I cooed, awkwardly taking the baby. She was wiggly, and I didn't quite know how to hold her. I'd never babysat, and none of my friends had babies. "You're a pretty little girl, to be playing a boy."

"Not the first time," the mother said.

The baby wrapped her chunky little arms around my neck and rested her head on my chest, gurgling happily to herself. I'd never been particularly fond of babies, but I felt a sudden rush of warmth for the child. Her skin was velvety soft and smelled of talcum powder. "Hi there." I smiled into her big brown eyes.

She grabbed my nose, and I laughed.

"Baby fever out here," Cole goaded as he entered the room. "Didn't know you had it in ya, Wasserman." He clapped me on the back.

I hurriedly handed the little girl back to her mother. "We should keep rolling," I declared. "It may rain this afternoon, and we need to be wrapped before it does."

Price announced the change of plans and gave everyone their marching orders as I took out my phone and checked my weather app, which claimed it was raining right now and predicted clear skies for the afternoon. Awesome.

# Stella

I've brought you six qualified candidates and you've turned them all down," Tawny said as Cherry, bouncing the baby on her hip. "I've run out of options."

I was curled in bed as Marguerite in the depths of depression, my hair a mess, my complexion paled by makeup. "They're not you," I mumbled.

"I'm due next week. I'm gonna have my own baby to take care of. I can't give you the help you need anymore." She said it with compassion, but it was clear Cherry's patience was wearing thin.

"Peyton's coming home this afternoon," she went on. "And he's bringing a girl from New York with him."

I sat up, my eyes wild. It wasn't a stretch to put myself in Marguerite's shoes. "A girl?"

"A nanny. Someone recommended by a friend. Her US visa is about to expire, but it won't be a problem for her to work here."

"And I'm supposed to trust a stranger with my child?" I demanded.

Cherry sat on the edge of the bed. "She's trained as a nurse, so she can help you as well."

"I don't need help!"

Lightning flashed out over the windswept sea, followed closely by a tremendous clap of thunder, which shook the walls of the house. The heavens opened, and the rain poured onto the roof like deafening applause. Dramatic timing, but the lighting and audio levels would never match with the angles of the scene we'd shot before the bottom fell out.

"And that's a wrap on today," Price called over the din.

It was just as well we were wrapping early. My horoscope this morning had been spot-on: undue stress and roadblocks in both career and love all day long.

Tawny was a fantastic actress, and working with her was a pleasure, but I was so frustrated by my earlier scene with Madison and Cole that I was off my game. I didn't feel guilty I hadn't been prepared—it wasn't my fault no one confirmed with me about what we were shooting—but attempting to emote while endeavoring to remember lines made for a taxing day. Cole and I improvised most of the scene, which should have been fine had Madison been able to keep up. But every time I went off-book, she looked lost and stopped, announcing that wasn't the line. Total nightmare.

It didn't help that I was already beyond annoyed with her for that damn picture she posted of me sleeping on the boat. She'd taken it down after my outburst this morning, but not before 107,498 people had liked it. I had to keep reminding myself she'd nearly died of cancer to avoid scratching her eyes out. I wished it were Felicity in her role. When she ran lines with me, she was so much better than Madison. A natural.

Cole, however, was unusually patient with Madison, gently encouraging her and guiding her back every time she got lost, and she ate it up with a spoon, gazing at him all googly-eyed even when she wasn't in character. I could practically see her salivating over what a fling with him would do for her celebrity status. I knew he'd blame their obvious flirtation on method acting if I confronted him about it, and that it was in fact probably good for my character work for me to feel what Marguerite was feeling; still, it was upsetting after what had happened between us last night.

Upstairs in the cheery yellow bedroom designated as my dressing room, I found Felicity sprawled across the flowery comforter on the brass bed, reading over the script changes we'd been handed this morning. "It would be so much more interesting," she said over the drum of rain on the roof, "if instead of fighting over the husband, the women bonded together against him."

"You're saying you want to give Madison a larger, more complicated role?" I scoffed, turning my back so she could unzip my dress. Out the rain-lashed window, palm trees bowed to the wind; the sea beyond was heaving and gray. "She can hardly handle one note. You want to hand her a symphony?"

She snickered as she unzipped me. "Too true. But think about it. What if...? What if it was the women who fell for each other?" She hopped off the bed, excited, and began pacing while I wiped off my sick makeup with a towelette and quickly applied a layer of tinted moisturizer and bronzer. "Your character's a former model. She could become a photographer—it's not uncommon—and Madison's character could become her muse. Perhaps she's the siren, not the younger woman. She'd shoot her with the female gaze instead of the male gaze; it would be a celebration of femininity!"

"Ha!" I threw my costume on the bed and pulled my favorite yellow and white sundress over my head. "Sounds dreamy. But it's not a story anyone wants to see."

"Are you kidding? Of course it is! It's modern," she insisted. I hid a smirk as I spritzed myself with perfume, amused by her enthusiasm. "I'll tell you what no one wants to see anymore is two women fighting over a man. Boring!"

I ran a brush through my tangled locks. "Well, if Jackson will listen to anyone, he'll listen to you." A little mascara and eye shadow, and I was beginning to look alive again. "Maybe you can get him to recast Madison's role while you're at it."

I heard heavy footsteps in the hallway coming from the direction of Cole's dressing room and flung open the door to find him headed down the stairs. "That was fast," I called, dabbing a coral stain on my lips.

"I have to make it to the bank before it closes."

Cole had been strangely distant toward me all day; I figured we could use some time alone to talk about what happened between us last night, so I could decide how best to proceed. My horoscope this morning had emphasized that as stressful as today might be, it would also bring clarity, but thus far I was just confused. "Give me a sec. I'll come with you."

"I'm in a rush—"

"It'll take two seconds."

I slipped my feet into my sandals and pointed to the dress on the bed. "Can you return that to wardrobe?" I asked Felicity.

"Sure." Felicity eyed me as I powdered my nose and checked my appearance in the mirror one last time. "You sure about this? He's been in a bad mood all day."

I lowered my voice. "You're the one who said a romance would be good press. That pic you posted of him with his arm around me on set the other day already has the trolls buzzing. A snap of us walking hand in hand on the beach could make the cover of *Star Weekly*."

"You're speaking my language, but—"

"I'm going." I cut her off before I could change my mind. "Do you have my A-pills?"

She nodded and checked her watch. "You still have another hour though."

I was already beginning to feel irritable, the need for another dose prickling beneath my skin like an itch I couldn't scratch. "I'll take them with me."

"You promise you'll wait?" she asked.

I batted my eyes. "I promise."

She deposited the precious little blue leather bag in my hand, and I blew her a kiss. "See you at home."

In the hall I passed Madison, pulling on an atrocious lime-green raincoat. She started to speak, but I held up a hand. "Sorry, in a rush."

I descended to the living room to find Cole already gone, but the driver lingered in the doorway, an umbrella dangling from his hand. He eyed my thin sundress. "Sure you don't wanna wait till the rain stops?"

I grabbed a bottle of water from the craft services table and quickly downed my pill. "I'll be fine."

Even with the umbrella, I was soaked by the time I reached the golf cart, twenty feet away. The driver unzipped the thick clear plastic rain coating, and I settled on the bench next to Cole. "Quite a storm," I commented as we pulled away.

He grunted.

"Not bad today, all things considered," I offered. He stared silently at the rain running down the plastic as we jostled along the road. "Just curious...What made you guys decide to cast Madison?"

He shrugged. "No one else was available on such short notice after the other girl dropped out. Taylor vouched for her."

Hmmm. That was odd; Taylor seemed to like Madison even less than she liked me. "Do you know why?" I asked.

"Does it matter?" he snapped.

His mood was darker than the skies overhead. I held my hands up, beginning to wish I hadn't insisted on coming along. "No, sorry."

We rode in silence the rest of the way to the bank. I was disconcerted; he was so into me last night—I'd been the one slowing things down. Perhaps I was too cold?

The golf cart pulled under the portico outside the small, coral-painted bank, and we both got out. "You don't need to come in," he said.

"Oh, I was going to get some cash. I thought I might—"

But he was already halfway through the door.

"I have to go back for the others," the driver called. "Probably take half an hour."

I hesitated, considering whether to head back with him. But I didn't want to give Cole the satisfaction of thinking I'd only come along to be with him, and I did need cash. I gave the driver a thumbs-up and swung open the door of the bank. I'd have half an hour alone with Cole. Surely I could turn things around. Maybe I could even get something out of him, see what the hell was going on with him. With us.

I acquired my colorful foreign cash from a friendly teller with striking pink and purple extensions woven into a French roll, then sat on a tropical printed couch looking out at the rain while he chatted with a banker in the bank's only office for a good fifteen minutes. By the time he emerged, the rain had cleared. He breezed out the front door without acknowledging me—probably thinking I'd headed back into town with the driver—and I hurried after him.

He stopped short when he saw the golf cart wasn't waiting beneath the portico. "Where's the guy?"

"He had to go get the others. He'll be back in fifteen."

"For fuck's sake."

"The rain's cleared. Let's take a walk," I suggested brightly, in an effort to lift his mood. "I've been wanting to check out the town."

We set out along the palm-lined cobblestone road that led down a slight incline to the small harbor, skirting puddles and dodging dripping palm fronds. Ahead of us in the port, mostly sailboats and fishing boats bobbed on the still choppy sea, but a sizable yacht was docked just outside the marina. A boardwalk curved around the little port, lined with shops and restaurants painted in bright colors. I noticed a group of probably thirty people huddled under an overhang beneath a sign that read "Ferry, 10:00 a.m. and 3:00 p.m."

"Ferry must be late due to the storm," I commented, scurrying to catch up with him, glancing up at the sky. Patches of clouds hid the sun, and the air was thick with moisture.

He spun to face me. "Oh my God, do you ever shut up?"

I inhaled sharply, taken aback.

"You never stop talking, do you? Is it all those pills you're always popping? Or do you actually think I give a shit about what you have to say?"

I stepped back, bewildered, but the ground wasn't where I expected it to be. I felt the water close over my ankle as I lost my balance, flailing my arms as I reached for him to catch me.

Only, he didn't catch me. He didn't even try. He simply stood by and watched as I tumbled hard on my ass into the muddy puddle, the wind knocked out of me. Behind him, I could see the people waiting for the ferry staring, cell phones raised.

Anger seared my chest. I reached my hand toward him and smiled, hissing through my teeth, "Take my hand, or I will walk off this film."

He snatched my hand and jerked me to my feet, his eyes cold. My dress was ruined. "Now smile for the cameras," I growled, keeping a death grip on his hand.

I turned to the people and made a show of laughing it off, taking a bow as they filmed. Cole fired up his movie star smile and waved. Out of the corner of my eye, I thought I saw a lime-green raincoat among the onlookers, but when I looked again she was gone, swallowed by the crowd. A woman with a baby strapped to her chest and three kids trailing behind her came running over wanting a selfie with Cole. He obliged, opening the floodgates. We were still trapped in a sea of cameras when our golf cart finally pulled up.

I dove through the plastic, refusing to even look at Cole as he piled in behind me.

"You okay?" the driver asked, glancing down at my dress.

I nodded. "Just took a spill. My butt's not as bruised as my ego."

He laughed. "I can't imagine what you guys put up with."

Cole shot from the golf cart when it pulled up to the pier leading to our bungalows, but I was hot on his heels. "Hey," I shouted, shading my eyes against the sun reflecting off the water as I trailed him down the wet planks all the way to the far end. I did my best to look nonchalant in case any of our crew were to see us, but I wasn't about to let him get away. By the time he got out his key and pushed his door open, I was close enough to force my way through the door behind him. "What the hell is wrong with you?"

I kicked the door shut, leaving us alone in his gargantuan bungalow. His television and glass floor windows were twice as large as those in the other bungalows, his kitchen a marble and steel full-size affair instead of a kitchenette, and his deck had a hot tub in addition to the plunge pool. Also, there was a giant, comfortable-looking suede sectional couch that didn't match the decor in the rest of the resort, and the walls were covered in what I could tell was real art—bright splashes of modernist color interspersed with movie posters featuring Cole's face. I guessed this was his private villa, not available for rent by the resort.

He spun to face me. "Wrong with me? What the fuck is wrong with you? Chasing me around like a love-sick puppy all day, acting like we're together—you should be embarrassed."

Tears sprang to my eyes. I hated myself for my desperation. "But last night—"

"We were drunk," he spat. "And you know how I get when I'm playing a character. Peyton had his claws in me. I got carried away."

My mouth hung open. "Are you saying you *method-fucked* me?"

He groaned. "My mistake."

I shivered in the blasting air-conditioning, my chest so tight I could hardly breathe. Behind him, his ten-years-younger face smirked down at me from a life-size poster of him as Bad Billy, cowboy hat askew, the same gun he showed me in the wine cellar in hand. "Why did you offer me this part?" I demanded.

"It wasn't my decision."

I felt the tears hot on my cheeks but didn't bother to wipe them away. "If you hate me so much, why did you let them cast me?"

"I don't hate you. I just...I didn't have a choice, okay? Jackson knows everything. He threatened to tell it all if I didn't give him the money for this project and star in it with you."

"What?" I sank into a rattan chair, my wet dress cold against my legs. "But you said—"

"He wasn't in his room doing homework that night. He saw."

My mind raced, piecing together elements of the night I'd tried so hard to forget. "What did he see?"

"It doesn't matter. Enough."

"But—" Carefully neglected memories began to rise from the lagoon where I'd buried them, nearly unrecognizable beneath thirteen years of lies. "Why didn't you tell me?"

He sighed. "It was better you didn't know."

"And now he's blackmailing you—to do a movie?" It was like sand was stuck in the gears of my mind. This couldn't be true. "That's insane. Why?"

"I don't know. I was a shitty father?"

"You didn't ask him?"

"I'm not in control of the situation," he growled. "Don't you see that?"

I'd never known Cole not to be in control of a situation. "Why me? And Madison...?" I was thinking out loud now. "What's his plan?"

"I don't think Madison has anything to do with it. And I don't know if there is a plan, other than to punish me, to make me pay for stealing his childhood—his words, not mine."

It was too strange to believe. Thoughtful, sensitive, considerate Jackson, a blackmailer? The guy meditated for an hour every morning *before* our 6:00 a.m. call time. "He didn't blackmail me."

"He didn't need to." Cole smirked. "You would've walked across hot coals for work that paid enough to fill your pool."

"Enough with the damn pool," I snapped. "The script is actually good."

The walls were closing in. I had too many questions. There were too many holes. Could I trust Cole? I stared down through the glass floor at the unsettled ocean, still murky from the storm. "We should have..." My voice trailed off. I couldn't imagine what it was we should have done. It was all so long ago. The lies had become indistinguishable from the truth.

"We had no choice." His eyes were hard. "We did what we had to do."

I pressed the heels of my hands into my eyes. "Maybe it's better for it to finally come out," I murmured. "Be done with it."

"No." He leaned forward and took me by the shoulders. "You're not sending us to jail."

I squinted hard at him. What else hadn't he told me? "I should speak with Jackson—"

"No."

"But—"

"He can't know you know." He squatted next to me, his gaze flinty. "Do you understand? It would only make things worse."

Again I nodded. "And how can you be sure he won't talk, after we've finished the movie?"

"I'll make sure of it by whatever means necessary." I didn't like the edge to his voice.

"Cole," I protested.

"He won't talk."

# Felicity

It's snowing again.

Everyone around here talks about how beautiful the snow is, but I hate it. Sure, it's pretty coming down, but it traps you inside for days at a time unless you want to completely freeze your ass off, and then it gets dirty and melts and makes a horrible muddy mess.

But the snow is the least of what I hate about this place. I hate the one stoplight that flashes yellow at night (completely unnecessary), I hate the school (full of small-minded bitches who whisper behind my back every time I turn around), I hate the Walmart (where we go for absolutely everything, and I know all the checkers because they go to our warehouse of a church, which I hate most of all). Strike me dead, but God I hate that church.

Every single person in a twenty-mile radius who has been saved by their Lord and Savior Jesus Christ (and that's literally everyone) shows up on Sunday morning and Wednesday night and whatever prayer group in between to sing and pray and gossip and pass judgment on one another and come up with new ways to hate anyone who doesn't hold the same beliefs they do. Like my beautiful mother, who, according to their rules, consorted with the devil and is currently burning in the fires of hell.

I tried with the church at first. I really did; I was lost, badly depressed. I'd hoped it would be like the church Jewel's foster parents took her to, where everyone was kind and she made friendship bracelets and learned to sing. I wanted something to believe in and naively thought a church full of people who called themselves Christians would, I don't know, *love thy brother* and *do unto others as you would have them do unto you*, but no such luck. Apparently, all churches are not created equal. Still, I kept going in hopes of meeting that one Sunday school teacher or friend who would be a life raft instead of a hypocrite who whispered behind my back and judged me for the "mistakes" of my mother.

The last straw came when I finally admitted to the church group that I was struggling to have faith in a God that would take away the single mother of a ten-year-old. After lots of hemming and hawing, they finally came up with the explanation that He had taken away my mother so that I would come to live with my grandparents and be brought back to the church. So basically they wanted me to put my trust in a God that murders mothers to get their daughters to worship Him. No thanks.

Iris was right to take the first bus to Miami. Good thing she got knocked up with me and her parents kicked her out (a claim they deny), or she might have wound up stuck here forever. Of course then she might still be alive, so there's no use playing the coulda-shoulda-woulda game. It's a game I play far too often, and it's holy shit depressing.

I have a lot of time to think because I don't have any friends.

Like right now, there's a study group going on at Ellie's house, and anyone who's not playing in or cheering at the varsity basketball game over in New Bethlehem is there cheating off one another's homework while Ellie's mom cooks spaghetti with meatballs for them. I know because I used to be invited. But now I'm here in my cold little room by myself doing my trigonometry homework under the quilt that hardly keeps me warm. Whatever. Their loss. I'm the one whose work they'd be copying. I'm smarter than any of them.

The first year I was a novelty, the only new girl in a class of townies who had known one another since kindergarten. But these kids didn't like novelty, and I was too shell-shocked to attempt to fit in. The second year I tried. That was the year I went to church and even joined the basketball team. I had a few friends for a while, but they all turned their backs on me around the time my waist slimmed down and my boobs showed up. For better or worse, I turned out looking exactly like my curvy, blond mother, save my nose, which I still haven't quite grown into. And now all the girls hate me because all the guys want to screw me. Yeah, that's right. Being a member of the Holy Cross Evangelist Church doesn't stop you from being a spiteful bitch or a rapey asshole.

But I'm not gonna make the same mistakes Iris made. Not that I'm into any of those meatheads anyway.

So I quarantine myself in the bedroom that used to be hers and stalk Cole, Stella, and Jackson on the internet. Jackson's pretty hard because he's my age and stays out of the public eye—even all his social accounts are locked—though every now and then I'll see a picture of him with his dad at an awards show or a charity event. Cole, of course, pops up on the internet all the time, but most of it's PR bullshit. Red carpet pictures, puff pieces, movie star smiles. But Stella…she's a fucking mess. And the bloodsuckers love nothing more than a fucking mess.

It was all downhill for her after she and Cole killed my mom. It seems like every time I open a tabloid, there's another juicy story about her losing her mind, and I relish every minute of her implosion. It's what she deserves after what she did to my mother, and it keeps me entertained here in Boring-sylvania.

I have to admit, though, Ruthanne and Fred aren't as bad as I'd thought they'd be. If I didn't know they'd kicked my pregnant mom out and then lied to me about it, I wouldn't mind them so much. They did take me in when no one else would.

My dad was a nonstarter. He now runs his family's chicken farm operation from Dallas, where he lives with his second wife. The social worker didn't know I could hear his end of the conversation when she called him up to tell him about me. He was very clear he'd given my mom the money for an abortion, so as far as he was concerned, I didn't exist. Despite evidence to the contrary.

But Ruthanne and Fred were happy to take me. They claimed they'd been looking for my mom for years, and the fact she hadn't aborted me led them to believe that she was in heaven. I didn't tell them about the stripping or the hooking.

They live in a blue two-bedroom shoebox on a flat two acres with two mutts, a goat, and a coop full of chickens. Fred's a big man with a love of Penn State football and deer hunting. He drives an eighteen-wheeler, and I think he's less about Jesus than Ruthanne, who's a Jesus freak by anyone's standards, but he goes along with it for her sake. Ruthanne works at the hardware store and has a big garden that provides all kinds of vegetables when the ground isn't frozen solid.

The first year was hard for all of us; I had residual hate for them because they kicked Iris out, and they didn't know how to handle a feisty ten-year-old who'd never had any rules and had just lost her mother. I got a lot of spankings and time-outs, like a toddler. The change came the following spring, when it was time to plant Ruthanne's garden. Bored, I asked if I could help one day and found I loved turning the soil, trimming the leaves, watching the new plants shoot up. Ruthanne was so pleased that the next morning when we were at Walmart, she took me to the juniors section and let me pick out a new church dress and a pair of heels, my first. It was then that I remembered something Iris had told me once when I asked how she became such a good dancer. "I'm a fine dancer, but what I'm really doing is selling a fantasy," she'd said. "If you listen, people will tell you what they want. Then all you have to do is give it to them, and you'll have them eating out of your hand."

That evening I helped Ruthanne in the kitchen too, and learned I liked cooking as much as I liked gardening. But what I liked even more was the fact that later that evening, when she caught me reading a copy of *Lolita* I'd found in a used bookstore in town, she simply shut my bedroom door.

I discovered that as long as I kept my opinions to myself, didn't take the Lord's name in vain, did my chores, got good grades, and went to church, Ruthanne and Fred were pretty okay. Besides the garden and cooking, I still have nothing in common with them except for my mother, and talking about her is hard for all of us, after everything. I've always maintained my account of what happened the night she died, but I can tell that even they don't believe me.

For years I've told my story to the police, to reporters, to anyone who would listen, but no one's been convinced. Every psychologist agreed: I was a scared kid in a bad situation making up fantasies to dispel the bleakness of her unhappy life. It happens all the time, they said.

Only, I wasn't unhappy. They assume that with the lifestyle Iris and I led, I must have been miserable. But I knew no other way to live. And to a ten-year-old, being able to walk to the store on your own and watch whatever show and say whatever bad words you want while eating frozen pizza curled up in the bed you share with your mom is a pretty awesome existence.

It's a lot better than huddling under a thin blanket in my cold bedroom with earbuds, watching movies I downloaded via torrent on the contraband iPhone I bought with my secret pile of money, because Ruthanne and Fred don't allow any entertainment that isn't church approved. I know all Cole's and Stella's movies by heart.

The secret pile of money and the thought of what I'm going to do with it when I turn eighteen is all that keeps me going most of the time.

A few days after the accident, Carol-the-social-worker had escorted me back to our apartment to collect my things, with the instruction that I should place whatever I wanted in two black garbage bags; everything else would be disposed of. The cops had already been through the place, and it was a wreck. Drawers were open, clothes strewn everywhere, pillows upturned. And yet somehow the entire apartment still smelled of jasmine. Overwhelmed, I sat on the end of the bed and started to cry. Carol patted my back and offered me a tissue. That woman always had a tissue. Part of the job, I guessed. "Can I help you pick which things you want?" she asked.

I blew my nose on the tissue and shook my head. "I'd like a minute alone, if that's okay."

"I'll be in the living room if you need me." She quietly closed the door behind her.

The second she was gone, I opened the closet and pushed aside the pile of clothes that hid the safe. I crouched before it and spun the code, then jerked the door open, my heart hammering. To my relief, the money was intact. I knew I probably didn't have much time before Carol came in trying to be helpful, so I snatched Iris's satin pillowcase off the bed and stuffed it with the cash. I heard a soft knock.

I wrapped the pillowcase in a sundress I grabbed from the floor and jammed it into my backpack beneath my schoolbooks right as Carol opened the door. I zipped the bag, trying to act nonchalant. "Just making sure I have all my schoolbooks," I said.

She wrinkled her brow in sympathy. "You're going to be attending a different school in Pennsylvania, so you'll probably need new books."

"But I really like these," I demurred, panicked she'd try to take my book bag away. "And they're already paid for. I'm gonna take them with me so I can keep learning."

She looked at me funny. "Okay."

When your mother dies, people will let you get away with all sorts of strange things.

She and I packed the garbage bags with a mixture of my clothes and the things of my mother's that most reminded me of her: her sketchbook and the larger folded sketches she did of me when I was little, the silver heels she bought herself the day after she met Cole, the little Dior saddlebag a suitor gave her, her jasmine perfume, her favorite jewelry, T-shirts, and dresses. It was hard leaving anything of hers behind, knowing it was all I'd have of her; I kept taking out things of my own to make room for things of hers, until Carol stopped me.

"You'll need clothes," she said.

I took one last look around, then lifted the framed poster of the Eiffel Tower off its hook above the bed, perched her most-loved sunglasses atop my head, and marched out of the apartment.

Only it wasn't actually my final time in the apartment. Two days later, when Ruthanne and Fred arrived in a blue Impala to collect me, they wanted to see where Iris had lived, so we went back. They tiptoed as though the floor might fall through if they stepped in the wrong place and glanced around tentatively, afraid to see something they didn't want to remember.

Fred spied the open safe first. "What was in here?"

"Some jewelry, a Dior purse," I fibbed. "It's all packed. She kept her money in there too, but there wasn't any left."

They shook their heads, disheartened by what their only daughter's life had come to. I could tell they were itching to argue about which of them was to blame, but thankfully they were too inhibited to do it in front of the grief-stricken girl freshly foisted upon them.

I rode all the way to Pennsylvania in silence with the backpack between my feet, next to the urn of my mother's ashes that now sits on the mantel beneath the big decorative iron cross. One day I'll take those ashes to Paris and release her into the city she always dreamed of visiting.

The picture of the Eiffel Tower hangs in my bedroom above the dresser, where an old teddy bear I gutted and packed with my mother's cash quietly waits for my eighteenth birthday, when I'll be free. Until then, I'm patient.

# CELEB SPOTTER

## TROUBLE IN PARADISE?

Cole Power and Stella Rivers took a break from filming on the beautiful Caribbean island of Saint Genesius Monday to visit the small port of Gen Town. We'd speculated a few weeks ago, when the report came out that Power had cast Rivers to star opposite him in *The Siren*, that the exes might be rekindling a romance, and Rivers's post last week, in which a smiling Power had his arm around her, seemed to support the theory. But bystanders say the two appeared to be arguing as they strolled along the port, and newly released video shows Rivers losing her footing and falling ass-first into a puddle while Power looks on, appearing to almost laugh [video]. Whoopsie! Rivers and Power were smiling minutes later as they posed for pictures with fans waiting for a nearby ferry, but the clip of Power watching Rivers drop has become a meme overnight. Sadly, it doesn't look like we'll be getting a Stole reprise anytime soon.

# Taylor

The greenhouse was set up as a photography studio for the initial seduction scene between Cole's and Madison's characters, with plants hung from the leaden glass ceiling and giant scrims filtering light through the walls of windows. Only, the light kept shifting as clouds rolled in. We were already behind, and if we didn't complete the scene before the storm, we'd be even further behind. It was doubly maddening because I'd been tracking the forecast and suggested we start with this location first thing to avoid this very predicament, but Cole refused to work before noon. Something about switching his body clock, since we were doing a night shoot tomorrow. So here we were, battling rapidly changing daylight for the second time this week and racing to finish before the heavens opened.

The scene wouldn't be so difficult if the babies didn't scream bloody murder at the sight of Madison, but we had to shoot Madison's coverage with a live baby stand-in, then switch to Felicity standing in for Madison to catch the baby's coverage. Felicity was now holding a baby on her hip, wearing Madison's skimpy white sundress and a wig to match Madison's long black hair.

On the sidelines I watched the monitor as the camera rolled, captivated by what I saw on-screen. Felicity disappeared into the role in a way Madison never could. There was nothing self-conscious or stilted about her performance; I felt like I was watching a real human being instead of an actor portraying a character.

Funny, as Stella's stand-in, Felicity was always professional—and it was clear the camera loved her—but she was too young for the role and must have been holding back, probably out of deference to Stella. She was perfectly cast in Madison's role though, and she absolutely glowed.

It was a particular form of sorcery, the ability to become someone else on command; I'd seen flashes of it in Stella's performance, but it was more that she was playing a role so close to herself that the line between her and her character blurred. Cole used to have the gift but had in recent years become a caricature of himself: every role was a more greatly exaggerated version of what had worked for him in the past, as though each time he reached into his bag of tricks, the tools he extracted became blunter.

Or perhaps the parts he'd played were somehow compounding inside of him: in real life he sometimes behaved so much like the fictional characters he'd portrayed in the past, I had to wonder whether the tables had turned and the roles were now playing him instead of the other way around. Like he lost a piece of himself and gained a piece of a character every time he stood before the camera, until he became a patchwork of gangsters, lovers, villains, and gentlemen. Regardless, today Felicity elevated him and brought his acting closer to truth than I'd seen yet.

A flash of lightning too close for comfort drew my eye to the window right as a deafening crack of thunder shook the house. The baby started squalling. To their credit, both Felicity and Cole stayed in the scene, but it was no use. Five seconds later, the lights went out. A collective groan went up from the crew.

"Cut," Jackson called.

"Everybody take five while we get the generator up and running," Price added.

Five minutes later, the generator was not up and running. Nor was it ten, twenty, or forty-five minutes later.

We were into our tenth hour of twelve now, Cole had disappeared, and the repair guy for the off-brand generator that our electrical engineer had never seen before was on Saint Ann and couldn't come until tomorrow. Price, Jackson, and I put our heads together and decided to call it a day. I sighed, frustrated that weather had cut us off for a second time this week. "I'll have the repair guy come out tomorrow; someone should learn how to run the generator so this doesn't happen again," I said.

"And I'm taking everyone out for dinner at Coco's," Jackson announced. Off my look, he continued. "As in, I'm paying for it. We don't even have to tell Cole, wherever he went. In fact, don't. I'd love to enjoy a night with just my crew. And cast. Everybody but my father."

Price and I exchanged a glance. "You know Madison's gonna tell him though," I pointed out. "She's been jocking his strap since day one."

"Well, they're both missing, as far as I can see," he returned.

It was true. Madison had disappeared as well, around the same time as Cole. I hoped that didn't mean what I thought it meant. I lowered my voice. "She's driving me as crazy as she is you, trust me. But you know we have to invite her. And him."

He nodded. "Let's get on it, then. We'll have at least twenty drama-free minutes before they arrive."


Coco's was an open-air seafood and burger joint situated at the end of the jetty that guided boats into the Gen Town harbor. One side of the thatched-roof restaurant overlooked the dinghies and fishing boats bobbing in the port, and the other side a small ironshore beach. Jackson sought out the manager and negotiated a flat rate for food and drinks while our rowdy group took over the place, swamping the bar so badly that one of the sound guys jumped behind the counter to help. Coco's was not the type of spot where this kind of behavior was looked down on. In fact, the barman, who seemed to have already knocked a few back himself, quickly poured each of them shots and turned up the reggae.

The air was misty and fresh once the rain cleared; the waves pounded the last of the storm's energy into the sand as the light faded from the sky. Someone handed me a beer and someone else handed me a dart. Before I knew it, I was three rounds deep with Price and Francisco, each of us with a win beneath our belt. And then the steel drums started up. I passed my darts to Brian, filled a plate with fried conch, and sat at a table with a red-and-white-checked tablecloth, swaying to the music in my seat. Stella slid into the chair next to me, picking a piece of conch from my plate with her fingers and dipping it into my tartar sauce, then popping it into her mouth.

"Mmmm..." she said. "I know I should stay away from fried food, but it's just so good!"

"Get your own," I teased, protecting my plate with my arm.

"Here, you can have some of my salad." She pushed a sad-looking plate of dry lettuce and tomatoes toward me, and I laughed.

Tawny sat on my other side with a plate full of conch, shrimp, and peas 'n' rice. "What's so funny?" she asked.

"Stella's stealing my conch and trying to push her salad on me," I said. "You better watch out; she'll steal yours too."

Stella snatched a piece of shrimp off Tawny's plate with a wink, then cut her eyes toward the bar. "Well, look what the cat dragged in," she drolled.

Cole sauntered over with a drink in each hand, Madison trailing after him like a schoolgirl in love with the prom king. Yep, they'd fucked. It was written all over her smug face. "Hey," he said when he reached our table. Tawny was the only one who smiled at him, but he sat down anyway, filling the last seat at our four-top. Madison hovered, staring at her phone like it held the answer to where to park herself.

Cole slid one of the drinks to Stella. "Tonic for you." He winked.

She eyed him, suspicious. "Thanks." She sipped the drink, her green eyes going wide as what was surely gin hit her tongue. "That's some tonic," she spluttered.

"Bottoms up." He chuckled.

"You have a nice morning off?" Tawny asked.

"Bought a boat," Cole replied.

"Fun!" Tawny looked out toward the harbor. "Is it out there?"

He shook his head. "Rick has to pick it up for me." His gaze landed on me. "Have you seen him?"

"Me? No." I shook my head. "Is he coming?"

"You tell me. You're the one who was eye-fucking him the entire time we were on the boat last weekend."

My jaw dropped. "We were just talking," I said.

"Sure." He smirked.

"Everyone else was occupied. What was I supposed to do?"

He held up his hands, snickering. "Whoa, whoa, whoa, sensitive, are we?" He leered at Stella as she tentatively sipped her drink. "Nothing wrong with a little action, right?"

I stood. "I need another drink."

Stella rose next to me. "I'll come with you."

"Nice pants, half-pint." Cole shot a mocking glance at my favorite cargo pants, which I'd cut into shorts only this morning.

"Pockets," I snapped.

"Careful," he called as we walked away. "You don't want to end up blackout drunk again."

I clenched my jaw as I threaded my way through the crowd to the bar, blind with anger. Fuck him, taunting me like that. Commenting on my personal life and calling me out in public for something that... I was more than unsettled I remained in the dark about what had happened that first night. "Are you okay?" Stella whispered when we were out of earshot.

"No," I managed. "I want to kill him."

"He's such a Scorpio," she hissed. "He always has something up his sleeve. And what was that about blacking out? He's the one that gave me this drink."

I glanced at her. "I don't think that was about you."

"Hey." I turned to see Tawny, her eyes full of compassion. "I told him that was unacceptable," she offered.

"Lemme guess—he said it was a joke," Stella said.

Tawny pointed at her. "You know him well."

"I wish I didn't, believe me."

The bartender approached, and Tawny promptly ordered three shots of tequila. "One more!" Felicity called, elbowing her way past the darts game to slide in next to Stella. "What's going on?"

Stella explained while I attempted in vain to free myself from the claws of rage with deep breaths. "Maybe you should quit," Felicity suggested. "See how long he can make it without you."

"Please don't quit," Stella said. "You're the only thing holding this film together."

"I can't anyway." I placed my fingers in the inside corners of my eyes to stop the tears, too upset to pretend anymore. "I need the money, and I have no other opportunities. I have to finish this fucking movie or sell my condo and change careers—which right now honestly doesn't sound too bad."

The bartender set the shots in front of us, and we all downed them without ceremony. The alcohol burned my throat, warming my chest and blunting the ire in my brain.

"I mean, but seriously…are you sleeping with Rick, though?" Felicity asked playfully. "Because he's really hot."

I laughed. "No! Are you sleeping with Jackson?"

She gaped at me. "No! We're just friends."

Stella snorted. "You keep saying that."

"Really!" Felicity insisted, looking over her shoulder to make sure no one was listening.

"I'll tell you who is screwing," Tawny said conspiratorially, shooting her eyes in the direction of Cole and Madison.

I got a strong whiff of what smelled like rubbing alcohol as Stella took a slurp of the "tonic" Cole had given her. "She can have him," she said. "He's not even good in bed."

"The best-looking ones never are," Tawny chimed in. "They've never had to work for it."

Stella snorted. "Exactly. It's all about him. He couldn't find your clit if you gave him a map."

We all roared with laughter.

"I tell you what," Tawny confided. "I knew I was gonna marry my husband the first time he went down on me. And thirteen years later I'm still glad!"

"You've been married thirteen years?" Felicity balked. "Don't you ever want to be with somebody else?"

Tawny shook her head. "Sure, I recognize an attractive man when I see one, but I know what I've got. He's my best friend. And our kids are pretty cute too."

An unconscionable yearning squeezed my heart. I didn't need anyone; I was totally fine alone—but a best friend who knew where my clit was? Man, that sounded nice.

"Well, you certainly have better taste in men than I do, so cheers to that." Stella raised her glass. By this point, she'd obviously forgotten she was supposed to be sober in front of me, but I didn't care. I knew I *should* care, but we weren't working, and I didn't have it in me today to fight another battle.

Tawny turned her attention to Felicity. "I know you're *just friends*, but look—" She cut her eyes in the direction of Jackson, who was indeed gazing at Felicity from across the bar. Stella waved, and he saluted us. "I mean, I don't know him well, but I can tell he's talented and he seems like a good guy."

"Also hot," Stella pointed out.

"Aaaand he's head over heels for you. Everybody knows it," I added.

"You like him too. I can tell you do!" Stella sang gleefully.

Felicity stared at her, a deer caught in the headlights. "I don't know," she said, all of a sudden uncharacteristically shy. "He's great. I'm not gonna lie... But I'm not looking for a relationship."

"That's when they find you," Tawny chimed in.

"It's more complicated than that," Felicity said. "I can't—"

"Oh," I said, suddenly realizing. "Is there someone at home?"

"Something like that," she said softly, looking into her drink. I sensed a sadness in her and felt perhaps I'd been too quick to judge her before.

"Okay, fine, we'll stop bothering you about it." Tawny squeezed her shoulder. The band started into an upbeat number. "Wanna dance?"

I wasn't normally much of a dancer, but what the hell. I was having fun tonight. We followed Tawny toward the half of the restaurant that had been cleared for the band, where the makeup and wardrobe girls danced with a handful of crew guys and locals. The overhead lights were dark, replaced with rotating colored ones that made for a festive lo-fi scene, and on the far side of the dance floor I immediately spotted Rick, leaning casually against an open window in conversation with Cole.

I didn't like the way I perked up at the sight of him. He smiled and raised his beer to me, but not wanting to give Cole any more ammunition, I pretended not to see and angled my back toward them. Cole was probably telling Rick how I'd gotten blackout drunk and thrown myself at him. Rick was probably laughing at my expense. Suddenly self-conscious, I no longer felt much like dancing, so I made my excuses and threaded my way toward a side exit leading down to the beach.

I wouldn't make a fool of myself over a man again. I was better off alone.

# Stella

Steel drums. Laughter. The burn of tequila in my throat. I preferred gin, but Tawny was funny! I liked this song. *You put the lime in the coconut.* It was the right thing to do. The coconut needed the lime and the lime needed the coconut. And they both needed the rum. The rum! I hadn't fully appreciated rum before. A travesty, really. *Travesty tragedy thespian lesbian tongue twister mama's mister.* I missed doing plays. The stage was where the real art was. And Taylor was nicer than I'd given her credit for. Cole was an asshole to her at the table. What had he said? I couldn't remember, but it wasn't nice. He wasn't a nice person, I remembered that much. Why had he asked me here? Madison could have him. That bitch. It was her who sold that picture of me in the puddle, I knew it was. I saw that atrocious lime-green raincoat—you couldn't miss it. I wanted to dance. The balmy breeze on my skin, the music, and the waves... This was the islands! Steel drums! I should dance. Felicity could read my mind, she was pulling me toward the dance floor. She would be so much better in Madison's role. Red and purple and green lights spinning. I needed to take off my shoes they were in my way, that must be why my limbs felt so slow. This beat was slippery. I moved across the dance floor, and suddenly my drink was on the floor. But no one seemed to mind. It was almost empty anyway. I would clean it up but my head was too heavy. I stumbled, but the wall caught me. The floor was uneven. Was it dark in here, or was it me?

Where was the bathroom? Cole was in the hallway, smiling. He caught me when I tripped. It was the shoes, I explained. You should really replace Madison. I know you're fucking her, but Felicity is so much better, Taylor agrees. Don't you want the movie to be good then you should fire Madison and hire Felicity. He was laughing, but it wasn't a nice laugh. He was saying something about my drink and helping me sit down against the wall. A flash, dots of green. I just wanted to take my shoes off. Oh hell there was Madison had she been there all along? She was an evil doll with empty eyes but my head was so heavy. Sleep. Cole said I needed to sleep right here. His teeth looked like a wolf's.

June 27, 2019

@MadisonMadeit

[PICTURE]

♡ 214,633 likes

Life is good when you get to pucker up to @ColePower and call it work! I don't think he minds either LOL. Having so much fun here at #GenesiusResort shooting #TheSiren. So excited to be starring opposite such a talented #actor!

#actress #model #me #survivor #warrior #blessed #yacht #movie #film #blogger #lifestyle #Madisonblogs #Madisonactress

# Taylor

I sat on a bench outside the entrance to Coco's, facing the sea and nursing my dark mood. The waxing moon was high and the tide was low, the shore only a stone's throw away. The sea gurgled as it raked broken bits of shells back and forth along the beach, oddly in sync with the music wafting through the open windows of the restaurant. I gazed across the moonlit water toward the shimmering lights of Saint Ann, considering whether anyone would notice if I cut out early and snuck back to my bungalow. Behind me, a screen door slammed.

"Hey."

I turned to see Rick, his muscular form backlit as he approached. Great.

"Hi." I gave him a perfunctory smile as he sat next to me, but he saw straight through me.

"Everything cool?"

"Yeah. I just needed a break," I fibbed.

He gave me the side-eye. "Okay."

"It's Cole, if you must know." I sighed. "He said some shit to me that...wasn't very nice."

"Wanna tell me about it?"

I shook my head. "I don't want to give him any more of my time tonight. Was he saying nasty things about me behind my back?"

"I thought you didn't want to give him any more of your time tonight."

I groaned and crossed my arms.

"No, he wasn't," he said. I could feel his eyes on me. "But even if he was, who cares? He's an asshole—you said it yourself."

"Fine." I met his steady gaze and felt the corners of my mouth involuntarily turn up. I couldn't help it. I felt good when I was around him. "No more Cole tonight."

He raised his beer in salute. I grabbed it and took a slug, and he laughed.

"So," I said.

"So."

I looked down at his cargo shorts. "Nice pants."

He noticed my matching pair. "Same. Pockets, right?"

"So useful," I agreed.

He stood and kicked off his flip-flops. "Wanna see something cool?" I knew I shouldn't, but I'd started to feel my mood lighten since he sat next to me, and he was only being friendly, right? I nodded. "This way." He moved down the pathway toward the ocean, and I slipped out of my sandals and followed him.

The breeze was stronger on the beach, away from the shelter of the trees and buildings. I wrapped my arms around myself to stay warm, looking up at the countless glinting stars as we shuffled through the sand. Rick must have noticed me shivering because he stopped walking and shed the button-down denim shirt he wore over his T-shirt, draping it across my shoulders.

"Thanks." The shirt was soft, still warm from his body heat. I slipped my arms through the roomy sleeves, unsure whether the sudden rush of heat I felt was from the extra layer of clothing or the feeling of his hand lingering on my back for a hair too long. We were just friends, taking a beach walk.

"Did you have a good week?" he asked.

I nodded, glad it was too dark for him to see the blush I felt in my cheeks. "After Monday. I kinda yelled at some people on Monday."

His eyes glinted in the moonlight, amused. "Tell me more."

"Just Madison and Stella. They deserved it. Well, Madison did. I've gotten to know Stella a little better, and she's not so bad."

I outlined what had happened as we trekked along the shore, and he assured me I was completely justified in berating them. "That girl with the phone—"

"Madison."

"She's obsessed with herself," he said.

"Yeah." I shuddered. "And her fans reflect it back at her, making her think she's really as important as she thinks she is. It's gross."

"It's not only celebrities who act like that, though," he added. "When I take fishing groups out on the boat, a lot of them don't even care about catching fish. They just want pictures with the fish, so it looks like they caught them. It drives me nuts."

I thought about when I'd driven out to see the super bloom in the California desert a few months ago and found hordes of people with cameras trampling the poppies to take pictures of themselves on the fluorescent orange carpet. As a child, I'd made the annual trek to the Antelope Valley or Santa Monica mountains to see the explosion of color that reappears every spring in Southern California with my mom, and we were always nearly alone on the trails. These days the trails were off-limits, due to crowds of careless Instagrammers who cared nothing about preserving nature. "It's like they're more interested in capturing the moment than experiencing it," I agreed.

"There is no moment. It's all capturing." He laughed.

I thought of JeanieBabie24's myriad bikini pictures and wondered what he thought of his girlfriend posing in a hot-pink thong. Had he shot those pictures? I had to ask him about her. Asking would make her real, make me stop fantasizing about a man who didn't belong to me. So what if he thought I was a crazy stalker? It didn't matter.

"Can I ask you something?" I asked before I could lose my nerve.

"Sure."

I gazed out at the sea, afraid to look at him. "Do you have a girlfriend?"

"No." He stopped walking and turned to me, but I still wouldn't give him my eyes, unsure whether to believe him. "Taylor? What's up?"

"It's...well, you were mentioned in one of the resort's pictures on Instagram, so I clicked on your profile, and I saw you were tagged—"

"Jeanette." He sighed. So that was JeanieBabie24's real name. "She's not my girlfriend. She's friends with a group of people I know, the younger half sister of a guy I went to school with. We dated, sort of, but not for long before I realized she wasn't—we weren't a fit. She's a sweet girl but misguided and she—we just don't have anything in common."

I frowned. I wanted to believe him, but... "But she was posting pictures of you guys together last week."

He nodded. "That was from months ago. She posts all these pictures of me—some she takes directly off my account. I've asked her to stop, but she says it's to make some guy jealous, or that she just liked the picture. I don't want to hurt her, and she's my friend's sister, so I don't know, I kinda gave up worrying about it. But I can see...how it looks a certain way."

We'd reached the end of the beach, where a path led up a small hill into the trees. "I wouldn't be here with you right now if I had a girlfriend," he said. "I'm not that kind of guy."

If he wouldn't be here with me if he had a girlfriend, did that mean what I thought it meant? I finally looked at him then, and his eyes were clear. He wasn't Rory or Cole, and he wasn't looking for a friend or a piece on the side or a fuck buddy. I wasn't sure why or what exactly he was looking for, but this guy was telling me point-blank he was interested in me. Heat bloomed in my chest and tingled all the way down my arms. I smiled, miraculously keeping my voice light. "Cool."

He returned my smile and jerked his head toward the path into the trees. "It's dark, but worth it, I promise," he said, holding his hand out to me.

I took it, aware of nothing but the touch of his skin against mine as we hiked along the shadowy trail. His palm was smooth with calluses, his grip firm. Everything about him was strong, steadying, solid. *And he doesn't have a girlfriend.* The world was suddenly full of possibility.

When we came out of the trees on the other side of the hill, I gasped. The bay before us was lit from within by an otherworldly blue-green light. The glimmering fluorescence was stronger around the edges and along the floating dock that stretched into the water.

"Firefly Bay," he said, sweeping his arm out at the bay.

"It's beautiful," I breathed.

"Bioluminescence," he explained. "The tiny plankton glow when they move or touch anything. They're especially bright tonight because the water's still disturbed from the storm. Watch this."

He walked out into the shallow water, ripples of eerie blue light cascading around his calves as he moved. "Is it safe to be in it?" I asked.

"Sure," he said.

I slowly walked toward him, dragging my feet through the warm sea to produce glowing waves. "This is incredible!" I trailed my hand through the water, amazed by the electric glimmer it produced. "The water's so warm, it's like bathwater."

"Yeah," he said, his face darkening. "It's a little too warm. Not a good sign for this time of year."

"Why?"

"Hurricane conditions."

I stared at him. "Are you serious?"

He tilted his head, amused. "You do realize you're in the Caribbean during hurricane season."

"But it's June," I protested. "Everyone assured us hurricanes never show up until August."

"Typically. But climate change is warming the water, bringing them earlier and making them bigger."

"Oh God." I pressed the heels of my hands to my eyes, the beauty of the bay suddenly forgotten. "A hurricane would end us."

"Not necessarily," he said. "We're far enough south that we don't usually get hit as hard. We more often get the beginning stages of a hurricane—a tropical storm or category one or two, before they turn and eviscerate our neighbors to the north."

"How do you live here, knowing everything could be destroyed?"

He laughed. "At least we don't have earthquakes and fires."

"Touché."

"We build to withstand storms the same way you build to withstand earthquakes. With the exception of those over-water bungalows and—well, a lot of the older, less expensively built buildings. But I love it here. The people, the ocean...I came back for a reason."

He seemed so at home here in his shorts and sunglasses with his perennial grin, it was hard to imagine him anywhere else. "You came back?"

"I went to college in Philadelphia, then lived in New York for a couple of years."

I gaped at him. "The city?"

He laughed at my shock. "I was in banking," he explained. "Wore suits every day. Never worked less than twelve hours."

I blinked at him, picturing him in a crisp suit in the snow. "Wow. I'm trying to imagine you in that world, and I have to admit, it's hard."

"It was hard," he agreed. "But I'd grown up seeing the rich bankers that kept their money in offshore accounts down here, so I figured if I wanted to be rich, I needed to go into banking."

"How'd that work out for ya?"

"I did make a lot of money—enough that it was difficult to give up even though I was miserable. And cold. So, so cold." He shivered.

"What made you come back here? Besides being cold."

He swept his hand through the glowing water. "Short story? I realized I'd become someone I didn't want to be."

"Long story?" I asked.

"My mom got sick. I came down for her first round of chemo. My sisters were frustrated with me because I was here, but I wasn't *here*—I was on my phone all the time, stressed about work. One night I was complaining to my mom that my siblings didn't understand—I made more money than all of them combined; that meant sacrifice. She said"—he cleared his throat, raised his voice an octave, and put on an island accent far thicker than his own—"'That is fine, Ricky. Just be sure you are not sacrificing the thing you desire most in the world.'" He laughed and shook his head. "She always knows exactly what to say to me."

"So when did you move back?"

"About five years ago. I sold all the bullshit, gave up the friends who only cared how much money I made. Down here, I had enough cash to live off for a long time, but I wanted to be around people and do something I enjoyed, so I started running boats and planes."

"And are you happier?"

He swung his arm out at the ocean. "What do you think?"

I thought a lot of things, not all of them G-rated, looking at this handsome man so comfortable in his own skin. "I think you're brave," I said. "To know what you want and give up the things society tells you you're supposed to desire to live your best life—I wish I could do that. I give you mad props."

He high-fived my raised palm. "Thanks. I'd love to show you my house sometime, if you want."

I wanted very much. "What's it like?"

"It's old—nearly a hundred years—but it was built well, and I've put in a lot of upgrades. It sits on top of a hill looking over the ocean, so it gets a nice breeze, and there's a sundeck on the roof. My sisters tease me though, because I live like a bachelor."

I laughed, brazenly laying a hand on his arm. "Lemme guess, a big TV and a brown couch, nothing on the walls?"

"The couch is blue, and my mom paints, so I have a lot of pictures of boats and flowers. And a wall of books, though I can't claim they're high literature or anything."

"What do you like to read?"

"Thrillers, mysteries." He shrugged. "Books with men and boats in them."

"Makes sense," I said. We'd been moving ever closer to each other as we talked, so that now our faces were only inches apart.

"What about you?" he asked.

The wind blew my hair into my face, and he tucked it behind my ear for me, brushing my cheek with his fingertips as he did. My skin buzzed where he'd touched it. "I like... This is a secret. You promise you won't tell?"

He locked his amber eyes on mine, and for once I didn't force myself to look away. "Promise."

"I like romance novels," I whispered. "The trashier, the better."

He tossed his head back in laughter. "I would never have guessed it." He placed a hand on my hip and once again found my gaze. "You are a surprise, you know that?"

"You too," I murmured.

This was a bad idea. I shouldn't get involved with someone while I was working. I needed to stay focused. This was a distraction. I needed to...

And his lips were on mine. Soft and smooth and strong, like him. His powerful arms were around me, our bodies pressed together, the bay glowing all around us. It was magical. Terribly, horribly magical. And absolutely wonderful.

My back pocket vibrated, and the ringer cut into the stillness. I didn't want to get it. I wanted to throw the damn phone in the sea and never answer it again. But I couldn't do that. Look at me. I was already distracted by this man beyond repair.

"You need to get that?" he asked, his breath hot on my neck.

I sighed, reluctantly reaching for my back pocket. "Yeah."

He smiled at my hesitation. "I'm not going anywhere."

The display showed it was Kara, the script supervisor. What could she want at this hour? "Hi, Kara," I answered.

"Taylor?"

"Yeah?"

"It's Stella. She's super wasted, I think." Her voice sounded distraught. "I found her slumped against the wall by the bathrooms and dragged her outside. I don't know what to do."

"Where are you?" I asked.

"By the bench on the beach side of the restaurant."

"I'll be right there."

I hung up the phone and put it back in my pocket. "We gotta go back," I said regretfully. "Stella's apparently trashed."

"She seemed fine last time I saw her," he said as we tromped out of the water and toward the path leading back to the restaurant. "But that was probably an hour ago."

"She has issues with substances," I said. "So...who knows."

He led me by the hand through the trees and back to the ironshore beach. We hurried across the sand to the restaurant, where Kara sat next to Stella's slumped form on the bench.

"What happened to her?" Rick asked as we approached, sliding in next to Stella and slipping his arm around her to sit her up. She wasn't quite unconscious, but her head lolled at an odd angle and she couldn't keep her eyes open.

"I don't know," Kara said. "I found her like this. I brought her out here because I figured she could use some fresh air."

"Thank you," I said, impressed that birdlike Kara had managed to carry Stella out here on her own. "Where's Felicity?"

"Not sure. I think I saw her leave with Jackson. That's why I called you."

I assessed Stella. "Could she have hit her head or something?"

Stella's eyes fluttered as Rick inspected her head. "She doesn't have any marks," he said. She didn't resist as he pulled back each eyelid, turning her face to the light. "Her pupils look normal. What was she drinking?"

"Gin, I think," I said. "She takes pills too. Maybe it's the way they mixed with the alcohol?"

"We should probably make her throw up if we can," Rick said.

"Not here," I said, checking over my shoulder to make sure Madison wasn't lurking in the shadows with her cell phone. "She'll be mortified if anyone sees her like this."

Rick scooped her up easily and carried her away from the hubbub of the restaurant, past the benches and onto the shadowy beach. I called Felicity. She answered on the first ring. "Taylor. What's up?"

"Where are you?"

"In the port."

Thank God this island was so small. "Can you come to the beach on the other side of the jetty? Stella's really wasted."

I waved from the pathway to the beach when Felicity came running around the front of the building two minutes later with Jackson hot on her heels. "Sorry. She was fine when I left her." She dropped to her knees next to Stella. "Where's her bag?"

Kara handed Felicity Stella's purse, and Felicity rifled through it, extracting a little blue pouch. She unzipped the pouch and removed four different-colored pill holders, carefully counting the pills in each.

"She hasn't taken any extra pills," Felicity said. "And her regular medication shouldn't interact this badly with alcohol."

"This badly?" I asked.

Felicity sat in the sand next to Stella, who rested her head in her lap. "I do my best to moderate, but she drinks. Often heavily, on more pills than she's on right now. And she doesn't become this incoherent. She's got a tolerance like a horse."

"How many drinks did she have tonight?" Rick asked.

"One, as far as I know, and a shot of tequila," Felicity replied.

"Who gave her the drink?" Jackson asked.

"Cole," I said.

Rick raised his brows, and we all exchanged a weighted glance.

"Dear old Dad," Jackson said bitterly. "I wouldn't put it past him."

"But *why?*" I asked.

Felicity looked up at me. "Same reason he said that shit to you tonight."

"To flex his power." Jackson clenched his jaw. "It's mind games. He's played them with me my entire life."

"Shit," Kara breathed. "I mean, I knew he was a dick, but...wow."

"I should never have taken his money," Jackson muttered. "Maybe I should pull the plug on this thing."

"Don't make any decisions tonight," Felicity said.

"She's right," I agreed. "And talk to Stella first. Maybe she remembers something or has different ideas about what happened. This is all just conjecture right now."

I talked a good line, but the memory of my own inexplicable blackout with Cole had reared its ugly head. Had I not overindulged that evening at all but been drugged by my boss? And if he'd drugged me, what else had he done to me? I desperately wanted to dismiss the idea, but the jack had popped out of the box.

# Part IV:

# Advisory

# Felicity

*Eighteen Months Ago*

Beyond a guarded, unmarked door in a dead-end alley a stone's throw from the tourists and junkies that trample the stars of Hollywood Boulevard, the walls of the dimly lit club shudder with throbbing bass. The beat reverberates through my platform stilettos and up my legs under my black leather minidress, where it quivers beneath my skin in sync with the pounding of my heart. The vibration shakes loose my thoughts, rattling them around in my head until they're as soft as powdered sugar; a trip to the dance floor melts them into sweet perspiration on my glistening skin.

I don't need to work at the Ninth Circle. My mother's lump of cash has only grown with wise investments in crypto.

But I can lose myself here.

The darkness and the drums negate the need for idle chitchat, and combined with the drugs and alcohol, allow a loosening of inhibition that compels authenticity. This is the place where the id comes to play.

I sling bottles of alcohol at more than ten times the price you'd pay in a store, with a side of fruit juice and a heavy dose of cleavage. Sometimes the customers get handsy (the women as often as the men), but I don't mind. Like Iris said, I'm selling a fantasy. I give them just enough of what it is they need—to feel sexy, special, wanted—then I retreat to my doorman building in West Hollywood and watch the sun come up from my balcony with a view all the way to the Pacific Ocean.

That's not to say I don't occasionally go home with one if he strikes my fancy—to his place, never mine, and I never stay overnight. If he comes back to the club hoping for another round, I make it clear that's impossible. If he doesn't get the hint, I have Marty throw him out. Marty's had more than his share of my body, but it's a fair exchange; he keeps me safe. Anyway, he's sexy in a Jason Statham way when he's not too drunk, and he never asks questions. I'm twenty-one now, but I've been working here off the record nearly two years, and I've never had to so much as show an ID.

I started at the Ninth Circle because I'd heard from a girl in my acting class that it was where Cole hung out. She'd apparently met him there the first time she slept with him. Yes, I take acting classes. Not because I still dream of becoming a movie star—I've long since given that up in favor of exacting revenge on my mother's killer—but because I have to be convincing in whatever role I need to play to achieve that goal.

Cole's an easier target than Stella, who had a rough ride in the years following my mother's death and has become somewhat of a recluse since the meat grinder of public opinion spat her out. Also, men like Cole are so simple. They all want one thing. I figured I'd meet Cole and worm my way into his life, find out what really happened to my mother, then figure out what to do about it. But around the time of my arrival, he took off for London to shoot a movie. After that, he went to rehab, then he got a sober girlfriend, and on like this for over a year.

Until tonight.

I spied him the moment he walked in, running his silver-ringed fingers through those famous dark locks. He was dressed in black—leather jacket, ripped jeans, motorcycle boots—traveling with a good-looking younger actor I recognized and another guy in a suit who was probably an agent or a producer or something. He didn't scan the room the way guests usually do as the velvet door closes behind them;

he didn't need to. Everyone continued right on dancing or drinking or hustling without any indication they'd registered the newly arrived star, but they knew he was there, and they were glad.

Celebrities are a common occurrence in the Ninth Circle—what it's known for even. It's a place they can go and fly under the radar, not be bothered or photographed while they let their hair down. Everyone's beautiful; everyone's cool. And yet each time a celebrity passes beneath the pink neon sign warning "Abandon all hope, ye who enter here," the energy in the room surges. On a night when multiple celebrities are in attendance, the electricity is palpable. This is one of those nights.

But I don't care about the others; I only want Cole.

I've imagined this moment so many times in the eleven years since I woke up motherless in the hospital; I should be ready. But I am in no way prepared for the onslaught of emotions that crashes over me as I saunter over to his table, my heart pounding harder than the bass that shakes the walls of the cave-like club.

Suddenly I'm eighteen again, climbing out of Fred's truck at the bus depot on a warm June evening, my suitcase in hand, the urn of my mother's ashes wrapped carefully among my clothes. I'd been touched they let me take her with me, surprised by the hard-earned $500 they gave me for graduation, moved they waited until the 180 West pulled out of the station, waving as we chugged away into the sunset. But I was so glad the Pennsylvania chapter of my life was over.

I slept fitfully on the bus through the night and got off in the morning somewhere in southern Illinois, where I dragged my roller bag down the road to a used car lot and bought a ten-year-old gold Accord with my pile of cash. Iris had always said Japanese cars never die. I drove recklessly across Missouri and Oklahoma with the windows down, eating kettle corn from a bag between my knees. I talked my way out of my first speeding ticket in Albuquerque, twirling my long blond ponytail nervously while allowing tears to pool in my big blue eyes. "I'm going to Hollywood to become an actress," I pleaded. "I only have enough money to get me through the first week till I can find a job. If I get a ticket, well—I'll have to go back home."

He caved.

When I got to Hollywood, it was love at first sight. The palm trees, the strip malls, the sunshine, the seediness. Los Angeles is awash in contradictions, a place where you can find a star who makes twenty mil a picture in line at a two-dollar taco stand with its sign written in Korean. Nobody cares who you are or where you came from unless you're a celebrity, in which case they care very, very much—but only as it applies to them. It's such an unabashedly selfish city. The last bastion of the Wild West, where anything can happen.

I promptly paid an exorbitant amount of money for a mostly clean apartment on the first floor of an old stucco building, got a job as a waitress at a café around the corner, and began taking advantage of all the city had to offer: acting lessons to change my personality on a dime, makeup classes to alter my appearance at will, Krav Maga to protect myself. Posing as an actor researching a role for a film, I befriended a pharmacist and learned the dosages and combinations of pills to induce sleep or cause death. I bought a 9mm Beretta and practiced at the shooting range downtown while cops in the next lane looked on, impressed with my steadily improving aim.

I didn't want to know anyone and didn't want anyone to know me, but I found it difficult not to make friends. For a place as cutthroat as LA, everyone was so incredibly friendly. I didn't show up for parties, turned down invitations to premieres and lunches and dinners with people's parents visiting from out of town, kept my romantic entanglements to one-night stands; still I was gifted random succulents and free Reiki sessions.

I resolved to move when my lease came up every year to prevent the neighbors from growing too attached and used an ever-changing stage name: Jasmine James became Olivia O'Hara became my current handle, Nikki Nimes. Everybody out here uses stage names anyway, so no one bats an eye when you christen yourself with a different moniker than the one your parents chose. I'm not a spy; I don't have a stash of false passports and wigs, but with each name change comes a new backstory and a makeover that includes a fashion overhaul as well as an eye color and hairstyle switch. I also swap acting studios every semester to evade my fellow thespians—although I have discovered that actors make the most suitable friends, so self-centered they rarely remember anything about you.

If I want to accomplish my goal—whatever it turns out to be—I have to be a blank slate, ready to take on whatever identity I need to succeed. I've achieved that mostly; with the exception of Marty and this one girl Lacey, who's worked at the Ninth Circle longer and probably has more to hide than me, I'm pretty much anonymous.

And now, nearly three years since I drew my first breath on the West Coast, Cole Power is finally in my crosshairs.

I catch my reflection in the gilded mirror above his table as I stand before him in the pool where the blue and pink lights converge, illuminating my body in their glow.

"Jesus," Cole says, staring up at me. "If I'd known they'd started hiring girls that looked like you, I'd have been back sooner."

*This may be easier than I thought.* "That's very kind of you." I lean down so that my boobs nearly spill out of my low-cut dress, right at eye level. "What can I get you guys to start tonight?"

"I'm a whiskey kinda guy myself, but get whatever you want." He doesn't even make an attempt to pretend he's not staring at my chest. "You're having a drink with us."

"Thank you," I purr, ever so lightly touching his knee. "So a bottle of Dom Pérignon and a bottle of Johnnie Walker—Black, Red, Blue?"

"Blue, as long as I can take it home with me." His eyes lock on mine. He raises an eyebrow. There is no subtlety in the gesture. He's brazen. No one's that brazen recently. Even the slimiest are more subdued of late, jolted by the sudden flare of the #metoo movement. But not Cole Power.

"I'm sure you know that's not allowed." I smile. "But if no one notices…" I shrug, allowing my spaghetti strap to slip from my shoulder.

"Perfect," he says. His fingertips linger on my arm as he brushes my strap back onto my shoulder.

It takes every ounce of self-control not to recoil at his touch. "Thanks." I bite my lip. "These dresses weren't made to stay on."

I cringe at the terribly cheesy line I've used an embarrassing number of times, but he swallows it whole, handing me a black card with a gleam in his eye. "Close it out and bring it back or I'll forget it. And give yourself an extra five hundred on top of whatever this place usually charges."

Wow, he is confident. Usually they don't tip until they're walking out the door—insurance you'll give them your phone number…or whatever else they might want. At the computer, Lacey looks over my shoulder while I run his card. "Ooh, Blue label and an extra bottle of champagne, good one." She flips a strand of her silky weave over her shoulder as she eyes him across the dance floor. "He likes you."

"He'd like you too if you were standing in front of him," I return.

She laughs, adjusting her boobs under her leather dress to show more cleavage. "Yeah, he's not too picky. I did that already though, years ago. Coke dick." She makes a face. "And he kept licking me and making comments about my *chocolate* skin I think he thought were compliments but were actually kinda racist."

I laugh. "Yeah, he hit on me more blatantly than I've been hit on in weeks."

"Can't teach an old dog new tricks." She winks. "Good luck."

The knot in the pit of my stomach tightens. She's totally right. What do I really think is going to happen? He's gonna take me back to his place and tell me all about how his ex-wife murdered my mother? Then cop to wrecking her car into a tree and fleeing the scene of the accident?

No. He's gonna take me home to screw me, then kick me out before the sun comes up.

My head swims.

While I'm not a sex worker like my mother was, I can usually separate myself from my body. But I won't go there with Cole. It's not possible. He turns every drop of blood in my body to ice.

I didn't realize what a visceral reaction I'd have to him when I finally met him. I'm completely thrown. Every decision I've made in the past ten years has been in preparation for this moment, and now that it's here, all of my plans seem so incredibly silly. Like something out of a spy novel. Who do I think I am, a Red Sparrow? Am I going to escort him out of the club to the flashing of the paparazzi, march right past the security guards and cameras at his luxury high-rise condo, and kill him?

I don't have my gun on me, but I do have sleeping pills in my purse; I could crush them up and put them in his drink. It would be easy enough to slit his throat once he was asleep.

The thought makes me queasy. If I knew for sure he was responsible for my mother's death, I could probably do it. I killed a deer once, hunting with Fred. He was so proud, he marked my cheeks with its blood and told all his friends how brave I was. I acted cool, but every time we ate venison that winter, I thought of the light fading from the buck's eyes as he gasped for breath before Fred shot him in the back of the skull, spattering my camouflage pants with warm blood.

If I killed Cole, I'd not only carry that weight the rest of my incarcerated life, but I'd never find out what happened to my mother. And what of Stella? She's likely more to blame for Iris's death than Cole.

It's too haphazard, too wasteful.

I follow the busboy to Cole's table, where a couple of hot girls have taken up residence between the other actor and Cole. Cole pays them no attention, never taking his eyes off me as I pour two tumblers of Scotch neat, then pop the cork on the champagne and hand each of the girls a flute.

"Here." Cole pours a glass of champagne and holds it out to me. "Sit." He pats the leather banquette beside him.

I take the glass and sit next to him, suddenly realizing that any interaction I have with him infringes on my future ability to get close to him. I have a role in his life now, albeit a walk-on one, as the waitress at the Ninth Circle. I clink my glass to his, desperately trying to figure out how to extricate myself from the situation.

"What's your name?" he asks.

"Nikki," I say. "What's yours?"

He laughs that throaty chuckle I've heard so many times on-screen. "Cole. Are you an actress, Nikki?" He leans toward me, his hair falling in his eyes. His breath is whiskey and smoke. "Or a model?"

"Neither." It's plenty dark, and he's drunk enough maybe he won't remember me at all. Surely I'm but a drop in the bucket of beautiful girls thrown at him every day.

"You should be." He places his hand on my thigh, his fingers creeping beneath my skirt. "You have the face for it."

I lay my hand on his. "Not here." He meets my gaze, and a flicker of recognition passes over his face. He shakes his head as if to rid himself of the thought. "What?" I ask.

"Nothing. It's just..." He furrows his brow. "You remind me of someone."

My breath grows shallow; the noise of the room subsides. "Who?"

"Just a girl I knew a long time ago. No one famous. But she was beautiful, like you."

"Was she important to you?" I ask, acutely aware that at the moment my hair is long and blond like my mother's once was, my eyes their natural blue.

For a split second his attention drifts, as though lost in memory; then he's back. "No."

I swallow the urge to strangle him, doing my best to hold my voice steady. "What happened to her?"

"Nothing," he says. "It's not important." He downs his drink. "Let's get out of here."

I force a smile but can't quite meet his eye. "Give me ten."

I rise and shimmy across the dance floor to the computer, where I find Lacey typing away at her phone. I grab her hand and tug her through the door marked "Employees Only."

"Need your help escaping," I say, flinging open the door to my locker.

"Cole?"

I nod, pulling on my jacket. "He wants me to go home with him, but that's not happening. I'm gonna get out of here before it turns into a thing. Can you close out my other tables? Keep the tips. Tell Marty I'm sorry."

She nods. "No problem. We can split the tips."

I shoulder my bag and give her a hug. "Not necessary."

"See you tomorrow," she calls as I push open the door to the alley.

But she won't. I'm not coming in tomorrow, or next week, or the week after that. The Ninth Circle has served its purpose. Nikki Nimes is burned. It's time for me to move on.

# Stella

*Friday, June 28*

I awoke to searing pain and murky blue darkness. An indigo trellis of liquid reflection wavered on the ceiling above me, in sync with the hollow sound of water swashing against something solid. I tried to sit up, but the burning sword through my brain held me in place. I heard my voice cry out—strangled, weak.

A hand on my arm. A bolt of fear shot through me as I turned to face my assailant in the dark, my voice stolen by the breathtaking pain of movement. Her profile was outlined by the flickering electric blue, her eyes two pricks of light in the gloaming, but I'd know her anywhere. My blood froze in my veins.

Iris.

Her hair was pulled back, and she was wearing the same aquamarine dress as when I last saw her thirteen years ago, looking not a day older. Was she here to torture me from beyond the grave? I tried to call out, but her name stuck in my throat. Surely I must be dreaming. But the pain...

She rolled away from me to turn on the bedside lamp, and the room flooded with light. I rubbed the sleep from my eyes.

I was in my bed, next to Felicity. She was wearing a turquoise night-gown, her hair gathered into a short ponytail, and the eerie blue glow had been the effect of the light beneath the bungalow on the water through the glass floor, which she must have forgotten to turn off. I blinked at her, disoriented.

"Are you okay?" she asked.

I closed my eyes, the vision still clear in my mind, Iris's face grafted on to Felicity's, so similar but for their coloring. I'd noticed a passing resemblance before but quickly dismissed it as my hazy, overactive imagination playing tricks on me. Now I tried to conjure up an image of Felicity without those bangs and the ever-present kohl liner around her eyes, picturing her tresses longer and blonder and her irises lighter...but my brain throbbed with the effort. Perhaps the differences were what made the imagined likeness so strong anyway.

"My head," I managed. The agony of speaking released a shower of stars across my vision. I was soaked in sweat quickly cooling in the blasting air-conditioner, my heart sprinting like it was being chased. "What happened last night?"

"Tonight," she corrected me, looking at the clock on the bedside table. "It's four a.m."

Mary Elizabeth uncurled from her post at the foot of the bed and gingerly approached, sniffing my clammy skin. The bungalow seemed to rock with the waves, churning in sync with my stomach.

Felicity must have been able to tell I was about to be sick because she jumped out of bed and rushed around to my side, where she grabbed the plastic garbage can next to the bed and held it up for me to retch in.

The retching did not make me feel better.

"Can you run me a bath?" I managed.

I stared at the wide woven blades of the motionless ceiling fan as she drew the bath, begging the room to stop spinning, the knife to stop stabbing.

Iris, here. So real I could reach out and touch her.

But she was long gone.

All of this unearthing of the past clearly wasn't good for my psyche.

But I had to keep it to myself. If anyone found out I was seeing ghosts, they'd throw me in the looney bin again. A health spa, they'd called it. Yeah, right. It might've cost an arm and a leg and had posh linens and a pool, but as far as I knew health spas didn't come with shrinks, unlockable doors, and ninety-day sentences. I couldn't go back there. I had to pull myself together.

The dreaded sense that something bad had happened lurked just out of reach in the shadows of my mind, but I was too weak to attempt to shine any light on it; I could taste the bile in my throat but lacked the strength to reach for the bottle of water on the bedside table. I focused on the sensation of Mary Elizabeth's small, dry tongue licking my hand.

Felicity supported me from the bed to the bathroom sink, where I gurgled mouthwash and downed Tylenol with a glass of water before she peeled my sweat-soaked clothes from my aching body and helped me into the bath. The water was deliciously hot and full of bubbles that smelled of lavender. I sank into the silence beneath the water, holding my breath until I felt Felicity's hand beneath my neck, pulling me up to sitting.

"Don't drown on me," she said.

I took a deep breath. The knife was still in my brain, but it no longer burned. "What happened to me?" I asked again.

"I don't know," she said. "One minute you were fine; then Kara found you slumped on the floor outside the bathroom."

"Where?"

"Coco's. You don't remember?"

Coco's. Right. It was murky, but I at least remembered being there. Everyone had been there. Damn. "Who saw me?"

She twisted her mouth into a frown. "I don't know. I was outside when it happened."

"Why did you leave me?"

"You were fine! It happened so fast. I'd gone for a short walk around the harbor with Jackson when Taylor called to say you were incoherent."

Oh God. "Taylor was there?"

She nodded. I sank into the silence beneath the bubbles again, wishing I could stay there forever.

When I surfaced, Felicity was holding a fresh glass of water. I drank it obediently. "Was Madison there?" She shook her head, and I let out a sigh of relief. "Thank heavens. Who else was there?" I asked.

"Rick and Jackson. We took you away from the bar so no one would see, and I made you throw up."

I groaned, imagining the scene. What they must think of me. "How?"

"I stuck my finger down your throat."

So it was over. Surely I'd be fired now. I'd squandered my chance at redemption and would be punished, tossed back into the void. Worse: shamed.

I sank into the womb of the bath. I couldn't face another round in the stockade. I wouldn't survive another public stoning. It had taken every ounce of my strength to pull myself through these thirteen years. I'd lost my career, my love, my friends. All I had left was my little dog and the fleeting reprieve provided by pills and booze—nothing more than small Band-Aids holding back a river of blood. I wasn't stupid. I knew the Band-Aids only made the wound worse in the long run, that I would eventually bleed out if things didn't turn around for me someday. All that had kept me going was hope for that day. Without it, I was finished.

Felicity's hand beneath my back. Air. And then she was lifting me out of the bath, wrapping me in a soft white robe, and guiding me to the bed.

# XRAY ONLINE

## BREAKING:
## STELLA RIVERS CAN'T KEEP HER ACT TOGETHER

Stella Rivers has been shooting *The Siren* with ex-husband, Cole Power, on the Caribbean island of Saint Genesius for only two weeks, and she appears to have already fallen off the wagon. Sources tell us a stipulation of her contract was that she remain sober for the duration of the shoot, but this morning a photo surfaced of her clearly inebriated and slumped against the wall of a local bar. Rumors of Power and Rivers rekindling their romance were swirling until a few days ago, when a video of Power laughing at her as she fell into a puddle came to light. Then last night influencer/actress Madison Kasabian posted a selfie kissing Cole Power. The kiss was on the cheek(!) but has everyone speculating that Power has turned his attention to his younger costar, leaving Rivers out in the cold. Looks like the beleaguered Rivers is once again drowning her sorrows.

# Taylor

ar too early the morning after Coco's, I awoke feeling as though a bomb had gone off in my head. Burning rage toward Cole mixed with the lingering effects of alcohol and lust for Rick made a firestorm that set my heart racing. I tossed and turned, fully aware I needed to sleep as late as humanly possible in preparation for our night shoot that evening, but it was no use.

At some point I gave in to the idea that going back to sleep wasn't going to happen and lounged half-conscious in bed with the blackout shades drawn, alternately reliving my kiss with Rick and imagining confronting Cole. I would be devastating, ripping apart his ideas about who he was and how the world saw him. I would write a scathing article exposing his true nature, which would turn the public against him, and he would be out in the cold where he belonged—if only I could prove what he'd done...and I were brave enough. Around mid-morning, the Tilt-A-Whirl of emotions gave way to a caffeine headache that forced me out of my cocoon to make a cup of coffee.

I took my mug outside and settled on a shaded lounger overlooking the miles and miles of turquoise sea. The day was still and bright, and a delicious breeze blew off the water. Next door, Brian and two other guys were having a contest to see who could jump farthest off the bungalow balcony into the sea, while overhead the gulls called to one another. I had to admit the place was growing on me, and not only because of a certain tall, dark stranger. That bioluminescent bay last night had been mind-blowing of its own accord. And the kiss...

I distracted myself from the cocktail of desire and rage coursing through my veins by opening the real estate app Rick had told me about and scrolling through homes on Saint Ann while allowing the morning sun to caress my lily-white legs. Obviously I wasn't looking to move to the islands, but it was crazy to see what I'd be able to afford if I were so inclined. For the price of my condo, I could buy a beachfront home twice its size and have money left to furnish it beautifully. It was fun to daydream, anyway. Gave me a reprieve from the shit storm that was *being in the employ of Cole Power.*

Fuck Cole Power. The very thought of him made me want to scream in fury. I yearned to feel my fist smash into his perfect jaw.

Once my legs were sufficiently pink, I indulged in a lingering shower, allowing the hot water to loosen the muscles in my sore lower back. I was dragging. Last night, Rick, Jackson, Felicity, and I had sat out on the porch of Stella and Felicity's bungalow talking for far too long after Rick carried Stella home and installed her in bed. Jackson strummed a guitar, playing songs we could all sing along to while fish jumped out in the water. Rick and I had played it cool in front of them, of course, and Jackson had walked out with us when we finally left, so I couldn't exactly invite him in. It was better that way, anyway. I needed to keep it in the road—and after the realization that Cole had likely drugged me, I was preoccupied to say the least.

When I'd asked Jackson why he'd agreed to let his father finance his film, he grimaced. "He wanted me to believe he'd changed, that he wanted a relationship with his son, and this was his way of making up for all the years of prioritizing his career and women and—hell, anything—above me. I accepted on that premise." He swirled the rum in the bottom of his glass, then downed it. "I'm not an idiot though. I knew the chances he'd somehow done a one-eighty when I wasn't looking were slim, but I figured the one thing my father can give me is a career. I'll take it." He cut his eyes toward the bedroom where Stella slept. "But not if it comes at someone else's expense."

We all agreed that we clearly couldn't allow Cole to go around drugging people and God knows what else, but I insisted that we hold off making any decisions until we consulted with Stella in the morning. I longed to share my undeniably similar blackout experience, but I knew it would likely be the final straw, and selfishly, I didn't want Jackson to pull the plug on the film for the sake of my own welfare.

I was ashamed of my cowardice; I admired women who called out their abusive bosses and sorely wished I were brave enough to join their ranks. But I knew if I spoke out against Cole, my prior alleged indiscretions would resurface and no one would believe me. And regardless of whether I spoke out, if I left Power Pictures I'd be jobless again, with nothing to show for these torturous months working for Cole—and no prospects.

Neither of these options was in the least bit appetizing; hence my escapist fantasy of looking at property on Saint Ann. I'd never really considered living in a small town, let alone on an island—and hadn't actually spent any time on Saint Ann, of course. But that didn't stop me from dreaming up a fictitious life on what (according to Rick) was an idyllic Caribbean island with a population of nearly 100,000, a lively town center, and a state-of-the-art hospital. I could...I wasn't sure what I could do; all my job skills were film-related. Maybe I'd run a small production company, produce locally? It was the kind of thing that would have depressed me to no end five years ago, but I had to admit was sounding better and better of late. But I was getting way ahead of myself. It was purely a fantasy.

I'd just emerged from the steam-filled bathroom when there was a knock at my door. "Who is it?" I called.

"Francisco."

I pulled on a robe and swung open the door. He was wearing a short-sleeved button-down, his hair pomaded to perfection, as usual. I cringed to think what a mess I must look, but he was scrolling through his phone. "Sorry to bother you," he said without looking up. "You weren't answering your phone."

"What's up?" I asked, concerned.

He clicked on something and handed me his phone. The blog picture was of Stella, slumped against the wall next to the bathroom at Coco's last night, and the caption read "Stella Rivers Can't Keep Her Act Together."

"Shit," I said.

"The insurance rep has already called," he said gravely.

I frowned. "Can you get Jackson and Stella over here as soon as possible?"

"Not Cole?"

"Not Cole," I confirmed.

He saluted. "Got it."

I barely had time to pull on clothes before Stella turned up looking like death warmed over despite her carefully made-up face, Felicity at her side.

"I need her." Stella gestured to Felicity as she entered without removing her sunglasses. She winced at the sunlight streaming through the wall of glass overlooking the calm sea. "Can we...?" She made a half-hearted gesture in the direction of the windows.

I hit the switch that lowered the transparent mahogany sunshade. "Blackout shades too?" I asked.

She sank onto the couch. "No, that's fine." She kicked off her sandals and curled up with her head on a turquoise silk pillow.

I pressed a cup of coffee into her hands and instructed Felicity to brew another pot while I opened the door to Jackson. He crept over to Stella like she was a dog that had been mistreated and might bite; I half expected him to extend his hand palm-up before squatting next to her.

"How you doing?" he asked quietly.

"I'm hungover, not dying," she said. "Though I feel like I'm dying."

He patted her hand with sympathy, and she recoiled. "Go sit. You're creeping me out."

Felicity giggled and perched at the end of the couch, catching Jackson's eye as he moved to a chair. I took the seat opposite him. "You've all seen the photos?" I asked.

Everyone nodded.

"We have to figure out how we want to play it with the insurance," I went on.

"Or whether we pull the plug," Jackson interrupted, tucking a strand of dark hair behind his ear.

This roused Stella. "Pull the plug?" she asked, sitting up. "Why?"

He looked at her incredulously. "Because my father drugged you last night?"

"Cole's an asshole." She shrugged. "It's no reason to can the film."

"What he did was criminal," Jackson protested.

"And we have no proof it was him," Stella pointed out. "The bigger question is who leaked the picture. I'm guessing Madison. I saw her in the crowd the day I fell in the puddle, and that picture was leaked too. She's so desperate for fame, she probably has some deal where she sends unflattering pictures of me in return for them printing flattering pictures of her."

Jackson furrowed his brow. "So you don't care that he drugged you?"

Stella finally took off her sunglasses and looked him in the eye. "I made twenty thousand dollars last year. My credit cards are maxed out, my house is reverse mortgaged, and I can't pay my property taxes. This job is a lifeline, and I'm not letting him—or you—take it away from me. Besides," she muttered, "drugging me is the least of his offenses."

She lay back down on the couch and flung her arm over her eyes with a dramatic sigh. Jackson looked to me expectantly.

"None of us wants to shut down the film," I said. "That's a last resort."

He nodded in agreement. "But if it comes to that, I'm not afraid to—"

"We *know*." Stella groaned without moving. "What you really need to do is fire Madison. She's going to ruin the film. Felicity would be much better."

"This was not my idea," Felicity piped up. "I'm not trying to steal anybody's part."

Jackson looked over at Felicity and smiled. "I know you're not. But she's right—I've thought of it myself. Problem is, getting rid of Madison isn't so easy. She's got a contract and is screwing my dad."

"Funny, she screwed my dad, too," I said dryly, debating whether to voice what else I knew about Madison. I'd sworn to myself I wouldn't, after what my father had put her through, but now that I'd gotten to know her, I realized perhaps she wasn't worthy of my empathy. Life was turning out never to be black-and-white. "I don't know if it helps, but... Madison never had leukemia," I blurted.

Felicity and Jackson gaped at me. Stella sat up, her bloodshot eyes wide. "Wait, what?"

"How do you know this?" Jackson asked.

"My dad found out. It's a long story..."

"Summarize," Stella demanded.

I sighed. I knew my part in the story wouldn't cast me in the best light, but at this point I had few fucks left to give. "Madison had a recurring part on one of my dad's shows when she first got to Hollywood. According to him, she threw herself at him and he accepted what she offered. Which, now that I know her, I don't doubt. Anyway, while they were involved, he did her the favor of making sure she got promoted to series regular on *Dallas Divas*. When it got canceled, she threatened to expose their relationship and say it wasn't consensual if he didn't put her on another show. So he dug up dirt on her in the event he needed to fight back and found out she'd never had cancer. The whole thing was a giant hoax designed to make her famous."

"Jesus," Stella breathed. "That's evil genius."

"It's the real reason I got fired," I admitted. I'd told Jackson and Cole my side of the Rory scenario when they hired me, though I withheld exactly what dirty work my father had asked me to do. "My dad wanted me to release all the info on Madison to preempt any attempt by her to accuse him of anything, and I refused. I didn't really know what had happened between them, and it just didn't seem right."

"So that's why you threw her into the mix for this," Jackson surmised.

"I knew he would hear about it and it would get under his skin," I admitted. "I didn't do the things my father accused me of," I explained to Stella and Felicity. "But that's a story for another day. Anyway, I'm sorry I ever brought Madison in for an audition."

"Wait, she *auditioned*?" Felicity asked.

Jackson nodded. "And she was actually good. Not first-choice good, but fifth on the list when the first four were unavailable."

"She must've been coached to within an inch of her life," Stella scoffed.

"By someone who's a better director than me," Jackson added.

Felicity rolled her eyes. "You don't have the time to spend hours a day coaxing a performance out of one of your actresses. You have an entire cast and crew to worry about."

"And a tight schedule," I added.

"Great." Stella beamed. "So we all agree we can get rid of her."

Jackson held up a hand. "Let's put a pin in this right now. We'll take the night off from filming." Off my look, he continued. "It's the scene where Marguerite tries to drown herself and the nanny saves her." He indicated Stella. "She's in no shape to be out in the ocean doing a physical scene tonight."

"We'll have to make it up," I pointed out.

"Fine. But I'm not putting anyone in danger again."

"Okay," I agreed. "Beyond that, we have two problems to solve to keep the film running." I held up two fingers. "How to keep our insurance in light of those pictures, and how to contain Cole. Anyone have any bright ideas?"

"Well, yeah," Felicity chimed in. "On the insurance thing, they need to know she wasn't drunk to keep her insured, right? So she releases a statement. Says she was roofied. Does a post about roofie awareness—how it can happen to anyone. Says she wants to share to prevent it from happening to other people."

Jackson nodded, thinking. "Great idea."

"What about Cole?" I asked.

For a moment no one spoke. Finally, Felicity shrugged. "We could kill him," she said lightly.

I involuntarily emitted a short bark of a laugh.

"Jackson would inherit his estate," she went on, "we'd recast his role, and violà!"

Jackson smirked. "Anyone have any ideas that don't end with us all in jail?"

"Oh, come on." Felicity laughed. "If I were going to murder someone, I think we all know I wouldn't get caught."

"Okay, okay," I said. Obviously she was joking, but it didn't feel right to be talking this way, no matter how much I detested Cole. Actually, it felt so wrong precisely because of how much I detested him: the idea of murdering him, if I were really honest, sounded *for just a moment*, like a good one. And that, I knew, was not good. Even if the world would totally be better off without him. "Nobody's murdering anyone."

"I'll talk to him," Jackson said.

"Way less exciting," Felicity drolled.

"I'm coming with you to talk to him," Stella asserted.

"No," Jackson said. "I need to do this alone."

# Felicity

'm curled up on the soft white couch in my apartment with a mug of chamomile on a rainy afternoon when my phone dings with a notification that an article mentioning Cole Power has been posted. I have alerts set for both Stella and Cole, though they rarely turn up anything useful. The only time Stella's name has come up at all in the past few months was in connection with an interview she gave to a horror fan site regarding a low-budget film she starred in that no one saw. Most of it was bullshit about her craft and rambling stories about bigger movies she'd shot a decade ago. But there was one memorable moment where she likened her "past mistakes" to the mistakes her character in the film makes that lead to her death—namely, attempting and failing to murder her husband's mistress, who later stalks and kills her. An odd admission for sure.

When the interviewer pressed her on it, she walked the comment back with a meandering statement about the importance of "coming clean" and living honestly and alluded to a memoir she wanted to write. The video only got 453 hits, so whatever she said didn't matter much. But it did get my attention.

Cole, on the other hand, comes up at least once a week, though usually it's a picture of him shopping with his latest model girlfriend or a promotion for a movie he has coming out. There were some juicy stories when one girlfriend broke up with him claiming he threw a cell phone at her head, but they went away when "sources close to the couple" revealed that she'd been on acid at the time and had threatened him with a knife. No report about why she felt the need to threaten him with a knife, and she of course denied the claims, but it was enough to throw doubt into the mix, and the rumors about Cole died down after a few weeks.

This latest alert, however, is a *Hollywood Gazette* report concerning his production company, Power Pictures—and to my shock, Stella:

Stella Rivers joins cast of *The Siren*.

My mouth falls open when I read the title. I immediately click on the alert, the seconds it takes to load stretching out like hours.

Stella Rivers, best known as Mary Elizabeth in *Under the Blue Moon*, will join the cast of *The Siren*, an indie thriller currently in preproduction at Cole Power's Power Pictures. Rivers will play Marguerite, a woman struggling with postpartum depression, who becomes paranoid when her husband (played by real-life ex-husband Power) hires a beautiful young nanny to watch their child.

Taylor Wasserman, formerly of Woodland Studios, is producing for Power Pictures, and Power's son Jackson Power is set to direct. *The Siren* is slated for production early summer in the Caribbean.

I reread the article until I have it memorized, then frantically search the internet for more information about the film, but this is apparently the first report. It's unbelievable; I immediately feel negligent for not knowing sooner. Cole, Stella, and Jackson together in one place—it's what I've been trying for months to figure out how to engineer.

After my run-in with Cole at the Ninth Circle, I never returned to work, never collected the money I was owed. I completely ghosted Marty and Lacey and all the other people who knew Nikki Nimes. I moved clear across the 101 to Echo Park, ditched acting classes, changed my email and phone, and became Felicity Fox—Felicity for luck and because I can use the nickname my mom used to call me, "Fee." Fox because I hope to be smart like a fox in this incarnation. Plus, it sounds cool.

My ID still reads Phoenix Pendley, though this time I'm taking the steps to change it legally.

Felicity is brown-eyed, with chin-length brunette hair and bangs. The thing I find the funniest is the difference in the men I attract. As a blonde, it was generally either guys with fast cars and lots of money or the really good-looking ones, both of whom predictably wanted a roll in the hay and a trophy on their arm. As a redhead it was the artsy ones in search of their own manic pixie dream girl. As a brunette, it's the more serious types looking for a girlfriend, who want to cook me dinner and discuss our dreams before they make sweet love to me. Barf.

One more adjustment I made to be totally sure Cole wouldn't remember me the next time we meet: I got a nose job. Expensive and painful, but worth it, I think. Though it was tempting to take a picture of my mother to the surgeon and ask for her nose, I didn't. I simply had the bump shaved off, leaving it smaller and straighter and slightly turned up at the end, when it had been turned down before. My profile is completely different now, and with the cut-and-dye-job and darker eyes, I really do look like another person. It's taken some time for me not to start when I see myself in the mirror, but I'm getting used to it.

Once the task of starting a new life was taken care of, I set about the business of devising a plan. There could be nothing haphazard this time; I needed to unearth what had happened to Iris that terrible night in Miami and carefully plot my retaliation accordingly.

The encounter with Cole had made me realize I couldn't exact revenge without total certainty of the truth and an airtight strategy, and I ruled out any interaction with him because he would inevitably want to fuck me, an option that was off the table.

That left Stella and Jackson.

After her reality show tanked, the tabloids finally tired of Stella, and she disappeared from the public eye. Time passed and people forgot about her. Then last year she got cast in a low-budget horror movie that released to no fanfare on Amazon, in support of which she gave the odd interview I saw. The thing was, she was really good in the film—as she was in the handful of other small roles she's done since. There's a rawness to her acting, a very real availability. She's no longer the sweet, spunky girl she was in the Harriet films or the manic madwoman she became after Cole dumped her. The chip on her shoulder is gone, as is the starry-eyed optimism, buried somewhere within her, covered by a thin layer of humble fragility that's both heartbreaking and fascinating to watch.

Jackson's story is much lighter fare. A year older than me, he took a year off to travel after high school, then went to college at NYU, returning to Hollywood for the directing program at the American Film Institute, unarguably the most prestigious film school in the world. He'd somehow managed to stay out of the spotlight growing up, despite the stardom of his father and, to a lesser degree, his mother, a model and party girl turned philanthropist after marrying a wealthy French businessman and birthing twins. She was even younger than Cole when she got pregnant with Jackson and has herself admitted she'd had him only in an effort to save their failing marriage. Now she lives in Paris, making up for her lackluster performance with Jackson by doting upon his little half siblings with every waking breath.

I have a couple of fake social media accounts I use to keep tabs on him, and as far as I can tell, he's not a partier like his parents were at his age. He rarely checks in at bars or clubs, and there are no photos with models or celebrities, nothing with Cole. His pictures are all black-and-white and of the artistic variety: bare tree branches across a full moon, the bottom half of a girl's face as she turns to smile.

I've been able to find little of his personal life online. He's a registered Democrat, an environmentalist, a supporter of the Black Lives Matter and #MeToo movements. He spent a year in India after high school and had a nerdy-cute girlfriend while in college in New York, but they amicably uncoupled when he moved to LA. His friends are as annoyingly artistic and benevolent as he seems to be. I've swiped and swiped trying to find him on various dating apps but come up empty-handed.

I spun my wheels for months after my run-in with Cole, but my machinations led nowhere and I'd begun to feel desperate. My ideas were all too complicated, with too many moving parts that depended upon one another to work. Was I intentionally making this harder than it had to be in order not to follow through? Surely poor Stella wouldn't be too difficult to get close to, and if her substance abuse problem was a fraction of what it used to be, it shouldn't be too hard to pry her secrets loose. I decided to make her my target.

A star map purchased on Hollywood Boulevard easily led me to her address, a crumbling Tudor home in Nichols Canyon. I began following her, studying her routines. Inspection of her recycling bin revealed she'd leaped off the wagon, deep into a fondness for gin and chardonnay—at least a bottle of wine per night. Many days she didn't leave her house except to take her little Chihuahua around the block, but I quickly learned her favorite coffee shop and dog park.

Then, a week after I started following her, she was suddenly gone. The dog had disappeared with her, the house closed up with timers on the lights that went on at seven and off again at ten. I tried to find evidence of where she'd gone, but there was none. No production reports containing her name, no travel itineraries in the trash. Finally a new credit popped up under her name on the Internet Movie Database, and I realized she must be off shooting what appeared to be a movie about a dog for the Hallmark Channel, not big enough to have been mentioned in any of the trades.

Two weeks went by. Three. I grew anxious. Her name was listed way down the cast list, which meant her role couldn't be large. How long could it possibly take? One evening I wandered down to the Blue Cat, my favorite hole-in-the-wall on the east end of Sunset Boulevard, in hopes of finding someone to take my mind off my failure to even begin to avenge my mother's death. The place was nearly empty, but I was already there, so I sat at the dimly lit bar and nursed a mezcal cocktail while watching the Mexican league soccer game play silently on the television above the bartender's head. He was cute—an actor, I was sure—and I'd considered taking him home with me a number of times, but had always stopped myself, valuing my ability to return to the bar above whatever brief thrills he might give me in bed.

I'd just paid my bill when Jackson walked in. He was with a guy and a girl I recognized from his Instagram account as a couple in his film school class. I'd been stalking him so long I felt as if I knew him, and not being a regular drinker, I was buzzed enough after a heavy cocktail that I nearly called out to him when his eyes grazed mine. I couldn't help but return the half smile he gave me, then ripped my gaze away, staring into the melting ice in my glass as I tried to still my wildly beating heart.

I shouldn't have been surprised to see him; I'd started coming to the Blue Cat after he tagged it in a post a year ago, but I found I liked it and kept coming back even after he failed to ever turn up. Finally, here he was, the grown version of the boy I'd met on that fateful night thirteen years ago. He was thin, but taller than I thought he'd be. He still had unruly dark hair with his mother's wide olive eyes, and his jawline had filled out to become an echo of his father's. He was unassumingly good-looking in fitted gray jeans and a faded black hoodie—exactly the type of guy I'd be into if he wasn't who he was. But he was... who he was.

I wrestled with myself over whether to chance talking to him as he and his friends seated themselves at a booth behind me. It would be so easy. There had been interest in his eyes when they'd grazed mine. It wasn't what I'd planned, but the opportunity was there, so tangible.

What would I say? Lying was the obvious answer—I knew enough about him that it wouldn't be difficult to pose as his perfect girl. I could be on a date with him in a matter of days. I could probably sleep with him tonight if I wanted. But then what? It would have to end at some point. He'd never volunteer the information I needed unprompted, and as soon as I started asking questions, he'd become suspicious. But if I told him the truth from the start, I'd scare him off.

"You follow Mexican soccer?" I spun to see him suddenly beside me, his hair falling into his eyes, the shadow of a dimple as his lips curled into a smile. "Sorry. Didn't mean to scare you." He laughed.

I gaped at him, my mind spinning through the options so quickly I felt dizzy. "You startled me," I managed.

"Let's start over," he said easily. "I'm Jackson."

I didn't take his extended hand. "I'm sorry," I sputtered, gathering my purse and jacket. "I have a boyfriend. I have to go."

I dove off the barstool and hastened to the door without a backward glance. When I was safely outside, I sprinted all the way up the hill to my apartment, impervious to the blisters forming on my heels from my impractical shoes. Finding I no longer felt the warm buzz of the mezcal, I poured myself straight tequila—the only liquor I had in the house—and sat on the couch, beating myself up.

Why was I so shaken? I was a terrible spy. First I botched the encounter with Cole, now Jackson. Luckily, it was dark and he'd seen my face for only about ten seconds, so I was sure he'd forget me in a matter of days. But I should have been cool. I should have been prepared. Now what? I opened my phone and stared at his Instagram account, willing him to post something. It would be so easy to slide into his DMs under one of my fake accounts... and what, ruin everything? I'd already been through this!

If I were going to contact him, it needed to be as myself—under an email he couldn't track and without a picture that would immediately lead him back to the girl who'd just run from him like Cinderella at midnight. Poor guy. I was sure his friends were still teasing him.

As I thought about him, my fingers began striking the keys on my computer to open a new email account. I should let it go, but I suddenly found I couldn't. I needed to know, and I needed to know now.

Hi Jackson,

I met you in Miami thirteen years ago behind your dad's house while my mother was inside. Her name was Iris and she was everything to me, the only person I've ever loved. Did you know she died that night? They said she'd been driving high and wrecked her car into a tree, but that's not true. Your father was driving the car, and she was already dead when he and Stella loaded her into it. I know you weren't responsible—you were a kid like I was. Did Cole force you to lie to the police? What did you really see that night? I know this will seem out of the blue to you, but I have thought about it every hour of every day since, and I have to know what really happened to her.

Please.

Phoenix

I attached a picture of my mother smiling on the beach a few weeks before her death with her arm around a chubby little blond me, keyed in the email address I found on his website, and hit send before I could second-guess myself.

But second-guess myself I have, a million times in the six weeks since I sent the email. He never responded. I considered sending a follow-up, but I never quite worked out what to say.

Stella came back, and I resumed my plan to ingratiate myself to her, though I've yet to succeed.

And now, like a lightning bolt from a blue sky, Cole's hired Stella and Jackson to shoot a movie—the three of them together, for the first time in thirteen years.

I finish my tea and set my mug on the windowsill, staring out at the wind whipping the pepper trees. Why now? It doesn't matter. What matters is that I will be on that movie set, and I will find out once and for all what happened to my mother.

@TheRealStellaRivers

[PICTURE]

♡ 19,394 likes

I was roofied last night while at a cast party at a restaurant on the island where I am shooting. There were a lot of people there (not only our cast/crew), and I don't know who roofied me, but someone took this picture of me slumped on the floor and sold it to Xray Online, who posted it this morning, claiming I was wasted. Well, I was. But not by my own hand. Luckily for me, members of our crew found me, took care of me, and made sure I got home without further incident. But not everyone who is drugged gets off so lucky. This is a reminder that it can happen to anyone, anywhere. Please, please be careful. Be aware. Don't take drinks from strangers, and keep tabs on your friends when you're out together. Stay safe out there, friends. Love, Stella

# Taylor

I was on the treadmill when the first wave of nausea hit. I slowed the belt and gulped down half the water in my thermos, figuring it was my body's payback for not having run in over a week. But the water only made it worse. Out the fogged window, the electric-blue horizon seemed warped, the phosphorescent green of the golf course too bright.

Thankful that I was alone in the ice-cold gym, I grabbed a eucalyptus-scented wet towel from the refrigerator and rubbed it over my face. My mouth watered; my peripheral vision darkened. I sat heavily into the chair next to the water dispenser and rested my head in my hands. What the hell? I'd been fine this morning. Well, fine-ish. But hangovers didn't usually make me nauseous.

I immediately thought of Cole and what he might have done to me while I was passed out—what that might mean in the context of my sudden nausea. Though surely I was being alarmist. *Please, God.* I was probably just hungry. It was early afternoon, and I'd had nothing in the way of sustenance today, other than the coffee I'd drunk this morning during my meeting with Jackson, Stella, and Felicity.

After a few minutes, the wave passed, but I was left feeling too weak to finish my workout. I grabbed another refrigerated towel and headed slowly back through the steamy day to my bungalow. I ate a nutrition bar and downed acetaminophen, which seemed to help some, then took a lukewarm shower.

Afterward, I wrapped myself in my bathrobe and lay down on the soft white bed, staring up at the steeply pitched thatched roof, light-headed. The light from the water bouncing off the walls was too much; I fumbled on the dresser for the remote control and lowered the black-out shades. The relative darkness provided some relief, but the water still reflected through the window in the floor. I forced myself off the bed and threw a blanket over the glass.

To make matters worse, I'd agreed to dinner with Rick after Jackson called off tonight's shoot and was very much looking forward to it, but I would obviously have to cancel if I continued feeling like this. Surely I'd be fine by then. I stumbled into the closet and yanked out the first clothes I saw. My favorite bra felt like it was strangling my tits, so I clasped it on the widest hook; still I had double boob. And they were sore too. Not a good sign. *Please let it be a bad case of PMS.* I hadn't gotten my period when I was supposed to last week, but that often happened when I was working crazy hours and stressing like a madwoman. It must be coming now, right?

My mouth watered in the bad way. I braced myself against the dresser.

I circled back to the obvious answer. If this had happened yesterday, I would have disregarded the idea: I couldn't be pregnant; I hadn't had sex. Cole told me point-blank we didn't sleep together.

But Cole had lied. Of course the asshole had lied. All evidence pointed to the fact that he'd drugged me, assaulted me, and then made out like I'd gotten too drunk and thrown myself at him. Acrid rage burned the back of my throat.

I ran to the shockingly sunlit bathroom and hurled into the toilet.

When there was nothing left in me to upchuck, I pulled on a base-ball cap and dark glasses and grudgingly slogged down the pier, across the sand, through the trees, and along the cobblestone road to the lone drugstore on the island, praying I wouldn't see anyone I knew. No such luck. One of the camera ops was in line with a basket full of stuff, and the two wardrobe girls were perusing the limited nail polish selection. I nodded and smiled at them, pretending to examine the vitamins and supplements until they'd vacated the store, at which point I grabbed a handful of different pregnancy tests and rushed to the cashier.

She smiled when she saw what I was purchasing. "Good luck, honey."

"Oh, they're not for me," I lied.

Back at the bungalow, I selected one of the tests at random and read the instructions as though it were more complicated than peeing on a stick. When I finally got down to business, I was shaking so much I could hardly keep the thing in place. I capped it and placed it on the slate counter beneath the giant window, then set the timer on my phone for three minutes. In thirty seconds, there were two blue lines in the window. I knew what it meant, but I consulted the instructions, hoping I was wrong.

I chugged a bottle of water and sat on the edge of the soaking tub staring across the mottled sea at the green hills of Saint Ann in the distance, waiting for the water to work its way through my body so that I could try again. Somewhere nestled among the palms was Rick's house, which I'd never see now.

A gull landed on the back of one of the loungers on the deck and cocked its head, judging me for my naivete. I'd wanted so badly for this movie to be my salvation that I'd willingly ignored all the blatant warning signs it was anything but. Now I was caught in the undertow, and this time there would be no one on a WaveRunner to save me.

When I could finally pee again, I took another test. Two lines appeared immediately.

I was pregnant.

# Stella

I trudged up the over-water walkway toward my bungalow, impervious to the breathtaking explosion of color reaching across the sky as the sun sank into the salmon-tinted sea. The hot stone massage Felicity had insisted I submit to had done little to dull the throbbing in my head, and my oiled skin felt sticky in the heavy air.

I was exhausted. I'd been unable to go back to sleep in the wake of this morning's meeting, strangled by panic over what would happen to me should Jackson decide to pull the plug on the film. I kept flipping between the things Cole had told me about Jackson the other day and what Jackson had said about Cole. Their stories didn't match up, but I couldn't piece together which of them was lying or why, and there was no one I could talk to about it.

Jackson had everyone believing that Cole had drugged me, and while that made logical sense, it made as much sense for Madison to have been the culprit—especially now that she seemed to be involved with Cole—or if Cole had been the one telling the truth, even Jackson himself. I wished I could remember a damn thing about what happened at Coco's, but my memory of the evening was nothing but a black hole.

Mary Elizabeth yapped excitedly when I pushed open the door, and

I scooped her up, allowing her to shower me with kisses. I didn't know where Felicity had gone but was glad to have some time to myself. Obviously I couldn't breathe a word to her of my suspicions about Jackson's motives, but it was hard to think of anything else, which suddenly made her constant companionship tedious.

The reflection of the sunset through the floor-to-ceiling glass bathed the deliciously silent bungalow in an otherworldly light. I considered the half-drunk bottle of rum on the counter. I knew with the renewed scrutiny of the insurance company and whatever was still coursing through my veins after last night that I shouldn't drink, but I also knew a glass of rum was the only thing that could make me feel better. I'd get sober when this was all over. I really would. But now was definitely not the time.

I poured the rum over ice and marched through the bedroom to the gorgeous bathroom, where I opened the sliding glass doors to the salty breeze and the sound of the sloshing ocean slapping the pilons beneath the bungalow then ran a bubble bath in the giant soaking tub. I did so love a hot bath. The sea was alive this evening, its surface rippled by the wind. A pelican dive-bombed a school of fish, coming up with a wriggling flash of silver in its large beak. The local rum was smooth and sweet on my tongue as I downed an extra anxiety pill, sure my current dose was insufficient for the amount of stress I was under.

I shed my clothes and slipped into the hot water. There was no denying the wound had been reopened inside of me; I was teetering. I could see the abyss, and I knew it would swallow me up if I let it. I'd sweat blood to bury the past; now it was all resurfacing, distorted from years of submersion. The harder I tried not to think about it, the more the memories pushed through. I wanted to run away and never see Cole or Jackson Power again. What had I been thinking, accepting this role? My psychic had said there would be forgiveness and healing, but for once she was wrong. My only recourse was self-medication.

When I emerged from the bath, my fingers were wrinkled and I was sufficiently anesthetized to face the rest of my evening. The sun had slipped beneath the horizon, leaving in its place a pearly sliver of moon that peeked through low clouds hovering above the luminous sea.

"Stella?" Felicity called out from the other room as I pulled a maxi dress over my head.

"Come in," I replied.

She entered holding Mary Elizabeth. "I'm going to take her to do her business. Want to come?"

After the bath and the rum, I was feeling better than I had all day, but I still didn't quite have it in me to put on makeup. "I'd love to, but I don't think I can pull myself together," I said, running a brush through my wet hair.

"Come on," she protested. "You look beautiful. And anyway, it's about to storm, so no one's out there."

I knew she was only being kind, but she was right that no one would be around, so I poured myself another splash in the darkening living room and we set out, barefoot. Stepping onto the pier without a stitch of makeup on, I felt more naked than if I'd walked out the door without any clothes. It was surprisingly freeing. The wind whipped our hair and dresses. I looked up to see clouds obscuring the stars. "Tut-tut, looks like rain," I quipped.

But Felicity apparently had not been exposed to *Winnie-the-Pooh* as a child.

When we reached the windswept beach, I set Mary Elizabeth down, and she immediately ran yapping toward the only occupied lounger on the beach. I chased after her, calling out an apology to the occupant of the lounger, who was curled up beneath one of the resort's oversize green and white beach towels with his face obscured by a raised hoodie.

The person turned, and I saw I'd been wrong. It wasn't a he. It was Taylor, and she looked an awful mess, her face puffy and streaked with tears. "Taylor," I exclaimed, kneeling next to her in the sand. "Are you okay?"

Embarrassed, she wiped at the tears with the towel. "Yeah, I'm fine." She took a ragged breath. "Sorry. Just personal shit."

Felicity sat on the other side of her. "Anything you want to talk about? We're good listeners."

I nodded agreement.

"Really, I'm fine." Taylor forced a smile.

"We have rum," I offered.

Felicity shot me a look, and I remembered that especially after last night I really shouldn't be drinking in front of Taylor, but she was too distraught to notice my slipup, or care. "I would, but..." She started crying again.

"Do you want us to leave you alone?" Felicity asked.

Taylor nodded. "Please don't tell anyone you saw me like this," she begged.

I patted her back. "Of course," I said.

"Invitation's open if you change your mind," Felicity added.

Fat raindrops started to fall as we walked away, back in the direction of our bungalow. We hadn't gotten halfway up the walkway above the surging sea when Taylor came running to catch up with us. "I changed my mind," she said.

The dark clouds ripped open, and sheets of rain cascaded down as the three of us hastened toward the bungalow. Inside, Felicity picked up the phone next to the purple orchid as we dried ourselves off. "I'm ordering dinner. What do you guys want?" she asked.

"A salmon burger," Taylor said. "And fries, and a ginger ale."

Felicity repeated the order into the phone, adding a cheeseburger for herself and a salad for me, then came to sit with us in the living room. Mary Elizabeth ran in circles, barking as lightning flashed and thunder shook the windows. "We never get thunderstorms in LA," I commented. Mary Elizabeth jumped into my lap, shaking. I stroked her little head as I gazed out at the rain. It was kind of frightening, being out here over the water, though surely we were safe. Cole certainly had bragged enough about the security of this place. "Exhilarating."

"Good thing Jackson canceled tonight's shoot," Taylor said.

"Has Madison been fired yet?" I asked hopefully.

Taylor shook her head. "Jackson's talking to Cole about it. I promise

I'll let you know when I hear anything." She took out her phone and checked her weather app. "Shit." She groaned. "This morning it said it was going to be clear tomorrow, and now it looks like thunderstorms the rest of the week. I guess we're just gonna have to go with it."

"Why don't we shoot the end then?" I suggested. "The part where I use the storm as cover to kill Peyton and the nanny. I'm especially looking forward to that part."

Taylor groaned. "Can we turn on the news? I want to see what the meteorologists have to say."

Felicity flicked on the flat-screen and selected the Weather Channel, but they were busy talking about the heat wave sweeping Western Europe. She muted the volume. "The food will be here in thirty. Does anybody need anything while we wait?"

I wanted rum, but I still wasn't totally sure whether I could quit pretending in front of Taylor. Instead I grabbed my pack of smokes and headed for the sliding glass door.

"I'm pregnant," Taylor blurted.

Felicity and I turned to her in sync, not even trying to hide our shock. No one said anything for a minute. I dropped my cigarettes on the end table and perched on the couch next to her.

"I'm guessing this was a surprise?" Felicity asked tenderly.

Taylor nodded. "I just found out today. Please don't tell anyone."

"We won't," Felicity and I promised in unison.

"Jinx," I said, and she threw a fuchsia pillow at me, which elicited a small smile from Taylor. "Who's the dad?" I ventured.

She furrowed her brow and looked down at her hands, blinking quickly. Damn, that had been the wrong question. It was the logical one, though, wasn't it? I'd been asked such invasive questions about private issues at every step of my life, I wasn't terribly good at knowing what was and wasn't socially acceptable anymore. "I'm sorry," I said.

She shook her head and wiped her eyes with her sleeve. "We're not together. It was a mistake—I don't even remember..." She choked back a sob.

Poor girl.

Felicity rubbed her back. "It's okay."

"It's not though." Taylor took a ragged breath. "I blacked out, and I'd only had two drinks that I know of. I think...I may have been drugged."

Felicity and I exchanged a glance, and I could see she was thinking the same four-letter name I was.

"Like Stella was last night?" Felicity asked.

Taylor peered at us from beneath a furrowed brow, her eyes guarded.

"It was the first night we arrived, before you all got here. I woke up the next morning all sandy and wet in my bed with his shirt on the bedside table, and I didn't remember anything. He said I'd gotten super wasted and tried to fuck him, but promised me we hadn't actually done it."

"That asshole," Felicity fumed.

"Are you sure it's his?" I asked.

Again she nodded. "There hasn't been anyone else. Well—there hadn't been. There is now, but it's new, and we haven't slept together."

"Rick," I sang gleefully, and Felicity gave me a sharp glance.

Taylor nodded, staring up at the bas-relief wood Buddha on the wall. "I guess that's over now. I already had to cancel going out with him tonight."

"Last night wasn't the first time Cole drugged me," I admitted. "He did it once years ago, when we were married."

Both girls gaped at me.

Veins of lightning shot across the sky out over the water as I dragged my mind for yet another sordid detail of our relationship I'd buried under an avalanche of drugs and therapy. "I'd been on a juice cleanse. I hadn't even had a drink. I was so confused when I woke up naked with no memory of the night before...I knew we'd had rough sex because I was sore, but also because I was on my period and our bed looked like a small animal had been sacrificed—sorry, TMI. I couldn't understand it; I would've had sex with him, done whatever nasty thing he wanted. I confronted him, and he laughed it off, saying he'd thought it was hot to fuck me while I was asleep. When I balked, he gave me a lecture about what a judgmental prude I'd become."

Felicity's eyes narrowed as though trying to understand something much more complicated than what I was saying, while Taylor furrowed her brow, disturbed. "Wow," she said. "That's…awful. I'm so sorry."

"I later found out it was kind of his thing," I went on. "He had a fetish, or whatever, for having sex with women while they were asleep. He'd hire hookers and consensually drug them, then have sex with them when they were passed out."

"He did this while you were married?" Taylor asked, aghast.

"And you knew about it?" Felicity piled on.

Reluctantly, I nodded. I couldn't believe I was confessing this to them, but the cat was out of the bag. "You have to understand, it was nearly fifteen years ago, long before #metoo or #timesup or any of that, and the circle we ran with at the time—people were into some weird shit. We had so much money and fame—everything at such a young age, people wanted more; they'd go to extremes to feel something. My arrangement with Cole was less than ideal, but it was part of who he was and I'd married him. Still, I didn't want him doing that stuff to me. The girls were clean and he paid them well; they knew what they were in for. Consenting adults. I figured that was better than the alternative—what happened to you."

Taylor picked at her cuticles, nodding slowly. "It makes sense now. I'd found his explanation hard to believe, but…" She wiped the tears that spilled from her eyes with the back of her hand. "I feel so violated. And I'm so mad at myself. It's like I'm two completely different people—professionally I've got my shit together, but personally I'm a fucking mess, and my personal shit gets in the way of my professional life and now I'm completely screwed and freaking pregnant and without this job working for a guy who *raped* me, I have nothing, and I just…" Her chest heaved. "I don't know what I'm gonna do."

"This is not your fault," Felicity said.

We put our arms around her as she broke down sobbing. "It's gonna be okay," I soothed. "At least you weren't arrested high on ketamine, half-naked and throwing pickle jars at bystanders in a Hollywood grocery store."

Taylor almost laughed through her tears as the picture on the television switched to a radar image of our corner of the Caribbean. The colorful patch of storm activity currently hovering over our island paled in comparison to the ominous splotch of angry red surrounded by yellow and green that seethed out in the Atlantic to the east of us. Felicity grabbed the remote and unmuted the volume.

"...tropical disturbance east of Barbados in the southern Caribbean has formed a tropical depression," said the weathercaster in the yellow dress. "We are currently issuing a storm watch for the area in red." Another map popped up, showing a swath of red over the long chain of islands that included ours. "This is a fast-moving depression, and there is a real possibility it could quickly turn into a tropical storm, though it's too early to accurately predict a path for the storm. Stay tuned as conditions develop."

The screen returned to the radar image of the storm as she went on about the early start to hurricane season this year. "Rick did say the unusual warmth of the water meant a hurricane was likely," Taylor said. She took a ragged breath and dried her tears on her sleeve. "I've gotta go talk to Price and Jackson."

"But your food," I protested.

"We'll send it to your bungalow when it comes," Felicity said.

"Thank you," she said, rising. "For everything. And please, please don't tell anyone what I told you."

"Of course," we answered in unison.

As we shut the door behind her, a flame of renewed fear flickered to life inside of me. I'd narrowly avoided Jackson shutting down the production this morning after I was drugged; if a hurricane were to hit, the film would be over, taking with it my career.

Felicity saw my sudden shift in mood and squeezed my shoulders. "It's gonna be okay," she said, echoing my words to Taylor.

But her voice was drowned out by the howling of the wind around the eaves.

# Felicity

*Two Months Ago*

At four p.m. on a Tuesday in mid-April, I take up residence on a park bench in the shade of a big sycamore tree along the path that leads to the enclosed dog run with a view of Lake Hollywood. My face is scrubbed clean of makeup, my pockets full of doggie treats, and I'm wearing an oversize T-shirt emblazoned with the name of a prestigious liberal arts college I didn't attend.

I open my copy of *Believe It and It Will Be* and let my mind wander, glancing up every time another hipster comes around the bend in the path, canine companion in tow. Twenty minutes pass. Thirty. I'm ready to give up and try again on Thursday when at long last I spot a small-boned woman in a big sun hat and dark glasses trailing an aging Chihuahua up the trail. Stella's dressed much too warmly for the weather, swathed head to toe in black Lululemons, only her pale hands protruding.

I stand and cross to the garbage can on the other side of the path, tossing in a crumpled piece of paper. As I cut back to my bench, the gold charm bracelet I picked up in a secondhand store last week slips from my wrist and lands in the packed dirt, glinting in the dappled sunlight as she approaches. I pretend not to notice.

Stella scoops up the bracelet and addresses me, just as she's meant to. "I'm sorry, miss?" She proffers the bracelet. "I think you lost this."

I look up, surprised—not that I dropped the bracelet, but that my ambush is for once going according to plan. "Oh my gosh, thank you so much!" I take the bracelet from her, smiling. "I didn't even feel it slip off! It's very special to me. My mother gave it to me before she passed away last year...Anyway, thank you." Feigning embarrassment, I bend to pet her Chihuahua, slipping her a kibble as I scratch under her chin. "Hi, sweetie." I look up at Stella. "She's adorable. What a good doggy."

The dog rubs against me, wanting more kibble. "That's Mary Elizabeth," she says.

Yeah, I know. I continue to scratch her ears. "A big name for such a little lady."

"It's silly—I got her when I was in Louisiana shooting this movie and named her after my character."

Wow, she is *desperate* to talk. This may be easier than I'd thought. I look up to see she's taken off her sunglasses, revealing a face at once familiar and strange. She's still beautiful, though her cheeks aren't quite as round as they used to be, and her brow is pinched with anxiety. Her big green eyes beg me to recognize her.

"*Under the Blue Moon*," I say with delight, as though only now placing her. "I love that movie. You're Stella Rivers. I didn't recognize you behind the hat and glasses."

"Yes," she says, relieved to be fondly recognized. "I have to wear them out; you know—tourists in the area. It can be difficult trying to live a normal life."

"I can imagine! Or really I can't. I'm just a nobody off the bus from New Hampshire." I laugh self-consciously, fiddling with the hem of my counterfeit T-shirt in hopes she'll bite.

Finally she notices the name of the school shouting from my chest. "Oh." She indicates the block letters. "How funny. That's where I went to conservatory! Well, I wasn't able to graduate. I was cast in the Harriet films after my first year and didn't have time to finish, but they gave me an honorary degree. Did you go there?"

I shake my head. "Grew up in the town, though."

"How lovely," she says wistfully. "New Hampshire is so beautiful. I always wanted to be from a small town; it's so romantic. I think maybe in a past life I was a professor. I'm wearing tweed and the leaves are changing colors..." Her gaze softens as though lost in memory.

"All I ever wanted was to get out."

Her eyes refocus on me. "Out?"

So the rumors would appear to be true: she's lost a few marbles. "I wanted to get out of New Hampshire and come here to Hollywood, where it's sunny and anything is possible." Now I'm making myself cringe.

"Oh," she says. "Yes. Hollywood. Here we are! I've been in the business since I was a child, of course. I can't imagine what it must be like starting from scratch, trying to get an agent and do the whole thing. It's a tough business; take it from me."

Okay, she's not totally out to lunch. At least she has some self-awareness. "Oh, I'm not an actress," I demur. "I just wanted to get away from the snow and my father."

She laughs. "My father was no walk in the park either. And I hate snow." She notices my book on the bench. "Are you reading *Believe It and It Will Be*?"

I nod, fleetingly worried the book is a step too far. But I have no choice but to commit now. "Again."

"I love that book. It changed my life."

"Positivity and gratitude are everything." Relieved, I bend and scratch the dog again. "Nice to meet you, Mary Elizabeth. You be good for your mama."

Stella cocks her head. "She likes you. She doesn't usually like people."

Here we go. "I love dogs," I admit, barely hiding my glee. "If you ever need a doggy sitter, you let me know."

"Actually"—she considers me—"I might do that. I shoot such long hours...I used to bring her to the set with me, but she's losing her sight and isn't so comfortable being in new places anymore. Do you have a card?"

"No," I say, internally berating myself for not having had cards made up. "But take my number."

She extracts her cell phone from a zippered pocket and inputs my number. "I'm Felicity," I say.

It's true. I officially became Felicity Fox last week.

She smiles to herself and shakes her head. "What?" I ask.

"Nothing. I was just thinking about my horoscope this morning."

"What sign are you?" I ask.

"Aquarius." She smiles. "What about you?"

"Gemini. With an Aquarius rising," I embellish.

"Oh, no way! Gemini is one of the signs Aquarians get along with the best."

"I know! Two of my best friends growing up were Aquarians," I fib.

We laugh together, and she fishes an amethyst pendant from beneath her sweatshirt. "Amethyst is supposed to be really good for Aquarians."

"What's good for Gemini?"

She lights up. "Agate or celestite are great. Tigereye too, for protection."

"Good to know." I bend to pet Mary Elizabeth again. "It was super nice to meet you two. Hopefully I can help you with Miss Mary Elizabeth."

"That would be great. I have your number."

I gather my things from the park bench as she and the dog scurry up the path toward the park.

At long last, the hunter snares her rabbit.

I can barely contain my joy. The weeks since I learned of her upcoming role opposite Cole have been a travesty of failed casual encounters at the coffee shop she frequents, the yoga class she attends, even the waxing salon she patronizes. Today marked the third time I've sat on this bench at this time in this stupid T-shirt I found on eBay. I'd been running out of time. If another week had gone by without success, I'd planned to head down to the islands to try to get a job at the resort where they're going to be staying while they shoot the movie.

Still, if she doesn't reach out to me within the week, I'll have to stage another chance meeting quickly; the clock is ticking. I need to have enough time to ingratiate myself with her and make my services indispensable before she leaves for the Caribbean in seven weeks, and I'm already cutting it close.

Jackson never responded to my email, and with today's interaction, I've burned my ability to get a job at the resort, so this has to work.

But I have faith. My entire life I've never had faith in anything, until now.

# Taylor

The bloodred blob wobbling westward across my computer screen had only just been named Tropical Storm Celia, but it already looked suspiciously like a hurricane to my anxious eye. "It's rotating counterclockwise," I pointed out, struggling to stay calm as Jackson and Price peered over my shoulders.

Price ran a hand through his shock of ginger hair, worried. "It hasn't got a center yet, so I guess that's good?"

"Shit. Nothing about this is good." Jackson squinted at the image and tilted his head. "They keep saying they can't predict the path, but it's headed straight for us, don't you think? It's so close that even if it turned, we'd still catch the outer bands."

"I spoke to the resort manager right before you guys got here," I said. "He told me a voluntary evacuation order has already been issued in Gen Town and the ferry will be running all day tomorrow to get people out. Hurricane prep is under way in Saint Vincent and Saint Ann as well." I didn't feel the need to mention that last bit was from Rick, who was adamant I evacuate as soon as possible and had offered his house to any of us who might need shelter, only adding to my growing panic.

Jackson paced to the windows, where he rested his forehead against the glass, staring out at the dark night. "There goes the movie." He groaned.

Price and I scooted our chairs closer to my glass kitchen table as I opened the information tab beneath the radar animation. "The system is currently moving west-northwest at thirteen miles per hour with sustained winds of up to seventy miles per hour," I read.

Price rubbed his temples. Even his perpetually calm exterior was showing cracks. "Seventy-four is a cat one hurricane."

I used the little graph at the bottom of the image to determine the distance. "Looks like it's about six hundred miles away."

Price did the math in his head. "So it'll be here in roughly forty-eight hours, if it maintains that speed."

Jackson turned from the window, his face tense. "Who knows how strong it'll be by the time it gets here. We've gotta get everyone out."

"I agree, but the budget to do that is gonna require approval from Cole," I said. "Did you talk to him yet?"

He sighed. "I tried to have a conversation with him about what he did to Stella last night, but he flat-out denied it. Swore it wasn't him. Said he's seen her popping pills constantly and that she probably took extras that interacted with the alcohol."

The blood rushed in my ears. "He's lying," I said, trying to control the rage in my voice.

"I know." The poor guy looked defeated. "What do you want me to do?"

"What did he say about replacing Madison?" I asked, then cut my eyes to Price. "You know about this?"

Price nodded.

"I filled him in," Jackson said. "Cole wouldn't hear of canning Madison. He doesn't seem to like Felicity for some reason."

"Probably because she doesn't want to sleep with him," I grumbled. "Did you tell him Madison lied about having cancer?"

He shook his head. "I thought we might want to keep that to ourselves, in case we wanted to use it."

I gave him a sly smile. "Look at you, becoming a shark."

"When it's kill or be killed..." He shrugged.

"Okay," Price stepped in. "We'll circle back if we still have a movie after this storm hits. For now we have to focus on the task at hand."

"Agreed," I said. "Let's talk to Cole and get him to approve the funds so that we can figure out an evacuation plan. The rest we'll deal with later."

I snapped my laptop closed and rose, the edges of the world going black as I stood. I gripped the edge of the table to steady myself, and Price took my elbow. "You okay?"

I nodded, cursing silently. "Stood up too fast. Let's do this."

Outside, the storm had cleared, but residual low clouds blocked the stars and the air was cool. I could see the lights of Cole's oversize bungalow reflecting in the still choppy sea below as we approached. Had the water risen? It looked higher beneath the wooden boards than usual, but in the dark I couldn't be sure. Price rapped on Cole's door. "You do the talking first," I whispered to him. "He's most likely to listen to you."

I could hear faint music coming from within, but nothing else. After a minute, I rang the doorbell. Nothing. Price knocked again. "Call him," I said. "Don't say we're with you."

Price took out his phone and raised it to his ear. "Hey, man," he said into the phone. "I need to talk to you about the schedule." We held our breath while he listened. "No. It's time sensitive. I'm at your door." He gave us the thumbs-up as he listened. "Okay."

He hung up the phone and the door swung in, revealing Cole wet and shirtless in board shorts, a longneck beer dangling from his hand. The slightest displeasure flashed across his face when he saw Jackson and me flanking Price, but he covered it quickly. "What's up?" Cole prowled into the living room, leaving a trail of water on the floor.

It was the first time I'd laid eyes on him since discovering he'd raped me, and it was all I could do not to grab the heavy Buddha statue that anchored the entry table and smash it over his head. But that would make me no better than him.

"There's a tropical storm—Celia, it's called—a few hundred miles east of here," Price said. Cole wandered out the open sliding glass door onto the deck, and we followed. "They think it may turn into a hurricane in the next day or so."

The jets on the Jacuzzi were firing at full tilt, the water changing from red to blue to purple and back again in time with the reggae blasting over the outdoor speakers. Cole took a slug of the beer. "What's that have to do with me?"

Price raised his voice over the noise. "It's likely headed this way. We need to come up with an evacuation plan."

Cole stepped into the hot tub and sank beneath the water. Jackson, Price, and I exchanged a weighted glance as we waited for him to emerge. When he did, he shook the water from his hair like a dog, splattering all of us with tiny droplets. "Saint Genesius is safe," he said.

"Not hurricane-safe," I protested.

"Yeah it is, up to a category five," Cole returned.

"You're trying to tell me these over-water bungalows can weather a category five?" I asked, incredulous. "That's insane."

He shrugged. "So everybody can come up to the lobby. It's made of concrete block."

"With tons of windows and surrounded by giant trees that could fall on it," I argued. "At the very least, we need to get people to shelters on Saint Ann, though I'd rather fly them out while we still can."

Cole laughed. "For a little tropical storm that may or may not hit us?"

I glared at him. "For once in your life, could you try not to be an asshole?" I snapped.

A small smile played around Cole's lips as he ignored me. I balled my hands into fists and bit my tongue so hard I tasted metal. Maybe murdering him was the right choice after all.

"Dad," Jackson said evenly. The word never sounded quite right when it came out of his mouth. "It's going to hit us. The storm surge alone will put most of the island underwater. Villagers are already evacuating. We need to get everyone to higher ground."

"So send them to Saint Ann." Cole shrugged. "I'm not spending fifty grand on plane tickets."

"You should at least give them the option," I said through my teeth.

"They have the option—to buy their own plane tickets if they're pussies that can't handle a little storm. But I'm not coddling them."

I shifted tactics. "It won't look good on you or the production company if any of them talks to the press."

He laughed. "They can't talk to the press. They all signed NDAs."

"I don't know that NDAs cover reckless endangerment," Price pointed out. "It's a crime."

"Only if someone gets hurt, and no one's going to get hurt. You said yourself the path of the supposed storm isn't even determined yet."

"The bungalows could flood in the storm surge, and we'd be sued for lost or damaged possessions," I pointed out.

"It would take a fifteen-foot swell to flood these bungalows." He laughed as though the idea were absurd. "But they can bring their shit up to the lobby if they're worried." He beckoned to someone behind us, and we turned to see Madison, wrapped in a bathrobe, her long hair in a plait over her shoulder. So their tryst was confirmed. "Let's talk in the morning."

Madison lifted the lid from one of the many room service meals strewn across the dining table and popped a grape in her mouth, then sauntered over to the hot tub with a smug smile.

After the door had shut behind us, Jackson stood on the pier with crossed arms, his eyes blazing. "I'll fucking pay for it if he won't. I'm not letting him put my crew in danger."

"Can you afford that?" I asked.

"Not as easily as he can, but I'll make it work."

"Call a team meeting for the morning," I instructed Price. "Let's get the ball rolling."

When this was all over, I would quit. To hell with the repercussions. I didn't care anymore whether I ever worked in Hollywood again. I'd rather sell the condo for pennies on the dollar and flip burgers at McDonald's than be in the employ of Cole Fucking Power. The very idea of being free of him made me want to jump for joy.

# Part V:

# Storm Surge

# Felicity

The day is still and clear, not a sign of the monster storm marching across the sea to destroy us. I shake the sand from a pair of cutoffs over the edge of the deck into the teal sea and grab my favorite beige bikini from where it's drying in the sun across the back of a cushioned lounger, then step back into the deliciously cool bungalow, sliding the glass door shut behind me.

Evidently I'll be packing for both of us, as Stella's at her most helpless today, drinking and binge-watching the weather while draped across the couch like Daisy Buchanan in *The Great Gatsby*. I keep expecting her to raise her wrist to her forehead and proclaim she always waits for the longest day of the year and then misses it. We are just past the longest day of the year, and it's exactly the sort of thing she'd do; I'm sure she wishes she'd played Daisy in the latest film adaptation.

As I gather discarded hats and shoes from around the bungalow, I can make out the reporters on TV debating whether newly upgraded Hurricane Celia, at the moment a category one, will turn north and head for Miami, or keep moving east, straight for us.

"Roberta's changed her dress," Stella announces. Roberta being the weather girl she's now on a first-name basis with. "Purple looks good on her," she adds with a flourish of her hand that sends the nearly empty cocktail glass perched on the arm of the couch crashing to the floor. "Oops," she says in reference to the glass, but she doesn't move to pick it up. "Fee, can you get me another glass of rum, pretty please?"

I take a bottle of fizzy water from the fridge and hand it to her. She looks at it like I've handed her a dirty diaper. "Drink this first," I say. Then, off her look, "Dehydration is terrible for your skin."

At this she sighs and twists off the cap. "I'm onto you," she slurs as I sweep up the broken glass. But she drinks the water.

Initially I encouraged her alcoholism, thinking it would make her more likely to spill what happened to my mother, but I quickly found that Stella's an incredibly frustrating person to try to get anything out of—largely because she has the memory of a goldfish—and the pills and alcohol only make it worse. The things she does remember, she's embellished so frequently that she's no longer sure herself what's real and what's fantasy. Every so often a memory will surface and I can see her gingerly lift it, dripping, out of the mire of her mind, then hold it up to the light to examine. Is it her memory or the memory of a character she played? Something that really happened or something she only wished or dreamed happened? It's hard enough for her to determine, and she was—or wasn't—there. I'm completely lost.

I'd thought the memoir she plans to write would be my ace in the hole; I've been sneaking glances at her journal every chance I get, but besides one interesting entry about the warning Jackson's mom gave her before she married Cole, all she's written are short, meaningless passages about things that don't matter in the context of Iris's death.

Nothing's going according to plan.

My sole objective, from the day my mother died, has been to determine who killed her and exact revenge. Every. Single. Thing I've done in the past thirteen years has been in pursuit of that goal. The move to Los Angeles, the backbreaking martial arts classes, the complete avoidance of any connection with other humans—it's all been in service of this singular objective. I've been a machine. I have an encyclopedic knowledge of pharmaceuticals and the doses needed for illness, sleep, or death; I can bring a two-hundred-pound man to his knees in a dozen ways, change identities at the drop of a hat, and dig up dirt on absolutely anyone; I've never had a romantic relationship, best friend, or even a real social media profile, and very few photographs of me exist in the world. The cherry on top: I've now miraculously managed to weasel my way onto a small island with the three people who know what really happened to Iris that night—at least one of whom must be responsible—and yet I've completely failed in my mission. I've not learned a thing about how Iris died, somehow ended up in front of the camera (and worse, liked it), and most inconveniently, developed what I'm beginning to think might be real feelings for the boy who perhaps could have saved her but didn't.

On the positive side, I've become indispensable to the woman who at best covered up her death and at worst murdered her—but now that I've gotten to know Stella, I honestly can't imagine her capable of murdering anyone, so I'm not sure that can go in the win column. I had to "humanely remove" a giant spider from the bathtub before she got in the other night because she was deathly afraid of it but couldn't stand to hurt it. And the mother that stole all her money when she was young? I later found out Stella continued to pay her rent for years afterward, until she could no longer afford it.

If I've learned anything from her, it's that tabloids are trash, so I shouldn't be surprised that I've yet to see a glimmer of her "famous temper." Nor have I noticed an ounce of jealousy—the opposite, really. She idolizes beauty and talent, even if it belongs to a younger woman, and has been most encouraging of my acting. Though she's never divulged the specific reason she and Cole broke up all those years ago, she has mentioned that he cheated, and there was the nugget she dropped about his fetish for sleeping beauties. So I guess my operation hasn't been a complete wash.

During the years I spent alone in my mother's old bedroom secretly watching every movie Cole and Stella ever did, I saw an independent film Cole starred in about men who had a sexual fascination with sleeping girls. He'd been young in the film, a good decade younger than when he met my mother, and his character had used drugs to put the girls to sleep. I'd never considered that fetish might live on in him and be the reason behind the holes in my mother's arms. But Cole does have that odd way of hanging on to pieces of the characters he's played, and it made so much sense when Stella mentioned it.

Cole had certainly paid Iris well, their relationship coincided with her drug habit, and it would be just like him to give his escorts heroin instead of sleeping pills. What didn't make sense was that she'd stayed with him after the holes in her arms disappeared, which was around the time the money also dried up. I could only assume that Cole fell in love with her and began seeing her regularly, while perhaps continuing to pay other women to do the unconscious sex. Now that I know him, it's nearly as hard to imagine Cole in love as it is to believe that my mother would fall for a man who preferred to fuck her when she was unconscious. But I have to admit there were likely things about her that, as her ten-year-old daughter, I couldn't have known.

Of course, this theory still explains nothing about Iris's death or Stella's involvement in it, though I've begun to think that maybe Stella never knew my mother at all. It's possible Stella assumed Iris was one of Cole's sleeping beauties, and her presence the night of her death was only coincidence.

I hope this is the case; for all her eccentricities, I've come to actually like Stella. I've never had girlfriends, and while I guess we aren't exactly friends in the traditional sense, seeing as I'm her employee and also lying to her about pretty much everything, I do enjoy her company. Her flair for the theatrical is exaggerated, but her wit is dry, and she has a way of making everything seem grand yet at the same time a little frivolous, as though we're characters in a high-society melodrama from a bygone era. Where at first I thought her delusional, I now see that she's only editing the film of her life as she goes. Some scenes—possibly some entire years—she's chosen to leave on the cutting room floor, focusing instead on the story she wants to tell, which she enhances for dramatic effect. Okay, so maybe she is delusional.

Madison was a curveball I didn't expect. Stella had only informed me on the plane that the original actress had been replaced, and I'd been so wrapped up in my own plans that I stupidly hadn't had the forethought to ask by whom. I nearly had a heart attack when I first saw her the day we arrived. I'd been in acting class with Madison as Nikki Nimes, and she was right—we'd even done a scene together. I now realized that acting classes were obviously a mistake, but when I first moved to LA I'd never imagined that in a city of ten million I'd cross paths with any of those people again. Hollywood, though, turned out to be just as small as everyone was always saying it was.

Madison was as terrible an actress then as she is now, and I hadn't expected she'd actually have a career beyond whatever show she'd snaked her way onto by dating the studio exec that turned out to be Taylor's father. Yet another example of how small Hollywood really is. I'd lied handily when Madison called me out the first day, but still wasn't sure she totally believed me, regardless of my "much better nose" and brown eyes and hair.

The room phone rings and Stella answers. "Felicity," she calls after a moment. "It's Taylor, confirming our info for our plane tickets."

Good damn thing I legally changed my name before all this. I take the handset from her. "Hi, Taylor. I thought you weren't booking tickets until five."

Taylor and Jackson had held a crew meeting this morning at breakfast, during which they'd announced the impending hurricane and given everyone until five this evening to decide whether they wanted to shelter on Saint Ann or fly out.

"The flights are all full," she says. "I'm gonna have to charter a jet, so I need to get a head count. Are you guys flying?"

"A jet?" I ask, surprised. "How'd you convince Cole to pay for that?"

"Jackson's paying for it."

My heart involuntarily swells with—I don't know what. "Jesus."

"What?" Stella asks.

"Jackson's chartering a jet," I tell her. "Do we want to go with them?"

Stella throws a thumbs-up as there's a rapping at the door.

"We're in," I say into the phone.

After I hang up, I answer the door to find none other than Jackson himself outside, shading his eyes against the noonday sun. "You talk to Taylor yet?" he asks.

"I just got off the phone with her. A jet, huh?"

He tucks a strand of unruly dark hair behind his ear, a mannerism I've come to recognize means he's stressed. "No other way out at this point, and I'm not gonna risk the lives of my crew. I'm headed up to the restaurant to grab some lunch. Come with?"

"Sure." I slip on my flip-flops and sunglasses and call out to Stella, "I'm going to get food with Jackson. You want anything?"

"I'm good," she returns.

I sneak a glance at Jackson as we stride down the dock together beneath the cloudless blue sky. He's tanned and has put on some muscle in his shoulders from working out with Cole's trainer, which he credits with reducing his stress level. There's no doubt that the shoot—and especially working with his father—has been trying. But he thrives on set. He's in his element working with the crew and the actors to make each scene come to life. He really encourages a collaborative creative environment, listening to the desires of each department and implementing them when possible, always holding on to the ideal of what's best for the film. He's well liked and respected by everyone except for Cole, who undermines him every chance he gets. Cole's the one with the jealous streak, not Stella, and he can't stand it that his son is more loved than he is.

Jackson did almost recognize me the first time he saw me, though of course I denied ever having met him. It was the first day we'd arrived, and I was sunbathing on a rock that jutted out over the turquoise water when he swam over to say hello. He welcomed me to the island, thanked me for coming down, and asked what department I was in. I noticed him looking at me funny as I told him I was Stella's assistant.

"Have we met?" he asked.

"I don't think so," I replied.

"You look so familiar."

"People always think I'm some girl on a show about teenage vampires," I said, rolling my eyes. "I've never seen it."

This was always a valid explanation in LA, where you could never be sure whether the cute guy in line behind you at the juice bar was familiar because you'd crossed paths in real life, or he was mildly famous.

"Maybe that's it." He shrugged. "Or maybe we met at a party or something and I embarrassed myself trying to talk to you."

"Maybe," I'd said, laughing to cover up my surprise at how close he was to the truth. "But I don't remember."

At which point he splashed me.

Part of my plan had been to get close to him in hopes of gleaning some information relating to my mother's death—a task I'd looked forward to after our brief meeting at the Blue Cat—but I've found myself unable to complete the seduction. The problem isn't a lack of desire. I see the way he looks at me; all it would take is a well-timed knock on his bungalow door and I'd be a permanent fixture in his bed. The problem is me.

It's not that I don't want him. Truth be told, I'd love nothing more than to dive into bed with him, and in the privacy of my own room at night I fantasize about it with an unfamiliar longing that's never satisfied when I finish myself off. But I can't deceive him. Or rather, I don't want to.

There's this infectious openness to him, an honesty about who he is and what he wants, a curiosity about life along with a willingness to embrace its beauty and strangeness without shying away from the unpleasant parts. He has no need for a coat of armor made of irony and cynicism; he comes bare-chested with sincerity and humor. If I make him sound unsophisticated or naive, then I misrepresent. He's generally the smartest person in the room; he chooses candor.

Complicating things is the fact that he's declared it his mission to make me laugh. I've never been a person who laughs a lot, not having had any friends, but he's sought out my sense of humor until he knows exactly what to say or what look to give me across a room to coax the unfamiliar fizz of delight from my throat.

He's confided in me about growing up with a mother more interested in partying with her model friends than raising a son and a father for whom he was nothing more than a photo op; told me horrifying tales of boarding school in Switzerland and wild stories about his gap year in India and the resulting passion for yoga, which he credits with saving his life. Never, though, has he come close to saying anything about Iris.

It would have been easier if he were self-centered and satisfied with talking about himself, but no such luck. He asks me endless questions about my life, my convictions, my aspirations—which I answer as truthfully as I can. The aspirations are easy: I don't know. I haven't gone to college. It's not too late, but I don't know what I'd study—I can't see myself as a lawyer or a doctor or an HR director. I enjoy acting— wearing the face of a character is both exhilarating and liberating— but especially after getting to know Stella, I'm not sure I want to be chewed up and spit out by the entertainment industry (a sentiment he understands). What I can't tell him, of course, is that the only thing I've ever really wanted is to take revenge on my mother's killer, which seems more and more likely to be his father.

Convictions are more difficult—what do I believe in? My go-to answer has always been *an eye for an eye*. But I'm beginning to under-stand that life is sometimes more complicated than that.

I've been as honest as I can about my history; I've shared that my mother died and I never knew my father, and he respected my wishes when I told him it was too painful to discuss. I've confessed my lonely adolescence with my grandparents and the horrors of their church, careful to substitute New Hampshire for Pennsylvania in keeping with what I'd told Stella. I haven't told him that in the past few weeks I've become closer with him than I've ever allowed myself to be with a man, or anyone for that matter—but I think he knows.

We tromp down the stairs to the empty beach and kick off our sandals to trek across the soft sand. The waves are high, but other than that, there's still no sign of the storm. "We never should have shot down here in hurricane season." He sighs. "Taylor and I tried and tried to talk Cole out of it, but he insisted. It was the only time he'd do it. It's all gonna be over if the storm comes this way. There won't be any more movie. It may already be over. The crew may not even come back."

"But they love you," I protest.

"Not as much as they hate my dad." He shakes his head. "It's strange—regardless of how he is to those closest to him, he can usually make a crew love him. But this time it's like he's not even trying. There's something different about him. I don't know. Maybe it's me."

"Hate to be the one to tell you, but your dad's a dick," I whisper.

"That's not exactly new information." At the tree line, we slip our shoes back on to walk up the shaded path through the ferns and white flowering plants toward the restaurant. "He's only producing this movie to bribe me, anyway."

My ears perk up. "What do you mean?"

He pushes his Wayfarers up on his nose as we start up the wide stairway that curves around the blue tiled waterfall wall to the pool area. "It's a long story."

"I got time," I return too quickly.

"It's not explicit. He didn't come out and say he was bribing me, but we both know it. There are...things that happened when I was a kid that he wishes I didn't know about."

This is the closest he's ever come to alluding to my mother. I try to keep the excitement out of my voice. "Like what?"

But we've reached the pool deck, and he gestures to the hive of activity on the restaurant patio up ahead. "Now's not the time."

I grab his arm and turn him toward me. "You're seriously gonna drop the bomb your father is bribing you and then you say it's 'not the time' to tell me why? That's mean!"

I expect him to laugh with me, but he doesn't. "I'm sorry." He lowers his voice and pulls me into the shade of an orange-flowering flamboyant tree at the edge of the deck. "I shouldn't have said anything. I'm just really angry at this whole situation—at myself as much as I am at him. The fact I let him bribe me and set the terms, the way he's behaved since we've been here, and now that the entire movie's going to just whoosh! Disappear because of a storm." He sighs. "It's appropriate though. He doesn't deserve success, and neither do I."

Is this what the guilt of keeping quiet about my mother's death has done to him? The irony is that it's exactly what I would have wanted before I got to know him. But now... Now my feelings are more complicated. "What are you talking about? Of course you deserve success. You're really good at what you do—you're a great writer and director and everybody loves you." It's all true. "No one deserves it more than you."

"The only reason I'm here is because my asshole dad is famous."

"So? What does that matter? Make it work for you. Do you know how many people would kill to be in your position? Don't be a little bitch."

He raises his eyebrows, and his dimple deepens, a sure sign he's holding back a smile. "A little bitch, huh?"

I shrug. "I'm surprised to hear this bullshit coming from you. You never seemed like the type to feel sorry for yourself."

He laughs. "No holds barred. See, this is why I like you, Felicity Fox." He narrows his eyes at me. "How'd you get a name like that, anyway?"

I mirror him. "Now's not the time." I smirk.

I can feel his eyes on me as I stride across the sun-splashed deck toward the restaurant.

# Stella

The calm before the storm stretched over the island like a cat in the sun. I stood on the porch of my bungalow gazing out at the line where the powder-blue sky met the cerulean of the sea, searching for signs of what was to come, but none were apparent. The air was still and thick, the heat oppressive with no wind to disrupt it. I raised my sweating glass to my lips and took a long, sweet draw of ice-cold rum and ginger. The trick was to drink quickly, before the ice melted. I considered the dive pool, but I simply didn't have the energy. Inside, Mary Elizabeth yapped at a school of fish visible through one of the glass windows on the floor. I stepped back into the blasting air-conditioning, silently glided the door closed behind me, and returned to my post on the couch.

After endless debate, the weather reporters all agreed: Hurricane Celia was headed straight for our idyllic island. All day, resort employees had been hastily closing the storm shutters, placing sandbags, and doing something to the edges of the roofs in preparation for her arrival. Felicity had thrown most of my clothes into my suitcase in anticipation of our departure tomorrow morning, but I hadn't let her pack my makeup and toiletries yet. We still had plenty of time.

Where was Felicity? It felt like it had been hours since she'd left for lunch with Jackson, but a check of my phone revealed she'd been gone only twenty minutes, which meant I still had two hours until it was time for another A-pill, regardless of how anxious I was. It was never time yet. I felt like my whole life I was always waiting for it to be time.

I still didn't quite know what to think of Jackson. I knew I should be suspicious of him now after all Cole told me, but was Cole really to be trusted? The fact that Jackson was spending God-only-knows-what to charter a plane to fly his crew to safety sure didn't line up with Cole's claims, and truth be told, I'd always liked Jackson when he was a boy. I'd only spent a short time with him, of course, but he never treated me like the evil stepmonster; he was always so kind and easy that he made me yearn for children of my own, which of course made my failed pregnancy only more crushing.

He'd been kind to me now as well, and he was obviously head over heels for Felicity. I was happy for her. He wasn't classically handsome like his father, but he had that dimple, and his complete lack of self-consciousness was sexy. Plus, if she decided she wanted a career as an actress, it couldn't hurt that he was a budding director with a famous father. It was obvious Felicity was equally as smitten with him as he was with her, but she assured me she wasn't sleeping with him. I couldn't fathom why; I sure would have been. I yearned for the foolish passion of young love, unfettered by caveats and baggage. They didn't know how lucky they were.

I poured myself another rum, skipping the ginger this time. My weather reporter friends Ed and Roberta (what a name, poor girl) weren't giving me any new information, so I finally grabbed the remote and switched the channel. Nothing but hurricane coverage on every station. I didn't need any more hurricane coverage. The hurricane was coming; I got it. I could have been the reporter at this point; I had all their lines memorized. Perhaps I should have been a weather girl. I liked the weather, and they always wore such cute outfits.

I switched to the resort's On Demand feature and scrolled through endless movie titles. There was a whole section devoted to movies with Cole in them—as a troubled trust fund kid in *Bad Boy*, a vigilante cop in *Bloodhound*, a charming but ruthless double agent in the Gentleman Gangster series, and of course, right there in the middle of the list was the film we did together. *Faster*. The catalyst. Ironic that it was about a relationship that moved at the speed of light and crashed spectacularly. If I'd never done that film, never met him, where would my life be today?

The poster featured our thirteen-years-younger faces staring longingly into each other's eyes. The passion was real; I was in love with him when we shot that poster and believed he was in love with me—though now I wondered if he was even capable of real love. The photo shoot had been the week before we ran off to Vegas and got married. We'd been fucking like rabbits for a whole six weeks, and he had me completely convinced he was my knight in shining armor—back when I thought I needed a knight in shining armor, which of course he wasn't anyway. But at the time I was addicted to him. Everyone on the crew was tittering behind our backs because we couldn't keep our hands off each other, but we didn't care. It would be funny if it hadn't all turned out so sad.

Sometimes I felt like the Ghost of Christmas Past, visiting myself in happier times. I drew out the golden moments with an appreciation I never had when living through them: nights in satin and diamonds, the scent of freshly applied lipstick and the pop of the flashbulbs as the velvet rope lifted; press junkets in foreign cities, signing autographs for smiling fans whose languages I didn't speak; the stick of pine needles beneath my knees and frost on my skin, fanning the ephemeral flame of truth for the camera. Watching an old movie I'd done was like a portal into the past.

I selected *Faster* and settled into the pillows with Mary Elizabeth in my lap. The piano riff to "Mad World" began to play beneath the familiar credit sequence, and there I was. Splendor in the springtime of life. My skin lustrous, my eyes bright, not a wrinkle in sight—I really was something. The deep emerald-green evening dress I was wearing clung to my curves and dipped nearly to my belly button, revealing legs for days and perky side boob every time I moved. I'd loved that dress. I kept it after we wrapped, but burned it after Iris...

Without warning, the vision of Iris wearing that dress filled my mind, spinning in circles so fast she crashed into my bed, dizzy. The moment I knew I wasn't in love with Cole anymore.

Iris loved that dress even more than I did. She liked to put it on and imitate my lines until we collapsed in a heap of giggles. That's the thing I remembered most about Iris: the laughter.

But I couldn't think of Iris.

Iris standing on the diving board of my pool, turning back to smile with the sun in her hair before plunging into the shimmering blue.

Iris humming off-key while cooking dinner in the kitchen, a glass of red wine in hand.

I'd been so good in recent years about not thinking of Iris, but spending time with Cole had opened Pandora's box. I couldn't help myself; all the memories from that time were fighting to get out, clawing their way to the surface.

Thirteen years and I hadn't told a soul.

I wiped my cheeks and realized that I was crying. Silly after so many years to still be so emotional. But I couldn't help it when I thought of the future we had planned, all gone in an instant, as though it had never even existed. She was the only person who had ever truly loved me for myself, and I'd never been allowed to mourn her.

I scooped up Mary Elizabeth and wandered into my room, where I rifled through my suitcase in search of the sketches I kept neatly folded inside the jacket of my signed copy of Uta Hagen's *Respect for Acting*. I sat on the bed and removed the jacket, carefully spreading the drawings out on the down comforter. The light streamed through the windows, illuminating the yellowed paper and faded colored pencil. The first sketch was of me, naked, looking over my shoulder at the artist, the green dress dangling from my hand. The second depicted

Iris, also naked and lying with her head on a pillow, her eyes closed and her flaxen hair spread out around her, the way she was when I first laid eyes on her. A sleeping beauty.

Suddenly inspired, I extracted the nearly empty journal that was to be my memoir from the bedside table and opened it. I didn't have to include it in the final version of the book, but I found I desperately needed to write it down. It could be cathartic, for my eyes only; no one ever needed to read it. I picked up a pen and began writing words I'd never spoken to a soul.

# The Love of My Life

I wasn't supposed to be home that day. I'd wrapped the film I was shooting early and caught a plane back to Miami without telling Cole, as a surprise for our nine-month anniversary. Oh, how things had changed between us in a few short months. We were caught in a vicious cycle of insults that could never be unsaid followed by flying plates and days without speaking. The makeup sex wasn't even good anymore. I'd thought the gesture might help heal things between us, so I had planned a romantic dinner at a swanky restaurant, followed by a night of molly and dancing at our favorite club.

He'd assured me that he'd be around all weekend studying lines for his next project, so I was disappointed when I arrived home that evening to find his G wagon missing and some kind of beat-up hatchback parked in the garage. The alarm was off as I entered the house; I called out and no one answered. I thought it odd, but the front door had been locked and nothing seemed amiss, so I ventured upstairs.

The door to our bedroom was ajar, the curtains drawn and the lights dimmed. Atop the huge mahogany four-poster bed that presided over the mostly beige room someone had placed a red velvet blanket, upon which was resting the most beautiful girl I'd ever seen. Her golden hair was spread across my pillow like a halo, her angelic face in repose; her naked body smooth and supple, as though she'd been airbrushed.

My first response was shock; I yelped, but she didn't budge.

My second response was envy: who was this girl and why was she in my bed? It was relatively obvious why she was in my bed—after all, I did share it with one of the most notorious playboys in the world, and I knew about his sleeping fetish—but I hadn't imagined he'd do it in our bed. And with a girl whose looks put me to shame!

My third response was concern. Why was she still sleeping? Why had he left her there? Was she alive?

I crept closer to her and gingerly placed my fingers on her wrist. I couldn't find a pulse, but I was no doctor, and remembering that I'd once checked for breath with a mirror in a film, I extracted my compact from my purse and held it beneath her nose. I had to position my head right next to hers to view the reflection, but was relieved to see a faint trace of fog on the mirror as she almost imperceptibly exhaled. She smelled of jasmine.

Next to the bed was a syringe, and the only blemish on her golden skin was a series of holes on the inside of her elbow. Heroin? My mind reeled. He was giving his sleeping girls heroin? I'd assumed sleeping pills were involved—or perhaps they pretended to sleep.

But heroin? He could kill her. I'd never tried it myself, but I'd had friends disappear down the slippery slope of opioid addiction, and it was not pretty.

I took her by the shoulders and shook her. She didn't respond. I gently slapped her cheek, then harder, but she continued to sleep. I tried to pull her up to sitting, but she was deadweight and I was dead tired from a night shoot followed by flying all day without having slept. I didn't know what to do. Should I call 911? But she didn't seem to be having any trouble breathing, and I couldn't have the press finding out there was a naked chick on heroin in my bed unless it was totally necessary. I went to the bathroom and filled a glass with cold water, then returned and threw it in her face.

She gasped as she sat up, disoriented. Her wild blue eyes landed on me and her brow furrowed, a flicker of recognition spreading across her face. I had the urge to apologize to her, but I squelched it, seeing as she'd been fucking my husband in my bed. "You wouldn't wake up," I said.

I threw a towel in her lap, but she disregarded it, continuing to stare at me with something akin to wonder. "Stella," she croaked.

"Yeah," I said. "You should probably get your shit together and get out of here. Where did Cole go?"

She looked around, as if realizing where she was for the first time. "I don't know. What time is it?"

I glanced at the little silver clock on the bedside table. "Seven."

"I'm sorry," she said.

"It's okay, I knew…about his fetish," I admitted. "I'm just surprised to find you here."

"I'm sorry to be in your space." She picked up the towel and began to dry herself. "I wouldn't usually go to someone's home, but he's paying me a lot of money." She met my eye, and I could tell she really was sorry. "I have a daughter," she added.

"Where is she now?"

"At home. She's ten and she's really mature, so..."

I picked up the syringe. "Heroin?"

A slight wince as she nodded. "His choice. I wasn't a user before."

I assessed her big blue eyes, her pert little nose and pouty lips. I wasn't jealous or angry with her, as I would have thought I'd been. Instead I found myself strangely drawn to her in a way I couldn't explain, and I overwhelmingly felt the need to protect her from my predator of a husband. "Whatever he's giving you, it's not worth it," I said. "You're ruining your life."

She pushed herself off the bed and wobbly stood to her feet, but her knees gave out. I caught her and eased her back onto the bed. "Stay here," I instructed.

Her clothes were neatly folded on a chair in front of the fireplace, where blue flames danced behind the glass—an unnecessary feature in a place where the temperature rarely dipped below seventy degrees. I deposited her little pile of belongings on the bed next to her, and she shimmied into a short silver party dress that hugged her every curve.

"Does he use condoms with you?" I asked.

"Yes," she answered quickly, then paused, thinking. "He's supposed to. But I'm asleep, so..."

We sat in silence for a moment, both of us realizing that he wasn't using condoms. "I'm trying to get a down payment for a place for my daughter and me," she offered. "I'm mostly a dancer, but that can't last forever, and I thought if I had a nest egg, it could cover the thin times while I learned to do something else."

I didn't know what to say. Her story was trite; I'd heard versions of it the handful of times I'd been in strip clubs, and always supposed it to be something the girls made up to get the guys to give them more money. But as it passed her lips, my heart went out to her, and I felt like a total bitch for having assumed all those other girls were lying. Well, probably some of them were, but I didn't think this one was.

Again she tried to stand, this time becoming so dizzy she dropped to her knees on the plush carpet before I could catch her. "You shouldn't drive yet," I said as I helped her back into the bed. "I'll get you something to eat."

"You're so nice." She smiled. "I always thought you'd be nice."

Downstairs I made us a flatbread and texted Cole that I'd found his whore in our bed and he should plan on sleeping elsewhere tonight. I poured myself a glass of wine and lit the half a joint I found in the ashtray, both of which I finished while the pizza cooked.

When I came back upstairs, I found her dozing again. I couldn't help but notice how long her lashes were as I shook her shoulder, realizing I didn't even know her name. She roused more easily this time and smiled when she saw me. "What's your name?" I asked.

"Iris." Her hand flew to her mouth. "Don't tell Cole. He thinks I'm Barbie."

I laughed. "Barbie? Really? He can't possibly think your name is really Barbie."

She shrugged. "You wouldn't believe how many guys have Barbie fantasies. It must be something left over from childhood."

I rolled my eyes. "Men."

"Tell me about it," she agreed.

We talked lightly as we ate on my bed with the tray between us, and she seemed to feel better with the food. It was odd though. I'd been working since I was so young that I'd never had many female friends, but this wasn't like getting to know a new female costar or the girlfriend of one of Cole's friends; there was something charged about our interaction. After dinner, we watched a show on HBO that turned explicitly sexual in a matter of minutes.

"I wonder if they get off sometimes," she said, watching two girls and a guy fondle one another on a bed bedecked with furs.

"It's usually pretty awkward with the crew in the room—and lights and privacy covers and getting the right angle," I said. "Plus, for some reason, they always seem to shoot love scenes in the first days, before you've even had a chance to get comfortable with your costar. But when you have chemistry with the other actor, it can be...different."

"You looked like you were into it with Cole. I got turned on watching that scene where you're in that hotel. You were so sensual."

The heat rose in my cheeks. "Yeah," I admitted. "Cole and I...Well, back when we first met, we were superhot for each other and we didn't always wear the protective coverings when we did our love scenes. Sometimes...well, it wasn't totally professional. I can't believe I'm telling you this."

Her gaze rested on me. "Naughty."

I felt flushed. "I've been traveling all day," I said. "I could use a shower."

"Why don't you make it a bath?" she asked, her eyes locked on mine. "I could use one as well."

There was nothing innocent in her suggestion. My breath grew shallow. I'd had threesomes with Cole on occasion and enjoyed it more than I cared to admit, but I had never been with a woman solo. This was before it was cool to be something other than straight, especially for a known actress. But I'd be lying if I said I wasn't attracted to her, and what would be the harm? It wasn't like I was cheating, really. My husband had been with her this very afternoon. It would be like a threesome, only at different times.

"Okay," I breathed.

I got up and walked to the bathroom, and she followed. Nervous, I dimmed the lights, started the water running, and went around lighting all the candles I'd put out as decoration and never used, as a way of distracting myself. When I turned around, she was again naked, standing before me in all her glory. "First time?" she whispered.

I nodded. "Are you . . . often with women?"

I cringed at how inexperienced I sounded, but she was unfazed. "I prefer women." She smiled. "Men are work."

She approached and grazed my body with hers as she untied my wrap dress and pushed it off my shoulders. I was glad I'd worn my La Perla, in anticipation of seeing Cole. But it didn't stay on for long. "You're so beautiful," she murmured before she touched her soft lips to mine.

The next few hours were a revelation to me. I'd always liked sex just fine, but I'd never known it could be what she showed me. Where I'd thought I would hook up with a woman to see what it was like, I discovered a whole new side of myself I didn't even know I was missing.

When she left at midnight to go home to her daughter, I asked her to please stop using the heroin, promising I would pay for rehab if she couldn't. "I know Cole's paying you a lot, but please..." I begged. "I'll pay you more."

"I don't want you to pay me," she said. "And I'll stop seeing Cole altogether if it means I can see you."

We got lucky: Cole left for a shoot in New York, and I was between projects, so we had the house to ourselves for the next few weeks. She detoxed from the drugs, which wasn't as horrible for her as it could have been, because she was so new to them. She was protective of her daughter and didn't want me to meet her until she was certain that I'd be in her life, but we spent every hour she wasn't with her daughter together, and I fell for her hard and fast. I've always been one to fall hard and fast, honestly, but she was different, and not just because she was a woman. Being with her was easy; there was no ego, no hidden agenda, no land mines waiting to be stepped on. I felt more myself with her than I'd ever felt with anyone in my life.

"Okay," I told her one night as we sat on the edge of my pool with our feet dangling into the water. "Let's do it. I'll leave Cole."

"But, Stella," she balked, "your career."

"It's the twenty-first century. It's okay," I said, trying to convince myself.

"It's one thing to say you like women as well as men," she pointed out, "or to allude to having had sex with women. Men, who you've said a million times are still the majority of the ones making the decisions in Hollywood, find that sexy. But to have a woman as a life partner is a different thing."

"Yes, darling, but you're gorgeous," I teased, stroking her beautiful face with the back of my hand. "How can they fault me?"

"Even if you identify as bisexual, when you leave Cole—the Sexiest Man in Hollywood—for me and they see us together in a relationship, all of a sudden you're gay, which makes you unfuckable, and therefore uncastable."

I recoiled at her harsh words.

"I'm sorry, but you're going to have to have a little thicker skin if you really want to do this," she said gently.

"What a screwed-up world we live in." I sighed.

"Yeah," she agreed. "There's no such thing as normal when it comes to sex—believe me, I've seen it all—but you have to understand most people don't even share their fantasies with their partners. Americans have these puritanical ideas about what sex is supposed to be, inherited from our prudish ancestors. My parents think that being gay is a sin. Of course, they also think sex before marriage is a sin. But so does a lot of our country, a lot of your fans."

She was right, obviously, and I'd never been brave. It wasn't in my genetic code. But she emboldened me. I'd learned more about sexuality in the few weeks I'd spent with her than I had in my entire twenty-seven years. I loved her. And if I couldn't be with her, then what was the point of any of this? "Maybe it's time to do something about it," I suggested. "We could set an example, show people it's okay to be different."

"Cole won't make it easy to leave him. You know that, right?"

I waved away her concern. "He'll be glad to be rid of me."

"Maybe." She bit her lip, thinking.

Later that evening, she spilled wine on her dress while we were cooking and went upstairs to borrow one of mine. I came up shortly afterward to find her standing in a thong in front of Cole's dresser, staring intently at something in her hand. "What is it?" I asked.

She dropped whatever it was back into the drawer. "Nothing. Wrong drawer." She turned and gave me a sexy smile. "But now that you're here and I'm already almost naked..."

She spun me around and slowly unzipped my dress, whispering in my ear as she did. "I have an idea, to make sure Cole lets you go without a struggle."

"I'm telling you, he'll be glad to be rid of me," I said as my dress fell to the floor.

"Divorce is never pretty. And the other women Cole's split with haven't fared so well." She pressed her body to my back and reached her hand down the front of my panties. "Remember the sex tape of Bar Salmaan that surfaced shortly after they divorced? And Keri Kline never worked as an actress again after the rumors about the racist slurs." The movement of her fingers made it difficult to concentrate. "I should let him sleep fuck me one more time and tape it, just in case he tries anything on you."

"Iris, you can't do heroin again. I won't allow it."

"I'd do it for you."

"Please don't."

We tumbled to the floor as one and never finished the conversation. But once she left, I opened the drawer where she'd stowed whatever she'd held in her hand earlier and took out a rainbow rabbit's foot. The initials "CS" were burned into the paw. I asked her about it a few days afterward, and when she didn't know what I was talking about, I opened the drawer to show her. But the rabbit's foot was gone.

A week later, so was she.

I closed the journal and spread the final drawing on the bed before me. It was the two of us holding hands, our shoulders squared, feet firmly planted upon a miniature globe. At the bottom in her handwriting was scrawled *The world is ours*. Only, the drawing was unfinished. Our bodies were filled out and colored in, but our feet and the earth were only a pencil outline, a perfect metaphor for the dreams that, with her death, evaporated like mist in the sun.

# Taylor

I sat at the table in my bungalow keying the passport numbers of our crew into the form on the jet charter company's website while Francisco paced with the phone to his ear, trying to find a decent hotel in Georgetown, Guyana, with a big enough block of rooms to accommodate everyone. We'd chosen Georgetown because the jet charged by the hour and it was the closest city that was definitely out of the path of the hurricane, but so far it looked like we were going to have to do three different hotels. Not ideal, but better than the alternative of going through the paperwork necessary to fly everyone elsewhere.

It felt odd to be doing all this work to avoid a storm when the day outside was sunny and clear. I gazed through the glass wall across the mottled sea toward the verdant slope of Saint Ann. Out on the water I spied Rick's fishing boat cruising toward the resort pier, hidden around the bend of the island where Cole's giant new yacht was docked. The asshole could buy a yacht, but he couldn't fly his crew to safety. No surprise there.

The immediate need for arrangements to move fifty-four people to a different country had briefly taken my mind off my physical and emotional troubles, but the sight of Rick's boat reminded me of the far-reaching impact this storm was likely to have. There was no denying the very real possibility that the island might no longer be a place we could shoot a film after this. Despite Cole's claims, I couldn't imagine these over-water bungalows weathering much more than a thunderstorm. Our cameras and computers would fly with us, but would the rest of our film equipment survive? Would there be electricity? Clean water?

I had the sinking feeling that a postponement of the film signaled the end. Which, I realized, meant I might never see Rick again. An uninvited lump formed in my throat at the thought. It wasn't fair. I liked him. I *really* liked him. But it didn't matter. As much as I hated it, with the recent turn of events, separation was probably for the best. I hadn't yet had the time or brain space to formulate a plan as to how to address my current predicament, but no matter what I decided, it didn't bode well for our budding romance.

"Okay," Francisco said, hanging up the phone. "I've got it down to two hotels, and they're across the street from each other. We can divide everyone up on the plane."

"Nice work." I raised my palm, and he slapped it. "Wheels up is at one tomorrow, so I've reserved a ferry at eleven and a bus to shuttle us to the airport on Saint Ann. Breakfast at nine thirty. The hotel staff that haven't already left will be traveling on the ferry with us to Saint Ann and sheltering in a church there."

"You're a rock star," he said.

"Thanks," I said, relieved we'd made all the arrangements. "Make sure you tell everyone to take all of their belongings with them. If the storm's a bad one..."

"Aw." He gave my shoulders a squeeze. "This is so sad. It's been fun, hasn't it?" Not exactly the adjective I would have chosen, but I was glad he thought so. He looked out at the sea. "I'm gonna go meet some guys for a last game of volleyball on the beach. You wanna join?"

"Thank you," I said, "but I need to pack. Have fun."

He gave me a little wave as he headed for the door, and I returned to my computer screen to check the names one last time.

"Look who I found," Francisco called from the doorway.

I heard the door slam behind him as I turned to see Rick, looking more serious than I ever recalled seeing him.

"What are you doing over here?" I asked with a smile. "I figured you'd be storm prepping."

"I'm in the middle of it. Came over to collect Cole's boat to put it in safe storage on Saint Ann, but he wouldn't let me take it."

"He wants to keep it here? Won't it—I don't know, sink?"

He shrugged. "Maybe. But it's his boat. I can't force him to protect it." He scanned the mess of papers spread across the table before me. "Is this a bad time?"

I shut my laptop and laughed. "It's always a bad time, but not for you. I'm glad you're here."

"I hear you guys are flying to Guyana tomorrow."

I rose to hug him. "Yeah." Time slowed as we lingered with our arms around each other. I rested my head on his chest, storing the memory of his strong body against mine, the light smell of his aftershave mixed with salt air. After a moment, he pulled away just enough to force me to look up at him.

"Hey," he said, his caramel eyes searching mine. "You okay?"

No. I wasn't. The lump in my throat swelled. "I..." I wiped away a stray tear with the back of my hand, unsure what to say. "I'm sorry."

"You have nothing to apologize for." He bear-hugged me, which only made me cry more. "It's okay."

But it wasn't. I took a deep breath and looked up at him.

"Do you wanna talk?" he asked.

Brave man.

I nodded. "I just need to get a tissue."

He smiled and released me. "Okay."

In the bathroom, I blew my nose, then splashed my face with cold water and rubbed depuffer under my eyes as I tried to figure out what exactly to say to him. I didn't have to tell him, of course. I'd only known him a couple of weeks, and it was unlikely I'd ever see him again after tomorrow. We hadn't even slept together. But he'd been kind to me; he'd reminded me that there were good guys out there.

And since we couldn't end up together anyway, what was the harm in telling him the truth? Sure, I didn't like the fact that I'd allowed myself to be taken advantage of—the optics weren't great, but I was sick of optics. I was sick of trying so freaking hard to be cool, of caring so freaking much what everyone else thought of me.

I found him outside, lounging on the daybed in the shade of the palapa. I sat next to him, and he took my hand. "I'm pregnant," I said. I waited for him to flinch and remove his hand, but he didn't. "I was raped."

At this, he sat up. "What?"

Rick listened intently as I clumsily unspooled the tale of my blackout night with Cole, his denial we'd slept together, and my realization that he'd drugged me. When I was finished, he pulled me into another bear hug as I shed more tears—though this time they were tears of relief. Just the act of voicing my story had lifted an enormous weight from my shoulders.

"I wanna kill him," Rick growled into my hair.

"Me too."

He pulled me into his lap and cupped my face in his hands. "I am so sorry this happened to you."

"On the bright side, at least I don't remember the rape part."

"Are you going to press charges?"

I sighed. "I don't know. I want to. But it's my word against his, and after the lies my father spread about me, my word isn't exactly golden. I am gonna quit working for him though."

"Shit. I'd hope so." He stopped himself. "I support you whatever you want to do, but..." His jaw tensed. "He should have to pay for what he's done. He shouldn't be allowed to do it to other women."

"Like Stella," I agreed. "I know."

"I don't want you to go to Guyana with him." He popped his knuckles. "I don't want you anywhere near him. I want to—" He balled his hand into a fist and slammed it into the mattress.

"He's not coming," I said. "He's staying here."

He looked at me sideways. "On the island?"

"Yep. Says it's safe, and we're all being crazy."

"Maybe he'll get blown away by the storm."

"One can dream," I agreed. "You could come to Guyana with us? There's room on the plane."

He sighed. "I need to stay here with my family. It's not so much the storm—a cat one won't be such a big a deal on Saint Ann—it's the cleanup. My parents—they aren't getting any younger."

I nodded. "You know we probably won't be coming back."

He pressed his forehead to mine. "I was afraid you'd say that."

"It's probably for the best though," I said. "I'm a wreck, in a complicated situation. You don't want to be involved with me right now."

He placed a finger lightly to my lips. "Don't tell me what I want." His eyes grew serious. "I know it's crazy because we just met, and we live thousands of miles apart—"

"And I'm pregnant and haven't decided yet what to do about it," I added. "Because I have to be honest, I haven't. If you'd asked me before this happened what I would do, what I should do..." I sighed. "It's different when it's hypothetical. I'm not sure yet, and you should know that."

He nodded, rubbing my palm with his thumb. "That too. But I guess I'm a romantic. I don't meet a lot of girls I like, and I like you. I'd like to..." He shrugged, and the corner of his mouth lifted. "See?"

My heart inflated like a balloon. "Even if where it goes is nowhere?"

He laughed. "With expectations that low, what do we have to lose?"

He wrapped my legs around his waist and kissed me. Every nerve in my body tingled as he ran his big hands up my back beneath my shirt. "Is this okay?" he asked, laying me gently back on the daybed.

The breeze caressed my skin as I lifted my shirt over my head in answer and pulled him to me.

# Felicity

Last sunset on the island. Last beach stroll in the rosy twilight, the crescent bay reflecting the radiant sky. The waves this evening are larger than I've seen them, cresting chest high before crashing onto the shore, leaving cliff-like ridges in their wake. The wind is cool on my bare shoulders, blowing my short hair into my face. In all my incarnations, this is the shortest my hair has been, and I like it. I do miss my eyes though. With all the sand and seawater, the contacts are irritating, and I never quite feel like I'm seeing myself when I look in the mirror.

Mary Elizabeth runs circles around my feet as I march across the sand toward where Jackson waits for me at the water's edge like a heartthrob from a teen movie, his locks tousled by the steady breeze.

"Hi." He goes in for a hug as I turn to start walking, leaving us in a clumsy spoon embrace. He laughs, and the awkwardness is immediately diffused. I allow myself a brief moment to enjoy the comfortable closeness of his arms around me before pulling away to give Mary Elizabeth a bit of kibble. Every inch I permit myself with him only makes me want another. It's a vicious cycle that can't last. "I can't believe this is all going to be destroyed tomorrow," I comment.

"Hopefully not completely destroyed. Maybe we'll be back to finish the film." Our eyes meet. "No, you're right. We're not finishing the film. Fuck."

"Are you okay?" I ask.

He shakes his head. "No. But maybe it's for the best. I knew going into it that working with my dad was going to be hard, but shit. This has been worse than I'd ever imagined." He laughs bitterly. "It's my fault for giving in to the lure of nepotism."

I roll my eyes. "Believe me, if nepotism had been available to me at any point in my life, I would have been on it like white on rice. And so would pretty much everyone else in the world."

He smiles. "So stop being a little bitch?"

I hit him playfully in the biceps. "Exactly."

"It helps having you around to talk to." I can feel his eyes on me, but I keep mine trained on the pink-tinged sand in front of me. "I hope we can keep it up when we're back in LA."

A crab scuttles across our path, and Mary Elizabeth scampers backward. My mouth struggles to form the words I don't want to say. "I don't know whether I'm going back to LA."

It's an idea I've been toying with but now realize I probably need to follow through on. I've grown too close to Stella and Taylor—and most of all, Jackson. As much as I'd love nothing more than to do all the dirty things I've been fantasizing about with Jackson in real life, I haven't been able to come up with a scenario that doesn't involve me hurting him in the end. So while it will be painful to sever ties, I need to start over—start honestly—somewhere else.

He stops and grabs my hand, forcing me to meet his gaze. "Why? Where would you go?"

"I don't know." I start to walk again, trailing my feet through the warm water. "Travel, maybe. You know I've never even left the United States?"

He looks at me sideways. "You're out of the United States right now."

"I mean besides this."

"I love to travel," he says. "And it looks like I'm gonna have some free time on my hands. Where do you want to go?"

Why does he have to be so awesome?

"I don't know."

I can tell he's disheartened by my lack of enthusiasm, but he doesn't push. When we reach the outcropping of rocks that marks the end of the beach, he scoops up Mary Elizabeth and we scramble up the boulders to the top, where we stand watching the sun sink into the sea in a blaze of amber.

The temptation to travel with Jackson is almost enough to make me reconsider. But if he knew the truth of who I am, of why I'm here, of the lies I've told him—he wouldn't want anything to do with me. And I can't live a lie anymore.

My revenge tour is coming to an abrupt end without my learning anything definitive about my mother's death or executing any part of my plan. Well, that's not totally true. I can almost say with certainty that Stella's not responsible, and whether or not he murdered anyone, the world would unquestionably be a better place without Cole Power in it. But what purpose would killing him serve, other than to ruin me? Iris is gone; nothing can change that. I'm finally starting to be able to imagine a life for myself beyond all this, and it seems wrong to allow him to steal both my mother's future and my own. It also seems wrong to let him walk free, but life isn't fair. Jackson talks a lot about allowing. Maybe this is my time to learn that.

I feel him looking at me but keep my eyes trained on the horizon. "I've always wanted to go to Paris," I murmur. "My mom had this poster of the Eiffel Tower in her room when I was a kid, and we dreamed about going, but it never happened. I want to spread her ashes there."

"Funny," he says. "My mom lives in Paris. I'd love to take you there."

His gaze is still on me, but I don't turn, for fear he might kiss me— or perhaps for fear he might not. Finally he laughs, and I meet his olive eyes. "What?"

"You're like a rosebud," he says. "Slowly opening to the sun."

Hot tears spring to my eyes, I don't know why. It was a cheesy thing to say, but the thing is, it's true. I've been so tightly closed for so long, and suddenly, terribly inconveniently, I've begun to open. He wraps his arms around me, and I bury my wet face in his T-shirt. We've never been so close. I can hear his heartbeat beneath the warmth of his skin, and for the first time in thirteen years, I feel almost hopeful. But I don't dare look up; what could he possibly want with me? Regardless of my plans for an honest future, right now I'm a lie, and he deserves better.

We stand like that, the ocean breeze soft on our skin, until the color has drained from the sky. Finally, Mary Elizabeth starts yapping, impatient for her dinner. "I have to feed her," I say, kneeling beside her as an excuse not to look at him.

I scratch behind her ears and scoop her up, then scamper down the rocks to the sand. The entire way back to the bungalows in the gloaming, we speak lightly of matters of no consequence, but something's shifted between us. Thickened. If only I were the girl he thinks I am.

His bungalow is closer to shore than mine, and when we reach it, he turns to me with an inviting half smile. "Wanna chill here?"

"I can't," I say. "I've gotta check on Stella—I've left her alone all day."

"Good luck," he says. "Hope she's not too drunk."

"Thanks." I blow him a kiss.

I push open the door to my bungalow to find it dark and quiet. "Stella?" I call out. No answer.

I flip on a lamp and pour Mary Elizabeth's dinner into a bowl in the kitchen, then call out again, "Hello? Anybody home?"

When she still doesn't answer, I shed my shoes and tromp back to her room. I nudge open her door to find her curled in a ball on top of the bed in the growing darkness, softly crying into a pillow. "Stella?"

I turn on the lamp next to the bed, and my heart detonates in my chest. A series of sketches are spread around her on the down comforter, unmistakably my mother's. I hear a strangled sound come out of my throat.

"Go away," she wails without looking up.

But I'm not going anywhere. All this time she's kept the truth shut up and locked away, and suddenly the door is open, light spilling through the crack. It's up to me to walk through it and learn the truth before she slams it shut again.

I gingerly pick up a sketch of Iris asleep on a red blanket, her golden hair spread around her. I notice the paper quivering slightly and realize my hand is shaking. I want nothing more than to examine each of the drawings, to see the world through my mother's eyes, taking in each detail of her sketch work, but I can't let Stella detect my desperate interest. I force myself to set the drawing back on the comforter before she notices I'm trembling. "These are beautiful," I venture, carefully controlling my voice.

She doesn't respond. I sit on the edge of the bed next to her, noting the empty bottle of rum on the bedside table. I have to get her to talk. "Did something happen?" I ask. Her shoulders shake as she cries, and I gently lay a hand on her arm. "It would help if you'd tell me what's going on."

She sits up, her eyes feral. "It's all his fault," she cries, pointing at the sketches. "He got her addicted, and now she's gone."

This is it, the moment I've been waiting for. Every nerve in my body stands at attention; the room pulses with hyperreality. I swallow, doing my best impression of calm. "Who is she?" I coax, not wanting to push too far and scare her off. But she's so insulated by the rum that she's not afraid of anything.

"Iris." She breaks into a fresh round of tears.

*Yes, that's how I feel too!* I want to scream. But I never expected to see Stella so upset over her death. "Who was she to you?" I ask.

"Everything," she sobs. "I loved her. We were going to start a family."

My mind snags. She *loved* her?

Stella collapses into a fresh round of tears, and I hug her to me like a child while my brain tries to grasp what she's saying.

Stella loved Iris? They were going to start a family? Her revelation is so opposite of everything I expected that I'm having trouble processing it. "You were in love?" I ask.

"We were in love." I can hear the pain in her voice as she whispers through her tears.

My world flips like a carnival ride, all my preconceived notions falling out. It's all I can do to stop myself from smiling.

Stella was Iris's lover, not Cole. Stella was the one who had her glowing, humming in the shower, thinking of a brighter future. Not Cole. My mother had said she was in love with a movie star, and my ten-year-old brain had unthinkingly assumed it was Cole. It never even crossed my mind that it could be Stella. How stupid I was! It made so much sense. The money had dried up and the holes in Iris's arms had healed, but she'd continued to go to Cole's house—to see Stella. She was planning to make a family for us—with Stella, not Cole. It was Stella who was telling Cole she was leaving him, not the other way around. All this time I've been thinking Stella hated my mother, when in fact she loved her.

A wave of relief rolls over me, consolation that my mother wasn't in love with a monster but with this poor woman who's mourned her all these years. No wonder Stella went crazy after Iris's death. She'd lost her lover and couldn't tell a soul.

I'm flooded with compassion for Stella, overcome by the urge to confess everything to her, but I remember the empty bottle on the bedside table and the coming hurricane and bite my tongue. If I give her that information now, I don't know what she'll do with it.

I swipe a tissue from the box next to the bed and hand it to her. "What happened to her?" I ask.

She wipes her bloodshot eyes and takes a ragged breath. "She overdosed."

"Was she an addict?"

She shrugs. "She'd done drugs before, but it had been a while. She was at my house—I was late to meet her. I'd had a stupid hair appointment that ran over. She got into Cole's supply while she was waiting and..." A sob escapes her lips.

"You found her?"

She shakes her head. "Cole did. He was supposed to be out of town, but he came back early."

The order of events match what I remember, but I find it hard to believe that the contented Iris I'd seen through the window that night left a pot on the burner and went upstairs to get into Cole's heroin supply. "What happened when you got there?"

"He was trying to revive her, but he couldn't. I wanted to call 911, but he said it would be faster for him to drive her to the hospital. She was gone by the time they got there."

So Cole had lied to Stella; she had no idea about the car wreck he'd staged. "How did the press never find out about this?" I ask.

She dabs at her tears with a tissue. "I don't know. Cole took care of it. He was really great about the whole thing actually. I was pretty messed up."

I'm walking a tightrope trying not to give away what I know. "Did the cops ever come around?"

She nods. "I didn't talk to them—he did. He said he told them he'd seen her slumped over the wheel of her car in a parking lot, and when he tried to check on her, saw she was in bad shape, so he pushed her aside and drove her to the hospital. He convinced me no one could know she'd OD'd on our property. It would've been a career-ending media circus. So I went along with his lie. I figured what did it matter. She was gone anyway."

"Did he know about you and Iris?"

She shakes her head. "We were planning on telling him the following week. But he knew her, from before. She was one of his sleeping beauties."

"So what did he think she was doing at your house?"

"He thought she'd come to see him, maybe to score some heroin. She knew where he kept it."

I wrinkle my brow, trying to understand how she couldn't see Cole's story was thin as gossamer, full of holes and happenstance. So many parts of her account—or rather, the narrative Cole told her—don't add up with what I know, and yet it's clear she's accepted his version of events as fact. But then, if she's spent the last thirteen years trying to forget, I guess she's likely to believe anything that allows her to do that. I want to know more but realize it's better not to press right now. She's wasted, and I need time to think.

One thing is certain: Cole Power is hiding something.

# Stella

*Sunday, June 30*

The morning of our departure, I felt like hammered dog shit. My head throbbed, my stomach lurched, my face was puffy, my skin splotchy.

I wasn't sure how much rum I'd had by the time Cole had texted the previous evening, insisting that Felicity and I meet him for a drink in the bar. Felicity had tried to stop me from going, but I wanted to hear whatever he had to say, so I somehow managed to pull myself together, and with the magic of hemorrhoid cream, contouring, and eye shadow, make it look like I hadn't been drinking and crying all day.

When we arrived, we found the majority of the crew there, toasting their last evening on the island. Madison had already retired for the night, thank God, and Cole was drunk and so adamant that he hadn't texted me that I had to take out my phone and show him the message. Typical Cole behavior. Felicity was right: we shouldn't have gone. But we were there, and the crew wanted to toast me, so I couldn't exactly turn them down.

This morning I was still furious with Cole and wanted nothing to do with the group breakfast at the restaurant. Unfortunately, room service was discontinued, our refrigerator had been emptied, and if I didn't eat something to soak up all the alcohol splashing around in my

316

stomach, I would most definitely hurl on the ferry. So I smeared more hemorrhoid cream and concealer beneath my eyes, applied a thick layer of foundation, and donned a sun hat and dark glasses. On the way out the door, I chucked my cigarettes in the trash. My throat burned from the number I'd smoked last night, and my mouth felt disgusting no matter how many times I'd brushed my teeth. I'd reached the end of the road with smoking.

Clouds were gathering, and the wind was strong enough I had to hold my hat in place as we trudged the million miles down the pier, across the beach, through the trees, and up the stairs to the restaurant. All the ocean-facing picture windows were boarded up, the East Asian paintings taken down, and the bottles removed from the display behind the bar. Without the views and glistening glassware, the restaurant was gloomy and bare. But there was plenty of food arranged on three wooden tables, pushed together to form a makeshift buffet.

Everyone else was already there, and the place was abuzz with the excitement of an impending emergency. Some people had even brought their bags with them so that they could board the first shuttle to the ferry directly after breakfast. There were conflicting reports about the strength and path of the storm. Some had heard it would be a category three by the time it reached Saint Genesius; others claimed they'd seen reports it might bypass us entirely. Regardless of where they fell on the prediction scale, everyone was glad to be evacuating before landfall.

Cole, however, was nowhere to be seen.

I was beginning to wonder whether something had happened to him when I felt someone grab my elbow and turned to see Kara, her dark eyes sympathetic. She hadn't been at the bar last night, and I hadn't seen her since she apparently rescued me from Coco's—which of course I didn't remember. I immediately felt the hot breath of shame on my neck and was glad for the screen of my hat and sunglasses. She gave me a little hug. "How are you?" she asked. "I've been thinking about you."

"I still feel like shit," I admitted. She didn't need to know that the reason I felt like shit was not the drug I'd been slipped on Thursday but the amount of alcohol I'd consumed in the days since. "Thank you for saving my ass."

She smiled. "Anytime."

"There won't be another time," I said. "I hope I didn't throw up on you or anything. I'm sorry."

She squeezed my hand. "It could have happened to any of us. Are you coming to Guyana?"

I nodded, surprised to find she was still holding my hand, lightly rubbing her thumb across the inside of my wrist. An electric zing pierced the heavy overcoat of my hangover. "Maybe I can buy you a drink once we're there, to say thanks," I said.

"I don't drink—"

"Oh." Perhaps I'd misunderstood. But she was still stroking my wrist.

"I used to, but I liked it too much," she explained. I could certainly understand that. "I'd love to have dinner though."

I smiled. "Okay."

"But you'll have to take off your sunglasses," she teased.

I interlaced my fingers through hers for a lingering moment before letting her hand go.

The sound of a fork hitting a glass drew our attention to the front of the restaurant, where Taylor stood on a chair. Everyone quieted down as they turned to her. "Hi, everybody," she said. "Thank you all for your hard work on this film, and thank you for being so cool about our evacuation. We've just had a weather update that our friend Celia has picked up speed in the open water, and we are going to be moving up our departure by thirty minutes to ensure a smooth ride to Guyana."

A murmur went through the crowd. "Mercury retrograde," I whispered to Kara. "Always messes with travel."

"The ferry is on its way now," Taylor continued. "So will everyone please kindly shove whatever you're eating in your mouth, gather your bags, and meet under the portico in front of reception ASAP? The first shuttle is already there, so anyone who has bags with them can go ahead and board. We are going to do roll call on the boat, but we're on a tight schedule if we want to make it out before the storm, and we cannot wait for stragglers, so please, hurry. If for any reason anyone does get left behind, go to the wine cellar below this room. Cole is staying, and that is where he'll ride out the storm. It is the most hurricane-proof place on the island. Thank you!"

The noise level in the room swelled as she stepped down from the chair. "I better go get my bag," Kara said.

I nodded. "Me too. See you on the ferry."

Felicity appeared at my side, proffering a blueberry bagel stuffed with cream cheese. "I know you don't do carbs, but this was the only thing that would travel."

I devoured the bagel as we hurried with the rest of the crowd down the stairs, across the windswept beach, and back to our bungalow. "I don't know that a golf cart's gonna happen now," Felicity said as she pushed open the door. "But I can help with your bags. I only have the one."

Our luggage was packed and waiting for us in the entryway, but Mary Elizabeth was not. Odd. She usually slept on the chair just inside the door until I returned. I whistled. "Mary Elizabeth!" Nothing. "Mimi!"

Felicity and I split up to sweep the bungalow, calling out as we moved from room to room. I pulled back the fluffy white duvet on my bed, then looked beneath it, checked the laundry basket, the giant bathtub—but they were all empty, and all the doors to the outside were firmly shut. My heart sank when we met back in the kitchen and I saw Felicity was as empty-handed as I was. "Maybe she got stuck in a closet or something," Felicity suggested.

We checked every closet and cabinet. Nothing. I was beginning to panic. I got down on my knees and looked beneath the couch, the chairs. But no sign of my little darling. Fear coursed through my veins. Where could she be?

A knock at the door. I rushed to open it, hoping she'd gotten out and it was someone bringing her back. But it was only Jackson, his roller bag in hand. "You guys ready?" he asked. "I can help with the suitcases."

"We can't find Mary Elizabeth," Felicity said.

"Shit. When did you see her last?" he asked.

"She was here when we went to breakfast," I replied, my heart racing.

Jackson dropped his bag and stepped inside. "You check the deck?"

He slid open the sliding glass doors, and the wind whipped around us as we followed him outside. The deck was slick with moisture, and whitecaps dotted the sea. My gaze immediately went to the pool. The cover was shut, but what if she'd somehow gotten in? "Where's the switch to the pool cover?" I asked.

Jackson flipped a lever on a panel next to the door, and I imagined her floating facedown as the pool cover slid open painstakingly slowly. I released a sigh of relief when she wasn't there. "We have to go, or we're gonna miss the ferry," Jackson said as the pool cover slid shut.

My hair lashed my face as I choked back a sob. "I can't leave her!"

Felicity put an arm around my shoulders. "Let's do another sweep of the bungalow, and we can check the beach and surrounding area on our way to the shuttle."

I blinked at her. Had she not understood? "I'm not leaving her."

"But we can't miss the ferry," she said. "It's not safe."

"She's right," Jackson chimed in. "It's not safe here."

The wheels in my mind spun. There were days I would have killed myself if it hadn't been for Mary Elizabeth. She was the only living creature that had stood by me through all my dark days, and I wasn't about to abandon her now, in her hour of need. "Cole said the wine cellar is safe," I asserted. "I'm staying."

"Stella," Jackson looked me in the eye, his countenance serious. "I hate to say this, but if she's not in the bungalow, she's probably in the ocean. Look around." He gestured to the turbulent sea, the strong wind. "She weighs nothing. She could easily get swept away in this weather."

"No! She was in the house!"

I tore into the house and ran from room to room, nearly blinded by the panic of losing her. "Mimi! Mimi!! Where are you?" I cried.

"She's not here," Felicity said, exchanging a glance with Jackson she must've thought I couldn't see. "Let's take the bags and go to the beach. Maybe she's there."

I ran out the door like a madwoman, yelling her name into the wind. A light rain was coming down now, whipped in every direction by the wind. I ran to the sea end of the pier, looking in every doorway, asking every passerby if they'd seen her. But no one had. Just as I reached Cole's bungalow at the far end, Madison emerged, dragging her suitcase behind her.

I stepped back, surprised. "Have you seen Mary Elizabeth?" I asked.

"Oh." She wrinkled her brow. "Yeah. I saw her down on the beach on the way back from breakfast. I wondered what she was doing out there, but figured you'd let her out to pee or something."

I stared at the bitch, all innocent, her hair as flawless as ever. "You didn't think maybe you should grab her?" I screeched.

"Sorry, no." She shrugged. "She's kinda not my responsibility."

"Fuck you!" I screamed over my shoulder as I sprinted down the pier, past Jackson and Felicity, who stood in front of our bungalow looking concerned, all the way to the beach. "Mary Elizabeth!"

By the time I reached the rain-pocked sand, Jackson and Felicity weren't far behind me. "What happened?" Felicity asked when she caught up.

"Madison saw her down here not long ago," I returned, jogging toward the tree line.

"You believe Madison?" Felicity asked.

"She's not drowned," I insisted, ignoring her jab. "She's here, probably scared out of her mind and looking for me. And I'm staying until I find her."

"The last shuttle is leaving now," Jackson said. "I'm so sorry, but we need to go."

"Then go," I yelled over the wind. "Both of you, go! Get out of here! But I'm not leaving." I pushed aside a clump of palms. "Mimi! Here, girl!"

"Stella, are you sure about this?" Felicity asked. "Once the ferry leaves, you're here. This is the last one going out."

"I told you, I'm staying."

"Okay." Felicity shrugged. "Then I guess I'm staying too."

Jackson turned to her, his face a mask of concern. "Are you serious? You're going to stay?"

"I'm not leaving Stella here alone," she said.

"I won't be alone," I said. "Cole's staying too."

"Even worse," Felicity said. "I'm definitely not leaving you here alone with him."

"Okay. Fine, then," Jackson said. "I'm staying too."

# Taylor

I did a final sweep of my bungalow, glancing furtively through the wall of glass at the landscape of turbulent seas and leaden skies, growing darker with every passing minute. Rick had warned me when he left this morning that the weather would change quickly, but this turn was much faster and earlier than expected. God, I hoped we still had time to make it to the plane. I unplugged the satellite phone he'd loaned me so that I could call him from Guyana, confirming that it was fully charged before I turned it off and slipped it into the lower pocket of my cargo pants.

One last thing to do before I left. Steeling my nerves, I rolled my bag out the door and let it slam behind me. A gust of wind nearly knocked me off-balance as I stepped onto the rain-slick pier and turned toward the horizon, the opposite direction of the last stragglers hurrying toward the shuttle. The boulder in the pit of my stomach grew heavier with every footstep. I hadn't told Rick I was going to confront Cole this morning. I hadn't told anyone. But I had to do it before I got on that plane, because I planned never to see him again after, and I wanted to look him in the eye when I stood up to him.

At the far end of the pier, I rang his bell and waited. He opened the door almost immediately, frowning when he saw me. "Not who you were expecting?" I asked.

"What do you need?" he asked.

I could still tell him I was just checking on him and walk away. But that wasn't the woman I wanted to be. "I need to talk to you. Can I come in?"

I ignored the snide glance he cast at my cargo pants as he opened the door wide, forcing my feet to follow him into the bungalow. Some kind of hard electronica was playing loudly over the surround-sound system while the sea pitched outside, but I could hear what sounded like the yapping of a dog coming from behind the door to his bedroom. "Is that Mary Elizabeth?" I asked, confused.

"No," he said. "Aren't you gonna miss your ferry?"

"This won't take long."

He flopped onto the couch and turned his attention to the baseball game playing silently on the television. "Spit it out."

My heart in my throat, I walked around the couch and stood in front of him, blocking his view of the television. "I'm quitting."

Unfazed, he craned his neck to look around me at the television. "You'll have a hard time getting hired anywhere else."

"I don't care."

He shrugged. "Your loss. I only hired you to piss off your dad anyway."

So I'd been right about that. But it didn't matter. "You should ask why I'm quitting."

He rolled his eyes. "Why are you quitting?"

I crossed my arms and steadied my voice. "I'm pregnant with your child."

That got his attention. "Impossible. We didn't have sex. It must be your townie boyfriend's."

I stared daggers into him, rage pumping through my body, but he wouldn't meet my gaze. "It's yours. It couldn't be anyone else's. You lied to me."

He sighed. "To protect you. You threw yourself at me. You begged for it. What was I supposed to do?"

"You drugged me," I said as evenly as I could muster, "the same way you did Stella, the same way you did all your—sleeping beauties, was it?"

His square jaw tightened. "Fucking Stella," he muttered under his breath.

"You raped me."

"You're accusing me of raping you?" He finally met my gaze, his pale eyes cold.

"Yes." I laid a shaking hand on my belly. "And I'm carrying the proof right here."

"Proof we fucked isn't the same as proof of assault." He rose to his feet, towering above me. "No one will believe you. With your reputation? All you'll do is dig your hole deeper."

I wanted nothing more than to turn and run, but I rooted my feet to the floor, adrenaline coursing through my veins. "I'm sure I'm not the only woman you've assaulted over the years."

"How much?" he spat.

"What?"

"The number. There's always a number." He rubbed his fingers together in front of my face, his eyes full of rancor. "How much money do you want to shut the fuck up and go away?"

I shook my head, holding back tears. "All I want is for you to never be able to do this to someone else."

At this he roughly grabbed my arm. I tried to wrest it away, but he only tightened his grip, bringing his eerily symmetrical face so close I could smell the whiskey on his breath. "I have the best lawyers money can buy. You'll never get past them. I'll sue you for libel. You'll go bankrupt fighting it."

Again I tried to wrench my arm free, this time using my opposite arm to dig my fingernails into the skin of his wrist. "Let go of me," I demanded, trying to keep the terror out of my voice. "They're waiting for me on the ferry."

The corner of his mouth twisted upward. "Not if I call them and tell them you decided to stay."

Dread gripped my throat. "Fuck you. Let me go."

"Afraid I can't do that." Without warning, he drove his knee into my belly. Sharp, deep pain. The air went out of me. I tried to gasp, but there was his knee again. The acrid taste of vomit in my throat. His fist flew toward my face, and everything went black.

# Felicity

L andfall should still be hours away, but the sky is dark and the wind is violent as I make my way along the deserted cobblestone road that leads to Gen Town. A dead palm frond rips from a tree and crashes to the ground not ten feet in front of me, sending me scuttling backward. Maybe splitting up to search for Mary Elizabeth in the rapidly deteriorating weather wasn't the best idea. Maybe staying on the island at all wasn't the best idea. But too late to worry about that now. The ferry is long gone.

"Mimi," I cry, the wind dampening my voice. "Mary Elizabeth!" I still don't understand how she could have gotten out while we were at breakfast, but it's been hours now, and the hope of finding her is quickly dwindling with the worsening weather. "Here, girl!"

The sound of a high-pitched horn close behind me makes me jump, and I spin to see Jackson behind the wheel of a golf cart. I hop in beside him, grateful for the shelter and the company.

"Any luck?" he asks.

"No." I brush my wet bangs out of my eyes. "You?"

"Nothing." He checks his watch and frowns. "Time's running out before landfall, and we need to sandbag all the entrances of the lobby to make sure it doesn't flood. The staff started to do it, but I noticed when I was up there a minute ago that they didn't finish before they left."

"Okay." I'm despondent that we haven't found Mary Elizabeth, but he's right. At some point we have to take the steps to ensure our own safety.

"I figure we check Coco's since the porch is open, then head back to the restaurant before it gets any worse," he suggests.

I look up at the heavy clouds and blowing branches as the cart bumps along the uneven road. "It's pretty bad out already."

"It'll get worse, trust me. I've been through a few hurricanes. They're the real deal."

"I know. I have too."

He stops the cart in front of Coco's. "What?"

"Yeah, I lived in Florida with my mom before she died," I admit.

He turns to me, searching my face. "You didn't tell me that."

"I haven't told you anything about that time in my life," I return. "Because it's hard—"

"Hard to talk about. I know." He nods, trying to wrap his head around it. "But I was there too. Isn't it funny? I'm only a year older than you. We could have known each other. Where did you live?"

"I don't want to talk about it."

I spring out of the golf cart and dash through the rain up the wooden steps to Coco's giant covered porch. All the tables have been removed save an old pool table, pushed against the inside wall and covered with a blue tarp.

Jackson scurries across the empty floor to catch up with me, taking my hand. "Hey." I turn to face him, and he looks at me with those soulful eyes. "Is it so bad to want to know more about you?"

I sigh, dropping my gaze to our interlaced fingers. I can't lie to him anymore, but I can't tell him the truth either. "I'm not the girl you think I am. You should stay away from me."

The words sound silly, made no less so by the fact that I don't seem to be able to release his hand. He draws closer, his eyes never leaving my face. "Whoever else you are, you are most definitely the girl I think you are."

His gaze travels down to my mouth. I should pull away. I should leave. But I don't. He tilts my chin up toward him and rubs his thumb across my lips. I can't help myself. I part my lips and take his thumb into my mouth. He replaces his thumb with his tongue, and I wrap my arms around his neck. The wall of ice within me thaws beneath his touch, the surrender almost unbearably sweet.

Without coming up for air, he lifts me and carries me to the pool table. Our hands are suddenly all over each other, tugging off shirts, our breath hot and fast, as every moment of tension from the past few weeks, every repressed fantasy explodes between us. I unbutton his pants while he fumbles in his wallet for a condom and wriggle out of my shorts as we tumble onto the pool table, impatient to have him inside me. I know it's wrong, but the movie's over now, and I might as well enjoy one good fuck before I never see him again.

He pushes into me, and I know with immediate clarity that this is not a parting fuck. It's not a fuck at all. It's something else entirely. Something I've never experienced before. My brain stops; my identity stops. We move in unison like the ocean I hear crashing against the shore, like the thunder that rolls overhead, the rain that drums the thatched roof outside. It's completely natural, like our bodies are puzzle pieces made to fit together, and it leaves me only wanting more.

Afterward, we lie entangled in each other's arms atop the pool table, panting as the wind cools our heated skin. I bury my face in the crook between his shoulder and his neck, dreading what comes next. I should have told him before I let this happen, but it's too late for that. I have to come clean now, before this goes any further. "I have to tell you something," I murmur into his neck.

He pulls back to look me in the eye, pushing my hair out of my face. "Yeah?"

The moment of truth. I take a deep breath and steel my nerves. "My name isn't Felicity; it's Phoenix." His eyes search mine, his face unreadable. I plow on. "Your father dated my mother, Iris, a long time ago. We met by your pool the night she died."

He goes completely still. My heart plummets. It's just how I'd thought it would be; he'll never forgive me for the lies. But that's how it has to be. It's right. It's what I deserve. I avert my gaze, terrified of the revulsion I'll see in his face.

He lifts my chin lightly with his fingers, studying my features. "You were blond then."

"And chubby," I confirm, "with blue eyes and a big nose."

I can tell he's comparing my current face to his memory of me as he scans my features. "I would never have recognized you."

"My eyes are still blue under these contacts, and the nose I had changed to lessen the chances of being recognized. But it's still me. I promise."

"I believe you." The noise of the storm subsides; time slows. He traces his finger over my nose, my cheeks. His voice is soft when he speaks again. "I've thought of you every single day since that terrible night. Wondered what happened to you. I wanted to look you up, but I didn't know your name."

"Phoenix," I choke. "Phoenix Pendley."

He wraps his arms around me, and I melt into his warm chest, so overcome I can hardly breathe. My shoulders shake as all the fear and exhaustion pours out of me. When I finally get ahold of myself, I look up at him. "I sent you an email a few months ago."

He nods. "That email is the reason we're here. It made me finally work up the courage to ask Cole the truth about the night your mom died, what it was I'd really seen."

"What did he say?"

"The same BS he'd said years ago—that she'd overdosed and he'd taken her to the hospital, but not in time to save her life. That we'd had to lie to the cops about her being in our home to protect his and Stella's careers. But this time we both knew I didn't believe a word of it. Then he offered to produce this film for me and star in it, as my film school graduation present. I knew he thought he was bribing me, but I took his money regardless, because fuck him. I figured I'd have a better chance of getting the truth out of him if I spent some time with him anyway. But that hasn't exactly worked out."

So the email had done its job; at least a part of my plan had succeeded. "What do you remember about that night?" I ask.

He searches my face, concerned. "Are you sure you want to hear this?"

I nod. "I've come a long way to hear it."

He closes his eyes for a moment, remembering. "When I went upstairs after I left you, I found Cole standing over your mom. She was unconscious, her arm tied off with a needle sticking out of it. The glass coffee table was broken, and there was blood on it. He said she'd taken drugs and he was trying to help her, then sent me to my room with a warning to keep my mouth shut. I was so afraid, I did what he said."

This fit with what Stella had told me about Iris being unconscious when she arrived. "And later," I prompt, "you lied to the police about having seen her."

He nods. "He told me I had to lie or they'd take his money and send him to jail and he wouldn't be able to take care of me and my mom anymore. So I lied. And every day since I've hated myself for it."

I have no words. I know I should be glad he hates himself, but I'm not. I want to despise him for lying, for letting her die, for continuing to have a relationship with his father afterward…but I can't. He was just a scared little boy. I feel the tenderness of his hand on my back; I hear the honesty in his voice, and I recognize with brilliant lucidity that improbably, he is the only person in the world I trust.

"It's the reason I went to India," he continues. "It's the reason I try so hard in the rest of my life to be a good person. But I know I can't ever make up for it, no matter what I do. I am so, so sorry."

I imagine my mother taking her last breaths with Cole standing over her, swearing to take her to the hospital while knowing he never will. But how did she end up there? Why was a deadly syringe in her arm when ten minutes earlier she'd been happily cooking dinner in anticipation of a night in with Stella? I comb over the details, my mind catching on one in particular. "You said her arm was tied off with a tourniquet," I say. He nods. "Do you remember what it was? A piece of rubber, a belt?"

"It was a belt," he says. "I remember thinking how big it looked on her little arm."

"So, a man's belt?" I ask.

He nods. "Probably."

"Your father's belt," I clarify.

"Most likely."

As much as I want it to, the simple fact of Cole's belt being around her arm doesn't prove anything. She was in Cole's room; she could easily have grabbed one of his belts; yet I know as clear as day that's not what happened. "He killed her," I say. "I don't know why or how, and I can't prove it; but I know it was him. I thought it was Stella at first, but I was wrong. She and Stella were in love."

A look of understanding washes over his face. "That makes so much sense. I knew Stella and your mother were close," he admits, "but I didn't understand what that meant at the time. My mom wasn't a fan of Stella and would send me over to Cole's for her to look after me when he wasn't home, as a sort of punishment for marrying him. But Stella didn't mind, and neither did I. We had fun together. She treated me like I was a grown-up—probably because she didn't have any experience with children—but I liked it. I met your mom a few times too. She was the most beautiful woman I'd ever seen; I had a mad crush on her." He laughs. "She told me about you. She thought we'd make great friends."

He tilts my chin up again, and this time I'm not afraid of what I'll see in his eyes. There's no need anymore to force myself to look away, to keep my emotions hidden behind the ramparts. A hint of a smile lifts the corners of his mouth as he leans in and again presses his lips to mine.

The constant pressure in my chest is suddenly gone, and in its place is a lightness, a vulnerability. For the first time in my adult life, I am known. Accepted. And it's a freedom unlike anything I've felt before.

**Part VI:**

# Landfall

# Stella

I lay sobbing on an espresso leather couch in the deserted lobby, my wails all but drowned out by the growing squall outside. I'd searched high and low for Mary Elizabeth, but she was nowhere to be found, and this storm was going to get a lot worse before it got better. My last hope was that Jackson or Felicity had located her, but the fact they hadn't shown up yet didn't bode well.

Through my tears I could make out thunderheads seething beyond the skylights in the vaulted-beam ceiling overhead. All the other windows were boarded up, making it nearly pitch black when the lights flickered, which they did with increasing frequency. I needed to get back to the bungalow and gather my things before sheltering in the wine cellar to ride out the storm. My pills, namely. I needed my pills. I'd only had one little A-pill this morning and hadn't touched a drop of liquor all day, not to mention thrown out my smokes. I was going crazy with worry; I needed something to steady my nerves.

Heavy footsteps on the tiles echoed in the cavernous room. I sat up and wiped my face on my shirt, hoping Jackson had returned with good news. But when I turned, I saw it was Cole who stalked across the lobby toward me, his face dark.

"You haven't seen Mary Elizabeth, have you?" I asked.

He shook his head. "I've been looking for you."

He tossed a lumpy envelope emblazoned with the name of the resort into my lap. "What's this?" I asked.

"Open it."

The flap wasn't sealed. I extracted a dime bag of bluish pills. "What are these?"

"Fentanyl."

I stared at him. Even in my darkest days, I'd never tried that one. "Why do you have fentanyl?"

"There's something else in there."

I scraped my nails along the inside of the envelope, extracting a photo, cut to wallet-size. I turned it faceup. My heart stopped. It was a picture of Iris. She was smiling before a birthday cake with lit candles, a chubby little blond girl I recognized as her daughter in her lap.

"What is this?" I managed.

"It's Felicity's."

I squinted at him, confused. "What?"

"She's—" He sat heavily on the couch next to me. "I had nothing to do with this. She didn't tell me until after she did it—"

I was beginning to panic. "Nothing to do with what? What are we talking about?"

He ran his fingers through his wet hair. "Last night when we were all at the bar, Madison swam over to your bungalow and entered through the deck. She's the one who sent the text from my phone, so you'd leave your room and she could break in."

A tremendous clap of thunder crashed overhead. "Madison broke into our bungalow? Why?"

"She'd overheard both you and Taylor trying to get me to replace her with Felicity, and she had this idea Felicity wasn't who she said she was. Something about being in acting class with a girl that looked exactly like her—anyway, she went over there and rooted around in Felicity's things, trying to prove it. Found the picture and the drugs zippered in her wallet."

My brain strained to run in a million different directions. I pressed the palms of my hands into my eye sockets until I saw stars, listening to the wind whistling around the boarded-up windows. The only reason Felicity would have a picture of Iris in her wallet…It couldn't be. It would mean she'd been lying to me from day one. I opened my eyes and scrutinized the picture. The little girl was seven or eight, and if you imagined what her round cheeks might look like slimmed down, it was true she bore a resemblance to Felicity, aside from the nose and the fact that she had blond hair and blue eyes. But eye color and hair color could be changed, as could a nose. And the fentanyl… "What are you saying?" I asked.

"Felicity is Iris's daughter."

The words I didn't want to hear.

"But why is she here?" I asked, bewildered.

"She targeted you, and you fell for it hook, line, and sinker. Who do you think has been leaking those photos to the press?"

"Madison," I responded, for the first time doubting my logic.

"Guess again." He crossed his arms. "Who's controlling your pills, huh? Who do you really think slipped something in your drink at Coco's? You know it wasn't me. Why would I do that? I'm producing the movie. I need you insured and ready to shoot. And now Mary Elizabeth—who you hired Felicity to care for—has disappeared, causing you to miss the ferry? Why do you think that is?"

I bit my lip, turning it over in my mind. I didn't want to believe it, but the math added up. God, I needed a drink. "Maybe she knew we were important to her mother and wanted to get to know us?"

He snorted. "Sure. The same girl who accused me of killing her mother years ago just wants to get to know us."

My head snapped up. "What the hell? You never told me that." His jaw tensed as he studied my face, clearly weighing whether to elaborate. I crossed my arms to match his as another crack of thunder exploded overhead. "For Godsake, spit it out, Cole."

"I didn't drive Iris to the hospital," he said evenly.

My blood ran cold. "What? But you—"

He placed his hands on my shoulders. "She was already gone. There was no saving her. I knew driving her to the hospital would only raise questions we didn't want to answer."

I shrugged his hands off. "What did you do, Cole?"

"I wrecked her car into a tree and put her in the driver's seat, then walked to a gas station and took a car home."

I stared daggers at him. "You let her die."

"She was already dead, Stella. News of an overdosed hooker in our house would have been worse for you than it was for me. I wasn't the one having an affair with her."

My breath caught in my throat. I reached for words, but none came.

"Yeah," he taunted over the howling of the wind. "I knew."

"How?" I managed.

"Oh, come on." He rolled his eyes. "She just happened to be in the house cooking dinner the night I wasn't supposed to be home? How did she get in unless someone gave her a key? And you lost your damn mind after she died, remember?"

I reached for memories of the time after Iris's death, but they were buried by a sea of booze and drugs. "But you never said anything."

He shrugged. "You were a wreck, and it was over between us anyway. I didn't want to fight. All I wanted was to get past it and get divorced. But then you got pregnant, and I had to stick around until that mercifully ended."

"Fuck you." The lights flickered as I narrowed my eyes at him. "Why did Felicity accuse you of murdering Iris?"

He sighed. "She was in the car."

I inhaled sharply. "Felicity was?"

He nodded. "Hiding in the back. I didn't know she was there. But she told the police I'd been driving the car and that Iris was already dead. No one believed her, but they still had to question me. Jackson corroborated my story about being home with him, and I asked the police not to bother you with the details because you'd been sick and didn't need any stress."

I could barely hear him over the blood rushing in my ears. "And they went along with that?"

"Of course they did. I'm Cole Power. I took pictures with them and signed autographs for their kids afterward. It was like they'd won tickets to Disneyland."

I took a deep breath, trying to still my rattled nerves. "And Felicity... What else did she see?"

"I don't know. I assume she was hiding in the car the whole time. She probably overheard us arguing about which hospital to go to."

"And then you didn't take her to one." I dropped my head back on the cold leather pillow. "The fentanyl... She wants revenge."

He nodded. "This entire time she's been giving you too many pills and leaking photos, developing the story that you're an addict that can't keep clean, so that when she slips you the fentanyl, it'll look like you accidently overdosed, just like her mother did. Symmetry."

The whole thing sounded somehow familiar—like the plot of a movie. Though I couldn't recall doing a movie with that plot. Had Cole? Maybe it was only something I'd seen on TV. At any rate, I'd had nothing to do with Iris's death, and Felicity had had ample opportunity to kill me and she hadn't. It made more sense for Cole to be the one she was after—if she was in fact after anyone at all. "How do you know she wasn't going to kill you?" I challenged. "You're the one who didn't take her mother to the hospital."

"Does it matter?" he asked. "She was going to kill someone, and logic states it's one of us."

Rain pattered on the skylights above us. "We're jumping to conclusions," I pointed out. "Maybe we should ask her."

"You think she'll tell the truth?" He laughed. "She's a fantastic actress. I'll give her that." He dropped his smile. "We have to get rid of her."

"What? No!" I protested. "Jesus. You're not serious."

He caught my gaze and held it, his eyes hard. "She was going to kill you, Stella."

"You don't know that. And anyway, she didn't."

My mind drifted to my conversation with Felicity last night. I'd been so drunk I didn't remember most of it, but I knew I'd disclosed my relationship with Iris to her. Which meant she had to understand I could never have had any part in Iris's death. So why hadn't Felicity confessed her true identity to me when she'd had the chance? I'd practically opened the door for her, and she hadn't stepped through it. My heart sank. As much as I didn't want to admit it, maybe Cole was right about her.

"The fact she hasn't killed you yet doesn't mean she's not planning to. That's why we have to get to her first," he said gently.

"Are you insane? This isn't some movie we're in. This is real life, and I'm not killing anyone. She can't do anything now anyway. We have the pills."

He waved the baggie before me. "How do you know this is the only trick she has up her sleeve? A hurricane would be the perfect cover for killing someone. No authorities on the island, no witnesses—"

"That's the end to *The Siren*—"

He shook my shoulder. "Wake up, Stella. I know you don't want to believe it because in that delusional head of yours you still think she's your friend, but she let Mary Elizabeth out knowing that you wouldn't leave the island without her."

Mary Elizabeth. My little darling, lost out there in the wind and the rain. Something inside me hardened. I wanted to punish Felicity for that injustice. But in no world would I have any part in killing her, no matter what she'd done. The very fact that Cole was suggesting it with a straight face was chilling. "We can report her to the authorities, give them evidence to put her in jail, but I'm not murdering her. That's insane."

"Okay." He scratched his chin, thinking. "If you insist. But we should at least put her somewhere she can't try anything on us for the duration of the storm, until we can get someone out here to pick her up."

"She's one small girl," I protested. "You're the Gentleman Gangster.

You do your own stunts. You know jujitsu, for godsake. Between the two of us, I think we'll be fine."

"I'm glad you think this is funny." His gaze was flinty. "But you're forgetting Jackson." The lights flickered again, then went dark. Gray light filtered through the skylights, leaving us in murky gloom.

"What about Jackson?" I asked.

"He's wrapped around her little finger; we have to assume he's on her side."

I didn't like the idea of colluding with Cole against Felicity and Jackson, but I didn't see any choice. "So what's your plan?" I asked, wishing I could see his face better in the darkened room. "Because you obviously have a plan."

"We'll have to knock her out, then—"

"No! Can't we just lock her in a room or something?"

"How do you plan to do that without sedating her?" he challenged.

"Me?" I shook my head vehemently. "I don't want anything to do with this."

"You have everything to do with this. It's your fault she's here. I can't get near her. She hates me. You made sure of that."

It was true. Felicity loathed Cole as much as I did. I'd thought her dislike of him was on my behalf, but I now realized it ran much deeper than that. "What are you suggesting?"

"You have sleeping pills, don't you?"

"Maybe. Why?"

"To drug her. You can put them in her drink. Then, once she's out, we'll lock her up somewhere safe till the storm clears. We'll have to knock Jackson out too."

I considered, uneasily listening to the rain patter on the roof. "But how are we going to explain who she is to the police?"

"There's already a record of her claiming we were responsible for her mother's death," he says calmly. "It works for us. She's an obsessed fan who stalked us because she wants revenge for something we were never involved in."

It was hard to wrap my mind around the idea that Felicity had targeted me with the intention of killing me. I knew logically that she wasn't my friend and I shouldn't feel any attachment to her, but she'd been so kind to me until now. And she was Iris's daughter. Iris, whom I'd loved. "I don't know," I said.

"Okay, how's this: give her the sleeping pills, and we'll talk to her when this is all over. We don't have to make any decisions about what to do beyond that."

It wasn't like Cole to be diplomatic. I assessed him, trying to read his features in the shadows. "Why not talk to her now?"

"Because we are literally the only people on the island. If it goes wrong, it could end very badly."

I nodded. "All right, but only as a stalling tactic. And we'll put her somewhere safe until the storm passes." As much as I hated to admit it, he was right. With the storm coming, we simply couldn't take the risk. We would have to do it his way.

# Felicity

Jackson and I are drenched and muddy by the time we place the last sandbag outside the restaurant. The two of us have put up a barricade in front of every doorway into the main building without any help from Cole or Stella, who are nowhere to be seen, and my muscles are wasted from lifting the forty-pound bags.

"We should go clean up and get back here before the storm gets any worse." He raises his voice over the wind, surveying our work.

I brush my wet bangs out of my eyes for the millionth time. I can't wait to grow them out when all this is over. "I hope Stella's okay."

"It's been what, four hours?"

We exchange a weighted look, and guilt snakes around my chest. "I shouldn't have left her alone for this long."

"You stayed in the path of a hurricane for her." He gestures at the rain coming down on us, growing heavier by the minute. "Let the guilt go."

"You did the same for me," I point out.

He hooks his finger through my belt loop and pulls my hips toward him. "And I'm glad I did."

I consider him. Once I'd realized he didn't hold my lies against me, I'd come clean, laying everything at his feet. He took it remarkably

343

well; but I wonder, once the storm has passed and this is all over, whether he'll change his mind. "Really?"

He pulls me in for a lingering kiss, his gaze steady when he releases me. "Really."

Something strange happens inside my chest, like a bird beating its wings. I turn away so he doesn't see the idiotic smile I can't seem to repress as we make our way down the stairs beyond the pool, dodging flying palm fronds and debris. Fighting our way through the increasingly horizontal rain toward the bungalows, I realize the storm has intensified far more quickly than we'd planned for. My heart sinks at the thought of Mary Elizabeth out in this weather. She could so easily be swept away, if she hasn't been already.

The water beneath the pier to the bungalows is startlingly close, sloshing up through the slats in the wood as we hurry over the slick boards to my bungalow.

"I'll be back for you in fifteen," he yells over the wind when we reach my doorstep.

Before he can depart, the door to the bungalow swings open, revealing a trembling Stella. Her puffy eyes are ringed with smudged mascara, and she's wearing some kind of gauzy swimsuit cover-up that's completely inappropriate for the weather. She waves both of us inside.

"I've gotta go clean up and grab my stuff." Jackson excuses himself, but Stella will have none of it.

"Come in, for just a minute," she says as a tear slides down her cheek.

Jackson and I step into the dimly lit living room, where the television blares a series of weather warnings as the anchors on the Weather Channel excitedly discuss the rapid approach of Hurricane Celia. I'm shocked we still have power—it's already gone out at the lobby. "We need to get up to the shelter as soon as possible, or we're gonna have to swim out of here," I say. "Any sign of Mimi?"

She shakes her head, wiping her tears. "I've been waiting for you. I made lemonade. I knew you'd be thirsty." She gestures to the table, where two highballs of pale-yellow liquid wait for us, the glasses sweating as the ice melts. Odd. But then, Stella is nothing if not odd. "Where have you been?"

"We've been placing sandbags up at the main building," Jackson says.

Stella grabs the cups from the table and hands one to each of us. Off our looks, she sighs. "I feel so bad I made you stay in a hurricane. It's the least I can do." She seizes a rocks glass off the side table next to the couch and rattles the ice, then drains what's left of it. "I added gin to mine."

Of course she did. Forcing smiles, we each take a tentative sip. The cold liquid is sweet and tart on my tongue, and I drink half of it in one draw. "This is delicious," I enthuse. "I didn't realize how thirsty I was. Thank you."

"I made it using the lemons from the tree by the pool," she says proudly.

Jackson takes another long sip. "It's great."

The television draws our attention with a prolonged discordant tone over color block. When the picture comes back, the weatherman is serious. "Hurricane Celia has been upgraded to a category two with sustained winds of 105 miles per hour and is likely to strengthen over open water as it moves west-northwest at a speed of thirty miles per hour toward the islands of Barbados, and Grenadine, and Saint Ann, now less than a hundred miles away. Storm surge in excess of ten feet is expected in low-lying areas. Please take shelter immediately."

"I gotta go." Jackson drains his glass and sets it on the table. "I'll be back for you in ten. If you're ready first, come get me on your way."

"See you then." I blow him a kiss, and he disappears out the door, into the deluge. "I'm gonna take a quick shower," I say to Stella. "You probably want to change. It's pretty nasty out there."

In my bathroom, I shed my muddy clothes and step into the shower, where I shampoo my hair and scrub the dirt from beneath my nails, feeling my tired body begin to relax as the hot water warms me. Poor Stella. I know losing Mary Elizabeth is a terrible blow to her, especially now that I'm privy to the details of her years of suffering. Though I do find solace in knowing my mother was so loved and mourned, my heart breaks for her.

They say time heals all wounds, but I know firsthand if you repress your trauma it only festers, becoming a poison that slowly turns your insides black with rot. It was such a relief to come clean with Jackson. Maybe I should throw caution to the wind and do the same with Stella now, rather than waiting until the "time is right." She's trusted me with her story; if I trusted her with mine, perhaps we could work together to bring Cole down. But there's no time now. We need to get up to the shelter, and presumably Cole will be there with us. I'll have to wait.

A wave of exhaustion rolls over me. The water feels divine, but I'm so drained that once I've conditioned my hair, I turn off the shower. I can take a pillow and blanket with me to the wine cellar and sleep there. I wrap myself in a plush white towel and wipe the steam from the mirror with my hand, starting when I catch my reflection. One of my brown contacts has fallen out, revealing one bright blue iris. I've grown so accustomed to my dark-eyed look that my natural color is shocking, more unreal than the counterfeit version.

My contact must have come out in the shower—it had to be; Jackson or Stella would have noticed if I'd lost it before. I open the drawer where I keep extra lenses and reach into the back, realizing as I come up empty-handed that my contacts are packed in the bag I meant to take to Guyana. Shit. But the bag's in my room. No harm done. I throw open the door to my bedroom to find Stella sitting on my bed, now dressed in yoga pants and a T-shirt. I jump. Since we've been here, she hasn't once come into my room.

"How are you feeling?" she asks.

My hand flies to my blue eye to cover it. "I hurt my eye," I say. "I think some sand may have gotten in it while we were doing storm prep."

"Hmmm." She crosses her arms, watching me intently. "Did you finish your lemonade?"

346

Why is she acting so strange? "Yeah, it was great. Thanks again."

I drag my suddenly heavy limbs to my suitcase and unzip it, overwhelmed by the prospect of choosing what to wear. I just want her to leave so that I can search for my contacts.

"How are you feeling?" she asks again. "You look kinda tired."

"Yeah." I face away from her so that she won't see my eye as I pull on my underwear and the first T-shirt and jeans shorts I see, then turn back to her, rubbing my eye. "I'm gonna take a blanket up to the main lodge."

I take a step toward the bed, but suddenly the floor isn't where it should be, and I find myself staring through the glass floor at the turbulent dark sea below. The room spins. I grab on to the bed to steady myself, noticing without judgment the strange sensation of my brain detaching itself from my body.

Somewhere far above me, Stella holds a small plastic bag of blue pills in her hand. The fentanyl I'd procured as a weapon, long ago in a land far, far away. "Looking for these?"

I grasp the comforter and drag my unwieldy body precariously up to her level, vaguely realizing I've forgotten to cover my eye, but the cotton candy in my brain prevents me from caring. Stella stares, her head tilting. Or maybe I'm tilting. "Did you give me those?" I manage.

"No. I wasn't trying to kill you like you were me. You've just had some of my S-pills, Phoenix." She smiles beatifically. "You'll be all right after you take a long nap."

Phoenix, that's my name. How does she know my name? Sleeping pills. I swing around and careen into the bathroom, banging into the door and landing on my knees on the cold tile before the toilet, where I jam my finger down my throat until I wretch into the bowl. I do it again and again until nothing comes up.

She hovers over me, her arms crossed. "It's already in your system."

I sit on the cold floor with my back against the vanity, staring at the rain lashing the windows. The gray day has turned to the blackest night, leaving us blind to the storm outside. "Not all of it."

"When were you going to kill me?" she asks, tossing the bag of pills onto the counter.

"I wasn't," I croak.

"I trusted you and you lied to me and used me." She looks genuinely hurt. "Has anything you've told me been true?"

"I'm sorry." I rest my cheek on the cabinet, warm in comparison to the floor. "I had to know what happened to my mother."

"I would've told you if you'd asked."

I shake my head, fighting to keep my eyes open. "I had to lie . . . to get to you. I thought you killed her."

"I loved her," she protests. "I would never have hurt her."

I allow my eyelids to close. "I didn't know. I wanted to tell you last night, but you were too drunk. You might've told Cole . . ." An idea pushes its way through the fog. "It was him, wasn't it?"

She sits next to me and takes my hand in hers. "No one killed your mother." The anger has drained from her voice. "She just overdosed."

"No." I desperately want to share the details of what I remember and the reasons I believe Cole murdered her, but I'm too drugged. "She hated heroin," I get out. "She was happy."

"That's the thing about heroin," Stella says. "Even when you hate it and think you're past it, it can come back and bite you."

I curl into a ball atop the soft bath mat, allowing my eyes to close. I can hear the ocean sloshing against the underside of the floor, rising higher and higher. "I was there that night." I force my mouth to continue pushing the words out. "I saw Cole come home. I was worried you would find them—I told Jackson to warn them."

"Have you talked about it with Jackson?" Her voice is tentative.

"This afternoon." It's becoming more and more difficult to speak.

"Why did you choose me?" she asks. "Why not him or Cole?"

"You said . . . a book. In an interview. You talked about coming clean. I thought you were ready to stop . . ."

She inhales sharply. I feel her move and hear her walking away, the cloud of sleep finally settling over me like a fuzzy blanket, melting my worries into oblivion. Sudden cold and wet. My eyes flutter open to see her standing above me with an empty glass. She pulls me up to sitting and pours a warm Red Bull down my throat. "What the hell?" I splutter.

"I'm sorry." She jams her knee into my back to keep me sitting. "You can't go to sleep."

I wipe the water from my eyes to see she's crying. But then she's always crying. The woman cries more than anyone I've ever met. "You shouldn't have drugged me if you didn't want me to sleep," I grumble. "I have caffeine pills in my purse."

I allow my eyes to close again while she rummages in my purse, coming up with the bottle of seven-hour Zing pills. She places one on my tongue, then puts the Red Bull to my lips to wash it down.

"It was Cole's idea to drug you," she admits. "He wanted me to kill you, but I refused."

The news would be more upsetting if I weren't so damn tired. "Why?"

She extracts a picture from her back pocket and thrusts it into my hands. It's the picture of Iris and me that I keep in my wallet. "You went in my wallet?" I ask, surprised. I never should have brought the picture with me, but it gave me strength, reminded me of why I was here. And I never thought anyone would be rummaging around in my wallet.

"Madison did. She broke in wanting to get dirt on you so you wouldn't take her role. She showed Cole, and he brought it to me." She shoves the Red Bull in my mouth again before I can respond. The effervescence is sharp on my throat. "You didn't let Mimi go, did you? Cole said—"

"God no. I adore her. That much is true," I swear.

Outside, the wind howls. "I'd wanted to meet you," Stella says. "But Iris was protective of you. She wouldn't introduce me until she was sure I'd stay in your life. Then after she died, I tried to find you—"

"You did?" Even in my diminished state, the irony of our situation does not escape me.

She nods. "But you'd disappeared. Your grandparents didn't want you to have anything to do with your former life."

I finish the Red Bull and wipe my chin on my shirt, feeling ever so slightly more alert. "I wish you'd found me. Things would be different." I yearn to talk more with her about all of this, but there's no time now. "What's Cole's plan with me?"

"He wanted me to kill you before you killed me, but I insisted we just put you to sleep until we could get the police to arrest you."

"For what?"

"Stalking, lying, attempted murder," she rattles off. "I don't know. Were you going to kill me?"

I shake my head. "I'd thought of it, in the beginning. But I decided not to, once I got to know you."

"Thanks, I guess," she says.

I feel hot tears on my cheeks, a sinking sensation in my chest. "I don't want to kill anyone," I whisper. "I just want to be normal."

Stella sits next to me on the bath mat and rests a hand on my back, gently patting me like I'm a child. "That stupid interview when I announced the memoir..." She closes her eyes. "Cole's call to do this movie came soon after. I didn't put the two together at the time, but now it seems obvious his offering me the part was more about bribing me than anything else—to make sure I kept my mouth shut. Not that I ever would have published anything about Cole's fetish—or Iris, no matter how desperate I was for cash. How would that have made me look? And it didn't matter anyway—as you know, no one wanted the damn thing. He mentioned it the night we hooked up though. I tried to set him straight about it, but then we were having sex and..." She sighs. "The next day he fed me this story about Jackson blackmailing him to hire me and do this film, so I didn't think about the interview again. I'm an idiot."

I rest my head on my knees, wishing my brain were working better. "Jackson did mention something about Cole bribing him too." I gasp. "Jackson! You gave him the lemonade too. We have to go get him."

I grip the counter with my free hand, and between the two of us, we manage to heave me to standing. "We have to get you both somewhere safe to hide so Cole still thinks I'm on his side," Stella says. "Otherwise he might kill us all."

I wish I thought she was only being dramatic. "I don't know how far I can go. Are you supposed to meet him somewhere?"

She nods. "In the wine cellar—once I drugged you."

I squint at her. "Leaving me here?"

"I didn't realize how high the water was going to get," she insists. "I made him promise he'd put you somewhere safe once you were asleep."

"Yeah, right." I snort.

"I'm sorry. I'm an idiot for listening to him." Her bloodshot green eyes plead with me to forgive her. "There's a storage closet and janitor's office next to the wine cellar—"

"Too close." I shake my head. "I won't be able to get down there without him seeing me."

She thinks. "There's an office off of reception. Apparently the walls up there are concrete, and at least you could lock the door."

The idea that a locked door is going to do anything for me is laughable, but with the sleeping pills smoothing the grooves of my brain, I can't come up with anything better. It'll have to do for now. I splash my face with cold water from the sink and discard my remaining brown contact, unexpectedly buoyed by the act.

Stella's breath suddenly catches. "He has guns. I just remembered. In the wine cellar."

Of course he does.

"Let's try to get to them before he does," I say.

I follow her into the living room, where she shoves bottles of water, flashlights, nutrition bars, and a towel into a backpack. "You ready?" she asks.

And then the lights go out.

# Stella

T he darkness was so complete, I couldn't remember which way I'd been facing in the room. It was like I was back in the womb. I fumbled for the power switch on the flashlight, and a bright beam cut through the black before Felicity snatched it and shut it off, sending us plummeting back into the inky void.

"We can't risk him seeing the light once we're outside, if he's out there." She grasped my hand in hers. "We need to let our eyes adjust."

We stood hand in hand, unmoving, while the wind roared around the eaves and the rain pounded the roof. Something crashed outside. The darkness remained.

"We have to go." Felicity pulled me toward the door.

"I still can't see," I protested.

"He won't be able to either," she pointed out.

She turned the handle and the door flew open with a thunk. "Ow," she cried.

"Was that your head?"

"My shoulder." She stepped out into the billowing rain, tugging me behind her.

Outdoors, the coal-black lessened to a dusky gloom punctuated by a gale so strong, I immediately lost my footing and had to grab on to the door frame to brace myself. A deck chair hurtled past, absorbed into the chaos before I could make out where it landed.

Felicity linked her arm through mine, and we steeled ourselves against the storm as we stepped onto the saturated pier. The sea rolled mere inches beneath the boards, pushing through the slats and surging over the sides as it seethed. When we reached Jackson's bungalow, Felicity banged on the door and rang the bell, shouting over the wind, but it was useless. "He's asleep," she cried, her voice edged with desperation. "We have to break in."

Water washed over our ankles as we assessed his bungalow. Like all the cabins, his had extensive decking on the front that faced the sea, but no windows on the back, and the windows on the sides were obscured by wooden slats, designed for privacy. A foot-wide ledge ran halfway around the outside of the bungalow, ending beneath the slatted windows, a good ten feet from the front deck. Felicity reared back and kicked the door with all her might, but it didn't budge.

She groaned and leaned her head against the door, her energy flagging.

"We have to go," I said. "I'll come back for him."

"No," she insisted, shaking her head to wake herself up. "These bungalows could go underwater at any minute. I'm not leaving him here to drown."

And with that, she lurched toward the side ledge.

"Felicity!" I called. "What are you doing?"

But she wasn't listening to me. I watched in sheer terror as she inched her way around the building, her fingers gripping the horizontal wooden slats. This was all my fault. I should never have listened to Cole. What was I thinking?

Felicity braced herself as a rogue wave slammed into her back, then continued her scrabble toward the window. It was so dark, I could hardly make out what she was doing, but I could tell she'd reached the end of the ledge and was climbing higher up the slats. Finally her body jerked inward, and she disappeared into the window. I breathed a sigh of relief.

A few seconds later, she flung open the front door. "What did you do?" I asked. "That was terrifying."

"There's a latch that opens the slats for airflow," she said. "I unhooked it and went through his bedroom window."

I felt terrible when I saw Jackson sprawled across the couch in his living room, still wearing the muddied clothes he'd had on when he left our bungalow. This was all my fault. How could I have trusted Cole? I knew better.

Felicity bent over his face, slapping his cheeks, to no avail. She put her ear to his chest.

"Oh God, he's not dead, is he?" I cried.

She shook her head. "Get me some water."

I extracted one of the bottles of water from my backpack, and she splashed it in his face the same way I'd done to her. He gurgled, but didn't wake up. "Jackson!" she shouted into his face.

I grabbed the water and dumped it over his head as she pushed him up to sitting, finally eliciting a gasp and splutter. "It's me," Felicity said. "You have to wake up. Stella drugged you with that lemonade." Disoriented, he looked from her to me and back. "It's okay. We worked it out. I'll explain everything later. But we have to go. The water's rising."

He rested his head on Felicity's shoulder. "Nope," she cajoled him. "You have to get up. The hurricane is here, and your father's trying to kill me." She turned to me. "Give me a caffeine pill."

I extracted one of the caffeine pills from the backpack and handed it to her.

"This should wake you up a little." Felicity placed it on his tongue and helped him wash it down with water. "We have to go now," she said, sliding her arm around him. I did the same on the other side, and we rose together, standing him precariously on his feet.

"Where are we going?" he asked, groggy.

"There's an office off of reception where you guys can sleep and wait for the storm to pass," I said, proud of myself for having a plan. "Cole will be in the wine cellar with me. I'll make sure he stays away." No part of me was excited about being stuck in a wine cellar with Cole for however long it took for this storm to pass; nor was I looking forward to the backlash when he discovered Felicity and Jackson were not, in fact, sleeping in their bungalows, but that was the way it had to be. Felicity was probably right that he wouldn't risk his own life to check on them during the storm or move them to safety, and if he decided to, I'd just have to stop him somehow. I'd gotten us into this mess, and I would have to get us out.

Outside, visibility was so low we could hardly see five feet in front of us. We stumbled down the flooded pier and onto the beach, where the storm surge had buried most of the sand underwater. Palm trees bent under the strain of the wind; the path that led to the main building had turned into a muddy river. As we mounted the stairs that ascended to the pool and lobby, I noticed one of the railings had been pried off, leaving a mess of twisted wood and nails behind.

Lightning flashed as we skirted the pool, illuminating a table and a number of loungers floating among the greenery that blanketed the surface. Somewhere a door banged; something rough and sharp scraped my leg. We moved past the restaurant, around the outside of the building toward the entrance to reception, where I groped desperately along the wall for the door handle until finally I felt something give.

"Got it." I exhaled, and the door swung in. "If I don't come back, hide somewhere else."

Felicity gave me a thumbs-up, and she and Jackson flattened themselves against the outside wall as I stepped inside. The darkness of the lobby was like a blindfold, but at least there was less danger of being swept out to sea or impaled by flying debris. I stood still, listening, straining my eyes to see. But I could make out very little definition in the shadows, and all I could hear was the scratching of a branch against the roof and the wailing wind.

The coast seemed to be clear, but I took a few tentative steps over the tiles to be sure, wincing at the loud squelching of my tennis shoes as I crept toward the wide hallway that led to the restaurant. I gasped as my hips collided with something solid and smooth—a leather couch, I determined, feeling along it with my fingers. Which meant I wasn't moving in the direction I thought I was. Without a wall to guide me, I was completely lost in the dark. I tried to picture the couch in the room to orient myself, but the room was full of furniture arranged into different sitting areas. It was hopeless.

I inched backward in the effort of retracing my steps to the door to find my bearings, but quickly slammed into a heavy table, sending a vase crashing to the floor. I flinched. Even the noise of the storm wouldn't drown that out. Somewhere a door banged open, and heavy footsteps trod over the tiles. My heart sank. I thought of Felicity and Jackson waiting outside, barely able to keep their eyes open, all because of me.

After a moment, the arc of a flashlight pierced the darkness.

"Hello?" I called out.

"What are you doing?"

The voice was Cole's. I made my way toward him, praying he hadn't seen Felicity and Jackson. "I was coming to meet you, but I couldn't find my flashlight in my bag. I bumped into a table." I gestured to the shattered vase.

"Did you do it?"

He shined his flashlight in my face, leaving me blinking and half-blind. "Jesus," I complained, shading my eyes. "Yeah, I did it. Crushed the pills up in lemonade."

"Where are they?"

"Felicity's passed out in her bed in our bungalow," I lied. "Jackson's in his. I watched him drink the whole thing, so I know he can't be awake. I'm worried about the water rising, though." This, I thought, was a good touch.

His eyes were in dark shadow, but his mouth twisted into a hard line. "Why are you lying to me?"

My mind raced. "I'm not lying."

"Yes, you are, Stella." Again he shone his light in my face. I winced and shielded my eyes with my forearm.

"I'm not, I swear! I did exactly what you told me to!"

His teeth glimmered in the dark as he pulled Bad Billy's antique six-shooter from his waistband. My heart leaped to my throat. So much for reaching the guns before he did.

"Then why"—he fingered the gun—"did I see the three of you together by the pool, not five minutes ago?"

I froze, searching for an answer that might satisfy him. "You didn't," I managed. "It must have been an optical illusion. It was probably a tree branch or something—it's so dark—"

"Lightning, Stella."

Damn. I remembered the ill-timed flash of lightning as we passed the pool. There'd be no convincing him.

"Where are they?" he demanded. He hovered over me, the gun dangling from his hand. "Don't make me ask twice."

My heart was now beating so wildly I could hardly breathe. But this was my ex-husband. I'd once loved this man and thought he'd loved me. Surely he wouldn't kill me. Courage. "Or what, you're gonna shoot me?" I challenged.

"I'd prefer not to," he said evenly.

Time slowed. I could feel my chest rising and falling with every inhale and exhale. "It wasn't Jackson who wanted to cast me in this film, was it?"

He gave a slight shrug.

I knew I should stop, but I had to know. "Why did you ask me here?"

"You were right for the part." His voice was flat. "I couldn't imagine anyone else in the role."

Now he was mocking me. "It didn't have anything to do with the memoir I wanted to write?"

He adjusted his grip on the gun. "What are you getting at, Stella?"

I steeled my nerves. I knew what had happened now, though I

still couldn't fathom why. "Iris didn't die of an overdose, did she? You killed her and covered it up with a car wreck so that no one would ask questions."

For the briefest moment, his eyes met mine, and I knew I was right. I sensed the movement of the arm that held the gun, but I never had a chance.

# Taylor

I awoke to pitch black and the sound of the wind and rain pummeling the roof above me with force. As I came to, a searing pain gripped my stomach. I gasped. It felt as though a cat was trying to claw its way out of me. I was disoriented, my brain foggy, my body heavy. My jaw throbbed. But it was nothing compared to the fire in my stomach.

Where was I? I could hear the violent ocean all around me but could see nothing. I felt along the surface I was lying on: cold and hard, walls about three feet high with rounded edges. A soaking tub. Why was I in a tub?

I felt something move at my side and shrieked, jumping out of the way. It was furry and small. A rat? What the hell? As I scrambled out of the bathtub, I stepped on the creature's foot and it yelped. Or barked. I reached into the tub and took out a shaking Mary Elizabeth. Thank God. But why was I in a tub with Mary Elizabeth?

My stomach cramped as I stood, and I sat down hard on the floor with the little dog in my arms. I felt a cold wet in my pants. Had I pissed myself? Miscarried? I was pregnant. I knew that much. Or I had been. If the pain in my stomach was any indication, I wasn't anymore. Unless, maybe I had food poisoning? I clung to the thought hopefully, though I knew that with the circumstances, it was unlikely. I closed my eyes and tried to conjure how I'd ended up here. I remembered last night with Rick. I remembered the storm approaching this morning, remembered moving the plane and boat up an hour...but then what?

Something nagged at the corners of my mind. I'd decided to quit my job. I was going to confront Cole. Had I? I set Mary Elizabeth on the floor and slowly stood, then felt my way along the wall to where the door to my bedroom should be. But it wasn't there. Instead I found the sink. Odd. I felt around the counter for anything that might produce light, coming up with a book of matches. Hardly believing my luck, I struck a match. Sulfur dioxide burned my nostrils as the dark came to life in flickering gold. I wasn't in my bathroom. This one was oriented opposite of mine, the countertop cluttered with high-end men's toiletries and prescription pill bottles. Resting between the sinks was a black baseball hat that read "POWER PICTURES."

Shit. I was at Cole's.

I had confronted him. I couldn't quite determine whether I was making it up or I actually remembered it, but regardless, the outcome seemed obvious. This was not food poisoning.

Another wave of pain seized my stomach, and something warm oozed down my leg. He'd done this to me. The memory lurked just outside of my reach, but I knew it with every cell in my body.

I lit another match and held it up to the crotch of my cargo pants. They were dark with blood. I screamed, pure rage filling every cell in my body. I didn't know whether I abhorred him more for knocking me up or for knocking it out of me, but it didn't matter. I loathed him with a hate as pure and deep as the darkness around me. If he'd stood in front of me in this moment, I would have killed him without a thought.

But he didn't stand in front of me. I was in the throes of a miscarriage during a hurricane; I needed to focus on the present. I struck another match and waved it over the vanity, then the ledge by the window, where I found what I was looking for: a big white jar candle emblazoned with the name of the resort. I touched the wick with the dying match flame and the candle sizzled to life.

Shadows danced on white marble and reflected off walls of glass as I carefully carried my new light source to the door that led to the bedroom and turned the knob. It didn't budge. My heart sank. Bathrooms weren't supposed to lock from the outside. I assessed the doorknob, only to find a dead bolt that required a key. Why Cole needed a dead bolt on his bathroom wasn't relevant. I was stuck, and I didn't dare consider what he planned to do to me when he came back.

Did he mean to kill me? He could have so easily thrown me into the sea to drown after knocking me out, instead of locking me here in this bathroom. The fact that he hadn't gave me a sliver of hope he wouldn't when he returned. Without the fetus I carried, I had no proof anything had ever happened between us. Would my word be enough? He obviously thought not. Or perhaps he figured that without evidence and after experiencing how vicious he could be, I'd be too afraid to speak up.

He was wrong. I didn't care anymore what it did to my career. I was more determined than ever to make sure that motherfucker never laid a hand on another woman. But to do that, I needed to survive. And that meant getting out of this godforsaken bathroom.

Gritting my teeth against the agony in my stomach, I set the candle on the sink and assessed my surroundings. The storm outside was fierce, and I could tell the ocean was high by the sound of the waves slapping the walls and the underside of the floor, but thus far the bungalow seemed intact. I had to assume Cole had gone up to the lobby to ride out the storm, so I ostensibly had some time to come up with a plan, if only I could think through this pain. I rummaged through his pill bottles, gladly downing a Vicodin with one of the half-empty water bottles that littered the countertop.

Mary Elizabeth whined. My blood-soaked pants stuck to my thighs as I squatted next to her and filled the empty soap dish with water, which she lapped up immediately. I grabbed the candle and wandered into Cole's walk-in closet, where I selected drawstring gym shorts and the smallest pair of boxer briefs I could find, figuring I could fold a washrag inside to absorb additional blood. As I peeled off my pants and dropped them on the floor, I was surprised to hear a thunk. I dropped to my knees and fingered the fabric, extracting a small gray plastic brick from the lower-leg pocket.

*Pockets are useful.*

I recognized it immediately as the satellite phone I'd forgotten Rick gave me before he left this morning. How had I not felt it until now? As if in answer, a sharp pang cut through my abdomen. I flipped the phone open and held down the power switch. As the buttons lit up green, a ray of hope flared to life inside me. The phone was fully charged, the number for Rick's parents' satellite phone stored right where he'd keyed it in a million years ago this morning. Could it possibly work in this weather? I extended the antenna the way he'd showed me and pressed dial.

The line crackled as it rang and rang. Finally the voice mail clicked on, sending my heart plummeting. I left a jumbled message detailing my situation, then set the phone on the vanity with the antenna angled toward the window. Lightning flashed, illuminating the world outside for the first time. I gasped at the sight. The lower deck was completely underwater and white-capped waves crashed violently over the terrace beyond the window, only a step down from where I stood. In context it was shocking the floor was still dry; if the sea rose any farther the bungalow would most certainly flood.

I needed to get out of here before that happened. But how? And if I did succeed in escaping the bathroom, would the pier that connected the bungalows to the beach still be above water and intact? Sharp claws of fear sank into my skin. I desperately scraped the recesses of my brain for a plan as I wiped myself down with a damp towel and donned the clothes of Cole's that I had selected, then combed every inch of the bathroom and closet for an escape route.

The closet was completely enclosed, but worst-case scenario had a high shelf about two feet wide that I could get up onto if the water got in and began to rise, and a decently solid step stool I could use to climb up. The door to the bedroom was crafted out of the same solid teak the rest of the bungalow was made of, but above it near the ceiling, a window about eighteen inches high ran the length of the wall between the bedroom and the bathroom. I would have to break it.

My stomach cramped, sending me to the floor, where I curled up in a ball and waited for the torment to pass. When I opened my eyes, I was facing the cabinet beneath the sink. A light bulb went off in my head as I remembered Rick's lesson in fixing a clogged sink.

Mary Elizabeth licked my ankle while I opened the cabinet and carefully unscrewed the two ends of the U-shaped pipe. It was made of a heavy metal that should work nicely for breaking the window, and the two straight pipes that attached to it could also be detached and used for backup.

A sudden ringing from the counter above me, and I jerked my head back, banging it into the inside of the cabinet as I rose to grab the sat phone. "Hello?" I screamed into the receiver.

"Taylor." Rick's voice was tinny and far away. "Are you okay?"

"No," I cried. "I'm locked in Cole's bathroom, and the water is almost floor level."

"…kill that…therfucker…was worried…happened when I didn't hear…called…too late."

"You're breaking up."

"…the storm. Need to get you out. I can…" The rest was lost in fuzz.

I moved closer to the window, hoping for better reception. "I think I can get into the bedroom by breaking the window above the door with a pipe, but I don't know if the pier is washed out."

"The storm tide…water so high…going out so the water…subside…hours."

"What? Are you saying the water will go higher?" I asked, watching as a wave splashed the window. I waited desperately for an answer, but none came. "Rick?"

The call had dropped. I sat on the edge of the soaking tub with a groan, willing the phone to ring again. After a moment, my wish was granted. "Rick?" I answered.

"Can you hear me better now?" His voice sounded like it was in a well, but at least I was catching all his words now. "I stepped outside."

"Yes."

"The tide is going out, so the water shouldn't rise any higher." I could hear the wind roaring around him as he shouted into the phone. "The water may seep in, but only a foot or two unless a window or door breaks. Down here the windows have to be made of safety glass, which means if they break, they shatter completely."

"So I'm safe here?"

"Safer than trying to traverse the pier right now. But you need to get out before Cole comes back. I won't be able to get over there until the storm passes."

"I know."

"Low tide is in two hours, which is around the time the eye should pass over Saint Genesius. The water will be lowest then. That's when you need to go."

"But where do I go? Cole's up at the main building."

"The post office is made of concrete block. You'll be fine there. The doors of buildings are left unlocked during storms so that cleanup crews can get in. I'll meet you there as soon as the storm is over."

"Okay."

"Keep this phone on you, and call me if you need me."

"I will."

I hung up and dragged the stepladder out of the closet, wishing I were taller. Even standing on the top step only brought me to eye level with the window, which meant I was going to have to rely on my upper-body strength to heave myself through it. *Please let it be safety glass.* I wrapped my hand in a towel and, shielding my eyes, slammed the pipe into the window. It shattered immediately, sending tiny pebbles of glass raining down and bouncing across the tiles. I breathed a sigh of relief.

As I came down from the ladder, Mary Elizabeth yapped at my ankles. Shit. How was I going to get her through the window? I had to come up with something in case I couldn't unlock the door from the outside. I'd need the sat phone and the candle as well. I went into Cole's closet, where I found a perforated gym bag with a long, detachable strap. It would have to do.

"I'm sorry about this, girl," I apologized to her as I unzipped the bag and placed her inside with the sat phone, a bottle of water, and matches. "This is the best I've got."

I continued talking to her as I climbed up the step stool. When I reached the top, I blew out the candle and wrapped it inside a towel, placing it gingerly next to the shaking dog, who whined and yelped as I zipped up the bag. Now in complete darkness, I gripped the strap of the bag in one hand, then pushed it through the window and slowly lowered it as far as I could, finally releasing it to fall the last inches to the floor below. Mary Elizabeth barked excitedly—what I thought sounded like a healthy bark, thankfully.

I gathered every ounce of strength I'd built up in CrossFit and hefted my upper body up and through the hole, then with much groaning, scooted myself lengthwise, lying facedown. My stomach cramped as it scraped the remainder of pebbled glass on the windowsill, but the Vicodin had begun to work, dulling the pain to an almost-manageable level. I swung my feet through the window and dropped to the ground.

# Felicity

The air is still and close behind the wall of pillows and blankets I fashioned in the housekeeping closet at the back of the spa building. I've been here for hours in the dark, vividly imagining the night of my mother's death while refereeing the battle within my body: head foggy from the pharmaceuticals Stella slipped me, heart racing with the caffeine pills. I feel as though I might tear in two and can't for the life of me understand why anyone would intentionally take uppers and downers at the same time.

Over the din of the storm outside, the sudden slamming of a door and heavy footsteps in the hall raises the hair on my arms. It can only be Stella or Cole, and from the weight of the tread, I'm guessing Cole. I listen as doors within the building are opened, unknown objects tossed about. I nervously check to ensure I remain completely hidden as the footsteps grow closer. The door of my closet opens; I don't dare to breathe. Petrified, I watch through the pillows as the beam of a flashlight sweeps the inky darkness.

It's a man, so it must be Cole. He's looking for someone. Me, likely. And Jackson. Or Stella, if...

I don't know what happened once Stella disappeared inside the lobby, but she never returned, and after five minutes Jackson and I bolted, finding refuge in the nearby spa building. We decided to split up to sleep off the pills in case anything happened to one of us, and he made sure I was concealed in my hiding place in the linen closet before tucking himself behind the extra mattresses in the storeroom.

He must have hidden me well because the door slams as Cole backs out of the closet, leaving me in complete darkness. I inhale, realizing I was holding my breath.

Over the noise of the storm outside, I can barely make out the sound of more doors opening and closing as Cole moves down the hall. Does this mean he's somehow discovered we're not in our bungalows? And if so, does he know Stella helped us? Worry prickles my spine.

Still foggy, I carefully push back my pillow fort and sit up, rubbing my eyes. At least I don't have to wear those irritating contacts anymore. Pins and needles tickle my feet as the blood flow returns. My watch reads 10:57 p.m., which means I've been here around three hours. Not enough to fully metabolize the heavy dose of sleeping pills Stella gave me, but the fear and caffeine pumping through my system work as an antidote, the need to live superseding the need to sleep. I remove the small metal flashlight I stored in the band of my shorts and grip it in my palm.

In the hallway, I suddenly hear men's voices talking excitedly. Cole must have found Jackson. My heart thumps faster as I strain to hear.

"I don't know." Jackson's voice. "I can't remember."

A decent line of defense, though I don't know how well it will work with Cole. "I saw you with them by the pool," Cole says. "Where is Felicity now?"

"I don't know. The last thing I remember, I was in my bungalow alone. What happened?"

Does he really not remember?

"Stella drugged you." Their voices are moving down the hall in the direction of the waiting room. "She's got it in her head I killed that woman who overdosed at our house when you were a kid and you helped me cover it up, and she wants revenge."

The fact that Jackson doesn't ask any of the myriad questions that flimsy fabrication should illicit makes me think he does remember and is only playing along. "Where is she now?" he ventures.

"Somewhere safe. Don't worry." It sounds like they've stopped right outside my closet. "We can deal with her once the storm has passed. The problem is Felicity. She's missing, and so are two of my guns."

Oh, come on. Like I'm some comic book vigilante running around in a hurricane, shooting people. Although, come to think of it, it's not actually that far from the truth. If only I'd known about those guns sooner. But I've decided not to kill anyone, I remind myself. Not even Cole.

Unless I have to.

In the hallway, Cole continues. "Good thing I still have this one."

The hairs on my arms stand up.

"What's Felicity have to do with this?" Jackson asks gamely.

"She's the dead woman's daughter."

"What?" To his credit, Jackson sounds genuinely shocked.

A tremendous crashing noise over the constant din of the storm outside drowns out their voices. When it subsides, I no longer hear them. Shit, where have they gone? Desperate not to lose them, I slide my feet into my still-wet sneakers and quietly open the door a crack to peer into the pitch-black hallway. Afraid to use my light, I feel my way along the wall and stand listening behind the door to the lobby to make sure they're gone before slipping through.

Outside I can hear the storm raging like a demon in heat. Every nerve in my body cries out to return to the linen closet and sleep until it's over, but that's not an option. What if Cole's discovered Stella helped me? I don't even want to think about what he might do to her. And where's he going with Jackson? I steel my nerves and nudge the front door of the spa open a crack. Immediately it flies wide, ripped from my hand by the vicious wind. A blast of air and water smacks my exposed face as I survey the area for any sign of Cole and Jackson.

Surely Cole won't harm Jackson; he's his son, and Cole's so

self-centered he would never imagine that Jackson would choose me over him. I try to convince myself, but my heart is sick with worry.

A flash of lightning illuminates the chaotic scene, sending me scuttling for cover behind the door frame. To my left, a giant oak has fallen into the restaurant, smashing the roof to bits, while ahead of me, so much debris is strewn about the pool deck that it's difficult to determine the exact location of the pool itself. A golf cart is upside down in the bushes, and the roof of some unseen building now litters the trees. A deafening clap of thunder draws my eyes toward the sky in search of flying debris.

Through the branches of the fallen tree I spot a winking pinprick of light moving toward the building beyond. Cole's flashlight. It disappears near where I have to guess the door to the main lobby must be. So I'll need a different entry point. I map the building in my mind, recalling all the doors Jackson and I shored up this afternoon. I decide on a staff entrance around the back of the building that opens into the employee locker rooms.

Before I can chicken out, I kick the door to the spa shut, lower my head, and sprint toward the main building. The wind pushes so hard I'm leaning at nearly a forty-five-degree angle as I fight my way through sheets of rain and flying detritus. A gust throws me into the muddy tangled roots of the oak, terrifyingly pinning me there for a moment before it changes directions. When it lets up, I run like hell around the corner of the building, narrowly missing being nailed by a falling branch before I yank open the staff door with all my might and dive into the relative safety of the locker room.

I click on my flashlight to creep toward the door, where I extinguish the light before softly pushing it open and slipping into the hallway like a ghost. I pause, listening intently for any human sounds, then grope my way back toward the lobby, where the complete blackout lessens to the darkest gloom. Though the high-beamed ceiling is still intact, a steady breeze buffets the leaves and sand now strewn about the tiled floor as a result of the compromised roof of the restaurant.

I can't make out much in the dark, but I note an overturned chair, a smashed lamp. No sign of Jackson and Cole, or Stella.

I steal across the lobby in the direction the breeze is coming from but don't make it halfway before I trip over something and tumble to the floor with a clamor that would wake the dead. My knee throbs where it struck the tile.

Footsteps.

I have to hide fast, but where, when I can't see? Recalling the overturned chair, I scuttle backward toward where it should be, fumbling as noiselessly as I can. My reaching hands land on soft upholstery, and I tuck myself behind the seat of the chair just as a shaft of light cuts through the darkness. I huddle in the shadows and hold my breath while Cole prowls the room, shining the light around the space. I'm nearly sure he can hear my heart thumping as the seconds drag on, but finally he must decide there's no one here because he turns and stalks briskly out the side door.

A whoosh of air sweeps in as the door shuts behind him. What has he done with Jackson and Stella? An image of my mother, her eyes fixed, her skin ashen, flashes before my eyes. I can't let the same thing happen to them.

As I unfurl my limbs, my hand strikes what feels like a wet tennis shoe. I tentatively trace my fingers over it. It's definitely a shoe. A woman's running shoe soaked in water and mud. A shoe that can only belong to one person. I grab it and creep blindly toward the hallway where Cole came from, fear driving me forward.

When I reach the hall that connects the lobby to the restaurant, I can feel the wind from above rushing through the splintered ceiling, blasting the branches of the fallen tree into a dangerous frenzy of bark and leaves. I drag my hand along the wall until I find the stairwell that leads down to the wine cellar, and gripping the handrail, carefully descend the steps. Once I'm safely around the bend in the stairs, I click on my flashlight. My breath catches in my throat as the beam illuminates the shoe in my hands. It's one of Stella's white tennis shoes, streaked with mud. On the toe is a single drop of blood.

I tear down the remaining steps to the basement, where a hallway lined with movie posters featuring Cole's face leads to a giant steel door that I can only imagine opens into the fabled wine room. "Jackson?" I call. "Stella? Hello?"

I grasp the long steel bar that holds the door in place and slide it back in its track, then pull the heavy door open and shine my light into the room. Jackson squints up at me from where he sits on the floor, filthy and wet. Thank God. "Are you hurt?" I ask, rushing over to him.

"I'm fine," he breathes. "Just glad you're okay."

As I kneel beside him, I bump into the stack of framed posters that leans against the wall next to him, sending one of them clattering to the floor. I right it, noting it's a framed poster of *The Gentleman Gangster 2*, featuring Cole in front of a bank vault with a hatch not dissimilar to the door I opened to enter this room.

"What happened?" I ask.

"He found me, told me you and Stella were—"

"I heard that part. I was in the linen closet listening. I never slept— the caffeine pills kept me awake. How'd you end up here?"

"He said it was the best place to ride out the storm, but when we got here, he pulled a gun on me and told me he was locking me in for my own good."

"At least we know he doesn't want to kill you."

"He doesn't know I'm on your side," he returns.

Cole's face taunts me from the poster behind Jackson's shoulder, and all of a sudden it hits me. "He locked you in here just like he locked the tellers in the bank vault so they wouldn't get caught in the shoot-out in *Gentleman Gangster 2*," I say. Something inside me clicks, like a crucial puzzle piece that, when it snaps into place, makes the rest of the picture clear. "Stella said the drugged lemonade was his idea too. It was from the fourth movie in the series," I add, realizing. "Only it was tea, used to put the guards of a museum to sleep while he lifted a painting."

Jackson stares at me, baffled. "What are you talking about?"

"Do you notice everything he does is from a movie he's been in? It's like he's taken pieces of his characters with him and is acting out the plotlines over and over again."

"Was being a shitty father one of the plotlines?"

He obviously means it as a rhetorical question, but I thumb through the file of his films I keep in my mind, snapping my fingers when it comes to me. "*Bad Boy*. His father bribed him to keep quiet about company secrets he'd discovered by giving him a large stake in the company. He played the son, but he's become the father. So yes, even that."

"Okay," he says slowly. "I see the pattern, but what are you getting at?"

"I found Stella's shoe in the lobby." I hold it up, and his gaze immediately lands on the drop of blood. "Did Cole say anything about her?"

"Only that she was somewhere safe, and he would deal with her after the storm passed."

"Anything else? Anything specific? Think."

He closes his eyes, thinking. "Something about her choosing her ship?"

I recognize the line. "To sail into a storm of her own making?"

He nods, eyeing me strangely.

"It's a line," I say. "In the third Gentleman Gangster movie, he says it before killing a man aboard a boat, then sending it sailing into a storm while he escapes on a Jet Ski. He's playing a character. Or a lot of them. Everything he's doing is something he's done in a film."

Jackson's countenance hardens. "We've gotta get to his yacht."

# Stella

The oblivion of unconsciousness morphed to thick darkness and violent lurching, underscored by the deafening roar of the sea and wind. Water sloshed around me; my throat stung with salt and thirst. One of my ankles throbbed with an unknown injury, and my hands were tied with rough rope around something solid above my head. The stabbing pain that split my skull pulsed with every plunge and toss, as though I'd been thrown into a washing machine in hell.

Confusion turned to panic as I realized where I must be. I remembered everything leading up to the moment the gun came down on my temple—the same gun Bad Billy had used to brain Wildman Sam, if Cole's story was to be believed—and then he must have tied me up out here on his boat in the middle of a hurricane. The only good news, if there was any, was that the boat seemed to still be tied to the dock. I felt a dull, jarring *thunk* every time a wave slammed it into the rubber bumpers.

I'd been a fool to think I could lie to him. I'd been a fool to get involved with him at all. I knew better, goddammit. Biggest mistake of my life, marrying him. And I'd made a lot of mistakes in my life. If only I'd stayed away from him, Felicity would still have a mother; I'd have a career. But that line of thought was useless now. I wouldn't let the heavy brick of regret drag me to the bottom of the sea. I had to fight.

My arms were sore and nearly numb from being trussed over my head; I wiggled my wrists against the rope and found they were already rubbed raw. I stretched my fingers, reaching for the tie, but no matter how I tried, I couldn't get them to even touch it, let alone unfasten the knots. A thorny coat of terror wrapped tight around my throat. Thinking I could use my teeth if I could get them close enough, I attempted to pull my feet in, only to find they were firmly tied to something else, too far away to give me enough leverage to reach my mouth anywhere near my wrist bindings. *Please, universe, give me some shred of hope to hold on to.*

I was still alive. Cole could easily have shot me, but he had only pistol-whipped me, which meant he must prefer me breathing, a positive sign to be sure. All I had to do was survive this horror carnival ride for the duration of the storm, then surely someone would come. But how long would that be? Cole must have gone to look for Felicity and Jackson. I had to believe he wouldn't find them; the alternative wasn't acceptable. I implored the universe to take Cole's life instead of theirs—instead of mine.

If I made it out of here alive, I swore to the heavens I was going to be healthy again inside and out, whatever it took. I'd give up drinking and pills for real this time, take responsibility for myself and my addiction. I'd sell my jewelry and fix the roof, like Felicity had suggested—live within my means. Hell, maybe I'd sell the house. I'd give back, actually do something positive for the world instead of pretending. I could take one of the acting teacher jobs that were sometimes offered, mentor young hopefuls as they reached for their dreams.

A powerful wave slammed into the boat, violently jerking my body away from the wall as the boat keened.

*If I make it out of here alive.*

Ever since Iris died I'd thought that my life was over, but as I pitched and tossed in the darkness at death's doorstep, I finally understood it was in fact quite full of possibility, and I wanted to live. Maybe my psychic's prediction that I'd be okay once I was true to myself had less to do with being a star and more about accepting myself for who I was, unphotoshopped. I didn't want to hide anymore. I wouldn't be a victim any longer. I could be better. I swore I could. *Please, universe, let me live.*

The door suddenly banged open, and a glaring light nailed me in the face. I recoiled and squeezed my eyes shut until I felt the beam leave my field of vision, then stole a glance around. I was in the waterlogged living room of Cole's new yacht, tied to a handrail next to a couch. Cole's dark bulk filled the doorway, his flashlight veering haphazardly as the vessel pitched in the surf, leaning steeply toward the side where the pier seemed to be.

Dread tightened my chest. "What are you doing?" My throat was dry, my voice scratchy.

He stomped over and squatted in front of me. "You're going for a sail, sweetheart."

Oh no. No, no. "Please don't do this, Cole," I begged.

"Oh, come on, Stella." He spat my name like it was distasteful to him. "You've been trying to kill yourself for years. I'm just helping you out. Something I should have done a long time ago."

"Why?"

"You want to ruin your own life, fine," he snarled. "But I'm not gonna let you ruin mine."

"I'm not gonna ruin your life," I pleaded. "I wouldn't have come here if I wanted to ruin your life. I was grateful for the opportunity to work with you again, to heal our past wounds—"

He howled with laughter, turning the hand that didn't clutch the gun into a talking mouth. "Soooo grateful for the opportunity to *heal our past wounds*, were you?" he mocked me. "You were so desperate, you would have fucked a donkey for five grand. *That's* why I invited you here."

I squinted at him. "What?"

"Don't even try to pretend with me, you manipulative cunt. You knew I'd see that interview you gave about *coming clean*. Big coincidence it happened to be right after I finally stopped giving you handouts, huh? You tried to call my bluff, and you lost."

I stared at him in shock. He'd hardly been giving me handouts. It was true the stream of residual payments from *Faster*, on which he'd added me as an executive producer, had turned to a trickle and then finally run dry shortly before I gave that interview, but I was only trying to drum up a new flow of revenue with a book deal, not to sell our secrets—*my* secrets—to the press.

But he had all the power in the situation, and I reasoned arguing with him on a literal sinking ship was not going to get me what I wanted. No, flattery was what I needed. "I told you I wasn't really going to write the memoir," I implored. "It was a stupid interview. You're right. I was desperate—"

"So desperate you tried to get my own son to blackmail me—"

I was genuinely baffled. "Jackson?"

A wave crashed into the side of the boat, washing over my legs and sending Cole scrabbling for support. "I'm not stupid, Stella. You give that interview, and then he reaches out after years of hardly speaking to me to ask what really happened to Barbie?"

"Iris," I corrected him.

"Whatever. She was a whore who was using both of us, and you should be thanking me for getting rid of her."

Fury flooded my brain. I wanted to tear into his flesh with my nails and hear him cry out in pain; it took every ounce of self-control to restrain my voice. "You said she died of an overdose," I managed.

He laughed. "And she did. Only she wasn't the one who administered the dose."

God damn him. "You killed her."

"She left me no choice."

"But why?" I cried.

"She'd taped our session a few days before—"

"What do you mean?"

His eyes lit up in the gloom with the realization I didn't know. "Sleep sex. She'd filmed it to blackmail me."

Oh, Iris. She'd gone ahead and done it—gone back to him—after I'd told her not to. But had she told him about us? "Blackmail you for what?" I asked, my heart in my throat.

"To keep quiet about your affair, I assume."

"Is that what she said?"

"She never listed her demands. She was as surprised to see me as I was her." He braced himself against the bulkhead as the boat keeled. "She was confrontational, angry about this rabbit's foot key chain that belonged to a friend of hers she'd found in my things—"

An image of the rainbow rabbit's foot that disappeared from his drawer flashed before my eyes. Iris had acted so strange about it. "What does that have to do with anything?"

We stared each other down as the ship pitched and tossed, sloshing water all around us. "The friend died of an overdose," he growled.

"So why did you have her rabbit's foot?" I asked through gritted teeth.

He adjusted his grip on the gun. "She was one of the sleeping girls, before Iris. I found it under the bed after she died."

"Did she die at our house?" I demanded, blinking seawater from my eyes.

He didn't answer, but the dark mask of his face told me everything I needed to know. My body burned with hate. "Had Iris known before, that her friend was one of your girls?"

He shook his head. "But she put it together. Accused me of killing her, then rushed at me and fell into the coffee table and knocked herself out."

I knew I was in no position to challenge him, but his story was bullshit. She didn't just fall and knock herself out. He'd pushed her or hit her, or both. "What did you do to her?"

"She was rushing me," he snapped. "I was defending myself."

"She weighed a hundred and ten pounds." I glared at him. "Then what happened?"

"She was unconscious." He clung to the railing on the wall with his free hand to steady himself as the boat seesawed. "There was blood, and her neck was all twisted. I couldn't have her dying like that, but I'd been shooting *Bloodhound*—you saw *Bloodhound*, right? The prostitutes whose murders were made to look like overdoses? So I thought quick and finished her off with the heroin before her heart stopped beating, then staged the car wreck to cover up the other injuries." He actually sounded proud of himself. "I did it to defend us. Our lives, our careers. Yours as well as mine."

The air left my lungs as though I'd been punched in the gut. I could see the scene in the bedroom like it was before me now: the shattered heavy glass coffee table, the blood, the syringe. He'd sworn she was shooting up when he found her and had fought him when he tried to stop her, falling into the table as she emptied the syringe into her arm.

When he'd related his version of events that night, I'd believed him, not inclined to suspect my husband, however rotten he might be, of murder. I also knew that overdosing after a period of sobriety was a common problem among addicts. I blamed myself—for not coming home earlier, for not making sure Cole's drugs were out of the house, for not insisting she go to rehab—but I hadn't questioned his explanation. I was so caught up in my personal cyclone of grief, I couldn't see past my own nose. It was becoming increasingly clear that I'd never been able to see past my own nose.

"I believed you." I choked back tears. "Is that why you cast me? To buy my silence?"

He laughed like a film villain. "You're not so stupid you think I ever intended for this movie to see the light of day?" He steadied himself on the back of a chair as the boat lurched, then swung the barrel of the gun at my forehead. "You were going to commit suicide while we were filming."

I struggled to make sense of what he was saying. "I'd never do that," I protested, though in the wake of Iris's death I had considered it more than once.

"Oh, yes you would." He smirked. "Everyone knows your history, your struggle with substance abuse. You finally get a chance at redemption working on a film with your ex-husband. You even start up a romance with him. Then he dumps you for your younger costar, and you can't handle it." He snorted. "I cast Madison because I knew she was such a fame whore, she'd jump on the opportunity to fuck a real movie star, and she'd be dying to make it public."

I finally understood. It all made sense: his flattery and flirtation in the first weeks of filming, culminating with sex in the wine cellar—before he abruptly turned his back on me and took up with Madison, making a fool out of me in front of the entire crew. Not to mention the pictures leaked to the press of him letting me fall into a puddle down by the marina, of me passed out. No wonder he drugged me that night at Coco's. "You were going to do to me what you did to Iris."

He raised the gun overhead. "Ding, ding, ding! We have a winner!"

"But after all these years, why now?"

A gust of wind sent the boat listing even more heavily to the side, but he managed to keep his footing. How long before the ship went under? "Even when you were out of control, I always thought your self-preservation instincts would keep you quiet. You'd never want it to come out that I was cheating on you, much less that you were a *lesbian*." He spat the word like it was repulsive. "And even if you said anything, it would have been your word against mine—no one would have believed you. But things have changed." His face contorted into a sour frown, as if lamenting days gone by. "These days no one gives a shit if you're gay, and people believe whatever women say. Especially after some of the bullshit about me that's been in the press lately, I figured the public might actually take your side. So when you started talking about coming clean, I knew what I had to do."

I was almost flattered he'd arranged this entire charade just for me, spent three million to kill me. Surely it would have been more practical to hire a hit man or something, but I supposed I wasn't the only one with a flair for the dramatic. This whole showdown was playing out like the ending of one of the Gentleman Gangster movies. Only this time Cole wasn't the hero but the villain, giving his final monologue before he goes down in a ball of flames.

*Please, universe, let it be him that goes down, not me.*

I had to keep Cole talking. The more he talked, the more time I'd buy before he shot me or sent the boat plunging into the violent sea. "How was I gonna kill myself, exactly?" I asked.

His laugh turned my blood to ice. "You down enough pills and booze every day to nearly kill yourself anyway. All you needed was a little extra one evening and you'd never wake up. But that cunt Felicity kept getting in the way."

"Put the gun down, Dad." Jackson's voice rose above the howling wind.

Hope sprang up in my chest.

Cole swung his flashlight to focus on Jackson, who stood in the doorway, bracing himself against the violent rocking of the ship. "How did you get out?" he demanded. "You shouldn't be here. Where is she?" He shone the flashlight around the boat, clearly torn between wanting to find Felicity and needing to keep us under surveillance.

Jackson ignored his question, slowly inching toward us. "What are you doing, Dad?"

"Protecting us," Cole snapped, his eyes darting from the windows to the doors.

"Against what?"

"If the truth comes out the way she wants it to"—Cole pointed at me—"we'll both go to jail."

"I was an eleven-year-old kid forced to lie by my violent father," Jackson said evenly. He was nearly at my side now. "I was afraid of you and didn't know the extent of the damage you'd done. But no more. It's over."

"Get off the boat," Cole barked.

"No."

Cole raised the gun and pointed it at Jackson's chest. "Don't make me do this, son."

Jackson held up his hands. "You can't buy our silence."

"You ungrateful little shit," Cole spat.

The boat pitched, sending Cole stumbling against the wall behind me. Jackson took advantage of the moment to make a move to wedge himself between us.

The sound of the gunshot was deafening.

Cole had fired the gun in Jackson's direction, so close it was impossible to tell whether it was a warning shot or simply a miss. My ears rang; every nerve in my body stood on end. "You weren't supposed to be here," Cole repeated. "I didn't want to do this to you."

"So don't," Jackson urged. "Put the gun down. We'll go somewhere safe for the rest of the storm—"

"And then you'll ruin me after?" Cole tightened his grip on the gun.

"We'll figure something out that satisfies everyone," Jackson said.

Cole narrowed his eyes, his jaw tight. "Betrayed by my own son."

"It's for your own good, Dad," Jackson said. "You think you won't get caught for this? Then what? I only want what's best for you. For all of us."

"I don't think so." Cole shook his head, his mind made up. "It's better for you to all go out now, victims of the storm."

"Hurricanes don't shoot people," I spat.

"But everyone will believe you would"—Cole turned on me—"after I tell them I just found out you killed Iris all those years ago because she was planning to tell the press about your affair."

"Fuck you," I muttered.

I detected a split second of movement in my peripheral vision before everything once again went black.

# Felicity

**H**idden outside the rocking portside door of the yacht with the rain lashing my back, I watch in horror as Cole smacks the gun into Stella's head with a sickening thunk.

"Dad, stop!" Jackson cries, but it's no good. She slumps forward, limp.

The boat lurches in the turbulent surf, the stern barely out of the water now. I grasp the door handle, my thumb resting on the release latch, and tighten my grip on the neck of the champagne bottle dangling from my free hand. Not the weapon I would have chosen if given an alternative, but the kitchen and restaurant were blocked by the fallen tree, so I had to find what I could in the wine cellar. In the cabin, Cole raises the gun and points it at Stella's head.

"You're gonna kill her!" Jackson dives at him, providing just enough distraction for me to fling the door open and spring through it, smashing the bottle into the back of Cole's skull with all my might.

He staggers and shoots, aiming toward Jackson's shoulder, but doesn't go down. Jackson attempts to wrestle the weapon away from him as I bring the champagne bottle down on Cole's head again. He's on his knees now, but strong as an ox. The gun goes off again, and Jackson cries out in pain. I clutch the heavy bottle in both hands and smash it over Cole's crown. Glass splinters as it makes contact, and the gun drops from his hand into the sloshing chaos of the floor. Jackson moans in agony. In the darkness, I can't tell where he's been hit, but he's on the ground where his still conscious father scrambles for the gun.

A towering wave crashes through the open door, flooding the cabin with a foot of water. My head jerks back as Cole grabs my hair and slams my face into the rushing water, holding me down. Unable to breathe, I flail, punching and kicking my arms and legs with all my might. But I connect with nothing. My lungs burn.

*Don't inhale.*

Suddenly the pressure releases, and I yank my head out of the water. A grunting tangle of limbs writhes next to me as Cole wrestles with Jackson, both of them reaching for the gun. The flashlight shines toward the ceiling at an odd angle, swinging wildly with the pitching of the boat. I lunge toward it, scrabbling in the dark until I have it in my hand, and sweep the cabin to locate my broken champagne bottle, wedged beneath Stella's limp legs. I grip the hard glass neck in my hand and point the light at the thrashing heap of men.

I hear myself screaming as I bring the sharp end of the bottle down on Cole's chest, but my body's gone numb and all I can see is red.

# Stella

*D*arkness splattered with shards of fragmented light, seawater crashing into a sinking ship. A woman screaming.

I tried to move but couldn't, a paralyzing night terror. I tasted salt, fought to breathe. Nausea welled in my stomach. The rocking. Stop the rocking. Pain—in my ribs, my head, my back.

The woman continued to scream. I fought to wake, but the dream wouldn't clear; the pitching and tossing persisted.

"Stop, stop!" A man's voice now, urgent. "He's gone. It's over."

The woman's screams turned to muffled sobs. "Shhhhh..." The man comforted her. "It's all over now."

I struggled to rise, but found my arms were trussed over my head, my legs bound. I closed my eyes against the beam of a flashlight. "Stella. Are you okay?"

Jackson. Everything came rushing back. Cole, the boat, the gun. It wasn't a dream. I felt the light move from my eyes and squinted at Felicity and Jackson, clinging to each other next to me on the floor, water sloshing around us. In the gloom I could see the arm of Jackson's sweatshirt was torn and soaked in blood; Felicity's tear-streaked face was speckled with drops of red.

"Where's Cole?" I asked.

"He's dead," Jackson said, helping a shaking Felicity to her feet while the boat rolled with the pounding surf. As he moved toward me to untie my hands, my gaze landed on something behind them, partially hidden by their bodies. I craned my neck to peer around their legs as they struggled to keep their balance. It was Cole, lying on his back, dark water washing over him. His eyes were open and fixed, his chest bloody.

And again the world went black.

# Felicity

Stella, Stella!" Jackson grabs her shoulders, trying to rouse her. He slaps her cheeks, and her eyes flutter open, struggling to focus. Her face is bruised; a deep cut gapes above her eye. She's not going to be happy about the scar it's sure to leave, but it could have been a lot worse.

"What happened?" she manages weakly.

"You fainted," Jackson says.

"Cole," she mumbles, straining to look around Jackson as he undoes the rope around her wrists. "He was..."

"He was going to kill all of us." His eyes flick to me. "We did what we had to do."

I register the *we* and appreciate it, strangely more moved by Jackson's fictionalization of the event than the event itself. What I've done. *Me.* I killed Cole. Stabbed him in the chest with the sharp end of the champagne bottle, long past his last breath, from the looks of it.

I know I did, though I can't recall it now, his blood cooling on my skin. After all these years, my mother's killer has finally paid for her death at my hands. I know I should feel something other than the heavy numbness that's settled over me now that he's stopped moving. Elation, anger, grief...something. But all I feel is oddly empty. After all my preparation, I hadn't really wanted to kill anyone, it turned out. And now that I have, I feel only a dull, aching disappointment.

Stella rubs her wrists as Jackson helps her to her feet, both of them stumbling as the boat lurches with the waves. "What are we gonna do with him?" she asks, gesturing to Cole's body.

"It's my fault," I volunteer. "I'll take the blame."

"No." Jackson looks at me pointedly. "We're gonna do the same thing he was going to do to us. Let the boat sink with him aboard and blame the storm."

My guilt-ridden conscience cries out for punishment, but at the same time, I'm enormously relieved he's clearly not going to let that happen.

"But his chest." Stella points out. "It doesn't look like he drowned."

"There are sharks at sea," Jackson reasons. "And he'll be in such bad shape by the time he washes ashore, no one will be suspicious."

"Do you know how to work the boat?" I ask. Jackson looks at me, and I can see in his eyes he doesn't. "I don't either."

"I know how to operate a boat," Stella pipes up.

We both turn to her, surprised.

"Oh, don't look so shocked. I'm not completely useless," she continues. "I learned for *Call of the Sea*. I haven't done it since, but it's not that hard."

Stella grabs the flashlight from Jackson's hand and steadies herself against the wall to step over Cole and mount the stairs to the bridge. After a moment, she nods. "Yeah, I can do this."

"Good." I meet her eye. "Thank you."

Water sloshes over Cole's lifeless form as waves toss the boat, but he's heavy enough his body stays put. "We've got to move him out onto the deck to make sure he goes into the ocean when the boat sinks," Jackson says. "It's already taking on water, so it shouldn't take long to go down. I'll grab his arms." Jackson kneels behind him, hooking his forearms beneath Cole's shoulders.

"But your shoulder," I protest.

"I'll be all right," he says. "The bullet only grazed me."

I grab an ankle in each hand and lift as Jackson drags him toward the ocean-side door behind him, stumbling beneath his weight. The boat tips, throwing Jackson into the bulkhead. He cries out in pain and drops Cole, gripping his injured shoulder. "Fuck!"

"Go sit," I say.

"I'm okay," he protests.

"I can help," Stella says.

I appraise her. She's in pretty bad shape herself, but at least she's not bleeding from a gunshot wound.

"We can both take his legs," Jackson offers.

I drop Cole's legs, moving to take his upper half as Stella stares at the mess I've made of Cole's chest, fighting nausea. "Look at me," I instruct. She lifts her eyes to meet mine, and I see the distress there. "You've got this," I say. She and Jackson each take a leg. "Now lift."

Cole's deadweight is far heavier than I'd imagined. Even tugging with all my might, moving him is painstaking work, made no easier by the erratic lurching of the boat. Once outside, I'm immediately slammed by a wave and lose my footing on the rain-slick deck. Jackson reaches out and grabs my arm as I hold on to Cole's bloody torso for dear life, wind threatening to throw me into the sea.

"That's enough," Jackson shouts over the din.

Another wave slaps me as I step over Cole's body into the cabin, spluttering salt water. The three of us push him as far out the door as we can without stepping onto the deck. "Okay," Jackson finally says. "That's good. We want the boat to get a ways out before he goes overboard so he doesn't wash ashore. Let's start the engines and untie the ropes."

Stella mounts the stairs to the bridge and inserts the key beneath the wheel. The engines roar to life. "It's gonna start pulling when I put it in gear. Get ready," she warns.

I nod. "We'll do the front, then the back."

She throws the boat into gear, and we all bolt out the back, holding on to the walls for stability as we stagger into the screaming storm. Standing at the sinking stern, I struggle to maintain my footing as the vessel pitches wildly in the surf, completely out of sync with the floating dock bobbing next to it.

We move to the edge of the boat, watching as the dock rises and drops, waiting for the two to fall into rhythm while the wind whips around us, threatening to throw us all into the roiling sea. "Okay," Jackson yells. "In one, two, three!"

We jump from the stern onto the dock and dart to the bow. My raw hands chafe against the rough ropes as we fight to untie the dock lines from the posts while the boat rolls with the waves, pulling and slacking the cords unpredictably. When the last loop is undone, the rope jerks from our hands and the front of the boat veers away from the pier, tugging the back line straight. Jackson and I scramble to the stern to unwind the rest of the rope until it rips from our hands.

We watch as the boat plunges into the oncoming waves, listing heavily to one side. In a matter of seconds, she's disappeared from view, swallowed up by the turbulent wall of wind and water that will doubtless soon sink her.

Stella sways, and I slip my arm around her waist to steady her, noticing the wind has suddenly downshifted. The change is slight but enough I no longer feel as though I'm going to be swept into the sea. "Are you okay?" I ask.

She nods, gingerly touching the gaping wound above her eyebrow. "Is it terrible?"

"It'll be hardly noticeable once a plastic surgeon is done with it," I assure her. "And the scar tissue will prevent you from ever needing Botox again."

She smiles wanly, her eyes tired. "A silver lining."

"Do you feel that?" Jackson asks, coming around to support Stella's other side. "The wind is dying."

I activate my flashlight. "The eye."

"We should get to the cellar," Jackson suggests. "There's a first aid kit in the supply closet next to it. We can patch everyone up and get our story straight."

"Just give me a little direction. I'm ready to play my part," Stella croaks.

A rush of gratitude warms my chest. I hide my emotion with a glance out toward where the ship has disappeared into the black night, hoping the pocket of relative calm allows it to sail far enough out that the ocean swallows Cole's body whole, never to be seen again.

We turn our backs on the roiling sea and climb the hill arm in arm.

# Taylor

The wind outside had abruptly stopped, the only noise the chaotic ocean sloshing against the boards of the bungalow.

"It's time," I said to Mary Elizabeth, scooping her from the cocoon of Cole's bed and zipping her into my bag. "Sorry."

She yelped as I slung the bag across my body and waded through the ankle-deep seawater swirling across the living room in the flickering candlelight.

Through the windows, the moon in the suddenly clear sky illuminated the storm-tossed sea in shimmering silver. The water was still high, the waves cresting over the porch outside, but I couldn't wait any longer for the tide to go out. The eye was upon us.

I said a silent prayer and swung open the door. The wind immediately blew out the candle, but after the total darkness of the storm, the moonlight was as bright as day. I was relieved to see the path of the pier stretching to the island seemingly intact. The water level was even with the deck, the peaks of waves periodically washing up and over the boards, like a bridge through the clouds. I took my first tentative step onto the wood. Then another, and another. The dock was stable. As I sprinted toward the beach, I could make out three shadows moving across the sand, a flashlight bouncing between them. Two women and a man too tall and thin to be Cole. Water crashed into my calves and thighs as I ran faster and faster over the planks toward the island, my heart soaring with each step closer to land.

## Part VII:

# The Aftermath

# The Biz Report

## NINTH WOMAN SPEAKS OUT AGAINST COLE POWER

Talia Goldman announced today that she is representing yet another woman who has come forward with allegations that the late Cole Power drugged and sexually assaulted her. The woman's name has at this time been withheld, but she detailed meeting Power at the Ninth Circle nightclub and going back to his home in the Hollywood Hills with a group of friends, only to wake up alone with him in his bed with no recollection of the prior evening and signs she'd had intercourse. The woman claims not to have been drinking heavily the evening in question and says she did not come forward earlier because she was ashamed of the incident.

This is the ninth woman to come forward with allegations of assault against Power in the two months since Taylor Wasserman wrote an op-ed detailing her alleged rape by Power while she was working with him as producer on *The Siren*, the film he was shooting when he died in June. Both Power's son, Jackson Power, and his ex-wife, Stella Rivers, have corroborated Wasserman's claims that the rape resulted in a pregnancy, which she miscarried, and the miscarriage was confirmed by a doctor on the island of Saint Ann, where Wasserman now resides.

Jackson Power is the sole heir of Cole Power and has said he plans to compensate his father's victims for the pain and suffering they endured at his hands.

# The Book Blog

## WHAT WE'RE READING THIS WEEK: "COMING CLEAN," BY STELLA RIVERS

Stella Rivers's memoir *Coming Clean* predictably reads like something between a tabloid and an after-school special . . . so why couldn't any of us over here at the Book Blog put it down?

I've been familiar with Stella Rivers since I was a child: first as the talented kid in *Under the Blue Moon* and the Harriet films, then as the sexy ingenue in *Call of the Sea* and *Faster*, but the image of Stella that's burned into my mind is the tawdry one we all remember, from a grocery store in Hollywood. Her pickle-jar-throwing fall from grace coincided with the pinnacle of tabloid culture, when paparazzi stalked celebrities like prey and the public gawked, ever hungry for more.

But the Stella pictured in the makeup-free, unedited black-and-white photo that graces the cover of *Coming Clean* is a Stella Rivers we haven't yet gotten to know. And the content of her memoir is just as honest as the jacket. Rivers unflinchingly details her troubled childhood, meteoric rise to fame, and rocky marriage to Cole Power with surprising candor and wit. But it's her candid account of the overdose death of the woman she loved, during a time (only fifteen years ago!) when neither bisexuality nor opioid addiction could be discussed without stigma that makes *Coming Clean* a must read this summer.

Everyone knows the press account of Rivers's miscarriage (thought to be an abortion at the time), divorce, and the substance abuse that led to her shocking fall from grace, but experiencing it from her viewpoint is both heartbreaking and eye-opening. The hindsight she's gained with her hard-won sobriety gives her a unique perspective on the ways she both benefited from and was destroyed by fame and provides her cautionary tale the happy ending it deserves.

Stella, forgive us, for we have misjudged you.

# HOLLYWOOD LIFE

## SMART LIKE A FOX:
## INSIDE THE WORLD OF BREAKOUT STAR FELICITY FOX

*By Max Jones*

On a bright spring morning in the Eighteenth Arrondissement of Paris, I find myself facing an ascent of what must be fifty stairs up to the faded cream building actress Felicity Fox calls home. As I contemplate the torture before me, I look up to see her backlit by the sun at the top of the stone staircase, her red dress billowing around her slim frame, shoulder-length blond hair framing her face like a halo. She waves, enveloping me in the warmth of her bright smile, and rushes down the stairs to meet me. "I know it's a climb," she says, laughing. "But wait'll you see the view."

We make our way through a heavy green door and up another flight of creaking wood stairs. A Chihuahua circles our legs as we enter an old-world apartment decorated with a bohemian flair. "This is Mimi," Felicity says, scooping up the dog and scratching her ears. "She's visiting while her mama is way across the world in China."

(Though Fox doesn't mention it, I'll later discover Mimi's mama is Fox's good friend Stella Rivers, who recently adopted her daughter, Iris, from mainland China.)

The view of Montmartre from the tall windows is, as promised, breathtaking, but it pales in comparison to Felicity Fox in person. Without a stitch of makeup, she glows as though lit from within—and for good reason. Her turn in the title role of this month's *Barbie*, which she co-wrote with boyfriend, Jackson Power (son of the late actor Cole Power), is being hailed as the must-see performance of the season. The film, directed by Power, is a dark fairy tale with elements of magical realism based on the life of Fox's mother, a sex worker who was forced into heroin use by an abusive client before finding love with a woman shortly before passing away of an overdose when Fox was ten. "I wanted to do something to honor my mother's memory," Fox explains. "The story isn't strictly factual, but more of an interpretation of who she was and who she could have been, set in 1890s Paris. I fell in love with the city while we were shooting, so here we are."

Fox and Power met on the set of the ill-fated *The Siren*, during which Power's now notorious father famously drowned when his boat capsized during Hurricane Celia. Fox was working as actress Stella Rivers's stand-in at the time, and director Power recognized her talent during blocking rehearsals, but she wasn't at first interested in acting. "It's not that I don't love acting. It's the fame I was afraid of," Fox admits. "I've seen what it does to people, and it's not pretty. It took some convincing, but Jackson can be very persuasive, and when he came to me with the idea to do something based on my mother's life, I couldn't turn him down."

When asked about her relationship with Power, Felicity instantly becomes demure. "Our relationship is private," she says. "But I will say it's very important to me. He's an incredible person."

Now the two are working on revamping Power's script for *The Siren*, in which Fox will play the role originated by disgraced YouTube star Madison Kasabian, who dropped off the radar after it came out that she'd never had the cancer she became famous for beating. Fox's friend and former boss, Stella Rivers, will star opposite her, and Taylor Wasserman, who produced the original film but has since moved on to a position as director of the Caribbean Film Commission, will executive produce.

"I'm really excited to be working with Taylor and Stella again, and to get to spend some time in the beautiful Caribbean," Fox says. "But we're still doing a little rewriting before we cast the male lead. I can't say too much because I don't want to give away any spoilers, but I really didn't want to do anything that wasn't going to be totally empowering to women. If having a platform is a side effect of doing what I love, then I want to use it for something positive, and to me that means empowering women and girls."

True to her word, Fox and Rivers founded the charity Women Care, which has to date raised more than two million for women's shelters in Fox's home state of Florida. "We started in Florida, but we're expanding across the United States in the coming months. Stella has started a program within Women Care where women write and perform their stories for one another in a supportive environment, which we've found really helps with self-acceptance and healing. Whether they're battling addiction or fleeing an abusive partner, it's so important for people to know they're not alone."

Meanwhile, Fox is unfazed by the rumors swirling about possible awards recognition for her breakout role in *Barbie*. "It's flattering," she says, "but it's not about me. All I've ever wanted was to give my mother a voice, and I'm grateful every day for the opportunity to do so."

## Epilogue

# Felicity

*Two Years after the Storm*

Paris teeters on the far edge of springtime, poised to plunge into sultry summer any day now. Pink buds litter the grass, and sunbathers line the shores of the Seine; in the parks, the daffodils and tulips of May are already giving way to the roses and peonies of June. I won't be needing the cardigan tucked into the canvas bag on my shoulder, next to the nearly empty urn of my mother's ashes.

Today marks the fifteenth anniversary of Iris's death, and I've finally followed through on my intention to spread her remains throughout the city she never got to visit before she died. Jackson was understanding of my need to spend the day treading the streets of Paris alone with her memory, dropping handfuls of ashes beneath willow trees and into banks of purple blossoms. I took her with me to the Louvre, where we lingered in front of the enigmatic *Mona Lisa* and the seductive *Bathsheba at Her Bath*, then to the Jardin des Tuileries, where we enjoyed a baguette next to a statue of a nude nymph with her dog. Along the wide Champ de Mars, we FaceTimed with Stella and her adorable daughter from a bench beneath a towering linden tree.

By the time the sun begins its dive toward the horizon, my feet are sore from all the walking and my shoulders are sunburned, but my heart is a little bit lighter. Saying a silent prayer for her spirit to find peace, I sprinkle the remainder of her ashes over a bed of colorful violets in the shade of the Eiffel Tower and return the urn to my bag.

It's been nearly two years since I killed Cole. For months afterward I was a nervous wreck, torn apart by pangs of conscience over taking a life, mixed with the fear that I'd be caught. But Stella, Taylor, and especially Jackson stood by me, reminding me persistently that I'd done the right thing. My apprehension peaked the following fall, when Cole's badly damaged boat was discovered deep beneath the sea miles off shore. But the alibi we provided one another—of helping Taylor through a miscarriage in the wine cellar during the storm—was never questioned. No foul play was ever suspected, and his body was never recovered. It won't be, they say. Eventually I realized that if Jackson could forgive me for killing his father, I had to forgive myself.

The soft evening is awash in muted apricot and rose as I hurry past the massive iron Tower and onto the Pont d'léna, crowded with Parisians whiling away the last minutes of the long day. I spy Jackson halfway across the bridge, looking out over the passing boats on the river that reflects the brilliant sky in swirls and ripples, the Jardins du Trocadéro behind him. My heart swells with the realization that he is Iris's last gift to me; after all the darkness, we are each a ray of light for the other.

Sensing my presence, he turns. "Everything okay?" he asks.

I close my eyes as he brushes his thumb across my cheek, wiping away an errant tear. "Better than okay." I can't help but laugh at myself; I've become such a softy. "They're happy tears."

He wraps me in his arms and presses his lips to mine, and everything stops, the same way it does every time he kisses me. As the sun dips beneath the horizon over the Seine, I'm certain that somehow, somewhere my mother is smiling, knowing that her little girl is going to be okay.

# Acknowledgments

So much goes into producing a book, and I am forever grateful to have the support of such a fantabulous team.

First and always, to my family: my husband, Alex, the best life partner a girl could ask for; my wonderful parents; and my adorable little girls, who remind me daily of what's truly important.

To my supercalifragilistic agent, Sarah Bedingfield, my rock and my guiding light, without whom there would be no books, and to the whole gang at Levine Greenberg Rostan Literary Agency.

To the unparalleled team at Grand Central Publishing, all of whom are such a delight to work with: my fantastic editor, Karen Kosztolnyik, for making this book the best it can be, and her terrific editorial assistant, Rachael Kelly; the superb Brian McLendon and Tiffany Porcelli in marketing; Andy Dodds and Matthew Ballast in publicity; and Albert Tang and Lynn Buckley for the gorgeous cover art. Additionally a huge thanks to Ben Sevier, Karen Torres, Alison Lazarus, Ali Cutrone, Nancy Wiese, Joelle Dieu, Kristen Lemire, Jeff Holt, Penina Lopez, and Tricia Tamburr, all of whom have worked so hard to usher this book into the world. I am so fortunate to work with all of you!

Before I wrote books, I worked in the film industry for many years as an actress, producer, director, and screenwriter, and this book draws on those experiences. As Taylor notes, a set can be a wonderful place to work if you're working with the right people, and I had the good fortune of working with many incredible artists and filmmakers over the years. So I'd like to say thank you to all of the dreamers and creators whose blood, sweat, and tears go into the content that entertains and inspires us every day. Keep dreaming and keep creating! We need artists now more than ever.

# About the Author

**Katherine St. John** is a native of Mississippi, a graduate of the University of Southern California, and the author of the critically acclaimed novel *The Lion's Den*. When she's not writing, she can be found hiking or on the beach with a good book. Katherine currently lives in Los Angeles with her husband and children.